Desperate Hunger

"You're going to regret this," she murmured.

He smiled, then pulled her to his chest, against the bright row of buttons adorning his front. Holding her face, he drew a deep, shuddering breath, then lowered his lashes. "I certainly hope so."

He kissed her, his mouth burning on hers. He had a firm, masculine kiss—possessive, straightforward, confident, and demanding. He held her so tight; brass, braid, and wool poked at her softness. In spite of the prickles, a hunger consumed her, voracious and swift. Not the tender longing she'd harbored for Philip, but passion, ardor, and another emotion—deeper and different. Spiritual in a way, but far, far more instinctive. His mouth worked against hers, claiming, exploring, pressing against hers. She struggled to keep some sense of composure, her insides melting . . .

Many Fires

Kathleen Sage

JOVE BOOKS, NEW YORK

MANY FIRES

A Jove Book / published by arrangement with
the author

PRINTING HISTORY
Jove edition / December 1995

ISBN: 0-515-11781-1

A JOVE BOOK®
Jove Books are published by The Berkley Publishing Group,
200 Madison Avenue, New York, New York 10016.
JOVE and the "J" design are trademarks
belonging to Jove Publications, Inc.

PRINTED IN THE UNITED STATES OF AMERICA

10 9 8 7 6 5 4 3 2 1

This book is dedicated from
the bottom of my heart
to my husband, Larry,
a genuine hero.

ACKNOWLEDGMENTS

Proper acknowledgments for a first novel would make a novel itself, and I am one of those women who never outgrew her penchant for fifteen best friends. So with my readers' indulgence, I would like to thank the following long list of supporters and helpers:

Eileen, my first fan and friend; Cathy and Tom, for teaching me to proofread; Ed, for the books; Cheryl, for listening; Amanda, for listening some more; Joan, who read every word; Stef, who read every word twice; Judy, who adopted me with such grace; and Rob for three years of faith and vision.

A special thanks to Frank Ryerson, investigator extraordinaire, whose vivid war stories inspired a wonderful character.

To my sons Todd, Tim, and Tony. And to my father and brothers. Their indulgence of my passion was made all the more precious by the fact that they couldn't believe I wanted to do this.

And, finally, to all my friends, neighbors, co-workers, clients, Cub Scouts, and fellow writers. Had anyone laughed, I couldn't have kept writing. None of you did, so I kept going.

On a more formal note, I truly appreciated the gracious assistance of Steve Alley, fort historian at Fort Leavenworth. My history of the Buffalo Soldiers was considerably fictionalized. Mr. Alley bears no responsibility for my views of the army, but he was very helpful with soldierly details, and I appreciate his patience enormously. Any errors and all opinions regarding the army's treatment of the Buffalo Soldiers are solely mine.

Vegetarian, Kansas, for those who must know, was a real place. For knowledge of its existence, I am indebted to Cathy Luchetti and Carol Olwell, two wonderful historians whose marvelous book, *Women of the West*, enormously expanded my views of the Western experience.

Thank you also to James Mellon, the editor of *Bullwhip Days: The Slaves Remember*. The interviews in his book formed the basis for the characters of the troopers. In general, I tried to reflect the ex-slaves' sentiments quite closely, because I could never have spoken for those hope-filled and downtrodden men better than they spoke for themselves.

Last but not least, thank you to Trooper Fred Jones, an admirable and fascinating man. The Buffalo Soldiers served on horseback, in segregated units, through World War II. They have an active veterans organization, the Ninth and Tenth Horse Cavalry Association, and do wonderful work with inner city youths. Anyone interested in the history of these soldiers—or their youth work—can contact Colonel Franklin Henderson, 5338 Garth Avenue, Los Angeles, CA 90056.

ONE

MAJOR JAMES RYERSON SCOWLED. HE HATED ASKING A woman for help, but his troopers were in desperate trouble, and the Osage had told him about a fine female healer. So he swallowed his pride, touched his heels to his gelding, and signaled his scout, White Bird, to follow. Hand on his side arm, Ryerson guided his chestnut down the bank of the creek. As he did, he studied the nearly abandoned encampment. So far his Indian guide had been right.

The town of Vegetarian moldered before them. Six modest cabins circled an eight-sided building, the whole crazy layout surrounded by acres of gardens. The founders had gone, but the commune's remains proclaimed their ambition: to live at peace with all of God's creatures. Ryerson wanted to scoff at that absurd ideal, but his wartime experience made the dream seem less foolish. Suppressing a sigh, he scanned the larkspur leading up to the only occupied cabin.

"Hold it right there."

At the sharp command, Ryerson halted. The cabin's one window had sprouted a gun. He stopped midstream, signaled his scout, then held his palm up in a gesture of greeting. A herd of goats bleated in the corral, then charged a full circle. Ignoring them, Ryerson kept an eye on the musket, wondering if the gun's owner would use her weapon. A slight wave of the barrel acknowledged Ryerson's salutation.

"Get out of here, Yankee." The lady's message was delivered with feeling, in a voice laced with culture and a soft Southern drawl.

Raising his hands, Ryerson edged his mount closer, acutely aware of his clipped Connecticut accent. "I'm sorry, madam, but I cannot leave you. I need to take you back to my troop."

"You're years too late, Yankee. Now get out of here before I forget the last of my manners."

Arms stretched high, eyes on the window, Ryerson swung one leg over the chestnut's neck and dropped down from the saddle. "I'm sorry. We're in need of a nurse."

To the side, the goats had stopped circling. They milled in their corral, worried and nervous. In the window, the gun barrel lowered a fraction.

"A sick child?"

"No, madam."

A boot scraped inside. Though Ryerson couldn't be certain, he thought he heard the rustle of cloth. He lowered his hands just a notch.

Elizabeth Wheaton appeared in the doorway, hesitated a moment, then stepped into the sunlight. "Many Fires," the Osage called her. At first the name had seemed odd, but now that Ryerson had seen her, he understood. She was one of those women lit from within. He loved her hair color, dark brown shot through with crimson. Not the wild reds of a fire on the prairie, but subtle and warm, like a regiment cooking at twilight. Her skin glowed, high-colored and creamy, awash in the kind of gold tones peculiar to auburn-haired women.

Wary, she moved into the yard. He noticed the dots accenting her cheekbones, the tattoos that marked her stint as a captive. About the size of small beauty marks, they'd been burned into her face with bone needles: two permanent rows of coal-colored spots. From White Bird's rather lurid description, Ryerson expected to find the strange markings repulsive, but she had such serene and remarkable beauty that he found the dots surprisingly pleasing.

She lowered the musket slightly. "Why do you want me?"

"I have a troop down with the ague."

"I buy my peace by tending sick children, but I don't nurse for soldiers. The Osage should have told you. And it doesn't matter which side." She fitted the butt to her shoulder. "Now go."

He would have liked to obey, but after six years of fighting, he had only one friend left in this life: the army—or at least the men he commanded. They needed his help. They needed her. He had no choice but to take her with him by force.

But first he'd have to disarm her. No simple task, considering their respective positions. She held her weapon, while his weighed down his hip. His hand itched for his pistol. He measured her more by instinct than reason. Five feet six and clearly not frightened. Still, not a killer, he felt. No, not a killer at all. He sensed that softness even seven feet away.

Ignoring the rising pace of his heartbeat, he crouched low and flung himself at her. His shoulder punched into her stomach. A cry of surprise escaped from her throat. He barely noted its sound. The next sensation he truly attended was the heat of supple and feminine curves as the woman fought to throw off his weight. He pinned her in the green grass, straddling her and wrenching the musket out of her grip.

Once overwhelmed, she stopped struggling. An eerie chill swept over him. The posture gave him control of her torso, but her eyes, cinnamon-colored and seething with hatred, reminded him of war's second rule: A soldier might conquer an army in battle, but a war is won in the hearts of a people.

She bucked. His emptiness fled in a hot rush of passion. It startled him, this lustful reaction. He found himself wishing he'd seen more of the whores.

Cursing himself, he tightened his grip on her wrist. "You're coming with me. You have no business out here on the prairie, living so far from the fort."

"I won't go," she said softly, her breasts straining against faded green calico. "I don't care if you kill me."

"I wouldn't do you the favor. You can come like a lady or you can come trussed over my saddle."

"That's happened before." She seemed almost to smile in triumph.

His muscles clenched, but he willed his fingers not to dig into her shoulder. "I don't think I care for your reference, but I don't dispute what you say." He rose. She'd classified him with her Indian captors. The idea stung. The army was her natural protector. To the Indians she'd been a slave. With his troop she'd be safe. Besides, he needed her help.

He offered his hand, holding her musket out to the side. "I don't care what you think of my methods. You can come peacefully, or I can force you."

Eyes wary, she rose without his assistance. "What shall I do with my goats?"

He was about to tell her the animals did not matter when the look in her eyes caught his attention. He scanned the prairie, the lonely plain barren of people. She lived here, he thought, with only these creatures for friends. For reasons he didn't care to examine, the idea seemed poignant to him.

"We'll take them." He kept his voice rough. He knew White Bird had to be laughing, and tried not to think how his troop would react. He knew it would make a good campfire story, how he, James Ryerson, notorious leader of Ryerson's Riders, ruthless despoiler of a thousand plantations, had returned to his men herding three goats. "But if they slow us down, we'll eat them for supper."

Elizabeth had recognized Ryerson immediately. She'd sketched him often enough, copying from the lithographs in *Collier's*. He was a good-looking man, grizzled and lean, though she usually drew him as some type of monster. Now he looked a little less fearsome. He never repeated his threat about eating the goats, only pointed out every few hundred feet that his men were suffering while she herded these beasts.

All these years she'd imagined his as a heart without mercy. As a girl, she'd stared for hours at his pictures. His looks matched his deeds. Hardened and weathered, his face glared from the pages, eyes fierce with his famous temper. His image seemed to bound out of the picture, almost as vivid as a living creature. Sometimes she'd shiver in fright. Even at fourteen she had noticed the taut, spring-wired body of the horseman said to outride the devil himself.

Shyly she glanced at the blue figure beside her. He'd startled her when he jumped her. Not just the attack, but the sensation of closeness—the warmth of his skin, the strength of his muscles, the scent of bay rum just like Philip had worn. Then the swift heat of his need, the urgency and the hardness, more desperate than she'd known from her husband.

She'd amazed herself when she hadn't killed him. He'd ruined her life. Not personally, of course, but as commander of his Riders. They'd burned her family's plantation, leaving only the blackened chimney standing above the smoldering ruin. Her family had seen many on their flight west. Silent remains marking Ryerson's path. The memory still chilled her. But that had been a long-ago hatred. The trembling and indignant girl who'd burned with fury at the sight of a Yankee had died and been buried ages ago on the prairie, replaced by a scarred and embattled survivor who'd eked out a peace in Vegetarian's ruins. Still, she was glad her cartoons were published under a pen name. Ryerson might not have been quite so civil had he found out he'd captured the army's chief gadfly.

Elizabeth wiped her palms on her skirt. Fortunately only one person knew. And he, because he fought the same battles, would never reveal that Elizabeth was the tart-penned defender of Indian women and children, the vitriolic political satirist, Lysistrata.

She laughed. The chuckle caught the Osage scout's attention, and she hurried up close to the rear of the goats.

Ryerson slowed his chestnut beside her. "You find this amusing?"

"In a manner of speaking. You know, your troops burned my home."

"Mississippi?"

She nodded.

He straightened himself in the saddle. The movement surprised her, for she'd perceived his carriage as perfect. She would not have thought he could sit any taller. But, starch upon starch, he stiffened his spine. Her chin snapped up at the sight. She'd seen that posture too many times in her life. She'd seen it in five of her six brothers, as one by one they'd joined up. She'd seen it among the bare-chested Cheyenne, as their breast-plated swagger took them proudly off to war. Most of all, she'd seen it in Philip, the downy-cheeked husband who'd marched off and been killed. Soldiers all, in love with their work, duty-bound, and feeling be hanged.

"Proud of those raids?" she asked tersely.

He ignored her. Annoyed, she lapsed back into her silence. She considered escape, but dismissed the notion. Common sense told her she couldn't outrun such a skilled horseman. No, she'd have to outwit him. She'd survived the war, the Cheyenne and Comanche, using grit, endurance, and adaptation. She'd do the same with the infamous raider. Outthink him, outlast him, and make herself useful.

Then make him take her back home.

"Do you mind if I ask where we're going?" After reflection, she'd decided there was no harm in the question.

"We've got an encampment about two miles north."

"What symptoms do your soldiers exhibit?"

"Fever and chills. One with lung problems."

"How many sick?"

"Pretty much the whole troop."

She prodded Nanny, her female goat, who'd stopped to crunch on the early grass. "Seems pretty careless, letting a whole troop take sick."

Ryerson froze, stopping his gelding dead in its tracks. "I'll thank you to keep your remarks to yourself." He brushed off his sleeve, an impatient, imperious gesture, as if dismissing an invisible servant.

Elizabeth shook out her calico skirts, intent on appearing fastidious. Nanny nibbled on her dress, apparently thinking the action meant crumbs. "I nursed for the Confederate army. If a whole troop turns up with an illness, the fact generally shows a want of good care."

She didn't see him dismount. He simply appeared at her side, his face dark with temper. "I'll repeat this just once: I'll thank you to keep your remarks to yourself."

"And if I don't?" She shoved the goat away from her, taking care not to tear her threadbare white apron. "I suppose you'll have me drawn and quartered?"

A glint of amusement appeared in his eyes. "There are some who might fear that fate."

"I told you. I'm not frightened by you. Your men burned my plantation."

Gripping her arm, he brought his beard-stubbled face close to her. "And you have no fear of their leader?"

She pulled out of his grasp. "Major—"

"Actually, Captain." He nodded at the braid on his shoulder. "I'm a brevet major. The army let me keep my wartime rank."

"Yes, well . . ." She glanced at the blue of his coat. "Whatever your office. I'm twenty years old. I've lost six brothers and both my parents. I've outlived one husband and been sold to another. I've seen countless men die and endless more suffer. I've watched the slow death of our wagon train's leader and had my own face marked for life. Now," she said, drawing a deep breath, steeling herself against the uniform's power, "if you have some special torture, I suggest you get on with it." She pulled away from the soldier, away from the Indian guide. "Otherwise you'll just have to put up with my scolding."

He smiled a genuine smile. He seemed to find it a diverting idea—a woman who did not fear the great raider. She wondered what he thought of his victims, women like her whose lives he'd destroyed.

Turning, she gathered her goats. He remounted his

horse. She supposed he must have some sense of the hatred and the heated emotions his wartime deeds fired. Not that he'd hurt women personally, or even killed that many soldiers, but he'd commanded his Riders for more than three years. The experience had made him a legend, famous for his hardness of heart, sharpness of glance, and, most notably, shortness of patience. Even powerful men trembled before him. At the Grand Review capping the war, Mr. Stanton, Lincoln's secretary of war, had gaped at him bug-eyed. The Southern newspapers went wild, reporting that Stanton feared the fighter he had unleashed.

Hurrying forward, she chased after Nanny. She glanced anxiously at the major and noticed him rubbing a scar on his hand. He tugged on the reins of the chestnut, riding the horse next to the goats. "Did my men kill your brothers?" he asked.

She grabbed the switch attached to her waist. "Only in a manner of speaking."

"Which means?"

Gathering her skirts, she drove the flock at a brisk pace. "They were killed by the war, but only Matthew had the doubtful distinction of dying in battle. He died at Shiloh. Robert and Andrew perished of typhus, Nathaniel of gangrene. One of them just turned up missing. In my heart I know he's gone forever. Isaac, the youngest, was killed with my parents while fleeing west."

He didn't answer for a few moments. "But one way or another they all died because of Yankees."

"Yes."

He guided the chestnut over a small knoll in the prairie. "So, you have plenty of reasons to hate me."

"No more you than anyone else. I've given up hating. I despise war and killing, but soldiers are just people. Beneath the uniform, one man's much the same as another."

"Still, the blue makes you sick."

"Yes." She tried to control the surprise in her voice.

"And the sound of a Yankee accent makes a knot in your stomach?"

She held her gaze straight and kept herding the goats. "You've talked to a few Southern ladies?"

"No." He smiled slightly. "I've tried to make friends with a couple of rebels. I found myself fighting the same reactions."

A small encampment poked up from the prairie. Elizabeth noted the grouping as she kept walking. One rectangular officer's tent. Two wigwamlike Sibleys. Ryerson's comments intrigued her so much, it wasn't until she saw the first soldier that the old fear rose.

She froze in place, pressing her hands over her tattoos. Nanny, Pappy, and Balthazar scattered, but Elizabeth stood still on the prairie, a thousand sensations swirling within her.

"They're sick. They won't even notice." Ryerson had softened his voice. It might not have belonged to the same man, so gentle had he been able to make its tone.

She felt the color rise in her face. "I hate the way people stare."

"I'm sure."

She expected he'd move, hustle her off to his troop, but instead he dismounted, standing quite close. To her absolute shock, he circled his arm around her shoulder. Her heartbeat sped. Furious questions whipped through her mind, then the pumping slowed down as the touch conveyed its own meaning. He intended a gesture of comfort.

Horrified, she shied away. She'd be the object of nobody's pity. Squaring her shoulders, she gathered her skirts and shooed her goats toward the dark silhouette guarding the encampment.

Ryerson followed. She could feel his gaze bore into her back. Eyes forward, she assessed the lone figure before her, a tall man, uniformed and broad-shouldered. Ryerson must have been telling the truth. Except for the sentry, she saw not a soldier.

Her spirits lifted. Perhaps there'd be some use for her here. Her interest piqued, she assessed Ryerson's camping arrangements. "I can't fault your sanitation. You've chosen high ground and dug the right trenches." She nodded at his string of horses. "You've even tethered the horses the correct distance away."

"Thank you," he said dryly.

She was about to launch into her lecture on the supreme importance of the right sanitary conditions when the guard's face came into focus.

She stopped, glancing sideways at Ryerson. "Is this some kind of joke?"

"No." Ryerson stilled, his expression carefully blank. "This is my friend, Sergeant Dixon."

Elizabeth slowly walked forward.

"Missus." The officer nodded as she approached. "I'm sure glad to see you."

Quietly Elizabeth inspected the soldier. He had a classically African face, dark-skinned and strong-featured. He spoke in low tones, guarded and respectful, his soft Southern accent completely at odds with the blue of his pants.

Elizabeth blinked, glancing again at Ryerson's face.

He smiled. "I take it you've never seen a colored trooper."

"No." She shoved her switch into her skirts. "Or infantry, either. I heard the Yankees used Negroes as soldiers."

"We did and we do. All your patients are newly freed slaves. I hope that won't be a problem."

Elizabeth stiffened. "Of course not. I'd never refuse to help because of that, but—"

"Good." Ryerson handed the reins to Dixon, then bent down and scratched Nanny's chin. "I expect you learned your nursing from Negroes."

"No." Elizabeth swallowed. She'd had an uncle murdered by slaves, an experience it didn't seem tactful to mention. "Daddy never let me go near our people."

Apparently startled, Ryerson glanced upward. "Not even the house servants?"

"No." Elizabeth took two slow steps back from the sergeant. He gazed steadily at her, his expression impassive. She stopped, checking her impulse to bolt. "We were pretty small farmers. We had field hands, that's all. Four to be exact. Mother and I kept our own house. I learned to nurse on Confederate soldiers, which is why I'd rather not care for your troopers. I've seen enough slaughter to last me a lifetime."

Ryerson pulled a cracker out of his pocket, using the hardtack to lure the goat. "You can hardly count these men as soldiers. They've been in the army less than a month."

"I don't see how that matters." Elizabeth slapped Balthazar's bottom, driving her pet toward the remuda. "I'm still patching them up to be sent off to war."

"I expect so." Ryerson tethered the first of the goats. "We're having trouble with the Cheyenne. I need these men fit for fighting."

Frowning, Elizabeth tied Balthazar down. "I'll have you know I like the Cheyenne. I count myself as one of their allies. Major, if this"—she turned and glared at the dark-skinned man in the blue uniform—"is what comes of befriending the Negro, you've granted that race a dubious freedom."

For all her objections, once put to work, Elizabeth Wheaton toiled unceasingly. Ryerson wasn't surprised. He'd seen nurses like her before, superficially flinty, but soft underneath. Much as he'd expected, she spent the day cleaning and fussing, making up special diets for each of the men. Next, she'd brought out her case full of powders and used them to brew sour-smelling tisanes. That evening, watching her from the door of the hospital tent, Ryerson noticed the fatigue in her face. He also saw the compassion.

She perched on a camp stool, bathed in the glow of a kerosene lamp, silently reading from a battered Bible. He'd listened to her for more than an hour. She'd sung three hymns, then recited out loud, declaiming the Old Testament scriptures. Her voice subsided into a singsong, then faded. He smiled to himself. He'd used that technique before, soothing homesick boarding school students in his faraway Maine teaching days.

"You should feel complimented," he whispered, nodding at the eight sleeping figures. "My men don't accept every white as their friend."

She looked up, surprised. "They don't accept me." She snapped shut the book in her lap. "What's going on here?" She looked to the left. "Not one will confess. How did all these Negroes get sick? And what are you doing out here on the prairie? You've got eight sick men in hostile country. I haven't seen such a troop of ragamuffins since the end of the war."

He stalked the small square of the tent. Reaching the stool, he grabbed her by the elbow and hustled her out into the night. Just outside the flap, she wriggled out of his grasp.

"Let's not go far." She peeked back at her patients. "The smallest private is in a hard way."

"They're all pretty sick."

"I know. Here." Evidently undaunted by his obvious irritation, she handed the leather-bound volume to him. "Hold this for me, please." She wore her hair in a chignon, and one of the pins had slipped to her neck. As Ryerson stood there holding the Good Book, she tugged the clip out, then pushed a wayward lock back into the bun. "So, do you want to tell me what's going on?"

Tucking the Bible in the crook of his elbow, he tightened the belt of his greatcoat. He considered her face. The hairstyle flattered in unlikely ways, the fashion accenting a lovely oval. And those tattoos. He found them intriguing. He'd never seen such marks before and he wondered briefly about their meaning. Mostly he admired the effect. Someone—an Indian artist, he supposed—had picked Elizabeth Wheaton's best feature, adorning her cheekbones with an exotic but flattering series of dots. Ryerson stifled the impulse to touch the small specks.

"We've been out on patrol." He considered himself an excellent liar. "One by one they took sick. I thought it best to rest and find help."

"Major, you may think me a foolish belle"—she jerked the pin out again, evidently unhappy with her rearrangement—"pampered and petted by adoring slaves, but I know a great deal about certain subjects, and nursing is one of my best. I know how these soldiers got sick. Someone's been neglecting them badly. You're not that person. I see your arrangements. You know what you're doing and you do it well, but some commander has done these men a disservice."

"They're all former slaves—"

"Don't try to blame their condition on slavery." Her hands froze at the back of her neck. "They're all strong and basically healthy." She twisted the thick lock again, then shoved the clip in. "You've got four cases of dysentery, three of malaria, and one of pneumonia. These are diseases of camp, of crowds and neglect. These soldiers didn't fall ill on the prairie. They haven't been slaves for more than two years. Some culprit, and I think it's the United States Army, has been mistreating these men."

He could feel the heat rise in his face. "Madam, do you accuse me of lying?"

"I do."

"I suggest you take your claim back."

"I shall not." She dropped her hands to her sides. The wayward ringlet tumbled over her shoulder.

Her questions set up a little war in him. She had excellent sense, this Indian-lover, unreformed rebel, and truly astonishing beauty. She'd pinpointed his problems exactly. His new colored troop had been sentenced to death, not by the hellish horror of war, but by a sadder and subtler outrage. The average Yankee fought for the Union and probably didn't like slavery much. Still, the war didn't mean that the typical white was ready to quarter next to a black. At Leavenworth, the new colored troop had been cramped into the fort's swampiest corner. Disease and neglect had killed recruits daily. Ryerson had taken a terrible risk bringing his men out on the prairie, but he'd already lost two thirds of his troop and had yet to see a single hostile.

Nevertheless, he didn't trust Elizabeth Wheaton. Whatever disagreements he had with the army, this woman's loyalties lay with all the wrong people. Females were an unpredictable sex; this one, with so many reasons to hate him, could turn out to be the worst of the lot.

He batted an insect away from his face. "I acknowledge, madam, that you're quite perceptive, but confine yourself to your nursing duties. These men have plenty of problems without adding a meddlesome nurse to their worries."

"As you wish." She lifted the tent flap. "Perhaps you could fetch me my things. I'd like to make a toilette before bed."

He grasped her wrist. "You're not planning to sleep in the tent?"

"I am."

"You don't think that indecent?"

"No. Nor would any good nurse. The pneumonia case is burning with fever. I know he'll need me during the night."

He let go. Stubborn, he thought, to the point of pigheadedness. He'd have to keep an eye on this woman. He'd seen nurses like her during the war. They'd start out in high feather, get in over their heads, work themselves into a sickness, then abandon their posts in a cloud of bad feeling. "I'll send Sergeant Dixon to help you."

A shadow passed over her eyes. "You trust Sergeant Dixon?"

"I do."

She picked at the frayed edge of her sleeve. "You know the others are sick."

He felt the color rise in his face. "What exactly are you implying?"

"Nothing. It's just"—she glanced over the prairie, as if half expecting some ghost to jump out—"I've never been left in the care of a Negro."

He shoved the Bible back in her grasp. "I have perfect confidence in my sergeant. In fact," he said, pulling back, unwilling to let her feel his hands shaking, "right at this moment, I have more faith in Dixon than I do in myself."

* * *

Elizabeth watched Ryerson leave, then ducked under the tent flap. She had no idea what the major meant by his comment, but she certainly did not like his decision. Sick men she could care for. Illness reduced all men to children. Dixon made her nervous, however. The thought of being left with a black man, hale and strong-bodied, brought back her childhood fears, the whispered rumors about her uncle's death, and her father's dire warnings about murderous Negroes.

Once in the tent, she made up her cot, unhappy and not daring to show it. She placed the bed next to the sickest man, a slender brown private, likely only sixteen years old. Dixon came in with her bag. The sergeant carried himself with natural grace, the kind that sent overseers quaking. He wore a full uniform, including a pistol, and she wondered what the Yankees were thinking, arming ex-slaves with weapons.

He must have guessed at her worries for he lay down the bag and touched the Colt's handle gently. "I know the guns make you uneasy, but you've got only the major and me for your protection."

"What about White Bird?" she asked.

"He's gone back to his people."

She retied the knot on her white apron. "Shouldn't you stand outside or something?"

"The major's standing guard duty. I'll relieve him at midnight. He sent me to see if you needed some help."

"No." She sat on her cot, still staring in rapt fascination, unable to get used to the sight of a black-skinned man in official regalia. Dixon must have been used to such rudeness. He approached the camp stool with grave dignity, commandeering the seat with a confident swagger.

Heat flamed in her cheeks. She brushed a tattoo, thinking about her life as a captive. She'd never liked slavery much; she liked it less now that she'd been someone's property. More to the point, she understood what Dixon's poise cost him. She smoothed back her hair, then smiled her brightest. "I think you do the uniform justice."

He grinned in return, flashing an even row of white teeth. "Why, thank you, missus."

She wanted to settle down on the cot, but having established the start of a friendship, she didn't feel right taking a rest. Shyly she ripped a small tear in a sheet, thinking the young soldier would soon need a compress.

"Have you and the major been friends for long?" She'd long ago mastered the exact tone of voice, soft, not quite a whisper, that did not disturb slumbering men.

"Yes." Dixon imitated her tone. "I've been with the major since '62."

"You served in the Rebellion together?"

He pulled out a knife, then quickly held up his whittling stick. "I was his orderly during the war."

"I suppose you're one of the Negroes he freed."

"No." He drew the knife over the bark. "I was a conductor on the underground railroad. Used to ferry slaves across the Ohio. When it looked like the Yankees was winnin', I just slipped across for myself."

Quietly as she could, she tore off the end of the sheet. "Where did you learn about abolition?"

"From a white man named Mr. John Freedom. He'd come around the plantations—he never let the owners see him—preachin' how one man could not own another."

"Is that how you started slave-running?"

Dixon sliced off a long peel of bark. "No, missus, not one bit of it. I got into that business because of a girl— brown-skinned and so pretty. She kept looking at me with those big, soulful eyes until I volunteered to take her across. She disappeared once her foot hit Ohio, but I'd found the only thrill that beats courtin'. I liked the danger. That's one thing the major and I got in common."

"Which is?"

"He made the war fun."

"What?"

"Sorry, missus. But that's the plain truth." He'd whittled the bark of the stick and a small pile of tendrils lay at his feet. "I can't stand a white who makes a pet out of a Negro. That's just an ownership of a different kind. Major, he wasn't a preacher. Fact is, we just got to like freein' the slaves."

A little more quickly, she ripped off another rectangular cloth. "I can see how you would enjoy that part of the war, but how can a white man find burning plantations amusing?"

"Oh, I think he learned. At one time he wouldn't have liked the destruction. He used to be a real gentle man. Did you know he taught poetry?"

"No." She stopped, intrigued. If she was going to outsmart the major, she would have to learn something about him.

"Yes, he did. At a fancy New England college." Dixon seemed to be carving a pipe stem. "I'm sure you'd never guess it, but Ryerson writes the most wonderful verses. Reads them, too. Used to spout ballads out loud. It's sad in a way. I haven't heard him recite since right after Vicksburg."

Pretending indifference, she folded the cotton. She believed Sergeant Dixon. Ryerson's speech had a rhythmic cadence, a precision and fury, that conveyed his feelings quite well. "Why?"

"Missus?"

"Why doesn't he write anymore?"

Dixon held up his stick, apparently measuring by eye.

"He had a son, also named James. A freckle-faced red-head, looked a lot like his father. Came to Vicksburg after the fall, stayed in camp for the summer. Brought Mama along." Slowly he turned the reed, examining it by the kerosene lamplight. "The boy died of typhus just after the visit. It changed Ryerson, losin' his son like that." Dixon peered over the pipe stem, an appreciative grin illuminating his face. "He got to be a regular bastard."

"But you liked this transformation?"

"Yes, missus, I did. I never liked being a slave. No one gave me a reason for hatred, but I still didn't like the idea. When Ryerson's Riders roared through Mississippi, I never had such fun in my life. Each day a new celebration, settin' all them colored folks free."

A chill swept down Elizabeth's back. "Not everyone thinks of those raids that way."

The lamp glinted off the trim on his sleeve. "No, missus, they don't. Even we did not like the killin', but we surely got to like that enjoyment, emancipatin' those chained-up people."

The young patient groaned. Elizabeth thought they should be quiet, but Dixon was a good storyteller, and it would help her to learn the great raider's soft spots. She lowered her voice a couple of notches. "How did the major's wife react to their loss?"

"Helen?" Dixon's smile disappeared. "Quite badly. She took to her bed and never really got better. She died nine months after the Vicksburg visit."

"In childbirth?"

"In a manner of speakin'."

"Did the baby survive?"

"No, missus, he didn't." He pressed his knifepoint into the end of the stick, slowly turning the twig in a circle. "Which is how I got to admire the major. He didn't set out

to do it, but he gave his whole life to freein' my people. So"
—he blew on invisible sawdust—"when he volunteered to
head this troop, I figured I would stick with him. Ryerson
thought it a good bit of work, startin' the first colored cavalry unit, but I had a nobler motive."

"Which was?"

"I thought I'd help him adapt to his new life."

Elizabeth arched a brow in surprise. "Does he know why
you joined?"

"No, I'm sure he doesn't. At least, I think he believed
my excuses." The smile returned, brighter than ever. "I
told him I liked chasin' women. That was one lesson I
learned on those raids. The girls love a cavalry trooper.
And it's not a bad life in the army. Sometimes you have to
be gone from your honey, but that just makes the female
heart fonder. The pay's regular, the uniform's nice, and
you never lose the sense of adventure." He tested the
newly carved pipe stem, then grinned. " 'Fun's over, Major,' I told him. 'We're going to do some serious courtin'.' "

TWO

ELIZABETH WHEATON REMINDED RYERSON OF THE LADIES who raised funds for the army, high-minded and idealistic, not naturally suited to life's rougher aspect. Funny, he mused as he walked through the darkness, how such a compassionate woman could survive so much hardship. Not that she wasn't courageous. Her valor showed in all her actions, but she had no viciousness in her, no meanness or anger to go with her hatred.

Passing the door of the hospital, he swatted a mosquito off the braid on his sleeve. At eight o'clock she'd sent Dixon to bed. Ryerson had allowed her that order, thinking the sergeant could use a few hours of sleep. She'd promised to get rest herself, but Ryerson had worried about her most of his picket. He'd seen that look in her eyes, that gritty composure that showed she refused to admit her own limits.

Ryerson stopped. He'd intended to sleep in one of the Sibley tents, but a soft silhouette held his attention. He wanted to see her. He had to admit that truth to himself. As he turned toward the door, he considered the reason. Perhaps he liked her luminous beauty or the memory of her plush woman's softness. Or maybe he wanted to check on his men. Then again, he didn't feel well himself. He flicked that reason away. She was, after all, part of his command. He did not need to justify his visit.

He entered the tent. She sat on the floor next to a cot, one hand holding a compress to young Carter's forehead. The gesture must have been instinctive, for her head slumped on her arm, and she appeared to be sound asleep. He strode to the side of the boy and whispered, "Mrs. Wheaton." He jiggled her shoulder, acutely aware of her soft cotton dress. "You've broken your promise."

"Yes, Doctor." She snapped her head up, bolted onto her feet, and stumbled headlong into Ryerson's chest. "Oh." She stepped back, shaking. "I'm sorry." She blinked. "I forgot where I was."

Still trembling, she turned back to Private Carter, replacing the compress on the sleeping boy's forehead, then gathered her hands in the folds of her skirt as she knelt down next to the cot.

Ryerson watched, stifling the impulse to hold her. Her hair had come loose and tumbled down over her shoulder. He thought the thick curls a blessing, for the threadbare material of her calico dress could scarcely have provided much warmth. He picked up a blanket, then paused. The rigid line of her back told him to wait. "Did you nurse a great deal during the war?"

She shook her head. "Only six months. I became ill with a fever. My parents took me back home."

"Six months is a good spell." He knelt down, unfolding the blanket. "Very few nurses last longer than that."

She nodded, her eyes on the soldier. "I must have seen a hundred men die." She turned her gaze full on his face. "How many did you see, all totaled?"

His hands stilled. "Die?"

She nodded again.

"I really don't know." He studied the nap of the scratchy

wool, absently noting the shoddy material. "I must have seen thousands of bodies, but actual deaths . . . less than a hundred. I never heard the question framed quite that way."

She rose, walked to the end of the tent, and took a small bundle out of the satchel she'd brought. "And how many did you kill yourself?"

"That I truly don't know. Not so very many. A commander doesn't shoot much, and even a soldier in battle rarely knows when he's hit his opponent. I lost four hundred and twelve in my command. I did keep track of that number."

"The Cheyenne count coup."

"What?"

"They count coup." She measured a powder into a cup. "They must touch a man before they kill him. In fact, it's the courage it takes to get close that they honor. Not the taking of a human life."

"A novel idea."

Returning, she stood before him. "I think the practice has merit."

"In a simpler world, I could see that it would."

"The Indians are not really simple." She sat down on her cot, her fingers curled tightly around the mug. "I know. I lived among them. At first their lives seem quite savage, but they have hearts and human feeling, not so different from whites."

He lifted the blanket. Her scent wafted up to him, a light hint of lilac, unpretentious and natural, as if she'd perfumed herself with the prairie. Laying the cover over her shoulders, he stifled the impulse to touch her cheek. "You're a remarkable woman."

She started, stood up, and edged toward the door.

"Come with me. I'll make you tea. You look as if you don't feel well yourself."

He followed her, ignoring the blanket pooled by the cot. He disagreed with her observation, but he wanted to stay by her side. She exerted a pull. He didn't know how to define the sensation, but he felt a calmness when talking to her, a kinship, almost a friendship. He supposed he should examine the feeling, but some part of his mind warned him away. He'd learned that, too, during the war. Wounds hurt less when left unexamined, and this part of his life, the painful emotions left by his past, was a part of himself that remained unexplored.

Outside, she approached the campfire's banked embers. Using her skirt, she took the pot's handle. It hurt his masculine pride, that gesture. It emphasized her poverty with no conscious intent. Her hem had been burned almost translucent by sparks.

He sat down, feeling a little bit dizzy. "I don't blame you for your hatred."

She poured out the tea, making no response to his comment. The mass of her hair fell to her waist, a thick, warming shelter allowing her to hide her expression.

Reaching out, he accepted the cup. "I ruined many lives, including yours, but those raids saved hundreds of soldiers." He had trouble gaining control of his voice, and his sentence came out a little bit gruff. "Believe me, I never took pleasure in them."

"That's not what Dixon says."

He smiled slightly. "Dixon liked freeing the slaves, and I grew to love Dixon. The raids left me few friends. I came to value the ones I made."

She drew back, replacing the pot on the fire. "Did Dixon really hate slavery so much?"

"Yes, he did."

She turned her face to him. "Was his master so cruel?"

"No, I don't really think so." He took a sip of the sour-tasting liquid. "But Dixon's a man. He loves his freedom—especially chasing beautiful women. I can't imagine him jumping over a broomstick."

"Broomstick?" She leaned toward the fire, seeking its warmth. She had the most beautiful skin, translucent and peachy, burnished rose-gold by the light.

He cradled the mug. "You really don't know much about the people you owned."

"No. I told you. My father never let me go near our Negroes." Sitting down on a log, she smoothed her skirt over her knees.

"That's how slaves marry." The metal cup warmed his hands. "The couple jumps over a broomstick. In the eyes of the world, the ceremony means nothing, but it means a great deal to the husband and wife. When we freed them, that's the first thing the poor bastards asked for. They'd bring me their wives and two or three children and ask to be legally married."

"That kind of marriage wouldn't be any more legal."

"I understand that, but most of them didn't. Half of them thought I was Lincoln himself."

"Not Dixon."

"No. Dixon understands quite well who I am."

She paused, picked up a stick, and poked an ember back toward the fire. "Don't you think he's just traded masters?"

He felt his cheeks heat in anger. "No."

She must have caught the edge in his voice, for she slanted a glance at him, then stared at the flames. "I didn't mean you. Life in the United States Army doesn't seem much of a freedom."

He gulped down another swallow. The brew had cooled, turning quite bitter. "The army isn't so bad."

"Hah!"

The tin bent in his hands. He tried to lessen his grip, but his suspicions held him. He found himself fighting his distrust of her. "Give me time." One by one, he loosened his fingers. "I can make the army do better."

"How?" She tossed the stick into the fire. "Do you think I'm stupid? Your men are sick because of how they've been treated. The Yankees might have bought off their consciences by freeing the slaves, but that doesn't mean they like the Negro or intend to treat him as an equal."

He sat the drink on a rock, careful to keep the liquid from spilling. "You really do hate us, don't you?"

"No, I don't." She stood up and adjusted her apron. The firelight danced on her glorious coloring. For the briefest of moments she seemed an illusion. Autumn in a Connecticut forest. The beauty, the promise, the brief hint of winter, all contained in an Indian summer. "I told you before, I hate war and killing, but give me credit for some common sense. Beneath the uniform, one soldier's the same as another."

He lost track of her sentence and barely made sense of her speech. His head ached. His own voice came from a far-distant place. "Would it hurt you if I didn't believe you?"

"I'm not sure."

She reached out and took hold of his hands. Blood throbbed in his temples. He'd only touched the gloved hands of ladies, excepting, of course, Helen, his wife. He thought Mrs. Wheaton's gesture quite brazen, but she seemed to view it in a different light. Slowly she turned his palm up, studied the pale crisscrossed lump of his scar, the calloused palm, the weathering tan.

She ran her fingers over the bump. "How did you get that?"

"Gunshot at Shiloh."

"Why?" Those cinnamon eyes burned with unspoken questions.

"Why not?" Slowly he withdrew from her grasp. "Do you think me so much a coward I'd hide in a schoolyard while my countrymen died?"

"The war took your wife and two children."

"Madam, you misspeak. They died of camp fever."

"Do you deny you blame their deaths on the rebels?"

He made no answer. He lied well in defense of his troopers, but he hid his own frailties more poorly. She reached for the cup. He tried to follow her actions, but his gaze remained fixed on the now-vacant rock. He wondered briefly if she'd fed him poison, but instantly dismissed that notion. He saw, in a quick burst of insight, that her weakness lay in a different direction.

She meant to forgive him.

He got up and strode onto the prairie. The night's insects rose in a hoard, springing swiftly into the darkness, tiny hopping insignificant creatures, bounding away from his blundering boots. He'd once destroyed people almost this simply. And what had it gained him? He'd had these thoughts so many times. Fame he'd have sacrificed gladly. Money. He had only Helen's. He'd made no fortune as a result of his exploits. A better life for his wife, son, and baby? He almost laughed at that notion. For all he knew, he'd cost his children entrance to heaven. Ryerson made an effort to swallow, but his throat had gone dry.

A rustle behind him caught his attention. She appeared at his side, still holding the cup. "The Rebellion stole your family from you. You avenged your loss by burning plantations. In an odd way, that gives me some peace."

He stared at her face, unable to comprehend what she meant.

Gently she placed the cool mug back in his grasp. "It's easy to imagine those motives. I would have found my fate much more painful had I been destroyed by a beast with no human feelings."

Soon after, Ryerson fell ill. All week Elizabeth worried. He alternated between severe chills and fever, but insisted on helping to care for the others. She knew he was suffering badly, and surreptitiously dosed him with quinine, but he brushed all suggestions of rest aside.

"Standards," he'd growled in response to her chiding. "A trooper fights in spite of his pain. These boys must prove a whole race of men worthy. I can't expect them to get soldiering right unless I provide a proper example."

Elizabeth made no reply, but she wondered if he would survive his own rules, for he drove himself at a terrible pace. At midnight he relieved Dixon on picket duty, watched for four hours, slept two, then made the whole troop a breakfast of spiced hardtack pudding. If men could be cured by ceaseless worry, Ryerson's soldiers should have been up and walking. Their grizzled commander not only cooked, but also prodded and prowled and fretted and questioned.

By the seventh day, Elizabeth reached the end of her patience. At breakfast, observing his pallor and two fever spots, she'd resorted to insult and physical force.

"You know, you're really quite hateful." She swiped at his shoulder, then attempted to push him out of the tent. He dodged. She searched through her pockets, determined to arm herself in some way. "Get out!" She retrieved a cloth and smacked his arm with it. "Remove yourself from my hospital, sir."

He grinned lopsidedly. She regretted the swat, for she never quite understood his sense of humor.

"Go on." She nudged his elbow, annoyed by his thick woolen jacket. She could not induce even that compromise, and the major wore his full uniform in spite of the temperature she knew he was running. "Go. Go." She pushed with both hands. "I allow only my patients in here."

Private Carter, the sickest, propped himself on his elbows. "Now you lissen, Major. We don't need your help. The mistus is takin' good care of us."

Ryerson lifted an eyebrow—stern, mocking, and paternal. "You trying to get rid of me?"

"No, suh," Carter said with a smile. "We like you just fine, but the mistus knows what she's doin'. Fort Leavenworth nearly killed us. We owe this lady our lives."

With that comment the patients sat up, one after another, nodding their heads in solemn assent. Ryerson sobered. He moved to the first cot, touched a young private's shoulder, then disappeared through the door. His departure left the small group of men quiet, and Elizabeth cleared away most of the dishes before Carter spoke up.

"Do you think we hurt his feelins'?"

"No," she said as she clunked a tin cup into her bucket. "He's a hard man to read, but I think he's happy you're all getting better."

Carter clambered out of his bed. He wore a loose cotton pajama, such as might be worn by some type of workman. Though Elizabeth made no request of him, he began to help straighten the tent. "He doesn't look so well hisself."

"He isn't. He's sick."

"You think so?" He took the bucket out of her hands.

"I know so. He's probably sicker than you are."

"Then you got to take care of him."

"Hah!" She shook out her apron. The garment had become awfully grubby. She washed the white cotton each night, but Ryerson, in the sole flaw she'd found in his management, had run low on laundry soap. "Have you ever tried giving him orders?"

"Mistus, you don't understand." Moving easily around each of the cots, Private Carter collected the rest of the flatware. "We can't lose the major. We could end up servin' under a bad man, somebody like that General Custer."

"Custer?"

"Yes, mistus." Carter had symmetrical features, clean-lined and serious and handsome enough that Elizabeth found herself wanting to sketch him. "They tried to give us to the boy general, but he took one look at our ugly black faces, tossed his pretty gold curls, and asked for a transfer."

"So, you have nothing to worry about." She whisked the wool blanket off the private's cot.

"That's where you've got some learnin' to do." He put down the bucket and rerolled the bedroll that served as his pillow. "I ain't sayin' the Yankees ain't good men, but very few of them got any love for the Negro. And then there's men like General Custer. He don't even treat white sojers right. I know Major Ryerson from his raids in Mississippi. He treats his boys like they's his own children."

Together they smoothed the wrinkles out of the sheet. Carter tucked under one side. Elizabeth folded the other.

"I thought you were through with being treated like children." She spoke softly—she hoped in the tone of a friend.

"We are."

Dixon walked in. Elizabeth looked in his direction. His expression attentive, he walked to the cot and picked up the bucket. "But you've got to wonder about President Lincoln. He must think a lot of the Negro. He freed the slaves without making provision for how a black man could earn his own livin'. It took us six months to find recruits who could read. These men can't ride, and they've never had guns. They better get a commander who loves them, or freedom won't be much of a blessin'."

Carter slumped onto his cot. "That's the plain truth of it, mistus."

Dixon frowned, then took Elizabeth by the arm and led her out of the tent. "What's this I hear about the major?"

Outside, Ryerson slept in the shade of a Sibley tent, his forearm thrown over his eyes, painfully haggard even in sleep. Stifling an impulse to unbutton his jacket, Elizabeth veered in the other direction. "He's sick."

Dixon followed her to the campfire. "Missus, Carter's right. You got to take care of the major. He's the only friend these men have got."

Elizabeth hefted the water off the andirons. "If you love him so much, perhaps you can help him."

"I'm not the nurse."

"I'm not the nurse, either." She bunched up her apron and tilted the water into a basin. "I told him when he first came to me. I only care for Indian children."

She could feel Dixon's gaze on her back. She dumped the dishes out of the bucket. Ryerson twitched at the clatter, turned to one side, then settled back into his slumber. She grabbed the bucket and strode to the spring. "I told him when he came to get me. I'm tired of nursing, tired of soldiers. I won't help any more men kill each other."

"You're tired of killin', so you'll let Ryerson die?"

She knelt at the bank. The cool water flowed over her hands, and mud squished beneath her knees. Evidently attracted by the sight of her mistress, Nanny trotted the length of her tether, gave Elizabeth a quizzical look, then bleated softly for some attention.

Ignoring the goat, Elizabeth filled the wooden container. "In some ways, the choice seems so simple. Let Ryerson die and save hundreds of lives."

Reaching down, Dixon lifted the bucket. "But you won't do that, will you?"

"No." She scrubbed the hem of her skirt, but only succeeded in smudging the bottom. Annoyed, she hopped to her feet. That was the trouble with nursing—noble objectives, but a mucky existence.

Dixon grinned, a smile that made the uniform dashing. "You like him."

"I don't." Elizabeth grabbed for the handle.

Dixon shied to one side, setting the dishes to rattling and sloshing water over his pants leg. "You like him in spite of yourself."

With a sidelong glance at her bleating goat, Elizabeth headed toward the hospital tent. "He has his good points. Look." She turned and faced Dixon. "If a man can be judged by the love of his comrades, then Ryerson has definite virtues. He's not the beast the newspapers portray, but he can't excuse any more killings. I *don't* count myself as one of his friends, and if you are contemplating any romantical follies, Sergeant," she said as she shook out her skirt, then retied the knot at the back of her apron, "banish those very thoughts from your devious mind."

Ryerson awoke in the hospital tent with no recollection of how he'd gotten there. He supposed he must have passed out, though he could not determine how long he'd been unconscious. He had no memory of his nightmares or dreams, but felt satisfied he hadn't cried out. Except for a sense that someone had touched him, he had no idea how he'd spent the day.

Still groggy, he struggled to a half-sitting position. The

sun had gone down, though not long ago. Its waning light bathed the room in a glow. For a brief moment, the room seemed to shimmer. He blinked, then looked around for his troopers.

Elizabeth Wheaton sat by his side, rolling a white linen bandage. Her head was bent to her task. One hand circled the other. She made a pretty, peaceful, almost heart-stopping picture. She wore a rust-colored dress, one he had not seen before, thinner, more worn than her green calico. He found its softness attractive—revealing—and he noticed the even pace of her breathing.

He grinned, weak, flushed, and a little bit dizzy. "Good evening."

She smiled, dropped her work in her lap, and reached over to fuss with his blanket. "Good evening."

Her gesture made him aware of his chest. "Did you undress me?"

"No." An inscrutable light flared in her eyes. "Dixon did that."

Glancing around, he noticed the cots. "What have you done with my boys?"

She tucked the roll in an apron pocket, sighed, rose, and moved to a bucket. "They're in the Sibleys."

He felt the heat rise in his cheeks, a painful sensation considering the fever. "I don't need the entire hospital to myself."

"They insisted."

"And you agreed?"

"They seemed to think it a sign of respect to not share their officer's quarters. You gave them your tent. They're giving it back." She reached down and wrung out a compress. "They can be pretty stubborn when they want to be. I thought it best to give them their way."

He fell back onto Carter's bedroll. "I've trained them too well."

Elizabeth smiled. "So it seems." Returning, she tugged the blanket down to his waist. "Lie still. I'm going to give you a bath."

He knew he should protest, should throw off the covers, leap out of the bed, and toss this presumptuous nurse out of his quarters. But her pronouncement aroused an indelicate passion. The gentleman in him thought he should leave, but a ghastly languor claimed all of his limbs. One part, however, responded with interest. He was lucky she seemed not to notice.

She pressed the cloth to his forehead. "You're struck with a malarial fever. Until your temperature's broken, it's best to keep you cooled down."

He found the gesture seductive. He watched her, unreal in her marked and exotic beauty, intensely aware of cool against hot. Her delicate lilac fragrance entranced him.

Softly he touched the dots on her cheek. " 'Nymph in thy orisons, be all my sins remembered.' "

She drew down her straight, no-nonsense brows. "Beg your pardon?"

"It's a line from *Hamlet,* when he greets Ophelia."

Gently she moistened the side of his mouth with a cool cloth. "I don't take its meaning."

He grinned, drowsing. "You're my punishment, I suppose."

"For what?"

"My transgressions."

Turning away, she twisted the washcloth. He noticed the pulse in the curve of her neck. She had such a delicate, feminine beauty, he found it remarkable that the war had not killed her.

She returned from the bucket and leaned toward his

chest. Capturing her hand, he turned her palm up, but stifled an impulse to kiss her. "They could have named you Aurora. Even your fingers have a rosy-tipped glow."

"You're babbling."

"I should say so." He caught the hint of a dimple. He had not noticed that before in her face, the slight hint of laughter implied by a crease in her cheek. It soothed him, that smile, and he found himself drifting toward sleep. "I think fate has a wry sense of humor, sending one of my victims to care for me."

"Be quiet. Don't talk like that."

He wanted to say something clever, but his illness truly had claimed him. He'd become soft everyplace. He smiled to himself. "I know. I'm mush-headed." He rolled over, preparing to sleep. "You know the line from *Hamlet?*"

"What line?"

" 'Frailty thy name is woman.' "

"Yes. I think I do. Yes."

He could hear the puzzlement in her answer. He knew he had some point to make, but the cool air wafted over his torso. "Well, for once . . ." What was it he wanted to say? A jumble of images passed through his mind. All he could grasp were the flowers. Lilacs and bright prairie lilies. ". . . For the first time in many long years . . . Shakespeare's truth does not seem to matter."

Elizabeth wondered what Ryerson meant by the quote, but she didn't dare ask. He needed his rest. For all her hard words to Dixon, she'd developed a soft spot for the major.

Stepping away, she stared at his back. His soldier's life had molded his muscles. Though she supposed him to be in his late thirties, he had the build of a much younger man, with a litheness to him that made his age hard to guess. Bending down, she dipped her cloth in the bucket.

Cool water washed over her fingers. She edged toward the cot, remembering the first day she'd met him. To her chagrin, warmth flared in the pit of her stomach. She found the sensation peculiar. He stirred something extraordinary in her, a low throb beneath conscious awareness, so strong and persistent she thought it might stay with her for years. She sighed. She supposed she had to accept this truth at least. The major radiated masculine essence, a combination of bay rum and bravado that must have belonged to men of his station at least as far back as George Washington.

She shivered, thinking her reaction foolish. She'd imagined Ryerson often over the years, sketching him over and over, as if by venting her spleen on the paper she could douse the pain he'd caused her. She'd wondered sometimes what he really looked like, and if he would be quite so fearsome in person. She'd even pictured him reading the papers and reveled in the sweet fantasy that her cartoons hurt him, if ever so slightly, and paid him back for some of the grief.

She shook out the compress, then touched his bare back with the cloth. Her heartbeat sped up. She could feel him through the thin linen. Smooth-textured skin and sinewy contours. *No, he doesn't seem younger,* she thought. *He's different, harder, leaner than I ever imagined.* She blushed. She had never expected to find him attractive. Thinking about her response, she decided isolation must have undone her and vowed, when she got back to the cabin, to spend more time with her Indian friends.

He turned, easing over. His eyes remained closed, but a ghost of a smile played on his face. She wondered what he was thinking. It would have been like him to find her dilemma amusing. Eyes narrowed, she touched his stubbled face. A low sigh escaped him.

Suspicious, she drifted back to her camp stool. She'd been lonely out there on the prairie, but had she really sunk so low as this? Hands shaking, she tossed the cloth in the bucket, then drew a bandage roll out of her pocket. None of Ryerson's men had been wounded, but a nurse never knew when she'd need a bandage.

Seeking to gather her thoughts, she perched on the rickety seat. She had no right to like Ryerson, no right to betray her family and husband. At the very idea, pain rose within her. She'd never thought of herself as a wanton, but Ryerson roused such complex emotions in her. She didn't know what to make of herself.

Hands still clasping the bandage, she struggled to get control of her breathing. Still trembling, she stared at the half-naked, half-sleeping figure. She'd already lost one soldier husband, and, as far-fetched as the notion of marriage might seem now, she'd not even start down the path to that grief. She wanted peace, a house on the prairie, maybe even a yard full of children. If that seemed too much to wish for, she wanted at least some sense of safety, some security from violence and destruction.

Ryerson groaned. She started, moved to help, but he settled back down before she could reach him. Edging closer, she watched him. For once, he seemed peaceful. To her surprise, his eyelashes softened his normally fearsome expression. Pale, almost silky, they rested on his war-weathered cheekbones and gave him the vulnerable look of a child. Friendship. She seized on that notion. Yes, they could establish that kind of accord. In spite of the cruel way she'd spoken about him, she actually did want to help with his troop.

She started in bandage-rolling, seeking some solace in the rhythm. Friendship. Her heartbeat slowed to the pace of the word. That seemed a good term for her feeling.

She'd help him get well, he'd be suitably grateful, take her back to her cabin, and they'd part as friends.

She stopped, took a look at her work. To her surprise she'd bungled the job. Generally she spooled without looking, but her inner skirmish had taken its toll. A lopsided lump filled her lap. Exasperated, she shook out the linen, glad he couldn't see her. He'd probably chide her for failing his standards, and laugh had he fathomed the reason. She held the strip up to the light, determined to get the task right. She might be lonely out there on the prairie, but at least she'd live her days out in peace.

Dixon entered the tent about midnight.

"Do you want me to spell you?" he asked.

Elizabeth had wrapped herself in a blanket. She sat on her camp stool next to the major, fighting off her impulse to sleep. "No. He's doing much better. Malaria is a cyclical illness. He'll be sick again in a couple of days, but he's over the worst."

The sergeant pulled up an empty cracker box. Sitting, he fished in his pocket, then drew out his unfinished pipe stem and his whittling knife. "Don't you think you should get rest yourself?"

"I'm fine."

Elizabeth watched for a minute, then turned her gaze back to the major. She liked this part of nursing, the nighttime vigils by a patient's bedside. She'd developed a taste for peaceable silence, especially when she also felt needed. Usually she read the Bible, but Ryerson drew her attention even in sleep. By day she found him magnetic. At night she found him a puzzle. Something about him worked on her insides. She tried to read his expression, decipher his eyebrows, and decode in the line of his cheekbone how this wry, compassionate man had come to do such terrible things.

The rasp of the knife drew her attention. Not bothering with the delicate whisper, she kept up her study of Ryerson's face. "Did you know his wife?"

"Yes, missus, I did." The sergeant's voice held a brief hint of sadness. Elizabeth knew that she shouldn't ask, but she'd wondered about this subject since their first conversation. Given Dixon's quest for a new life for the major, she knew better than to exhibit an interest. Still, she thought, this was Ryerson's soft spot, the best way to figure him out.

Squelching her doubts, she drew in a breath and asked her question outright. "Did he love her so very much?"

"Yes, missus, I think he did." The knife scraped the wood. "She was a real pretty woman. Rich—with a powerful father. She bore him a son and then a second. She would have made any man happy."

Elizabeth's heart sank in her bosom. She shouldn't care what Ryerson had suffered. Nevertheless, Dixon's answer hurt her. It would have seemed a less painful loss had Ryerson not been fond of his wife. She drew the blanket around her and listened for the sound of the crickets, or wolves, or even a falling ember. Unfortunately all the prairie sounds had deserted the night, leaving only her own interior questions and the sound of Dixon's whittling knife.

"What did she look like?" She blurted out the sentence, knowing exactly how stupid she sounded.

She couldn't see Dixon, but she thought she heard a soft chuckle. "Why do you ask?"

She jumped to her feet, paced to the side of the tent, and dumped her satchel out on a cot. "It's not what you think. I simply wondered about him, how such a decent man became such an ogre."

"Like I said, she was pretty." The cracker box creaked as he lifted off and sauntered over to sit next to her. "She had hair a little like yours and the air of a great New England lady."

She fiddled with her medicine packets, annoyed with her own devious motives, but unable to stifle her interest or think of a way to make her questions a bit less direct. "Did she make him happy?"

"I believe so, at least before Jamie's death." He shut his knife softly. " 'Course, her passin' affected him greatly, in particular the way that it happened."

"Dying in childbirth?" For some reason, this part of the story made her heart ache.

"Not exactly."

The man had a cruel streak, parsing his information this way. Affecting an air of forced calculation, she lay her tisanes out in a row. "I don't follow what you're saying."

"She died by her own hand."

She stilled. She'd intended to straighten the contents of her bag, but suddenly the powders looked foreign, and no logical order suggested itself. "I'm sorry." Elizabeth thought her comment quite stupid and looked at the ceiling in her distress.

Dixon's soothing bass wafted her way. "No need." Dixon paused, then hitched one thumb in his belt. "She had a lot on her mind. She'd been weakened by fever. Her Jamie had died: The major couldn't be with her. When she lost the baby, she took to bed and never got better, the way it happens sometimes after childbirth. She died in the worst possible way."

Elizabeth jumped to her feet, paced the length of the tent, turned at the door, and stared out at the prairie. So that was his ghost, the memory he kept pushing away, the invisible creature that always annoyed him.

Comprehension made the beast human. She wasn't sure she was ready for that.

Slowly she returned to the cot. She lowered her eyes and studied her packets again. Suddenly she seized on an order. She separated the herbs into two piles, those she knew to be true medicines and those with merely a good reputation. Quietly she picked up one of her herbs. The scent of balsam drifted to her. She held the packet up to her nose, breathing deeply to let the smell sharpen her senses, and stifled the impulse to ask any more questions. "I'm sorry. I should not have asked."

"That's all right, missus." Dixon looked down, shoved his knife in his pocket, and made a good pretense at feeling for something. "I'm sure you had the best of intentions." He picked up the pipe he'd been whittling, shoved it into his mouth and chewed on the stem. Moving to Ryerson's side, he stared at his sleeping commander. Tenderly he adjusted the blanket, watched for a moment, then strode toward the door. Lifting the flap, he glanced at Elizabeth, then spoke in a pain-laced and barely audible whisper, "She slit her wrists on Ryerson's dress sword."

THREE

"YOU CAN'T GO BACK TO THE CABIN." MAJOR RYERSON
mounted his chestnut. He pressed with his legs, rode
to the head of his troop, and waited, straight-backed and
indifferent, while Elizabeth gathered her goats. She hated
to quarrel. During the two weeks in which he'd been sick,
she'd grown almost fond of the man. Watching him command the magnificent warhorse, she understood why—and
how much—his troops loved him.

She glanced at the line formed by the soldiers, at the
young, proud faces trying to disguise their fear of their
mounts. "I don't care to discuss this in front of the troopers."

"Fine. Don't. Just come back to the fort."

She fidgeted with the nosegay tucked under her apron
string, a small token she'd intended to give him. "Can't we
talk someplace more private?"

Ryerson nodded, first at her, then at his sergeant. While
Dixon gave a command to dismount, Elizabeth turned,
hiding her offering in the folds of her dress. With one hand
she gestured to Carter, who came and took charge of her
pets. Turning, she walked to the stream fed by the spring,
ignoring the creak of Ryerson's saddle. She had made it
about halfway to the water when Ryerson's footfalls

clumped up behind her. He wore his full major's regalia, including a sword that clanked with every step.

Elizabeth kept her gaze forward, thinking about the morning's events. The soldiers must have begun their work early. She'd slept in a Sibley tent, arising to find the whole camp had been struck, her hospital loaded into an ambulance wagon. Ryerson had ordered her to pack, a command she'd obeyed promptly, selecting the nosegay as Carter took down her tent.

Only when she'd gathered her flock, and the whole troop stood at attention, had Ryerson stiffly informed her he intended to take her to the fort. She should have been angry, but somehow she wasn't. She'd gotten to know him by now. Of course he'd want to abduct her. He thought she needed protection. Years of command honed certain impulses to reflex. She even forgave his unscrupulous methods. He had, after all, planned Ryerson's Raid. She could hardly expect a skilled and ruthless tactician to change his ways to suit a mere woman.

Reaching the stream, she lifted her skirts, making her way along the banks. "Why can't I return to my home?"

"There's a war on the plains." He strode to her side, guiding her progress with a hand at the elbow. "There's a very good chance the Cheyenne will kill you."

"No. They won't." She tried to ignore her response to his touch. She'd discovered in caring for him that there was something electric in him, a fierce energy that transported itself from his being to hers every time he came anywhere near her. "I told you before, I have friends among them."

"I'm sure you do," he said as he offered his arm, "but war often erases those types of distinctions. Even your friends may find they don't know you."

Ignoring his gesture, she walked beside him in silence. The grace of his stride surprised her. The sword clanked in a dissonant clatter, like a full suit of armor somehow come to life, but he moved with a lithe suppleness completely at odds with his martial bearing. Warmth crept through her limbs. "You don't understand. I was married to one of their chiefs."

A high color came into his face. She'd come to recognize this sign of his temper, the darkening of his swarthy complexion. "Then I'm sure you can grasp this fact, madam." He curled his fingers over the hilt of his sword. "Even the greatest leaders can't control their own warriors once the young bucks get their blood up."

"I know. You used that excuse on the raids."

He snatched back his hand. Instantly she regretted her jibe, her reference to those of his Riders who had exceeded even his fearsome orders.

"Here." She held out the nosegay. "I didn't want to part with an argument, but you have a way of making things hard."

He frowned. A light breeze ruffled the blossoms. Briefly Elizabeth worried about the coolness. The wind meant they ought to hurry. Kansas weather had only two moods— bright blue, sunny, and true; and black, swift, and decisive. Ryerson's mood matched the latter.

"Look." She offered the flowers again. "I gathered them for you. It was an honor to serve you, in a way. I learned a great deal nursing these Negroes. I'll always regret the loss of my home, but I can see now the war served some purpose."

He touched one of the petals. The wind danced in the tendrils, tangling butterfly weed and wild indigo. "You'll come back to the fort?"

"No." She turned. A single raindrop splashed her face. "Please don't ask that of me."

Ryerson gripped Elizabeth's shoulder. "We don't have time for this nonsense. You're coming with us."

She shrugged, pulling out of his grasp. "I'll go where I want. I mean to go back to the cabin."

"And if I don't take you?"

"I'll walk by myself." She thrust her chin up, trying to look a little more forceful. Tightening her fingers over the nosegay, she swished her skirts and headed in a southward direction.

"What are you doing?" He'd reined in his temper, but his voice had an edge, thick, taut, and lethal. She reconsidered her course of action.

"All right." She turned to face him. Three fat droplets hit her, one on her nose and two on her shoulder. "I want to go home. No one will hurt me."

"No." He grabbed her wrist, holding so tight that pain shot up to her shoulder. A look had come into his eyes, a kind of mad panic, and she wondered about the rumors, the ones that labeled the major a madman. "You think you're different, but really you aren't." The wind gusted up, bringing a shadow. "Go tell your stories to somebody else. I've seen hundreds of women like you in action, defending yourself with outdated weapons and foolish illusions. Do you think that I, of all people"—he paused, startled, then brushed at his sleeve, as if a raindrop had touched and annoyed him—"would abandon a woman to war's vagaries?"

A bolt of lightning hit the horizon, followed by the boom of thunder. Elizabeth jumped, dropping the nosegay. A shout caught her attention. Dixon led the small line of troopers down the draw to the stream.

Ryerson threw her a look of disgust, snapped toward his troopers, then bellowed above the storm's growing rumble,

"Dismount! Hang onto your reins! Unroll your shelters—
and quick!"

She bent to retrieve the bouquet, then abandoned the
effort as she felt a tug on her elbow. His hand on her waist,
Ryerson pulled her toward the troop. Halfway there, he
stopped next to Private Carter, who struggled to make a
pole of his rifle.

"No time for that." Ryerson shook out the square of the
shelter, the small tent employed on maneuvers. "Use this
for cover, along with your slicker." Almost tenderly, Ryerson covered the boy with the canvas. "We don't need any
more sickness."

Carter nodded. "Yes, suh. But, please, git yourself covered."

Elizabeth shot him her best look of thanks. The sky had
opened itself, and cold droplets of rain smacked her face.

Elizabeth glanced at the rest of the men. Following Ryerson's orders, they had tucked into improvised quarters.

A soft huff escaped the major. "Come on."

Elizabeth found herself once again in his grip. Wind
whipped her cheeks. Rain slapped her face. The prairie
turned muddy beneath her. James Ryerson, the beast
who'd haunted her maidenly dreams, swept her up and
carried her forward.

His hand hurt her waist. She thought she should try to
gain her own footing, but his painful grip also felt solid, a
fixed point in a world turned to water. She buried her face
in his chest. He lifted her higher, then whistled, a long,
eerie blast through the grumble of thunder. She glanced
around, but the rain filled her vision. Before she could
figure out what Ryerson wanted, his chestnut nickered beside them.

Ryerson set her on her feet, the water sluicing off the
brim of his hat. Reaching out, he tugged on the reins, issu-

ing sharp commands to the horse. To her surprise, the charger rolled to his side, making a great sucking noise in the mud. Ryerson grabbed Elizabeth's arm, shoved her next to the animal's belly, then unfastened the roll on the front of his saddle. Another lightning bolt struck in the distance. The chestnut jerked, and Elizabeth scrambled.

Ryerson steadied her with his hand. "Don't worry. He'll stay."

Elizabeth looked at the chestnut's wide, frightened eyes and realized with a cold shiver that he'd learned to do this trick in battle. Ryerson shook out the canvas, then settled the square over her head. Thunder boomed in the distance, then rumbled over the grassland.

"Come here." Ducking under, Ryerson pulled her onto his lap. He removed his hat, opened his greatcoat and circled his arms around her. Horrified and embarrassed, she tried to squirm forward, but he clasped her tight to his chest, and she found herself cocooned in his warmth. She wiped one muddy hand on her skirt, then drew in her breath, trying to find a more modest position. She regretted the threadbare state of her skirt, the dearth of ladylike undergarments. Three layers—skirt, pantaloons, and his wool cavalry pants—failed to disguise the sinewy cords of Ryerson's muscles.

He leaned back, tugging gently to bring her closer. She tried to stay forward, but he kept up the pressure, until, to her frustration, he'd established her in a nested position. Reluctantly she hunkered back. A small sigh escaped him. Settling in, she tried to relax. His breath on her neck, the damp scent of horseflesh, managed to make the world almost cozy, but she remained edgy, wondering how long this rain would last and if the chill would affect the health of her patients.

"So," he said as he planted a booted foot next to hers, "why don't you want to come back to the fort?"

She shivered, staring out at the rain and the fuzzy landscape it made of the prairie. "This is a fine time to ask me."

At first he didn't seem to respond to her comment. He remained tucked in the shelter, apparently watching the rainstorm. Gradually, though, she could sense his reaction. Snuggled this close, she found it hard not to feel the tension in his muscular thighs and the growing thickness and hardness between them.

His fingers brushed the back of her neck, and he pulled a strand of wet hair from her face. She shivered. Gently he turned her toward him. He examined her face, his eyes bright and incisive, then frowned.

She flushed, hating her weakness. Alone, she forgot the tattoos. But people were mirrors, their eyes reflecting their feelings too well. His expression—like that of all whites she'd met since her freedom—mingled horror with pity. She tilted her chin up, tamping back an impulse to flee. Let him look all he wanted. She'd never been any great beauty, but she felt certain of one truth at least. Inside, she'd gotten better. If her outside could not match the healing, at least a frank gaze would show him that the markings meant nothing. In her soul she'd made peace with her past.

He touched her lightly, grazing the pad of his thumb over her cheekbone. A ghost of a smile played on his face. He drew her silently to him, pressing his lips to her forehead. Then he shifted beneath her, balancing her on both of his thighs. He lifted the canvas, staring into the storm as he absently rubbed the scar on his hand. "We could pretend to be married."

She blinked. Jerking around, she stared into his eyes,

searching for a trace of amusement. "Are you making a joke?"

Wind gusted into the shelter. Adjusting the covering, he folded her into his chest. "No one at the fort would dare cause you pain if they thought you were my wife."

Heat flushed in her cheeks. Her breath came in little short bursts. "I think you've gone crazy."

"The newspapers have sometimes alleged that." He smiled, his mouth close to hers. "Perhaps a marriage would squelch that scurrilous rumor."

"Are you ill?" She pressed her hand to his forehead, sincerely concerned for his health. "Do you hear what you're saying?"

"I know what I'm proposing. Now, why don't you listen?" Closing his eyes, he leaned into the chestnut. "For all you think you know me, there's one question you never asked."

She stilled, watching his face. "What?"

"How many times I nearly died."

Slowly she withdrew her hand. The truth of his comment stabbed at her heart, for she'd never thought of him that way before—vulnerable, frightened of death. She clenched her fists in her lap. "How many?"

"Seven, exactly." He readjusted his legs, drawing her closer. Eyes still shut, he held out one hand, using his fingers to count. "Once at Bull Run. This palm wound at Shiloh. Twice on the raids. Once reconnoitering the Tennessee River, once in a train station just south of Corinth —a cannonball took off my first orderly's head. And the time I shot Nathaniel Greenstreet." He opened his eyes. She'd never noticed their color and couldn't say that she noticed it now, but his gaze had the strangest effect. He'd lost none of his intense energy, but somehow he'd softened, his face becoming more tender. "This time makes eight. You saved my life, and also the lives of my troopers. I hate to admit this, but we only survived because of your help."

She averted her face, trying to make sense of his proposition. He'd truly surprised her, and as she turned the idea around in her mind, she found just one explanation for his peculiar behavior. She placed her hand on his sleeve. "You don't have to protect me." The rain eased to a gentle patter. "It's not your fault I was out on the prairie."

He didn't answer. Self-conscious, she pushed the rest of her hair off her shoulder. She found this position un-nerving—seductive. For all his fierce reputation, he could make her believe in this kind of peace—the private world of a man and a woman. She had a wild, poignant thought. What if they found themselves an island far away from mankind and wars?

She twined her fingers in his and squeezed. "I know you feel grateful, but that's just your illness, the isolation you felt out on the prairie. You're going back to the army, where people adore you. Soon your sickness will be just a bad memory."

He lifted her hand. "We could say we were married by an itinerant preacher." His lips brushed over her knuckles, inducing a rapid, hot-and-cold shiver. "My men won't contradict me." He kissed her palm, then rubbed his thumb over her cheekbone again. "No one would dare make fun of my wife."

A riot broke out inside her. Apparently Ryerson meant this suggestion. "What would you do in the future? What if Di—you—found a second wife?"

A smile quirked the side of his face. "Likelier the devil marry an angel that I contract a true second marriage."

She drew back slightly. "And what of the army? What would happen to you if they found out?"

He shrugged, leaning forward. "I've eluded whole armies bent on my destruction." His mouth hovered near hers. "I think I can manage this minor maneuver."

He drew down the canvas, making the shelter a warm, private retreat. Pain bloomed inside her breast, desire rebelling against common sense. Ryerson's touch made her crazy. She'd been happy out there on the prairie. Serene and content, but very alone, and he, with his electrical presence, forced every nerve to remember the bleakness.

"You're going to regret this," she murmured.

He smiled, then pulled her into his chest, against the bright row of buttons adorning his front. Holding her face, he drew a deep, shuddering breath, then lowered his lashes. "I certainly hope so."

He kissed her, his mouth burning on hers. He had a firm, masculine kiss—possessive, straightforward, confident, and demanding. He held her so tight he hurt her; brass, braid, and wool poked at her softness. In spite of the prickles, a hunger consumed her, voracious and swift. Not the tender longing she'd harbored for Philip, but passion, ardor, and another emotion, deeper and different. Spiritual in a way, but far, far more instinctive. His mouth worked against hers, claiming, exploring, pressing against her. She struggled to keep some sense of composure, her insides melting, her nipples gone taut.

"Why?" Pulling back, she searched his expression. A darkness had come into his eyes, a feral and bottomless black.

"Don't ask," he whispered, his breath warm on her earlobe. The chestnut moved beneath them. Ryerson placed a hand on the animal's neck. Panic surged through Elizabeth. She kissed Ryerson back, thinking herself ten kinds of fool and probably something baser than that. She hated her weakness, but she hungered to taste him and yearned for his touch. Only half-consciously, she arched her hips into his. A thrill spiraled inside her. Some part of her knew why she loved this gesture, why she adored the sensation of hardness. She felt her distress as an ache in her muscles, as a jangle of nerves and blood rushing with madness. He'd aroused her desire for a partner. He'd awakened her need for a man.

Gently, as if he sensed her weakness, he cupped his hand under her breast. She moaned. He froze, watching until her breathing slowed down. Then he raised the canvas, allowing the rain to splash in his face. "My apologies, madam. I forgot myself."

She watched the water course down his cheeks. Beads bright as teardrops formed on his stubble. Her hammering heart regained its old pace. "No need—"

"I'd forgotten." He clamped his hand on her shoulder. "Four years—the war before that."

Letting go, he swept back the shelter, baring himself to the storm. Eyes lowered, he dropped back on his elbows, almost as if he'd lost track of her presence. Elizabeth bit her lip. Thick droplets spattered his uniform blouse. She feared for his health and wanted to pull him into the shelter. One sign and she would have, but he'd retreated inside himself, locked in a fierce and eloquent stillness. She crossed her arms over her bosom.

"I'd forgotten," he whispered, speaking either to God or himself.

FOUR

THE STORM HAD CLEANSED THE PRAIRIE OF DUST, AND THE midmorning light lent a heartbreaking beauty to the wide, clear expanse of the plains. Ryerson breathed in the scent of the newly washed grass. Riding at the head of the troop, he found it hard to keep his eyes focused on the horizon. Elizabeth's kiss had shaken him badly. He had forgotten the power of lust. In the years since Helen's death, he thought he'd reconciled himself to a bachelor soldier's existence, long months of celibate life relieved by the occasional whore. Unfortunately the ache in his groin told him quite clearly that he'd been mistaken in that self-assessment. He wanted this woman—and badly.

He tugged on the reins of the chestnut and dropped back. The line of his soldiers passed him, riding a little more gaily, having survived their first open storm on the prairie. Briefly he considered Elizabeth's observations. He thought them perceptive, if melodramatic. He didn't need her forgiveness. He needed—he batted that thought away —he didn't want to know what he needed. He didn't like giving a name to those urges. She'd saved his life. Hell, she'd saved his whole troop. Given the chance to return the favor, Ryerson thought that he ought to. After all, his raid in a way had put her out on that prairie. He had no intention of wedding her truly, but if he could shelter her through this Indian war, he might make up in very small measure for some of the damage he'd caused in her life.

He glanced at her in the ambulance seat. She sat beside Private Carter, the small line of goats trotting behind. For reasons he couldn't define, he liked the idea of this pretend marriage. Her poverty pained him. It pleased him to think of buying her dresses and finding her some decent housing. He'd have to displace one of the less senior captains, but that should pose no particular problem. The married officers' quarters were spacious enough. No one need know of their sleeping arrangements. He'd make a visit to a few of the ladies and rid himself of his baser urges. And he'd buy her a bonnet to cover her hair. Real wife or not, he wanted that glorious sight to himself. And besides, he rationalized to himself, she'd have a less painful experience if he found her a way to hide the tattoos.

He studied her profile, her classical features. He believed her description of the people's reaction, for he knew well enough how westerners felt. They hated the Indian, saw him as evil. The tattoos would provoke some lurid assumptions. Ryerson had wondered about that himself— what exactly she'd suffered at the hands of her captors. What did those strange markings mean? Her defense of the Indians struck him as strange, but she was a remarkable woman in many ways. She had, after all, forgiven Ryerson his raid, and how many women in her position could claim that peculiar distinction?

He smiled. She caught his grin.

"Private." He halted the chestnut. "I'm going to spell you."

Ryerson dismounted. Carter jumped down off the wagon.

Ryerson held out the reins. "Would you like to try him?"

"Suh?" Fear, delight, and apprehension all crossed the boy's face.

"You'll find this an easier ride. A skilled cossack couldn't control the half-broken, hammerhead, spavined nags the army's seen fit to issue this troop."

Carter accepted the offering, planted one hand on the horn, and scrambled into the saddle. To his obvious surprise, Ryerson's charger held steady, ears pricked upward and backward, as attentive as any well-trained human soldier. Ryerson gestured toward the head of the line. "Take the place behind Sergeant Dixon. I'd like the boys to see how much difference a decent mount makes."

"Yes, suh." The young private nodded, touched his spurs to the chestnut, and bounded toward his comrades. The troop rode to the front and the side, a straggling line of awkward, bobbing young riders. A tight pride squeezed in Ryerson's chest.

"You really do love them, don't you?"

Ryerson glanced at her. The sun shone through the ambulance canvas. The cloth framed Elizabeth's face, making a backdrop a painter might envy. The light played in her hair, muting its reds and turning it golden. The sight made him dizzy, wild and poetic. He remembered her as she worked in the tent, incandescent and glowing, as if Apollo had loved her and wished to lend her some of his treasure. He batted that last nonsense away, thinking the illness still affected his thinking. He slapped a mosquito, then vaulted onto the seat. The troop bounded ahead, bouncing behind Private Carter. Ryerson flicked the whip, and the ambulance leaped to a start.

Elizabeth jumped to her feet, clutching the post that held up the canvas. "Wait!" She turned and climbed into the back.

Startled, Ryerson tugged. He bellowed to Dixon. Troop

and ambulance came to a halt, the chestnut pawing the prairie and some of the joy leaching out of Carter's face.

"Mrs. Wheaton?" Ryerson twisted around and got a view of Elizabeth's bottom. Pleasant enough, were it not for her peculiar behavior. "What are you doing?"

"Balthazar." She clambered over the ambulance gate. "He can't keep up this pace." She dropped out of sight. A high bleat floated Ryerson's way. Elizabeth reappeared to the side, arms full of brown-and-white goat. "If you'll have the men go a little bit slower, Nanny and Pappy will do all right. I'll just bring the little one up here with us."

She lifted the bundle. Ryerson scowled. He threw the troop one quelling glance. Dixon grinned and ordered eyes front. Ryerson grabbed the goat by the scruff.

"Be careful." Elizabeth kept her hands under the animal's stomach. "He's just a baby, you know."

Ryerson tugged, lifting the kid out of her grasp. Balthazar squabbled and kicked, missing Ryerson's stomach by half an inch. With a mild curse to himself, Ryerson dumped the beast into his lap.

He stretched out his hand. "Would you care to join us?"

Elizabeth climbed up without help. Reaching out, she brushed Ryerson lightly, then folded Balthazar into her apron.

"Don't be scared," she crooned, as if speaking to a human infant. "Mama will take good care of you."

Ryerson nodded to Dixon, who had the good sense to keep his face neutral. The whole procession started again, this time a little more slowly. Only Carter had trouble. The chestnut warhorse had gotten inspired. He intermittently quivered and twitched, as if he smelled some excitement out there on the prairie and couldn't quite understand why his new master wished to proceed at this tranquil pace.

Elizabeth settled down, snuggling the goat beneath the

soft curve of her bosom. Desire hit Ryerson like a physical jolt. He tried not to be petty, but he found himself jealous of the kid's position. He fought off the bawdiest thoughts, tried to distract himself with speeches from *Hamlet*, but kept wondering what it would be like to lie in Elizabeth's lap.

They'd driven maybe three miles in silence before Elizabeth interrupted Ryerson's struggle. "How did you become friends with Dixon?"

The question surprised Ryerson. He still wasn't sure how she felt about his colored troopers. She'd nursed his men with devoted care, but her feelings against them must have run deep, considering how she'd acquired her terror. He knew from his own experience with horses that childhood fears die the hardest. He decided to answer in detail.

"At Vicksburg my son fell in love with Dixon." Pain welled inside Ryerson. Elizabeth didn't react to his discomfort, simply sat there, serene as always, stroking Balthazar's neck. He clucked to the horses, wondering why he should dredge up this old, sad memory, then reminded himself how much he owed her. He tightened his grip on the leather. "The sergeant was my orderly then, but he wanted to be a cavalry trooper. The army didn't have a Negro horse unit, so Dixon and Jamie drilled every day." In spite of his grief, he smiled to himself. "You should have seen them. Crisp and perfect in their presentation, a redheaded boy and a nappy-haired servant. They should have been funny, but somehow they weren't. Even General Sherman came out to watch them, declaring he'd never seen better soldiers. Helen, my wife, thought their antics delightful, but I viewed them with more mixed emotions. I knew what Dixon wanted, and when Jamie died, I promised myself I'd help my orderly achieve his ambition."

Shifting, she rearranged the goat in her lap. "You lost

your son, so now you've adopted a whole troop of Negroes."

"Mrs. Wheaton"—he straightened his posture—"you're
given to odd observations. My motives are far more
straightforward than that. By purest chance, Sergeant
Dixon became my son's best friend, and his last. I felt I
owed the man something. I like to pay off my debts."

She patted the kid's furry back. "You founded this troop
to help Sergeant Dixon?"

"Yes."

A smile quirked at the side of her mouth.

"You find that amusing?" he asked.

"Not exactly." She continued to stroke the beast on her
lap. Ryerson flushed. To his displeasure, he found the gesture extremely erotic. The caress reminded him of those
hazy moments of illness when she had thought he'd dozed
off. She'd brushed out her hair, then anointed her hands
with sweet-smelling creams. He'd watched her from beneath lowered lashes, wondering at the mysteries of
women and the myriad ways they kept themselves soft.

As if she sensed the drift of his thoughts, she left off the
petting and straightened her apron. "If we're to pretend to
be married, you ought to call me by my Christian name."

Fierce delight shot through Ryerson. He wanted to hug
her, but supposed he shouldn't. "You've decided to accept
my proposal?"

Her fingers curled in the animal's fur. "I'd rather go
back to the cabin."

"And if I don't permit you that freedom?"

"I'd as soon be a wife as a captive."

"Sensible view."

Balthazar slipped to her knees. She grabbed him and
tucked him back in her lap. "I can see this arrangement
would buy me some peace." In spite of her words, her

voice telegraphed her distress. He could tell from its tone, a certain forced flatness, that she strove to conceal the depth of her worry. "But I'm still concerned about some of its details. You have no reason to want to help me. There's nothing for you in this agreement."

"You think not?"

"I know not. And I hope you do, too. For all the unorthodoxy of my past, I still consider myself a lady."

He straightened himself in the seat. "Madam, you need not concern yourself for your virtue. I have no illusions in that direction."

"Even after the kiss?"

"Especially after the kiss."

He couldn't see her expression. They'd caught up to the troop, but he kept to the side in order to spare her a shower of dirt clods. As always, her nerve served her well. She kept a grip on the baby, and an eye on the parents, holding steady by tucking her feet under the seat. "Well, then, back to my point. You owe me nothing because of the raid."

Annoyance flashed through him. He hated that characteristic of women. They'd make pets out of goats and reduce a man's past to drawing room theories. "Elizabeth, let me make myself clear." The sun burned through the canvas. The scent of wet grass filled his nostrils. The whole world seemed hopeful, green and at peace, in startling contrast to the morning's dark storm. "I'm not offering to protect you because of the raids. I did what I did. I don't regret one single dark deed. It's true the war haunts me, but not in the way that you think. For all the cruelty of my pillage, those forays were only war's remote shadows. I don't like to describe the scenes I've experienced—bloated bodies and too-shallow graves or mangled limbs eaten by maggots. I only want you to know—I never caused the death of a woman."

She pulled the kid tight to her bosom. "But, in a way, what you did was worse."

"Why?"

"Because"—Balthazar bleated as if her grip pained him. He lifted his pink nose up to her—"the women did nothing to hurt you."

He felt like an ogre. He didn't want to debate this matter, didn't want to wound for no purpose, but her comments touched a sore point with him. "They sent their men to serve in the army. Do you think soldiers would join without that incentive?"

Her breath came in small bursts. "You made war on innocent victims."

"Should only men die in a war?"

"Only men become soldiers."

"Soldiers are husbands, brothers, and fathers." By now, he couldn't help his anger, couldn't keep the harsh tone out of his voice. "I struck at men's homes. The places where they sheltered their women and children. Their gardens and cellars. Their family treasures." All the memories welled up inside him, the fury and anguish, the sense of despair. "I plundered their hearts and trampled their heirlooms. Made them pay for Helen and Jamie." His voice rolled over the prairie. He knew the troop heard him, but he still couldn't stop. "I liked General Sherman. He made war hell. This country won't resort to its fiendish solutions for ten generations—maybe more." He thought he'd said enough, but anger propelled him to keep up this one-sided skirmish. "You think I regret those infamous raids? You're mistaken. I know what I did. I saved thousands of lives. Traded hardship and hunger and famine for blood and death and much-mangled bodies. I think I got the best of the bargain."

"I refuse to believe you're as hardened as that," she whispered.

"Then you delude yourself, madam."

"Why, then, this peculiar marriage proposal?"

He tugged on the reins, slowing the ambulance to a stop. "I told you before, you saved my life—and the lives of my troopers."

She watched him with a wary gaze. He hated to see that expression. Not frightened, but distrustful and leery. "Well, I must say"—she took a deep, calming breath—"considering your upside-down sense of justice, I don't think I like being one of your debtors."

"Fort Leavenworth is quite pretty." Elizabeth touched Carter's sleeve as she pointed out a neat row of white buildings, precisely arranged around a central square. "More civilized than I thought it would be."

"Yes, mistus." The soldier frowned, his expression a visual grumble. He tugged on the reins, guiding the ambulance onto the road leading to the parade ground. A shadow shifted at the end of the commons—an inky blur of pattern and movement that turned and flowed in their direction.

"Of course . . ." Elizabeth dropped her hand. "Appearances can be deceiving."

The dark shape rumbled toward them. Light glinted off a bristle of rifles. Elizabeth shuddered. An infantry company marched into focus, reminding her a bit too abruptly that this seemingly peaceful expanse of deep green was really a place where men learned to kill.

Ryerson's troop trotted past. From her perch in the wagon, Elizabeth noted the drilling foot soldiers' reactions.

They stared, not overtly or rudely. Rather, their scrutiny took the form of disruption, a dissonance in their rhythm, a twist of the shoulders, a tilt of the neck, and a twitch of the muscles. Elizabeth glanced at Ryerson's back. Predictably he ignored the disturbance, riding upright on his charger as if the infantry company had turned out to greet him.

At the stables, however, the mood of the spectators changed. The horses, of course, were indifferent, but the troopers working around the long building took conspicuous notice of Ryerson's group. At first one or two men simply stared. Elizabeth added a fillip of interest. As the ambulance neared, a low buzz ran through the stalls. A burly man shouted in German. Somebody answered. Carter clicked with his tongue, driving the team to the side of the cavalry line. The maneuver put the wagon out of view, but word of Elizabeth's presence had spread. A hum to the rear caught her attention. Glancing back, she caught sight of a crowd, not large, probably less than a dozen individuals, but sufficiently vocal that the tone of their chatter carried over the sound of the hooves.

Elizabeth lifted her chin. She'd learned this one lesson at least. Don't hide. Stare them down. Pretend to be proud, and never, *never* let the gawkers know how much you hate their rudeness. Evidently Ryerson's troop had been schooled in the same kind of experience. They rode the length of the stables, eyes forward, halting in the fort's farthest corner.

The major signaled, dismounted, then nodded to Dixon. Without a glance at either troopers or audience, Ryerson strode to the rear, raised his arms up, and lifted Elizabeth out of the seat. His light touch amazed her. Ryerson had leashed both his fierceness and harshness. He held her so gently she wondered if he'd noticed the hubbub. A glint of steel in his eyes reassured her.

Carter's voice floated down. "Good luck to you, mistus."

Ryerson set Elizabeth on her feet, bent down, and whispered, "Chin up, Libbie. Soon the worst will be over."

Warmth feathered through her. The nickname came as a pleasant surprise. No one had used her pet name in years. She could not even guess how Ryerson knew it. Her astonishment must have showed, for he grinned, cocky and pleased with himself. "Instinct. You had to be Libbie."

Elizabeth's heart squeezed in her chest. Only Papa had used that nickname with her. Philip, as well as her mother and brothers, had always preferred the more ladylike Beth. Her father, however, had enjoyed being different. As a child, Elizabeth had chafed under his teasing, suspecting the tomboyish tag reflected a father's discomfort with his one female offspring. Over time, she'd found a certain joy in his habit. She took the name as his way of admitting he looked at his girl as a person. And Ryerson?

She smiled as she tucked her arm in his elbow. She liked the sound of her name on his tongue. She'd gotten used to the clipped Connecticut accent, learned to hear some of the softness that leaked through the edges of his short, seemingly harsh Yankee speech.

Ryerson covered her fingers, snugging her close, using height, weight, and momentum to guide her. She followed along, thinking she must be crazy. The fort frightened her. The soldiers, the noise, and the movement brought back memories, painful and vivid. Worse, she knew the crowd followed. She wanted to hide. Turn herself into a bird or a rabbit or some smaller, more peaceable creature, the kind nobody noticed. Only Ryerson's stride, graceful and rhythmic, kept her from bolting. She allowed herself one moment of hope, then tensed.

They'd reached the parade ground. The blue-clad Yankees still drilled with precision. Elizabeth fixed her gaze on

Ryerson's sleeve, ignoring the growing lump in her stomach.

They'd traversed most of the length of the green when Elizabeth caught sight of the women. Three ladies, officers' wives, she supposed, strolled in the shade. As Ryerson approached, a pretty girl broke off from the others. Her pale parasol bobbed in the sunlight. She'd crossed half the distance between them before she slowed down, stopped, and shied to the side. The swift shift of crinoline satin largely obscured an audible gasp. Ryerson must have noticed the lass's reaction, for he stiffened his back, tucking Elizabeth's hand a little more tightly into the crook of his arm.

Eyes forward, Ryerson steered Elizabeth toward a tree-lined path. The smell of lush grass made her homesick. She'd been away from civilization so long. She fervently wished her return could be peaceful, but the low hum behind them reminded her in no uncertain way of what supposedly civilized people thought of her background.

Ryerson marched past the girl, past the other two women, past the row of cannons and the length of the path before halting in front of a stately two-story building.

"Ready?" He glanced down at Elizabeth.

She shook her head, acutely aware of her drabness, her oddness, and the peculiarity of the events about to transpire. Hesitating, she stared up at the white-columned porch. Ryerson would proceed with his plan. She felt quite certain of his resolve. Approaching the fort, he'd had a short conversation with Dixon, who'd halted the troop and announced, with no prelude, that Major Ryerson had made Mrs. Wheaton his wife. As Ryerson had predicted, not a single man balked. At the time, Elizabeth attributed the troopers' indifference to their irregular notions of marriage. Standing before this prim structure, a genteel reminder of all the army thought proper, Elizabeth realized the troop's acceptance reflected a quite different meaning. Like Dixon, they loved their commander and wished to show him their friendship.

With his hand on her waist, Ryerson pressed Elizabeth upward. Putting her weight on his arm, she lifted her high-buttoned boot. Her feet felt heavy, along with her stomach. He must have sensed her discomfort. He braced the small of her back with his palm. She focused on that sensation, stiff leather gauntlet against threadbare cotton.

Gathering her skirt, she mounted the stairs. As she scaled the first step, she found herself grateful for his support. He was wrong, dead wrong, in his decision to bring her, but she couldn't fault his goodness of heart. This course of action took courage. The tour of the fort must have showed him how much, but he remained by her side, steadfast as always, prepared to endure as much public censure as if he'd contracted a genuine marriage—and worse, should their ruse be discovered.

"You can still change your mind." She paused at the top. "Your men will say nothing."

He let go of her waist and strode the width of the porch. He swept the door open and held it for her. She could have wept at the gesture, for he stood in the doorway, courtly and proud, as if he escorted a very great lady, rather than herself, a shabby, discarded, well-worn bit of flotsam, the disfigured survivor of two violent wars. She lifted her chin and sailed past, cringing inwardly, but loath to fail his elegant manners.

Inside, a bespectacled private manned a federal-style desk. Letting go of the handle, Ryerson crossed to the boy, squared his shoulders, and halted. "Major Ryerson reporting to the post commander. Company L is returned from maneuvers, and I am requesting a change of quarters."

The owlish private leaped to his feet and saluted. "Welcome back." He shot Ryerson a questioning glance. "Sir?"

Ryerson stepped to the side, beckoning to Elizabeth. "May I present the former Elizabeth Wheaton, now Mrs. Major James Ryerson, my wife."

The boy blinked, his face soft and pudgy. "Sir?"

Ryerson clasped his hand over his sword hilt. "I wish to rank a married captain."

"Tonight?"

"Tonight."

Elizabeth reached Ryerson's side. His expression confused her, for his jaw had tightened, and his face had gone flinty, as if he expected intense opposition and had made up his mind to resist.

The clerk looked uneasy. Ryerson adopted his warning look—the one that preceded his temper. He recaptured her elbow, drew her close to his side, and straightened his already strictly martial posture. "I'm senior by brevet to every post captain."

"Yes, sir." The clerk ransacked a drawer, dropping three maps and a handful of papers.

Ryerson shifted his weight, a subtle gesture, but one that rattled his saber. "Do you doubt my rights in this matter?"

"No, sir."

"Then hop to it, Private. I'm tired."

Hands trembling, the clerk riffled through a neatly lined ledger. Elizabeth felt a stab of empathy for the boy. She had not understood Ryerson's discourse, but she knew something of his methods by now. For all his sometimes softhearted kindness, he wielded authority like a rapier. She gathered he wanted some privilege, some tribute the boy felt loath to give out.

Wetting his lips, the private peered at a name on the page. "I'll need orders—"

"Then get them."

The boy nodded, then scurried through a door to the side of the office. Ryerson relaxed. Elizabeth marveled at his self-possession. His carriage expressed minute variations in starch, starting at perfect and proceeding by subtle degrees to commanding. Sometimes he even seemed to grow larger, radiating a presence that filled a room. At other, quieter moments, he shrank, though he never seemed entirely human. At the very least she remembered the lithos. That wartime image stayed with him, like a constant shadow of the genuine man, the vivid picture his fame had created of the terrible raider who'd pillaged the South. A scuffle of boots brought Elizabeth out of her thoughts. The clerk hustled in a plump, bewhiskered officer, a shade past middle age.

"Colonel." Ryerson touched the brim of his hat.

"Major." The portly commander returned the salute. He circled the room, then came to a stop before Elizabeth. Carefully he studied her cheekbones, gawking a little less rudely than most of the soldiers. "Mrs. Major." He cut off his gaze, then stalked to a window. "Such a tactician, Major, Major. Always full of surprises."

"My specialty during the war."

"I suppose you have papers."

"They're in her Bible. You can send your private to get them."

"No need. We're all gentlemen here." He left the pool of afternoon sunlight, returned to the desk and perused the book. "Mrs. Captain Jennings is lowest. Perhaps you could give her a few days' notice."

"Tonight."

The word struck Elizabeth like a blow. Suddenly she took Ryerson's meaning.

"Wait." She took one quick step forward.

"Mrs. Major?" The colonel turned, his expression repeating his question.

Elizabeth's heartbeat sped up. "What's going on here?"

No one answered. Ryerson had drawn into his presence, his magnificent, electrical pose, the one she remembered from *Collier's*. The private whipped off his glasses and cleaned them. The colonel picked up a pen and studied its nib.

Elizabeth's heart whooshed in her bosom. She'd finally grasped this disagreement. She'd supposed Ryerson had some kind of house. The notion that he might have to change quarters had not crossed her mind. "Do I understand this conversation correctly? Are we putting another officer out?"

The colonel nodded, brief and tense, without looking up from the paper.

"And his wife is living there now?" She turned to Ryerson. He stood, arms crossed and scowling, the neat row of brass buttons studding his chest.

"Major." Briefly she touched his gauntlet. "James."

He gave her one fierce glance of disgust. "Gentlemen," Ryerson snapped out the word. "If you'll excuse us."

Hand on her elbow, Ryerson propelled Elizabeth out of the room. He hustled her the length of the porch, then stormed down the steps, taking her with him. Reaching the bottom, he charged the path in furious silence. The crowd scattered before his onslaught. Nobody followed. Reaching the end of the neat line of trees, he turned to the right, hauling Elizabeth after him, and planted her next to one of the cannons.

He circled the massive weapon, sword clinking in time with his spurs. "Mrs. Wheaton."

"Mrs. Ryerson now."

"Yes, well." He flicked a bit of lint off his sleeve. "Mrs.

Major Ryerson, then. You've just become an officer's wife. You're expected to live in the married officers' quarters."

Casually as she could, she edged toward the trees. "I'll not displace another woman."

He cut her off by commandeering her elbow. "This is a matter of rank, not sentiment."

"I don't care about rank." She struggled to free herself from his grasp, but he held her tight, guiding her firmly back toward the guns. She grabbed one of the wheel spokes and jerked. "You may be the perfect soldier, but I don't give one fig for those rules. Can't they just let us live someplace that's empty?"

"There are no vacant officers' quarters."

"But you have a place now."

"I have exactly one room to myself."

"Then we'll just stay there."

Dropping her arm, he clasped his hands behind his back. He paced from one cannon to the other, his face in high color, clenching and unclenching his fists. "Madam, I have the greatest respect for your scruples, but I cannot consent to this plan. Not to put too fine a point on the matter, but I have one room—one bedroom—to myself."

She thought her knees would buckle beneath her. She hadn't thought about where she'd sleep. Nevertheless, she held firm. She knew something about James Ryerson. He waged war like a vandal, but held to a gentleman's personal ethics—she hoped.

Briefly she touched the cannon behind her. "I'll sleep on the floor."

He turned on his heel, a tic in his jaw revealing how far she'd pushed him. "Are you out of your mind?"

Pretending a calmness she didn't feel, she sat down, took a deep breath, then deliberately fanned out her skirt. "For heaven's sake, James." She folded her hands in her lap. "I live in a cabin. Before that a tepee. At this point in my life, even wooden floors sound quite grand to me."

He scowled. "You were not my wife in that tepee."

"I'm not your wife now."

"Not in that sense," he said, brushing his left forearm, "but I'm pledged to protect you. If I take you into my bachelor quarters, the soldiers will think of you as a squaw." He jabbed his finger toward the parade ground. "You've already seen what your treatment will be. Don't hurt yourself by displaying a weakness." Turning, he stalked the artillery again, outlining his thoughts in short, staccato phrases. "If I treat you like an officer's wife, these people will see I intend to defend you."

She smoothed the carpet of grass, ignoring his fit. If they meant to weather this Indian war, she'd have to learn to handle his temper. She searched for a chink in his armor, then smiled. She spoke to her lap, in a calm voice she knew he could hear. "I know you mean well, but command has spoiled you rotten."

He looked up, surprised.

Without lifting her head, she kept on with her speech. "For four years or more you've gotten your way. You've moved history—and men—with these tantrums. I'm sure this is effective for slaughter and pillage, but you won't find these tactics so useful with me." She raised her chin, awaiting the next burst of anger.

He grinned, that wry smile she found so distracting.

"Please," she said as she drew another deep breath, then patted the ground by her side. "Sit next to me."

He marched back, sword clinking, hesitated a moment, then came down on one knee in a courtier's position. Bending low from the waist, he brushed his lips over her fingers. "Elizabeth, please. Let me do you this favor."

She glanced around, but no one could see his outrageous

behavior. She thought his gesture might be sarcastic, but his face remained still and composed. He stared at her from beneath lowered lashes, his breathing harsh beneath his stiff collar. Suddenly she wanted to hold him. He might not be her actual husband but he was offering her a husband's protection—and meant it.

She squeezed the gloved hand that held her bare fingers. "I won't stand on the fact that we're not really married." She swallowed, feeling the weight of her vow. "I'll submit to you in practical matters, but there are some favors you cannot ask."

He frowned. "I can't ask you to live in suitable quarters?"

"That's not the problem."

"And what, pray tell, is the problem, madam?"

Shyly she brushed his stubbled cheek. "You don't understand, do you?"

"No, frankly, I don't."

She jumped to her feet. "I don't suppose that you do." It was her turn to pace the artillery row. The brass cannons stood at attention. She hurried past three, then returned. "After all that you've done, this must seem so minor." He remained in his half-kneeling position, hand on his sword hilt, his face vaguely bemused. "James." She dropped down to meet him. "I know what this woman will feel like. You've done the same thing to me. Not once, but twice." She placed her hand on his sleeve. "You've burned my plantation. Kidnapped me from my cabin. I can forgive you, even admire your motives, but from this day forward, for as long as I'm with you, there's one rule I'd ask you to follow."

A glint of suspicion flared in his eyes. "Dare I ask what that precept might be?"

"You'll not drive any more women out of their homes."

FIVE

RYERSON SURRENDERED. HE STORMED BACK TO THE colonel and withdrew his request. After growling out his report in very poor humor, he escorted Elizabeth onto the porch. He found his troopers waiting for him. The crowd of spectators had gone, replaced by Dixon and most of the troop milling anxiously at the foot of the steps.

"We brought something for you." Dixon flashed a devilish grin. Ryerson nodded. One of the soldiers brandished a broomstick. Ryerson wondered where Carter had gone, but stifled his question as four laughing privates gestured Elizabeth off the veranda.

Ryerson rested his boot on the railing as she and the soldiers retired for a brief whispered conference. He thought her pretty in the falling daylight, a small, auburn-haired figure, consulting earnestly with his brown-skinned troopers.

She returned with the following news: "They want to find out who'll be boss in our marriage."

"I see." Ryerson descended the stairs. He held out his hand for the broomstick. Dixon could barely contain his amusement as Ryerson examined the unpainted handle, then hefted the pole. After a leisurely study of the homely broom, he skimmed his fingers over the wood. "Seems sturdy enough." He slanted a glance at Elizabeth. She'd gone pale beneath the tattoos, but she kept her chin raised, and her breathing seemed even beneath the thin cotton that covered her bosom. He cleared his throat with a cough. "Perhaps we should go someplace less public."

Dixon grinned. The troopers whooped in delight. Their cries traveled the length of the parade ground, the hubbub bouncing off newly green trees and echoing in the lowering twilight.

Ryerson took Elizabeth's arm. "To the river?" He paused, cocked one eyebrow, and waited.

She nodded, either completely confused or simply struck speechless. He wasn't sure whether she thought this idea peculiar or was simply too stunned to make a fuss. He waited until they reached the tree-covered bluffs before he tried an explanation.

Turning onto the path that led toward the river, he lowered his voice. "This is one of slavery's customs. It's the way slaves marry, but there's a little more to it. This ceremony also predicts the course of the marriage." Elizabeth gaped at him, wide-eyed, as if she couldn't believe what she was hearing. He swallowed, regretting this false marriage idea. His plan had seemed simple out on the prairie. He had enough rank to command his own house, which should have made the arrangement straightforward. She'd surprised him with her resistance, and now, of course, the rules had changed. They'd be sharing his quarters, one room exactly, in a house he split with two English cousins. The Hazletts were friendly enough. They would dine in the mess if he requested, but given his supposed newlywed status, he could hardly ask to move out of his bedroom.

He scowled, tightening his grip on her elbow. "The ritual works this way. We each jump backward over the broomstick. If my feet touch, I will be henpecked." He thought he caught a glimpse of a dimple. "If you miss, I will be boss. If we both get over the wood without touching, that means we'll have a congenial marriage."

She ducked her head under a low-hanging branch, then continued her tromp down the path. She seemed tired by the time the group reached a clearing, but she smiled when two troopers went down on their knees. They grinned in return, then balanced the broomstick between them.

"Lower," she prompted, but both soldiers laughed and raised the handle a little bit higher. She sobered, turned backward, and bunched up her skirts. Pausing, she chewed on her full lower lip, her gaze fixed on the yellow-green grass. Without warning, she jumped. Ryerson caught a glimpse of pale calf. He scowled at the obvious absence of stockings, the lack of even one petticoat, but he was the only man who seemed to notice these details. To much merriment and general good humor, she sailed easily over the stick.

"Your turn." She smiled. He liked seeing her happy. The sight made her surpassingly lovely. It also kindled a warmth in his chest.

Suppressing his grin, Ryerson backed up to the handle and jumped. His feet cleared the pole, but his sword caught on it. The mishap set off gales of soft laughter and a lively debate over its meaning. Dixon claimed that the blade didn't count, but none of the troopers agreed. A bottle of wine appeared out of nowhere, and immediately after, a fiddle.

"To the bride." Dixon held up the amber-colored flagon. "We declare her the winner."

Ryerson nodded. He accepted the glass and took a long swig. Honeyed fire burned his mouth. Persimmon brandy slipped over his tongue, warmed the back of his throat, and slipped sweetly into his stomach. He'd intended only a sip, but the fruity concoction had a thirst-quenching freshness. He drained the bottle of a good two inches of liquid. Passing the wine to one of the troopers, he glanced Elizabeth's way.

She sat on a log, tired and abstracted, seemingly lost in the low, velvety song of the fiddle. Her cinnamon eyes were dreamy and glazed. An apricot flush tinged her cheeks.

"Let's go." He took hold of her fingers. The drink's fire had warmed him. She felt precious and soft in his hands. On impulse, he pulled off his glove. Holding her hand in his, he escorted her to the top of the bluff. He caught Dixon's smile in the side of his vision.

The troop said good-bye at the parade ground, heading back toward the low ground by the river. Ryerson frowned, making a note to check on their quarters, then turned and faced his impostor bride. She seemed subdued, wary, and exceedingly pretty. Snugging his hand around her waist, he led her quietly through the long lane of trees. As he did, Ryerson had a chance to reflect on the broom ceremony and all that this false marriage implied.

She had in fact won the first round, an idea he found mildly annoying. Although he respected her feelings, his pride had suffered a serious setback. On the prairie, she'd seemed vulnerable and helpless, knowledgeable about certain matters, but too softhearted to survive another war's rigors. Life as his wife had seemed such a fine offer; he'd expected her grateful, subservient compliance. She surprised him when she'd come up with opinions, especially in areas she knew nothing about.

So it was with some satisfaction that he noticed the shock on her face as she preceded him through the door of his house and encountered his roommates completely absorbed in their Friday night game of cutthroat poker.

"Ryerson, ho!" Lieutenant Charles Hazlett barely looked up from his cards. "Back from the wars."

His cousin, Randalph, rose at the sight of a woman. He studied her tattoos. "Major." He nodded with grave courtesy. "Private Carter came by with some of your troopers. They made a few—rearrangements. They said you'd like their surprise, but they didn't tell us you had one of your own. Madam." Randalph Hazlett bowed from the waist. Elizabeth flinched. The dip hid the English lieutenant's expression. Ryerson noticed her watch intently as the dapper young officer straightened his back. He smiled, gesturing toward Elizabeth's bag neatly stashed in a corner. "I deduce this is yours. The troop brought it by. They were as closemouthed as my uncle at Christmas. I wondered what all the fuss was about."

Ryerson guided Elizabeth into the room. A chain of emotions played on her face. Some of his anger abated. He knew she expected a refuge, some little room where she'd find some peace, not a pair of raffish English lieutenants, young, blond, and cavalry-dashing, sprawled in a spacious, if masculine, parlor.

Still, she held up well enough. She advanced to her suitcase, dodging a fine set of antlers, the head of a pronghorn, and a row of stuffed prairie chickens, all neatly displayed on the wall. Though clearly exhausted, she lifted her bag by herself. "Thank you for watching my things."

Ryerson strode forward. He lifted the suitcase out of her hands. "Sirs, I'd like to present the former Mrs. Elizabeth Wheaton, now Mrs. Major Ryerson, my wife."

Even Charles stood up at that statement. "What, ho?" He cleared his throat and tugged at the edge of a pale, wispy mustache. "What did you say?"

She faced them full on, ignoring their stunned, disbelieving expressions and their efforts to control their surprise.

"I'm quite tired. Do you think you could show me my room?"

Randalph regained his composure first. Though Elizabeth's curtness bordered on rudeness, he seemed inclined to leave her in peace. "Certainly, madam." He slicked his hair back from its center part and threw Ryerson one rueful glance.

Crossing the hall, he opened the door to Ryerson's room. Ryerson didn't like ignoring his friends; however, the tone of Elizabeth's voice—the shortness, strain, and lack of good humor—told him he ought to stay by her side. He nodded briefly to his two roommates. Following her into his room, he shut the door silently behind her.

Inside, she leaned on the wall. Eyes shut, valise at her feet, she pressed her fingers over her mouth. To Ryerson's surprise, tears seeped from beneath her dark lashes.

He went to her swiftly, drawing her gently to his chest. "Don't cry, Libbie." His voice came out husky. "Please don't. You'll make me sorry I brought you."

She shied away, still fighting back tears. "I'm sorry. It isn't your fault. This is harder than I thought it would be. I tried to warn you—"

"You did."

"No." Quickly she searched through the folds of her dress. "I mean—" She ransacked her pockets. "I did, but not very hard. I thought this time things might be different."

"They will be. I promise." He enclosed her with a hand to each side of her face. "My troopers already love you. The rest of the soldiers will leave you alone once they realize I intend to protect you."

She gazed at him with brimming eyes. Tears had deepened their color. The anger had drained from her expression, replaced by fatigue and a sense of defeat. "Ah, yes.

Ryerson the Raider. The Yankees adore you. No one would dare make fun of your wife."

He smiled. Her hair had come loose. He pushed several damp locks back from her face and brushed his thumb over her cheekbone. "Not quite." She had fine skin, high-colored and golden, made all the more so by this burst of emotion. "They'll leave you alone because they fear me."

"I thought the whole United States Army viewed you as a hero."

"Not really." She smelled of dust and a light hint of lilac, a combination he found profoundly erotic. He wanted to kiss her. The impulse unnerved him, for he'd accepted her notion that illness had deepened his sense of attraction. Standing here, suffused in her scent, he realized he'd been deluded in that idea. He felt sick to his stomach. His desires had increased since his health had improved. "In fact, regular soldiers judge me quite harshly. I gave war a bad reputation. Took the chivalry out of a fine occupation —not to mention compounding my error by introducing the horse to the Negro. Added to that—" A hairpin poked out of her hair, distracting him. He fought back an impulse to remove it. "The newspaper scribblers said I was crazy."

Her face softened a little. Her tears had stopped flowing, and she swiped at her eyes with the cuff of her dress. He grinned.

"What's so funny?" she asked.

"You are." He pulled a kerchief out of his pocket. "In two weeks of nursing my troop, I have yet to see you without compress or bandage. Need help yourself and you're reduced to a sleeve."

He offered the cloth. She dabbed at her cheek, then rested a hand on his chest. He ached to embrace her. To fold her into himself and make her forget all her worries. Right at this moment, however, he doubted his motives.

He felt tense in his arms and his chest, and in a lower, singularly masculine place. He meant to protect her, to give her a haven. But how would he shield her from his own baser nature? Cursing himself, he pushed back from the wall. She bent down, picked up her valise, then slowly walked forward.

He turned. Exasperation flared through him. Carter had clearly been busy. A double-wide bed loomed in the corner, piled three deep in quilts, the pillows fluffed up. Self-conscious, he paced to the side of the bed and tugged on the quilt. "I'm sorry. I generally sleep on a cot. I'm afraid I've taught my sergeant too well. He's got Private Carter in on his plot."

She scanned the room, evidently a little bewildered. "Plot?"

"You know, his plan to see me married."

She stared at the bedstead. He wondered what she thought of the piece. Dixon had picked rather nicely. The bed had a deeply carved mahogany headboard, masculine in its color, but ornamental enough that even a female should like it. Shyly she touched one of the bedposts. "You know . . ." A high color crept into her cheeks. "You know . . . about that?"

He nodded, then crossed to his night table. To his surprise, someone had filled a chamber set with water. He lifted the pitcher from its basin and poured. "Yes." Perfume wafted out of the shallow dish. "You know the troop really does like you."

She threw him a questioning glance.

"They've been working quite hard. The bed, the flowers, even this." He nodded at the porcelain bowl, lightly touching the pink sprig on its side. "This has been put here for you. Generally this room's pretty barren."

"They're trying to make me a home." She said this softly, her voice subdued and thoughtful.

He brushed at his sleeve, unnerved by the thought. "Would you like to wash up?"

She nodded. She drifted past him, moving slowly, as if in a dream. Reaching the small table, she touched the pine drawer, then ran her finger over the basin, as spellbound by the mundane piece of crockery as a Boston blue blood might be by a plate of bone china. She touched the liquid. Almost reverently, she picked up the fresh bar of soap. "Oh, God." She brought the square to her nose. "Do you know how long it's been?" She shut her eyes for a long, passionate second. Finally she pulled up her sleeves and dipped her hands in the water. "Oh, James, this is lovely. Warm water, real soap, and a porcelain basin." She slipped the suds through her fingers. "I take back my complaints. A bath would make the whole afternoon worth all the grief."

Ryerson strode to the door. "Hazlett!" He barked out the name. "Get me Private Carter, and quick."

"Aye, sir," Charles shot back, in a fake Cockney accent he used when he was inclined to be funny.

Turning, Ryerson watched her. She pulled the wayward pin from her chignon. To his immense satisfaction, her hair tumbled down. He wanted to run his hands through the curls, but contented himself with moving her case to the nightstand. "You know, I was wrong about you."

"I'm sorry?" She shook out the waves. Gaslight played on the fiery cascade, and he wondered if he'd ever tire of the sight. He fantasized about her hair's scent and texture. The spectacle of it intrigued him the most, however. Cool fire on a living creature, liquid as water, but touched with the colors of autumn.

"At first your constant questions upset me." He opened

his trunk. Removing his gauntlets, he laid them in a small drawer. "All that harping about my past." He unbuckled his sword, hanging the saber on one of his pegs. "I thought it a silly, female obsession. Poking around in my memories, as if my mind were a cupboard you wished to straighten."

"And now?" She unlatched the suitcase and pulled out a brush. Their intimacy struck him with force, and he realized how much he'd missed the companionship of a woman. There was something comforting in her presence. Different from a friendship with men, more delicate, but also more binding. And spiced by the other hunger, of course.

She turned. "And now? What do you think?"

"I see there's a certain point to it." He sat on the bed, testing its softness. He could not quite imagine where Dixon had gotten this. In his sly and conniving way, the sergeant had done him a favor. "Sometimes you see better than I do myself the weight and effect of the past."

"So?"

He wanted to remove his boots, but that seemed a presumptuous gesture considering the sleeping arrangements —and the fact that they hadn't discussed them. "Come here. Sit down."

She eyed him warily. She'd dipped her face in the water, making her sweet, fresh-faced, and dewy, with a little sparkle to her peach-colored complexion.

"So." He patted the quilt, the kind with blue double circles. "Your thinking needs some rearrangement. I know you hate this experience. I can't blame you. But you can't live out your life in complete isolation. You're a beautiful woman."

Her hands flew up to her cheekbones.

He stood, drew her to him, and cradled her face. "Yes, you are." Gently he pried her fingers loose. "Even with the tattoos." She struggled to free herself from his hold. He held her firmly. "You're twenty years old. Someday some man will love you. How will you find him if you're holed up in that soddy?"

She froze, her eyes assessing. "Are you making a joke?"

"Elizabeth, please." He locked her chin in his grasp. "I know what you think of my raids, but surely I haven't struck you as being a cruel man in person."

"No," she answered softly. "No, you haven't."

"Then why should I mock you?"

She wriggled out of his grasp. Slowly she circled back to the nightstand. "How do you propose I find a new husband when everyone thinks I'm already married?"

He clasped his hands behind his back. "I've been considering that." He paced to one side of the room. "After this Indian war, you'll divorce me." He prowled to the other side. "No one will blame you, given the infamy of my reputation. No one need ever know of our ruse." Completing the circle, he peered out the window. "We don't need a consummation. You're twice married already. You've already accomplished what we need on those lines."

She made a sound, a swift intake of breath.

"I'm sorry." He flashed her a look of contrition. "Sometimes I'm too blunt. The harsh facts of your life sometimes obscure your delicate nature." He glared out the window, regretting the gaffe. The tattoos bedeviled him just a bit. Not their appearance. He meant what he said. He found them lovely, a flaw that accented perfect proportions and drew out her beauty instead of obscuring it. Still, he wondered about their meaning. He'd heard of captives with Indian husbands and children who'd died of grief when returned to the whites. She did not seem to have formed that kind of attachment, but she did defend the Cheyenne. That odd tendency reflected well on her Indian marriage.

He straightened his uniform jacket. "I apologize if I made a crude reference. Back to my point, however. You must have known you would have to face this experience someday. You're too good a nurse not to know how healing works. The time for rest and retreat is over. If you're going to recover your spirit completely, you have to come out of that hole in the prairie."

She sat down on the bed, still watching him closely. "Why do the newspapers say that you're crazy?"

He joined her, drawing her hands into his. She felt warm and alive and incredibly soft. To his surprise, he wanted to answer her question. Her persistence had made an impression. Suddenly it seemed very important that she understand his wartime experience. Maybe even important to understand it himself. He brushed a lock back from her cheekbone. "Because I was nearly crazy at one point in time."

"After the death of your wife?"

"No." He touched one strand of her hair. He found it so lovely, its thickness and color. He'd dreamed about her like this, the shining mass flowing over her shoulder. "After I lost my first troopers in battle. I had to go home for a while."

She widened her eyes, as if trying to read him. "Is that really true?"

"Yes."

Ducking, she turned his palm over. "That's hard to believe."

"Why?"

"You seem to be such a natural soldier."

"Hardly." A slight rap interrupted his answer. He slipped his hands out of hers and strode to the door, regretting even this slight separation. "I barely like horses."

"But you ride so well." He could hear the disbelief in her voice.

"A learned skill, I assure you. See this?" He paused, turned, and showed her the scar on his cheek. It had faded, he knew, but still made a dent on closer inspection. "I was kicked in the head when I was a boy. Scared to death of the beasts. I only rode in buggies before the war started."

Swiftly he opened the door, a little self-conscious about his revelation.

Private Carter saluted, standing outside. "Suh?"

Ryerson stepped back. "Did you bring the water I found in the basin?"

"Yes, suh."

"Who found the bed?"

Peeking inside, a shy grin spread across Carter's face. "Sergeant Dixon."

"How did I guess that?" Squelching a chuckle, Ryerson gestured the private into the room. "Where on earth did he get it?"

Carter seemed uneasy. He snatched off his forage cap and darted a glance Elizabeth's way. She readjusted her apron as if caught unprepared, then composed her expression into a semblance of welcome. "Go ahead, Private. I'm fond of the sergeant. Nothing you say will get him in trouble."

The young man looked down at his shoes. "You promise that, mistus?"

"Of course."

A broad grin split Carter's brown face. "The news spread in less than five minutes. How the new Mistus Major refused to take the Mistus Cap'n's wife's place."

Elizabeth rose. "Oh?"

He nodded, his worries abated. "So, we borrowed her bed."

"Whose?" she asked.

"Why, the Mistus Cap'n's, of course."

"With her permission?" Ryerson snapped out his question a little too harshly.

"Yes, suh." Carter nodded again. "Don't seem like they've got much need for something so fancy, seein' as how she's expectin' a baby and all."

Elizabeth shot Ryerson a glance of outrage, then frowned. She addressed her question to Carter. "Surely you left her something to sleep on?"

The private took an anxious step forward. "Why, sure we did, Mistus." He twisted the cap in his hands. "And the Mistus Cap'n was happy, considerin' she's still got her home. She said she'd consider it a privilege to help you—" Carter embellished his sentence with a small throwaway gesture. "You know—" He added a slight nonverbal flourish, then shrugged. "Get a good start on married life."

"I see." Elizabeth spoke in a tremulous whisper, though Ryerson couldn't read the tone of her voice.

Eyes forward, Ryerson suppressed a snort of amusement. He had to give Dixon credit. Three years with Ryerson's Riders had taught the sergeant to forage. Perhaps this false marriage would work after all. He still hadn't figured out all its details, but at least he knew how to take care of her simpler needs.

"Private Carter." Ryerson snapped out the name.

The soldier threw back his shoulders and stood at attention. "Suh?"

"I'm detailing you as my wife's striker. Ten dollars a month is the going rate. You'll assist in the household and see to her comfort."

"Very good, suh," the boy answered back, his voice as precise as his thick Mississippi accent could make it.

"Good. If you'll heat up some water, I believe your new mistress would like a hot bath."

The water felt good, but not as good as the peace and quiet. Elizabeth had gotten used to that on the prairie, the luxury of vast space and silence. She hadn't realized how much she'd missed it until she sank into the tub, alone for the first time in weeks.

Feeling guilty, she drizzled some bubbles over her shoulder. She shouldn't take long. The water was already cooling, and she had no one to help her rewarm the bath. Besides, she told herself, dark had fallen, and she had to face Ryerson sooner or later. He was waiting outside in the parlor, by mutual agreement. She thought for the sake of appearance that she shouldn't keep him tarrying there.

Sighing, she sank into the soapy water. She saw now why Ryerson had been so angry. In the heat of their disagreement, she hadn't considered the sleeping arrangements. Still, she didn't think it would be much of a problem. She'd slept on corn husks in the cabin, buffalo robes before that. The feather bed looked awfully lovely, but she'd just have to forgo that civilized pleasure. Ryerson could sneak in some quilts and some pillows, and she'd make do with the floor.

She rose, grabbing a towel. She'd laid out her nightgown at the friendly prompting of Private Carter. He'd insisted on bringing the tub to the bedroom, taking great pleasure in the idea.

"You got to relax," he had told her sincerely. "This is a big day for you."

She supposed he must be in league with Dixon. She didn't know what the sergeant thought of their marriage, though she supposed he knew that the broomstick ceremony wouldn't be legal. Still, he must have approved of their peculiar union, as he seemed to be doing all that he could to make their mock marriage successful.

She shrugged the white cotton night rail over her head. She hesitated, then hopped under the covers, thinking to wait there until Ryerson made up a bed on the floor. She pushed her bare feet under the blanket. The idea hurt her a little, to be fooling such good-hearted men. She thought Ryerson lucky in his choice of friends, and hoped the troop wouldn't be too disappointed when this outlandish arrangement came to an end.

She cleared her throat, pulling the quilts up to her neck. "I'm ready."

Ryerson opened the door. Striding in, he nodded at the brass tub. "You want Carter to take it?"

"No. Leave the tub for a minute. We need to talk."

He nodded tersely. He'd unbuttoned his uniform jacket and he looked quite different. He looked younger and less formal. More like a man and less like a soldier. He leaned on the bedpost, tense and expectant. "You look very pretty."

"Listen, I'll take the floor."

"Hardly." He shrugged out of the jacket. He wore a white cotton shirt, now gray from trail dust. With his eyes on her, he neatly flicked open a button. "Do you mind?" He gestured toward the tub. "I'm awfully dirty myself."

"No." She burrowed down under the blankets. "You're not planning—" She flinched, her feet touching a hot, flannel-wrapped brick Carter had secreted under the blanket. "You won't do anything ungentlemanly?"

He smiled as he hung his shirt on one of his pegs. "You should have thought of that problem when you gave poor Mrs. Captain Jennings your quarters."

She didn't know how to answer. She hadn't thought

about this part at all. Though even after reflection, she didn't regret her decision.

"I trust you," she said simply.

"Yes, well . . ." His hands paused at his buckle. "Close your eyes."

She did as he asked, though an afterimage stayed with her of muscular shoulders and the flat planes of his waist leading into blue cavalry pants. She found the picture disturbing, more so than when he'd been sick. Those contours spoke of his life in the saddle, the life that had made him more of a man than she knew how to handle. She bunched up the sheets and tightened her eyes, but a second, more lewd picture formed in her brain. The splash of the water confirmed the image. He had in fact removed his clothes.

"You can open them now if you wish."

He faced her. He was submerged to his nipples. A swirl of dark curls adorned his chest. He clamped an unlit cheroot in his mouth. "Do you mind?" He waved the cigar. "Usually I just like to chew them, but I think I could use a small smoke."

She shook her head.

"A barbaric habit, I know. And a poor substitute for slaughter and pillage. But a man has to have one or two vices. Since you're bound to reform me, I'll make you this bargain and keep it for the rest of our marriage. I'll give up burning plantations if you'll allow cigars in the bedroom."

"Fair enough."

He nodded, then chewed the unlit cheroot, his eyes bright but unfocused. For the first time, she noticed their pigment. Not brown, not really hazel, but an unusual greenish-brown color that did not call attention to itself. Contemplating his face, which was relaxed and amused, she realized with a small jolt that he'd lost his fierce and characteristic expression. For the first time since she'd known him, she felt she looked at a man. Not an image or picture. Not the famous soldier. He seemed more than naked there in the tub. At last, he seemed truly human.

"Isn't the water cold?" she asked quietly.

"Tepid." He grinned. He seemed happy and unaccountably pleased with himself. "But a damn sight warmer than most Kansas rivers."

He lit the cigar and sucked in a miserly mouthful of smoke. She searched her mind for something to say. She wanted to think of him as a patient, but decided the subject of baths would be a little too risky. "Is it really true that you don't like horses?"

"Of course." He pulled the cigar from his mouth, sinking more deeply into the water. An involuntary shiver ran through her. She didn't know how he could stand it. The water had been cool when she left it; it must be freezing by now.

She snuggled down, her feet touching the flannel. "So how'd you end up with a cavalry troop?"

"My father-in-law."

"I beg your pardon?"

"Senator Charles Parker." He doused the cigar, tossed it over the edge, then pushed himself up with a soft sloshing noise. Grabbing a washcloth, he began to soap up. "He raised a volunteer unit for me."

"He couldn't have raised a foot company?"

"No." He washed briskly, efficient and neat, and she wondered if he did anything slowly—and what it would take to help him relax. "He had political ambitions for me. The cavalry's the most popular arm of the service."

"You couldn't refuse?"

"Yes." He stopped, lowering the soap cake. "I could have refused him."

Suddenly her stomach went hollow. She regretted asking

these questions. She envisioned his marriage as supremely happy. Worse, he must have adored his wife to work so hard at pleasing her father. "I see." Her mouth had gone dry, and she thought she should stop, but the question came out in spite of herself. "Did you love her so very much?"

"She was my life." He gave her a look she couldn't interpret. "Shut your eyes," he said in a low voice.

She did as he asked, but her mind cheated on his request. Once more, she pictured him by the sounds that he made. The slosh of water on sinew and muscle. The splash of his rising. The rasp of the towel. She sensed the last part acutely. Lean and naked he'd be. Eyes squeezed tightly shut, she followed the soft whisper of clothes. The rustle of cotton. The scrape of wool pants. Bare feet slapping the floor. She felt his presence next to the mattress.

She opened her eyes.

"But she's gone." He sat on the edge of the bed, stockings in hand. "And you're as close as I'm likely to come to a second. Which is why I won't let you sleep on the floor."

She wondered what he'd do next. He'd dressed himself in his uniform. She supposed he meant to sleep in his clothes, which seemed peculiar but somehow reassuring. "I don't want to argue, but I wouldn't feel right putting you out." She slipped to the far side of the bed. "I'll share if you'll lie on top of the quilts."

His hands froze. He gave her a swift, startled look.

"I mean . . ." She felt herself flush. "You can get your own blankets. You'll lie on the top. I'll lie underneath."

He laughed, shaking his head. "You know," he said as he pulled a sock over his foot, "it's a shame I can't keep you."

Her cheeks heated up. She wondered what he found so amusing. He didn't help one little bit, breaking into a resonant chuckle as he pulled the wool stocking up to his calf and slipped his foot into his boot. Standing, he stamped his heel against the floor. "It speaks well of your husbands, my dear, that you'd trust me that far. But their situations were different. A hunter's apt to exhibit a great deal more patience when he knows he has something to gain by inaction."

"I beg your pardon?"

He sat down, holding her by the chin. "Libbie, I brought you here to protect you."

Her breathing slowed down. He had marvelous hands, warm and strong. They were calloused, but also quite supple, like finely worked leather. His touch made her feel stifled and dizzy. "I don't understand what you are saying."

"I want very much to make love with you."

She resisted the impulse to push his hands away. Her cheeks glowed like embers, and she knew he must feel it. He was right in one sense. Her first two husbands had been different. Ryerson had this disarming directness. He spoke about subjects Philip would never have broached, and Sleeps With Eagle, well, that marriage had been odd altogether. She struggled in vain to regain her voice, but his words rattled around in her head, blotting out more logical thoughts. *I want very much to make love with you.*

When she finally spoke, her sentence came out a tremulous whisper. "I don't think that's a good idea."

He chuckled, rose from the mattress, and stared out of the window. "Sad to say, dearest, but I think you're right." Grinning, he lifted the sash, then threw one leg over the ledge.

"What are you doing?" she asked.

"I'm going to check on my troopers."

"This late?"

He poked his head out and looked to the left. "I want to see how they're quartered."

Bolting upright, she stopped in a sitting position, loath to exit the bed in her thin cotton night rail. "You can't go out the front door?"

He shook his head, then peered to the left. "Close the window behind me. Just before dawn, you'll hear a tap on the pane. Don't be frightened. That will be me. I'd be truly appreciative, wife, if you'd let me back through in the morning."

Ryerson kicked off his boots, tucking his stockinged feet beneath the scratchy wool blanket. He didn't so much mind the tent. In four years of war and two on the prairie, he'd grown rather fond of sleeping outdoors. Instead, he regretted his own sense of honor and how badly the death of his Jamie had hurt him. His son. Not just his life's blood and heir, but the child of his dreams. The beginning and end of his life. The possibility of creating more children bothered Ryerson, even with whores. He considered it fate's great joke and blessing. Man could not control mortal existence. In the end, that had been the greatest aftereffect of the war. Ryerson never again took life—or death—for granted.

Ryerson turned in his bedroll. It pained him to sleep on his stomach, given his still-stiffened state of arousal. Libbie. So soft and sweet-smelling. Sleeping half a mile away. Dixon had laughed outright when Ryerson had sneaked into his quarters and given his sergeant an order. Set up an enlisted man's shelter tent in a secluded spot by the river. Dixon had shaken his head; then, loyal as ever, he had set off to do his friend and commander's bidding. Still, Ryerson had sensed his comrade's disapproval. Clearly Dixon liked this false marriage and looked upon it as a means to an end. A real marriage. A state Ryerson did not want. He'd debated the matter with Dixon, who always maintained that his commander would be better off with a woman.

"There's two kinds of men in this life: ones like me that like the chasin' and ones like you that like the havin'," Dixon had often advised him. And Ryerson certainly had liked the having. At least until after Vicksburg.

Restless, Ryerson turned back onto his stomach, re-arranging himself against the hard ground. The punishment suited his mood, and he endured with grim satisfaction the half pain, half pleasure of his unfulfilled arousal.

How would he arrange his false marriage?

He didn't want to share Elizabeth's bedroom. He found the woman attractive. Worse, he found her erotic. He knew damn well he couldn't sleep in her bed and resist her, especially considering his recent past. Since the war's end, his acute sense of grief had faded away, replaced by the dull ache of constant yearning. He hated how his own passion ruled him. His mind and his heart might have forgotten, but part of him remembered how much pleasure a woman could give him.

Unfortunately this tent ploy would not work forever. While no one was likely to notice him out by the river, the enlisted man's tent offered scanty protection. In the spring it rained on the prairie. Even now a thunderstorm rumbled off in the distance.

Hunching down, Ryerson centered himself away from the canvas. He shivered, though not really from cold. Freezing to death was his secret terror. He'd seen a man die that way at Vicksburg. Not, as Ryerson would have expected, in true freezing weather, but in a cold drizzle while sleeping alone in a shelter like this. The army issued shelters in halves, just to force two men to share them.

Ryerson shivered. He pulled the wool blanket up to his

shoulders. No, this ruse wouldn't work. Of all the deaths he'd seen on campaign, he thought freezing the worst. There seemed something despicable in it. A slow death, not even fighting. Ryerson had little use for most women, and none at all for Elizabeth, but that trooper's fate had taught him a lesson. A lonely man paid a terrible price. And a man could survive wretched conditions, given a suitable partner to sleep with.

SIX

ELIZABETH AWOKE THE NEXT MORNING CRABBY AND tense. During the night, one of the Hazletts had knocked on the door. Elizabeth nearly fainted from fright. Gathering all of her courage, she'd whispered through the wood panel, asking Ryerson's roommate what he wanted.

"One of the soldiers has brought you an invite," he said, then shoved a thick square of vellum under the door.

Elizabeth read the handmade invitation, then stumbled into the bed. The note created worries for her. It also gave her a faint ray of hope. She spent the whole night agonizing over it, rising and dressing before the sun rose. Tucking the paper into her pocket, she awaited Ryerson's return. He reappeared just before dawn. Climbing in through the window, he scowled at the faded blue frock she'd put on and hustled her into the parlor.

Elizabeth caught her breath as they entered. The hunting trophies had vanished, along with Ryerson's two English roommates. Bouquets of spring wildflowers festooned the pegged walls, hung upside-down with bright yellow ribbons. A chocolate-skinned girl sat by the heavy mahogany table. She stood as Elizabeth entered, nearly dropping a large wicker clothes basket.

Ryerson brushed past, touching Elizabeth's arm.

Brusquely he grasped the girl's basket and slipped it out of her grip. "This is Mary. She brought these from town." He held up the woven laundry basket, bulging with bolts of richly colored fabrics and a fat selection of ladies' pattern books. Elizabeth frowned, smoothed back her hair, and presented her face to the dressmaker's assistant. The girl peered back shyly, her gaze fixed on Elizabeth's cheekbones.

Ryerson shifted his load to one hip, took the girl by the elbow, and marched her to the front of the parlor. "You can return at noon for the order."

"Yes, suh." She spoke in a soft Mississippi accent, so much like home that Elizabeth wanted to weep at the memories it evoked. "And, mistus." From beneath a cascade of dark waves, the seamstress slanted a glance Elizabeth's way. "I'm sorry for staring."

Ryerson scowled and opened the door. The girl gifted Elizabeth with a tentative smile, then vanished into the soft light of dawn. Ryerson turned. He should have looked funny, loaded down with feminine trifles, but the pose tripped Elizabeth's heartbeat. She liked the idea of ordering new clothes. She'd never been a fashionable dresser, but clothing appealed to the artist in her. She liked color and texture, the chance to create. And, she had to admit, the invitation would give her a place to wear something new and a chance to look pretty for James Ryerson. She was about to bring up the letter when a sound from the kitchen caught her attention.

"Morning, mistus." Carter appeared, his hands filled with a tray and a silver tea service. "Breakfast." He lay the dishes down on the table, pulled back a chair, gestured Elizabeth toward it, and waited.

Hesitating, Elizabeth glanced at the stripe on his pants.

"Do you mind this? You did not join the army in order to work as a servant."

Leaning forward, Carter picked up a napkin. "No. And don't you go gettin' tighter across the breast than a baked field hen." He snapped the cloth over his forearm and nodded again at the cane-back seat. "I don't mind takin' keer of the major, 'cause he's doin' his best to take keer of me."

Gaze forward, Carter waited, as straight-backed as the chair he stood next to. Ryerson posted himself at the head of the table. Drawn by the scent of food, Elizabeth edged toward the table, wondering what manners applied to this situation. As she worked through the problem, Carter lifted a towel off of the platter. Steam wafted off baked goods so fresh they looked to be straight out of the oven. Awestruck, Elizabeth allowed the private to seat her.

She waited until Ryerson had seated himself before she ventured her first observation. "You're very thorough."

"Tactics." Reaching over, he snagged one of the treats. He broke the hot dough open, releasing a mouthwatering apple-cinnamon scent. "I told you. My specialty during the war."

He popped a morsel into his mouth, chewing with an efficient gusto. Elizabeth picked up a roll. Carter lifted the lids off three pots of jam and one crock of meltingly pale creamery butter. Elizabeth broke her roll in fours, trying to decide which jam to taste first. She glanced at the major. He smiled. Reaching over the table, he picked up a jam pot. Without saying a word, he slathered his muffin, then handed the sweet-smelling jelly to her. Irritated, she took a plain roll and bit into it. She was learning to hate his supreme confidence. He knew just what he wanted, while she felt like a bumbling idiot.

She picked up a knife, aimed for a jar, reconsidered her action, and dropped the utensil. "I'm sorry." She worried a crumb with the tip of her finger. "I know you mean well, but I'd much prefer to eat breakfast in private."

An inscrutable light flared in Ryerson's eyes. He glanced briefly at Carter. Elizabeth gauged the private's retreat by the clump of his boots and Ryerson's poised and expectant expression. As the parlor grew silent, Ryerson's face grew more somber. "Do you want me to go also?"

She shook her head. She wanted to speak about the invitation, but did not quite know how to bring up the subject. Without looking at her, he lifted the pitcher and poured her coffee. Its scent drifted to her, lovely, seductive, redolent of morning and civilized breakfasts in her parents' kitchen.

She shoved her hands beneath the table and crumpled her napkin into a ball. "I didn't say I wanted a drink."

He glanced up, surprised. "Do you?"

"Yes." She smoothed out the napkin. "But I wish you'd ask."

"Fair enough." He filled his own cup, then lifted it to his lips. Pausing, he took a second to savor the scent. The action surprised her. She'd seen him slow down for so little.

"You like coffee?" she asked.

He nodded, taking a gingerly swallow, as if he expected the liquid to burn him. "I learned to love it during the war." He took a second swift sip. "There's almost no situation so grim that a cup of this does not improve it." He sucked in a deep breath. "The smell alone is halfway to heaven. I've seen men sit down in a lull of a battle and lose themselves in a good cup of coffee."

She smiled in spite of herself. She could picture the scene he described. She found herself wanting to sketch him, grizzled and hatless, sitting down on a log beneath a leafless tree denuded in battle, to brew himself a bit of refreshment. Slowly she fingered the porcelain handle. "You know, we're in this together."

"I'm sorry?"

"This ruse." She grasped the cup tightly, using the heat to keep her attention focused. "There's no turning back."

He looked up quizzically, the coffee forgotten. "What are you talking about?"

"I need to know where you slept."

"In a shelter tent down by the river."

Her cup clattered against the saucer. "I hate you." Jumping up, she strode to the side of the room, stopping beneath a spray of larkspur. Pausing a moment to regain her composure, she smoothed her hands over her worn gingham skirt. "You did that to spite me. Well, I refuse to feel bad about putting you out, but we have to have a different sleeping arrangement."

He wolfed down half a muffin and chewed the remainder serenely. When he finished, he pushed back his chair. "I can rank Captain Jennings."

"No."

"Better suggestion?" He brushed a crumb off his sleeve.

"Yes." She inspected the bright blue flowers hanging from the wall. Last night Ryerson had disarmed her by speaking of love. No, not love, she corrected, lovemaking. Sex. Something quite different. "You're sleeping with me."

"I thought we agreed that was out of the question." He made no sound of surprise, but she thought she caught an edge in his voice.

She didn't dare look at his expression. "We did." This was a lie. She had agreed that lovemaking was a poor idea. Out of the question was a bit more far-fetched. This seemed like a subtle distinction, however. One she did not need to debate. "I don't like the idea of sharing close quarters, but we have to have a masquerade that will fool people. The curiosity seekers have already started."

"What are you talking about?"

"Here." She took the invitation out of her pocket.

He took the thick square of vellum from her and scowled. "Where did you get this?"

She shrugged. "I'm not sure exactly. One of the Englishmen said you were wanted. I made an excuse that you were sleeping and had him slip it under the door."

"A hop?" As he read, one side of his mouth curved into a malicious grin. "How ironic." He tossed the paper onto the floor.

"You find that amusing?" Elizabeth asked, genuinely bemused.

He rose from his chair. Without speaking a word, he cleared the dishes off his side of the table, retrieved the dressmaker's basket, then unfolded a swath of green taffeta. "Yes. I find that funny." He held up a swag to the light.

His gesture brought her to full alertness. All morning she'd been worried and tense, but the sight of the cloth cheered her up. She crossed the room just to stand next to the splendid material. "You find parties funny?"

"Sometimes." He held the color up to her hair. "Civilization brings out the savage in me. I hate dancing in boots. Also, I find it peculiar that I would receive my first invitation the day after I'm married."

Pausing, he assessed her with relish. His gaze swept over her figure. He placed the cloth on one side of the table. A brief shiver ran up her spine. She still hadn't gotten used to his nearness.

She wiped her palms on her skirt. "Surely your raids were not so reviled by the army that the women would snub you?"

"For the raids, no." He picked up a gray silk, a serious color Elizabeth hoped he wouldn't like. "You forget, my dear, my current command."

"Truly?" Outrage bloomed in Elizabeth's breast. Whatever her preconceived notions, she'd come to like Ryerson's troopers. She couldn't quite imagine the mind that would hold to a hatred when faced with such hopeful and downtrodden people. "They would shun you for that?"

Had glances been arrows, Ryerson's look would have pinned Elizabeth to the wall.

"Well, get used to the invitations." She nodded at the white square on the floor. "It's the first of many, I'm sure."

"What makes you think so?" He scanned the gray fabric, frowned, then tossed the piece next to the invitation.

She wondered what he was doing, but did not feel like changing the subject. Standing, she popped a quarter of a muffin into her mouth. She wiped her fingers off on a napkin, then picked up a green-and-red plaid. "I got used to these ploys in Kansas City. Polite invitations. Smiles for the captive." She quirked her lips into a false grin. "Then outrage"—she grimaced—"as my hosts learned the truth. I liked the Indian. I defended their habits. Worse, I refused to be used as an excuse for more fighting."

Slowly he took the silk from her hand. He unfurled it carefully, hefting its weight over his arm. "Is that how you came to live on the prairie?"

She nodded. "I tried to live in Kansas City, but I could not abide whites anymore. The Indians had not meant to hurt me. They liked the tattoos. They marked their own women. To them, these make me pretty—"

She stopped.

Ryerson smiled, wry and arresting. "Go on," he said softly.

She flushed, embarrassed, and unfolded a square of

brown calico. Ryerson's reaction confused her. Most men leered at the tattoos, as if the markings confirmed some twisted theory. Ryerson claimed to find them attractive, an assertion she refused to believe. Still, he looked at her with a piercing expression, as if her face were a puzzle he wished to read. And, for all his arrogant ways, he'd come to breakfast in a blue flannel shirt, still military in its appearance, but civilian enough that she realized he meant to use his clothing as a symbol of truce.

She smoothed down the cotton, the plainest material the dressmaker's assistant had brought. "I know this will seem odd to you, but I'd like to go to the dance." The fabric cooled her hands. She tried to focus on that sensation and calm her sense of unease. "I thought a great deal about what you said. You're probably right. I have to face this sooner or later, and the more they see me, the quicker people will get used to the markings."

"And how does this alter our sleeping arrangements?"

"Please don't misunderstand. I'm not suggesting . . . you know . . ."

"Improper involvements?"

"Right."

"Then what are you doing?"

"I'm trying . . . I'm trying to protect you."

"Now there's a novel idea. One of my victims trying to help me."

"Don't be so damnably arch. The war is over, you know. A colored command might make you a misfit, but a fraudulent marriage to a cruelly disfigured former Indian captive is the basest kind of illicit conduct."

"Flattering description."

"Don't toy with me. Exposure for fraud would make you an outcast. I don't want to have your fate on my conscience."

"Noble emotion." He tossed the plaid to the right. "You could help me by keeping your political sympathies quiet."

"I know. And I will. That will be hard, but for your sake I'll do it." She ran her fingers over the selvage, then inspected the raveling edge of the piece. He'd managed to mollify her somewhat, but their situation niggled at her. They might fool the rest of the world, but their false marriage would never work out unless they learned to work as a team. "I'd like to explain my feelings to you."

He nodded.

"I know it seems odd, loving a people that made me a captive. Sometimes it even seems strange to me. But it's not the marks on my face that cause me such pain. It's the memories I carry inside. That's why I tried to help the Cheyenne. I lived through the same experience myself. The Yankees destroyed my way of life."

"Help?" He narrowed his gaze.

Hesitating, she unfolded the plain cloth. She thought she should tell Ryerson about her sketches. It seemed disloyal, considering the risks he was taking, that she was keeping a secret from him. Still, she hated his temper and flinched at the thought that she'd have to face it once she revealed what she'd done for her friends. Besides, he'd kidnapped her from her home on the prairie. She'd tried to do some good for her Indians. The essence of her story was all Ryerson needed to know. "I offered to nurse for the Indian children." She lied through her teeth, felt guilty for it, and hid her falsehood by closely inspecting the drab bolt of cloth. "Perhaps I'll pick this one."

He frowned. "You've missed the point. We're taking the green, the red-and-green plaid, and maybe something in a dark yellow."

She dropped the cotton and picked up a pattern. "Did you choose clothes for your first wife?"

"Never."

"Then why treat me differently?"

He prowled the room, poking the bolts he'd thrown down. "Because you're not like her."

The pattern paper shook in her hands. Though she tried to control it, a soft rustle gave her away. Reluctantly she put down the sketch, drew in her breath, and asked the question that had been bothering her. "Do you like the fact that I'm different?"

"In certain ways, yes."

"Why?"

He hefted the stack of material off the floor, the one containing the fabrics he'd chosen. "Because she hurt me." Without looking at her, he swept the plain cloth off the table. The bolt hit the floor with a thunk. "I'd like to think that you won't."

"But you're not certain of that?"

"No." He lay the material out, then picked up the stack of ladies' pattern books, sorting quickly through them, then lay his selections out on the cloth.

"So why are you picking clothes out for me?"

He laid down the picture and scowled. Clasping his hands behind his back, he strode the length of the parlor. As he paced, the gold stripe on his trousers flashed in a rhythm. "Helen was more sure of herself."

Elizabeth watched. She couldn't figure him out. Worse, she couldn't figure herself. Even if she ignored his past, she hated the way he'd disrupted her life. What should it matter that he'd had his reasons? He was a violent man with a terrible temper, who'd caused nothing but pain in her life. She might accept his protection, but did she have to return his affection? Very quietly, she perused the pattern picture. "Did you like that in her? Her self-confidence?"

"At the time. Yes." He halted to one side of the parlor.

"And now?"

"And now," he said, turning as he pinioned her with a look, "I like you."

She lifted her chin, but inside she melted, her reaction betraying good common sense. His gaze expressed his every desire. Four years of passion and fury. His thwarted love for his wife. His desperate fight with himself. And how badly, how very badly, he wanted to give his heart to a woman. She hid her trembling hands in her skirts. "And you're afraid that I'll hurt you."

"Yes."

He broke off the look and strode to the table. As he passed, a warm pressure whispered against her. She found herself enmeshed in his presence, flustered by the power of his touch.

He lay the pictures down by the cloth. "Do you like my choices?"

She nodded, unable to speak. He was probably right to sleep in the tent. If he affected her with such force, how much stronger must be his male reaction? She'd always felt in control with her husbands, but Ryerson seemed very different from Philip, or even her dear Sleeps With Eagle. Not only fully mature and virile, but in control of all but his temper. It unnerved her to think that she couldn't trust him, for she'd come to the painful—and novel—conclusion that she didn't have faith in herself.

"You can't just keep sleeping inside that tent." The words danced over her doubts and popped out of her mouth before she could stop them.

"I'd pretty much come to the same conclusion."

She trembled, and not just for herself. She knew why she envied Helen. Not the status as wife. Not even the passion. Helen had taken a special treasure. One that Ryerson couldn't get back. Innocent love, boundless and hopeful.

The kind of devotion she'd commanded from Philip. The kind of love she knew how to manage. "So," she said as she steadied herself by touching the table, "what do you suggest?"

He smiled, brushed his lips over her forehead, then strode to the table and picked up the thick square of vellum. "I propose we attend our first dance together."

The hop was held in the arsenal hall. Ryerson sucked in his breath as he led Elizabeth into the brightly lit building. She'd stayed in all week, making her gown. Swiftly he snugged his hand to her waist. "Buck up, little one. This won't be so bad."

"I'm all right." She tightened her fingers over his. The puff of lace at her neck trembled slightly. "It's not—it's just—" She raised her head high and stared past the bustle and movement of dancers. "I'm just looking. That's all."

Ryerson followed the line of her gaze. The dance floor glistened and rippled. The couples waltzed in a slow circle, gold braid gleaming on indigo frock coats, graceful women shimmering in satin. Elizabeth seemed unaffected, however. She fixed her gaze on the far wall, staring at a row of crossed sabers, as if mesmerized by the cool and elegant splendor of these cruelest weapons of war.

Bracing her on his arm, Ryerson swept her into the room. He intended to guide her straight to the punch bowl. She followed politely, but as the first couple turned, the male partner caught a glimpse of Elizabeth's face. He lost his rhythm completely and stopped. The variation in pattern attracted attention. A few more dancers slowed down. A low hum traveled over the room. Not all at once, but slowly, almost one by one, the dancing couples came to a halt.

Hot blood pulsed in Ryerson's temples. He felt Elizabeth's back muscles tighten. He knew she looked lovely, decked out in emerald, her taffeta gown highlighting her hair. He wanted to kill the Indian who'd tattooed her and shoot every one of these staring bastards. He felt helpless and angry, frustrated and stupid. He wished he could wipe the marks from her face and give her the knowledge, certain and sweet, that her beauty would have attracted attention without them.

He scowled at the first man who moved, a cocky young captain with flowing blond hair and highly fashionable sideburns. Shoving past the dandified soldier, Ryerson pulled Elizabeth onto the dance floor. The captain's dress saber rattled, but Ryerson barely attended the sound.

"I can manage, you know." She lifted her chin, her gaze sweeping over the crowd. A breath of white netting feathered her bosom, accenting her fragile and delicate beauty. He loved her dress. Ignoring all conventional wisdom, she'd chosen a pattern without a hoop. The gown draped instead like a medieval princess's. She and Mary had trimmed it by hand, a frothy concoction of dainty lace and handmade silk flowers, showing no fashion judgment at all, but a unique and startling sense of aesthetics.

Ryerson tightened his hand over hers. The crowd fanned out in a circle, leaving him and Elizabeth standing alone. Turning, he drew her into his arms. He fixed his gaze on those cinnamon eyes, hesitated a moment, then took the first step. The taffeta skirt whispered against him immediately, turning fury to passion. He planted a kiss on her throat.

She started, pulling away. "What are you doing?"

"Showing these fools how much I adore you." He grinned, though he worried his smile came out more like a grimace. Her touch worked like a gunpowder charge. He'd slept at the foot of her bed for a week, a painful experience in more ways than one.

"You don't need to protect me so fiercely."

Reluctantly he loosened his grip. Stepping back slightly, he struggled to distance himself from the feminine press of her softness. "It's not you I'm protecting."

"No?" She followed him through a series of turns, neatly ignoring the roomful of gawkers. "Then why did you glare at that captain that way?"

"I'm upholding my standards."

"Ah."

He tightened his grip. Red, white, and blue bunting billowed down from the ceiling. The brass band kept on pumping. The crowd still gaped in rapt fascination, having abandoned all pretense of manners. Ryerson wanted to tear out their eyes. He could imagine the rumors, given the infamy of his own reputation, but couldn't these idiots see how their rude staring hurt her?

Scowling as fiercely as he could manage, he pulled Elizabeth closer, intent on hiding the disfiguring marks, but she held her chin high, her face in deliberate profile. He stiffened his back, trying to control the pace of his dancing. She followed him with too-graceful steps. He would have preferred awkward distraction, a period of adjustment where he could be clumsy, but she fell in with his lead, and the ease of her movement unnerved him further. He planted a thigh next to hers, determined to keep his rhythm gracious. "Do you doubt what I say about standards?"

"Yes." She lowered her eyes, her hand on his shoulder.

"That's a mistake."

"Why?"

He whirled her in a wide circle, forcing the dandified captain to stand farther back. She seemed to have lost herself in the music, but he kept track of their hostile watchers. To his relief, some of the couples started dancing again.

He turned her, deriving some satisfaction from his increasing mastery. His ankle boots hurt, and he hated the sash required by the dress code, but some of the pleasure of dancing came back. "You may question my courage, even my sense of honor, but never question my sense of justice. Many, many plantation owners had their homes wiped off the face of the earth for less pertinacity than that captain is showing."

"And I suppose you think that justice?"

He scowled. She might forgive but she'd never forget. Their conversations always came back to this subject. She stared at his chest, as if to signal her disapproval of the eagle-embossed double row of gold buttons. He glanced briefly around at the crowd.

The brash, dandified captain had moved to the edge of the circle. He was speaking a little too loudly, throwing occasional glances Elizabeth's way. Ryerson glared at the booming-voiced boor. Most of the couples had gone back to dancing. Only this man kept on provoking. Very discreetly, Ryerson checked the knot at his sword hilt.

"That's a beautiful weapon." Elizabeth softened her voice.

"Yes." Ryerson glanced at the jeweled handle, fighting off the burn in his stomach. "It's special. It's a presentation sword, given to me right after Vicksburg."

A look came into her cinnamon eyes, half-frightened, half-startled, and suspiciously bright. Ryerson realized with an intense sense of displeasure that Dixon had told her about his wife's suicide.

"You know?" he asked hoarsely.

She nodded, eyes still wary, distrustful, and most of all filled with questions.

He stumbled, then regained his balance. He hadn't anticipated her knowing. Dixon had always been loyal. He had never considered the notion that his friend and sergeant would have revealed the details of a subject he considered so private. Still, the business had come up, and it seemed a suitable test of his mettle to talk about his wife's death while dancing in front of a roomful of people. "Yes. This is the one. If that's what you're wondering. My men gave it to me after James died. And Helen used it to join him."

She trembled. He could feel it though sash, shirt, and frock coat. Her eyes formed a question, but no words came out. Though she did not speak it, he felt compelled to answer her question.

"I seldom wear it, but I admired your courage in attending this dance." He sensed her shock in the line of her muscles, the stiffness, the tension, the sense of unbending. Frowning, he whirled her toward the far side of the room. "I wanted to ask something equally brave of myself."

SEVEN

A HARD HAND CLAMPED DOWN ON ELIZABETH'S SHOUL-
der. The touch threw her slightly off-balance. As Ryerson steadied her by the waist, she whirled to face the
golden-haired captain.

"Excuse me." A sneer marred his face, but Elizabeth
couldn't help thinking him handsome, though in a young
and insolent way. He bowed, wildly mocking. "May I have
this dance?"

"No." Ryerson planted himself in front of the boy.

The blond appeared not to have heard him. He stared at
Elizabeth's cheekbones, his smirk fading into his sideburns.
"I'd like to dance with the new Mrs. Major."

"No." Ryerson repeated, his voice taut with a threat. He
stilled, hand on his sword hilt, his fierce gaze turned on the
soldier, the picture of coiled concentration.

Elizabeth trembled. She'd seen Ryerson angry. What
worried her now was the fact that he wasn't. His composure conveyed a state beyond temper, a mood both focused
and lethal.

She smoothed the wide front of her taffeta skirt. "Perhaps—"

"No." Ryerson cut off her sentence, but kept both eyes
on the captain. "My wife does not care to dance."

The room stirred behind them. To Elizabeth's dismay, the foolish young officer did not seem to grasp his own danger. Anger distorted his freckled features. His fingers curled over his pistol grip. "Don't like to share her?" His bold stare did not leave her cheekbones. "Don't seem like you've got a right to be picky."

Ryerson's saber flashed out of the scabbard. The captain reached for his pistol, but Ryerson grabbed the boy by the throat, bringing the blade to rest above his gold-braided collar.

"I said no," Ryerson repeated, his chest moving beneath his blue frock coat. "If you wish to dispute my rights in this matter, we'll settle our difference away from the lady."

Elizabeth's heart hammered like thunder. In Mississippi, soldiers still dueled. She didn't know much about the habits of Yankees, but she took Ryerson's statement to be that kind of challenge.

She moved close to his elbow. "James." She wanted to touch Ryerson's hand, but he kept it clenched over the sword hilt. "Please. I cannot allow this violence." She used the calmest voice she could manage. "I will not allow you to kill a man in my defense."

Ryerson moved the sword's point up to the boy's cheekbone. "What if I just scar him a little?" The long-haired captain still did not move. Though Ryerson gripped him by the throat, the foolish, fiery officer still glared through blue eyes dark with revulsion.

"Don't." She tugged Ryerson's sleeve. "Please." Grimly she clutched his arm. "Don't risk your life for so little reason."

Ryerson ignored her. His breathing had slowed, but he kept his gaze on the captain's eyes, his sword pressed to the highest point on his face.

Breaking away, Elizabeth swept into the room's center,

facing the glittering crowd of astounded onlookers. "Look." She filled her lungs, then spoke distinctly in her best Southern accent. "Look if you must." She made a slow turn, her hands at her sides. "You know how I got the marks on my face. They don't come off and they really can't be changed. I know they make me look peculiar, but they don't mean I've lost all human feeling."

A low murmur swept through the room. Sabers rattled, and stiff satin rustled. Elizabeth did not acknowledge the sounds, but lifted her gaze to the swords on the walls. No one moved in the field of her vision. One of the Hazletts appeared by her side.

Bending a little, he took Elizabeth by the arm. "I've got her, Major. Would you like me to take her back home?"

"No." Elizabeth pulled herself from his grasp. She continued her speech to the crowd. "Thank you, but no. I don't want to run and I don't want to fight. I need a brief refuge. If you leave me in peace, I'll go back to the prairie after this war."

The whole room had stilled. A hundred eyes stared, first at her, then at the major, who was still locked with the captain in a lethal embrace. Ryerson's face had a curious expression, not angry, not hostile, just grim and determined. She knew from the set of his jaw, from the line of his posture, that he could still kill in a heartbeat.

Involuntarily Elizabeth shuddered. Peace, she thought, would always elude her, married to someone as fierce as the major. Still, she had married him, in at least certain senses. And she saw in that moment quite clearly how hard it would be to leave him. For all his wildness, hardness, and harshness, she'd come to respect this fearsome soldier. She cleared her throat, then spoke in the steadiest voice she could muster. "I'm Major Ryerson's new wife. I'd like very much to be left alone."

Without warning, Ryerson let go of the swashbuckling captain. A tiny scratch marred the plane of his cheekbone. For all his showy bravado, the golden-haired boy must finally have come to his senses. Stumbling backward, he touched the nick on his face, sobering at the blood on his fingers. Ryerson watched, then resheathed his saber. He strode to Elizabeth's side. Hand on his sword hilt, he faced the restless throng of amazed party-goers.

"Truce?" he asked them quietly.

Elizabeth had no idea where Ryerson slept after the party. He'd dropped her off at his house, refusing to touch her, not saying a word. She'd tried to thank him, but he'd simply smiled grimly, then disappeared out the window. He returned at dawn by the same route. Elizabeth thought he looked exhausted. Gray morning light painted lines in his face, ravaged his generally rugged complexion, and turned his eyes a much darker color. He shook off her efforts to help him.

"We've our first drill this morning." He shrugged out of his rumpled frock coat.

She wasn't sure what his comment implied, but this seemed a poor time for ignorant questions. In truth, last night's scene had frightened her. The incident brought out a fact she'd ignored. The civilian reaction to her had often been hostile, but in the hard world of the Indian-fighting army, a man who undertook to protect her might have to defend her with his life.

She felt subdued and discouraged as she reached out her hand for his coat. "Is there anything I can do to help?"

Pausing, he grinned. "You can stop looking so lovely."

She blushed, glancing down at her nightdress and robe. Of all the extravagant clothes he'd bought her, this frilly peignoir amazed her the most. He'd spent more on this intimate outfit than on both the party dresses together.

"Standards," he had growled in response to her protest. "I can't stand a man who treats his wife better in public than he does in the privacy of his own home."

She'd suspected there was another reason for the robe, however. Beautiful as it was, it was also modest compared to her night rail, covering her from neck to foot in layers of lace and heavy satin. She suspected he welcomed the tiers of elaborate ruffles. After the first rainy night on the prairie, he had spent his nights at the end of her bed, sleeping on an army camp cot which he folded each morning and hid in his trunk. For dressing, he brought in a screen and set it up in the corner, reasoning this would cause no suspicions as even long-married couples preferred the convenience of disrobing in private.

Draping his frock coat over her arm, she walked to his trunk and opened the lid. "What do you wear to a drill?"

His boot scraped behind her. Her heartbeat sped up. In their week of false marriage, her physical awareness of him had grown. He'd made no improper advances, or even spoken about his frustration, but there was an unvoiced tension between them, and she sensed it was growing.

Softly he touched her shoulder. "Are you all right, Libbie?"

"Yes."

"You look upset."

She searched carefully through the neat piles of clothes. "I don't know how to do this."

"What?"

"Anything." She lifted up a pair of his gloves. "You've got your clothes arranged in some kind of order. I know there's a logic, but I can't grasp its details. I can't even hand the right uniform to you." Frustrated, she lay down the gauntlets. "You pick out my dresses. Order my meals. Find me a servant and conjure a house. Lay a glittering world at my feet, and for what? You don't even touch me."

Fatigue lined his face, but deep in his eyes she detected a flicker. "Do you want that? Do you want me to hold you?"

"No."

He ran his finger over her cheekbone. "Then what are you wailing about? Are you ill? You don't look as if you feel well."

"Actually—" She paused, trying to make her voice matter of fact. "I don't. Last night was a bit of a shock."

Gently he moved her off to the side. He pulled one of the uniforms out and surveyed it. "The army has dress regulations. I'll get you a copy. As officers go, I'm not much for polish, but rules make life simple. You're quite correct in your observation. I arrange these in order, so I won't have to search. If you want to help with such a wifely task, you'll have to learn the army's dress codes." He strode to the screen and threw the coat over. "As for the shock, you're just not used to fighting."

Returning to the bed, Elizabeth slumped onto the mattress. He'd made her part of a world she hated, and now, God forgive her, she wanted to help him. "That's where you're wrong. I'm quite used to fighting. In fact, that's the problem. Half my life I thought of you as a monster—this beast—like my . . . like the newspaper sketches. Then I got to know you. I found you were simply a person, not so different from me in terms of your feelings. But up until last night's fight, I never thought you could be hurt—at least not in a physical sense."

He turned, evidently surprised. Stopping short of the screen, he stripped off his shirt. "Well, that's progress of sorts. May I ask to what I owe this sudden insight?"

"Well—to the fight." She averted her eyes from the sight

of his chest. She wished he would duck behind the partition, for she found his muscles attractive. "It got me thinking. You might have to risk your life to protect me."

"The beast is less fearsome when he's on your side?"

"Yes. No." She knotted her fingers. "Oh, James. I don't know what I mean." She kept her eyes lowered, but her wretched brain, so skilled at conjuring pictures, summoned an image. Ryerson, bare-chested, hand on his waistband. Frowning, she blinked. "I know I sound like an ingrate. But it's so hard for me to justify fighting, especially after all that I've seen."

She did not see him move, but he appeared at her side, dark eyes glinting amusement. Her heartbeat sped up. Sometimes she felt wicked, living with him and wanting him so.

She swallowed. "I do appreciate what you've done for me. I'd like to return the favor in some way."

"You can help with my boots."

"Of course—"

"Good." He sat on the bed. "I'm glad we've straightened that problem out. You can practice on these," he said as he stretched out one leg and scowled at his foot, "but it's the knee boots that really require a helper."

"What?" She stared helplessly at him. "Oh!" She leaped off the mattress, then dropped to her knees. Removing his boots wasn't quite what she'd meant, but having proffered her offer, she didn't see a graceful way out. She grimaced, examining the finely worked footgear.

"This isn't so bad." He removed a cigar stub from his pants pocket and clamped the end in his mouth. "I could get used to this arrangement."

He smelled of cigar smoke, outdoors, and leather. Male and familiar, these scents made her homesick. Scowling, she grasped his heel firmly. "Maybe I could help with the troopers."

"You've done enough."

"I've done nothing." The short boot slipped off easily. "That's part of my problem. I've nothing to give you, nothing to offer except my friendship."

"You saved my life and the lives of my troopers."

She switched to the other boot and removed it. "I suppose you marry all of your nurses?"

"An impertinent question."

"Answer me, James."

"No. Never."

She stood. To her surprise, she had liked performing this humble service. He seemed precious to her, precious and sacred. A flesh-and-blood man, bound by a pledge, maybe not a marriage exactly, but a bond that seemed somehow sweeter and dearer. "Then what can I possibly give you that's worth all you're risking?"

"I told you before. It's already given. Tit for tat. You gave me my life."

Softly she touched his shoulder. He had another scar there, a thickened, shiny patch on his skin reminding her that he could be wounded. "That's foolish, almost feminine prattle."

"Elizabeth." He stilled her hand. "I never use words foolishly. I don't just refer to the nursing. I . . ." He paused, his mouth drawing down. "I . . . desire . . . you." He locked his fingers over her wrist. "In some ways that's a gift worth life itself."

Warmth shimmered upward and outward. She didn't know why she had these desires, but his touch fuddled both her head and her body. "Ah, yes. Ryerson the poet. Is that why you're talking in riddles?"

Their eyes met. He remained seated, fire in his gaze.

Tightening his grip, he drew her slowly between his thighs. Though they didn't quite touch her, she sensed their warmth and their muscular tension. She stilled, not daring to move or lower her body. "What are you saying?"

"I'm not sure I should put this in words." He took her hand, then drew her closer. A whirl of dizziness whooshed in her stomach. Shutting his eyes, he pressed her palm to his cheek. Its grizzled stubble abraded her skin.

"I see . . ." She could scarcely call up her voice. "I mean . . . ," she continued a little more bravely, "I mean, of course, this is a very difficult subject, so—but—" She sucked in her breath. "How will we ever make this false marriage work if we cannot describe how we feel?"

He leaped to his feet, almost knocking her over. "I'm not proposing discussing our feelings! It's lust, not emotions, we are talking about." He strode to the trunk. "Primitive, maybe, and simple." Yanking out a pair of blue cavalry pants, he ducked behind the screen in the corner. "But vital."

He stripped off his pants. He'd set up the screen as a precaution, but she could make out his silhouette through the canvas. She knew she ought to avert her eyes, but he'd angered her with his statement. She wanted to watch him, figure him out. She did not understand what he wanted from her or what he expected in this situation.

Balancing on one foot, he thrust one leg into a clean pair of trousers. "Lust is a man's most primal impulse." She caught a shadowy glimpse of his thigh, strong and well-molded. "It's springtime and hope. The desire to create children." Without glancing at her, he pushed in the other leg and pulled his pants over his buttocks. Though she'd never seen his thighs and calves naked, her mind concocted an illicit vision. She felt her cheeks pink at the lewd speculation.

He continued his swift, staccato speech, completely oblivious to this subject's effect on her senses. "I want you, at least on a primitive level. To a man, that's a gift worth life itself. It's difficult for me to admit this, but I haven't truly desired a woman since Vicksburg."

Somebody knocked on the door. It took Elizabeth a moment to hear it, but the rap in her ears wasn't her heartbeat.

"Major?" Charles Hazlett's voice traveled under notes of a trumpet. "They're forming."

Ryerson stepped out from behind the screen. He'd thrown on his frock coat, but left it unbuttoned. As he fastened the uniform jacket, Elizabeth bolted off the bed. She reached for his sword.

"Here." She retrieved the rigid blade from its peg. "Let me help."

He glanced up, assessing. She flushed hot and cold, both chilled and warmed by his frank appraisal. Only when she felt stripped to her soul did he drop his gaze and say thank you.

He raised his arm for the saber. She hefted its weight, awed by its power, its beauty, and the thought that his wife had killed herself with this weapon. She did up his buckle with trembling fingers. She ignored the indelicate part, of course. She was aware that her actions aroused him.

"So you see," he said and pressed a swift kiss to her forehead, "you've already made yourself useful."

Ryerson staggered back less than half an hour later, quarreling furiously with the Hazletts, Carter, and Dixon, who were trying, without much success, to support him from either side. Fighting back a sickening clench in her stomach, Elizabeth led the squabbling group into the bedroom.

"What happened?" she asked, appalled by the swelling lump on Ryerson's forehead.

Jerking away, Ryerson unbuckled his saber, tossed it over a peg, and flung himself on the bed. Once there, he grunted, rolled to his back, and crossed his arms over his eyes. "It's nothing. Merely a scuffle."

A chill swept Elizabeth's body. "Not over me?"

"No," Ryerson snapped.

"Yes," Dixon corrected.

"No." Ryerson lifted his hands, glared at his sergeant, then sank his head into the pillow. "I had a scuffle with that devil captain, the one who bothered you at the hop. He refused to drill his men with my troopers, claimed that whites should not share the field with the colored."

Dixon stepped up to the bed. Working with grim efficiency, he started undoing the major's frock coat. Charles Hazlett made a signal to Carter, who disappeared toward the kitchen. Elizabeth hovered, unable to quite reach her husband through his fussing circle of masculine minions.

"Nonsense." Randalph Hazlett tugged on one of Ryerson's boots. "He was spoiling for you after last night. You wouldn't have got this," he said, nodding at Ryerson's goose egg, "except he had three flunkies jump you."

"The major did real well by us, mistus." Carter reappeared in the doorway, carrying a basin and a porcelain pitcher. "You should have seen him take down those Yankees." He poured steaming water, while Hazlett struggled with Ryerson's knee boot.

Dixon meanwhile tried to touch Ryerson's forehead. "Stop!" The major knocked his hand away. "I'm all right, I tell you." His voice bounced off the walls, rolled to the ceiling, and tumbled back into the room's center. All the occupants stilled. No wounded lion roared better than James Ryerson in a temper. "Leave me in peace."

"Yes, suh." Stepping back, Dixon slanted a glance Elizabeth's way. Carter and the Hazletts looked at the floor. The sergeant touched each of their elbows and grinned. "We got to remember that he's got a wife."

Head ducked down, Elizabeth waited as her four helpers retreated, shutting the door to the bedroom behind them. Without saying a word, she walked to the bed and finished removing Ryerson's boot. He stayed silent through that whole procedure, keeping the top half of his face firmly covered and his mouth set in a frown. Grim-faced and deliberate, Elizabeth dropped the footgear onto the floor. The thud of its heel broke the silence.

With a sigh to herself, she folded her hands in her lap. "You'll have to cooperate sooner or later."

He slouched down, crossing his arms over his chest. "Don't look so self-satisfied. I'm not very much in need of your nursing, and you were not the cause of this fight."

She stripped off his sock and inspected his feet, closely observing each of his toes.

"What are you doing?" he asked.

"Looking to see if you have feet of clay."

"Very funny."

Rising, she crossed to the nightstand and retrieved her lye soap. The scent stung her nose. "This scrubbing won't be so pleasant as when you were down with the fever. The forehead wound will require harsh cleaning."

"I'm sure it will sate your innate sense of vengeance. Inflicting pain on a cavalry raider."

She lathered a cloth, then returned to the bed. "No. It won't. I cannot understand why you don't believe me. I harbor no hatred because of the war."

Leaning forward, she rubbed the rough cloth over his scrape. He grimaced, eyes shut, but did not flinch or pull away from her touch. She worked carefully, hoping she was not hurting him much, but she could not help but notice the lines on his face or the whiteness that pinched the edge of his nostrils. She stopped for an instant, took a short breath, then restarted. A tremor passed under his lashes. He pulled his cigar butt out of his pocket. Clamping down on the end, he chewed as she continued her washing.

"No." He moved the stub to one side of his mouth. "I don't believe your denials. Hatred is a natural emotion, especially considering what you've been through."

"Love's equally natural." She set the cloth down, then carefully felt over his sides. "And a painful experience teaches a person compassion."

She touched his lower right rib cage.

He flinched. "Are you saying you love me?"

"No." Laughing, she gently unbuttoned the top of his frock coat. "But I do feel a friendship. I'm sorry you're hurt, but I am grateful to you and glad to do you a service."

She undid the brass buttons in silence. He endured the attention, watching steadily from beneath lowered lashes. When she finished, he tried to shrug out of the jacket himself, but pain crossed his face with each movement. He fell back on the pillow. Slowly she pushed his uniform open. A crimson welt marred his lower ribs. A round, punishing bruise purpled his stomach. To her surprise, the sight made her queasy. She generally handled the sight of blood well. His injuries, though they clearly went deep, weren't shockingly ugly or visibly gory. Still, there was something distressing about them. Perhaps the injustice of his being ambushed, she thought, or maybe her part in inspiring the fracas, made his wounds affect her more than they should. For whatever reason, a wave of illness passed through her, and she turned away for a moment.

"Are you all right?" He touched her hand briefly.

"Yes." She pulled in a lungful of air. "But I'm very sorry you're hurt."

"Mistus." Elizabeth started, snatching her hand from Ryerson's stomach. "Mistus." Carter rattled the doorknob. His soft voice sounded urgent. "Can I come in? Sergeant Dixon sent me to warn you."

Elizabeth turned. "Come in." She smoothed down her skirt and folded her hands in her lap. "What's the matter?"

"We got trouble, mistus." Carter peered in, looking dolefully at Ryerson's bruised and disheveled figure. "They're going to arrest the major. The colonel's already sending his men."

"What?" Elizabeth jumped to her feet. "Arrest him for what?"

The private pulled off his forage cap, twisting the cloth in his hand. "Conduct unbecoming an officer, mistus."

Indignation spurted through her. "Since when is fighting a fault in a soldier?"

"Don't know, mistus." The dark-skinned young private toyed with the tiny crossed sabers festooning his hat. "Probably when you fight for a black man." He straightened his shoulders. "Don't matter, really. Sergeant Dixon says there's goin' to be a court-martial. He's gone to plead with the colonel, but the sojers is already comin' this way."

"Stay here." Elizabeth charged toward the door. "Guard the door. Don't let them in until I get back."

"Woman!" Ryerson vaulted out of the bed with a curse.

Elizabeth turned, glaring fiercely. "And you stay put." Ryerson lunged. Elizabeth dodged. Before she could think what she was doing, she jerked his sword from its peg on the wall. He froze, palms upraised in a gesture of peace. She ignored his display and pointed the blade straight at his stomach. To her absolute shock, her hands did not tremble. "Just once in our marriage take an order from me." Advancing a step, she kept the weapon aimed at his center. "Look sick and stay in that bed." He opened his mouth as if to speak, but she brandished the weapon, and he remained silent. "Don't you say one word about standards. You're hurt. I'm your nurse. My standards count in this situation. Just this once," she said and lifted the blade a little bit higher, "it won't hurt to admit that you're wounded."

To Ryerson's outrage, Carter did as she asked. He drew out his pistol, ordering Ryerson into the bed, then posted himself at the door. When the detachment arrived to arrest Ryerson, the foolish, loyal, misguided private refused to move, claiming to be obeying Elizabeth's orders. Ryerson let him. He wanted to break up the fracas, but during Elizabeth's absence he'd discovered he really was dizzy, and sick to his stomach to boot. The squad's sergeant hollered and cursed, reasoned and commanded, but Carter stood guard, holding off the bemused group until Elizabeth reappeared forty-five minutes later.

"Thank you, Private." She stepped in front of the door. From the bed, Ryerson couldn't hear what she said, but she had a low, fierce conversation with the sergeant who'd come to arrest him.

Combat became her. The sergeant hitched up his pistol holster, but she stood her ground. She ignored the threat implied by his gesture and continued to argue with great earnestness. He crossed his arms over his chest. She kept on with her speech, debating the matter with impassive brass buttons.

The sergeant just glared. A dazed look crept into her eyes. Ryerson recognized the high flush of battle, the darkened pupils and rosy complexion that soldiers wore in their excitement. At length, she produced a white paper that seemed to persuade the indignant squad leader to her way of thinking. Carter relinquished his post, replaced by a short, Irish-looking foot soldier. But to Ryerson's amazement, the sergeant did not arrest the private. He sent him off toward the kitchen instead. As he walked away, Elizabeth entered the bedroom, closing the door softly behind her.

"I've failed," she said miserably. "I can't even get you a doctor."

"What about Private Carter?" He wanted to shake her, so worried was he that she'd gotten the private in trouble. "Why didn't your antics get him arrested?"

"Antics?" She slumped onto the mattress. "I don't understand. The sergeant thought the same way. He wanted to charge Private Carter with obstruction of justice, interfering with an officer in the line of his duties, and refusal to obey a lawful order. I told him that you'd made the private my striker, and Private Carter was only obeying my orders. The sergeant seemed unimpressed with my reasoning."

"I see." Ryerson's head throbbed.

"Well." She lifted her chin. "He is my striker. Why can't I have him watch over my husband?"

"Elizabeth." His stomach burned, and his ribs pained him badly. "You may be my wife, but you're not in the army. Carter is detailed to help you. That doesn't mean you're his commander. You can't contradict an officer's orders."

"Yes." She fiddled with the sleeve of her day dress. "The captain thought the same thing."

Closing his eyes, he pressed his palms over his face. "So how did you get Carter off?"

"I convinced the sergeant the colonel agreed with my orders."

"What?"

"The colonel refused to rescind the charges. I pleaded your illness, however, and he agreed to a house arrest. I showed the captain the paper and persuaded him to the opinion that Carter's action conformed with the colonel's intentions."

He thought he was going to be sick. "House arrest?" he asked grimly.

"Yes."

He peered through his fingers. "I'm confined to this house?"

"Actually," she said as she cast her eyes down and worried her lip with her teeth, "to this bedroom."

"And I suppose you've detailed yourself as my nurse?"

She frowned, petulant, almost sulky. "Don't look so unhappy." She flounced off the bed, snatched a cloth from a peg, carried it back to the basin, and rinsed it. "Worse things have happened. I promise I'll take good care of you."

Slowly he eased off the mattress.

Turning, she hurried over. "Wait just a minute." He froze. It hurt him to move, but he wanted to slip under the quilt. He didn't like the bruise on his stomach, or the notion of lying half-naked before her. Reaching his side, she gently pushed on his chest, then dropped to her knees.

He jerked. "What are you doing?"

"You have to lie still." She clamped her hands over his ankles. "Take them off." With a brief nod, she indicated his pants. "I'll help you if it's too painful."

"Are you insane?" He tried to stand up, but she and the stitch in his side held him prisoner. He struggled for a brief instant, than sank back onto the bed. "A female nurse does not undress her patient."

"Generally not." Letting go, she moved her hands to his waistband. He felt himself respond to her. She stilled, fixing that cinnamon gaze on his face. "But our situation is different. The doctor won't come. He says he's too busy. They won't send a steward"—she colored slightly, a peach tinge he'd become very fond of—"because . . ." She sucked in her breath. "You know—" She lowered her even row of dark lashes. "Because they know I'm a nurse and they think you're my husband." The green braid on her sleeves trembled slightly as she tugged at a pants button.

Swiftly he grabbed her hands. "Wait." He sat up. Pain, sharp as a hot bayonet, poked him. He gritted his teeth and kept his voice steady. "Close your eyes."

She did as he asked. He stood. He tried to shuck out of his trousers, but a sick headache pounded his temple, sending daggers of pain into his brain. The room slipped sideways, and he went with it. His arm grazed her shoulder. She steadied him with a full waist embrace, taking his weight onto herself.

She flipped back the quilt and lowered him onto the bed. Hunkering down, he pulled the cool weight of the sheet over his chest. She tucked him in with a neat motion, then lifted the quilt up from the bottom. Quickly she tugged on the cuffs of his pants. "Let's try it this way."

He raised his hips. She pulled, freeing his legs in an awkward motion. Finishing, she slung his pants over her arm, then moved to a wooden chest by the side of the room. He'd acquired it for her, an accomplishment really, by showing a settler how to cook on a Sibley stove.

Maneuvering sideways, Ryerson stared at the neat line of her back. He seldom savored her figure. Her graceful movements and ladylike carriage somehow discouraged baseness of thought. Except when his body betrayed him. Like now. Then her loveliness tempted. The softness. The curves. The plush bottom and tidy waist, nicely encased in wool plaid and waiting for the right man to free it. He bunched the quilt over his growing hardness.

She opened the chest lid. "I think the ribs are bruised but not broken, so bandages won't help very much. I can give you a tonic to help with the pain."

"Fine. Just don't make me sleepy."

"Why not?"

"I don't like those kinds of powders. Women—" He cut short his thought. It wouldn't do to insult her when she was working so hard to assist him. "I like staying awake."

She pulled out one of her sour-smelling packets, a bottle of whiskey, and a small vial of clear liquid. "It wouldn't hurt you to sleep. Rest is healing."

He wanted to answer, but more than that he wanted to watch her. He liked it when she turned her back. He thought her face lovely, but she had a proud, unswerving gaze that never let him scrutinize her. Propping his head on a bunched-up pillow, he watched her prepare. She took her job seriously, lifting out packets and bottles, organizing them on a tray, arranging the objects this way and that until she'd lined up an impressive array into a neat little medicinal army. Without looking at him, she retrieved a glass from the nightstand and measured in two fingers of whiskey. Standing back, she studied her display for a moment, then dumped two powders and stirred. Finally she brought back the flower-sprigged pitcher and added some water.

"You're being too fussy. I'm not badly hurt."

Ignoring his protest, she scooped up the tumbler, plus a crystal vial of clear liquid. Reaching the bed, she put down the cruet and held the whiskey mixture up in her hand. "Sit up."

He narrowed his gaze. "What for?"

She eased onto the mattress. "Sit up. You're going to drink it."

He tried to peer into the glass, but it hurt to bend at the waist. "That?"

"Yes." She pulled back the quilt. "It's an herbal remedy. Raspberry tea and dandelion bitters, and a little liquor, of course. It will make you sleepy and help you relax."

Gently she cradled his head. "Now." She lifted the potion up to his lips. "Drink."

He swallowed the brew without argument. He found it more sour than he expected, but hid his disgust by gulping it quickly.

"Good." She set down the drink. "Now slide down and turn on your stomach."

"What for?"

Bending down, she picked up the crystal vial and poured a clear, oily liquid onto her palms. "Turn over. For once in your life, surrender a bit."

He scowled. "The mere suggestion makes me want to oppose you."

She rubbed her hands briskly together. "Please." She placed her warm hands on his shoulders, stroking gently down toward his biceps. He turned over swiftly, though more to hide his illicit interest than because he needed more nursing.

"Thank you." Softly she touched his back. "I want you to sleep. You know perfectly well how poorly you rest. This will help you, I think." She stroked lightly over his muscles. "Do you like this?"

She'd warmed her hands by the rubbing. They felt hot, sensual, more intimate than he thought proper. "What are you doing?"

"Just touching." She pressed on his spine, smoothing upward with the pad of her palm. The oil made her movement quite slick. "This is called effleurage. I learned it from the Grahamite settlers. Evidently they left Vegetarian in a hurry. Quite a few pamphlets remained in the ruins."

"Graham." He tried to turn over, but the crick in his side kept him from bending. "You mean the quack who makes those funny brown crackers?"

"Yes. And those crackers are good for your health."

"Thank you so much for your advice, but I survived a whole war on hardtack. I'm not going to take up eating brown flour just to placate—"

"Quiet." Reaching his shoulders, she feathered her hands off to the side. "I didn't ask you to follow his physical laws, but you ought to respect some of his theories. These techniques are described by the Greeks. The pamphlet says that ten minutes of rubbing, scientifically applied, is equal to one hour of sleep."

"I see." He swore his voice sounded drugged. Her ministrations increased his frustration, but also brought on a profound sense of stupor. He wanted to drag her into the bed, into the fog in his head. All week he'd dreamt about her. He couldn't recall a single image, only the vivid, painful experience of thrashing around in a state of arousal, trying half the night to fall back to sleep. "You didn't do this to Confederate soldiers?"

Without skipping a beat, she smoothed her hands up toward his shoulders. "No. Only my Indian husband. When he had a neuralgia, we'd call in a shaman and work on his aches and pains together."

"I don't require miraculous measures. A few hours in bed ought to suffice."

"A few days would be more precise."

She had him. He knew that she did. He was stuck in this bedroom. With her. Pledged to protect her, when every nerve, fiber, bone, and bruised sinew wanted nothing more than to plunder and ravage. He bit down on the edge of the pillow. A quill worked through the fabric, pricking the side of his mouth. He scowled. His vow had cost him a great deal of sleep. It began to steal his sanity.

Moving away from the feather, he recited a long, boring verse from the Bible. He'd intended to wait until his excitement subsided, but his body craved this form of attention. Though he doubted she knew it, she pleasured him quite thoroughly, pausing every few strokes to slather on more of the oil. With a curse to himself, he dropped his chin over the edge of the bed.

"Are you all right?" she asked softly.

"Not really." He spoke through clenched teeth.

"Does this hurt? Are you in pain?"

Ribs creaking, he pushed himself onto his good side. A light sheen misted her face. A pin had come loose, and a thick, auburn swath masked her expression.

"Libbie."

"Yes."

"You know I like you."

She did not answer. Propping himself, he pushed back the curl, running his thumb over her cheekbone. She blushed, pulling back. He cupped his hand at the back of her neck, twisting a tendril over his finger. Cool silk caressed him. He'd wondered about this since he'd met her. What did she feel like? Her hair, her skin, all those soft, delicate places. He'd noticed her curves at their first meeting. Lately, however, he'd been struck by her fitness. Her captivity had molded her body. She had contours quite different from other white women. Seeing her next to the other officers' ladies, he'd noticed her strength—and he liked it. He caressed her softly, his nerves singing with both pain and passion. "Do you regret marrying me?"

Rising, she returned to the wooden chest. "We're not really married."

"Not legally."

"Not illegally, either." Bending down, she searched through the contents. "We're friends, that's all." She pulled out half a dozen packets, dropping them in a pile on the floor. "And now I'm your nurse."

"That's all?"

Frowning, she lined up the powders in a neat row. "Yes." She opened one of the bags and tasted. "What else would you think?"

The pain in his side had come back. It had faded away with her stroking, but returned when the glow in his muscles subsided. "I'd think, when a man risks his life to protect you, you'd offer him a bit of affection."

She looked up, surprised. "I offered to help with the troop."

He wanted to pace. He felt incredibly crabby. Stuck in a room with a beautiful woman. He'd sworn to protect her, but right at this moment that seemed like an amazingly farfetched idea. "I appreciate that, but I was thinking of something more like a kiss."

"Don't be silly. I never kiss patients."

"How about husbands?"

Returning, she fluffed up his pillow. "Now you're being impertinent. You're hurt. And drugged. So I'll make some allowance. But we've already made this decision."

"No exceptions for illness?"

"Don't be a child."

"Children don't think what I'm thinking."

"Neither do you when you're well."

He prayed for strength. He wanted to grab her. Luckily he knew he couldn't. Had he been a bit more himself, he would have pinned her flat to the bed. "That's where you're wrong."

"I don't believe you." She picked up his boots. "You pretend you're a beast, but you can be perfectly gentle." She crossed to his trunk and bent down, a movement that should have been modest, except that her weird Greek massage techniques had every molecule of him worked into a passion.

He shut his eyes against the distraction of the lovely curve to her bottom. "Believe me, Libbie, I have monstrous thoughts. It's just, when I'm stronger, I hide my fantasies better."

"Of course." She returned for her bottle, leaning over to get it. The delicate swell of her bosom distorted the red-and-green plaid.

He stifled a groan. "You want to know what I'm thinking?"

Lifting the tray, she stood up. "Not really."

The morning sunlight poured through the liquid. Tiny patches of light danced on her day dress. "You're all my holidays wrapped together. You look like Christmas."

She turned, keeping her back perfectly straight.

"Smell like Easter."

The medicines rattled. She caught herself, but he saw that she'd stumbled.

"When you let down your hair—" Though it hurt him to do it, he struggled to a sitting position. Once upright, a rush of pain, tempered by pleasure, surged through him. "I feel like the Fourth of July."

EIGHT

RYERSON SEEMED TO BE SERIOUS. HE CONTROLLED HIM-self well, but Elizabeth knew he'd spent the week in a pitched battle with his masculine nature. She'd been desired before, but never in such a violent way. He violated her sleep, bolting awake during the night, then lying in bed so tense and restless she sensed his disturbance from seven feet back.

Worse, she felt the same way herself. They spent the small hours of the morning locked in a silent contest of wills, each unable to reclaim slumber, each bent on hiding that fact.

He wanted the kiss. And a good deal more.

"You're raving." Returning to the bed, she smoothed back a brown lock, pretending to study the lump on his forehead. Surreptitiously she glanced at the sheet. Thin as it was, the starchy white covering did not quite disguise his virile reaction. For once, however, she did not fear him. She doubted sincerely that he could act on his impulse. He had three injured ribs and a bruise on his stomach, not to mention the bump and the stiff dose of whiskey she'd given him. Still, it never hurt to be careful. The whiskey mixture would have knocked out Sleeps With Eagle. It barely slowed Ryerson down.

Releasing the lock, she retrieved her last medicine bottle and tucked it back in her dresser. It felt good to be useful. She regretted Ryerson's wounds, especially the way he'd gotten them, but she didn't like a frivolous life. Rummaging through her belongings, she pulled out the sketchbook and charcoals she'd used to design her dress for the party.

Tucking her notebook under her elbow, Elizabeth pulled a chair next to Ryerson's bed. "Are you all right? I could get you a nightshirt, but I think you'd sleep better without one."

He grinned. "Do you mind seeing my chest hair?"

"No." Ignoring his jibe, she flipped open to the first sheet of blank paper.

"No Bible?" he asked, his voice sardonic.

"No." She grasped her chalk firmly. "I'm on to your tricks. You probably know half of the verses by heart. If I start reading, you'll start reciting. I'm going to sketch you. You're going to pose. It's the best way I know to make you be quiet."

Ducking her head, she busied herself with her picture. She found the drawing pretty hard going, as she usually looked at her subjects. With Ryerson, however, that approach didn't feel right. She wanted to catch his true likeness. Her lampoons missed something vivid in him—his passion, precision, and deep sense of honor. She wanted to work from an interior vision, trying to capture his essence.

She glanced briefly at him, then lay her chalk sideways and stroked. Massing black for a background, she shaded with the palm of her hand. Silent and attentive, he propped his head on the pillow. The alcohol seemed to have loosened his normal reserve. He studied her cheekbones in frank appraisal, as if she were the one who was posing and he were the artist doing the sketch.

Frowning, she shaded two hollows for his eye sockets.

His fierceness began to emerge from the shadows. Pausing, she studied the drawing, then quickly filled in his pupils. She left a dash of brightness to offset the darkness, a gleam of hope in his eyes. Next, she started in on his mouth. He remained grim in this feature, tight-lipped and determined, more like the monster she'd always drawn. She cringed at the thought of how she'd portrayed him. She hoped he'd never find out. One of her drawings had become quite famous. In it Ryerson sported the horns of a devil, an Indian maiden splayed at his feet, and smoke from a village curling around him.

"Do you really want to help with the troop?" he asked suddenly.

"Yes." The charcoal bit into the paper and broke. Annoyed, she wrapped the broken piece in a scrap of paper and tossed it onto the floor. "Not that I like helping the army. But your colored troopers are different. Life hasn't left them a lot of choices. I don't mind helping them out."

He picked up the bundle and pulled out the chalk. "Then I'll make you a bargain. I'll rest if you do me a favor."

She selected a thick piece and outlined his shoulders. "What favor?"

"Look in on the troop. Make sure no one got hurt in the fracas. Tell them I'm well. And also," he added as he dusted a smudge off his fingers, "I'd like you to check on a small project."

"Project?" She narrowed her eyes.

He held out his hand. "Can I have some paper?"

"Yes." She tore out a page and handed it to him. "What kind of project?"

Ignoring her question, he sketched for a moment, using bold strokes to trace out a figure. "Barracks improvement. I could use your advice."

"Fort design is not one of my talents." She tried to go back to her drawing, but she found herself looking at his sketch instead.

He scowled. He drew steadily, his eyes dark and assessing. "You know a great deal about camp sanitation."

Her heartbeat sped up. She'd speculated about this since the beginning. Why had the troop been out on the prairie? How had all those soldiers gotten sick? Pretending indifference, she fiddled with the frayed edge of her notebook. "Yes."

"We're trying to make their quarters healthier."

"I see." She went back to her sketch, sharpening the point of the charcoal by scraping it over the paper. She wanted to ask a lot of questions, but considered it wiser to continue working.

He turned his page sideways. He seemed to be printing. "You were pretty much right in your accusations. The army's divided on how my troop ought to be treated. They're in a regular barracks with a genuine outhouse. That's fancy living for a bunch of ex-slaves. So, some officers think my troop ought to be grateful and ignore the fact that they're badly neglected and dying like flies from their living conditions."

"But you disagree?"

"Of course. It's morally wrong. We insult everything the war stood for if we apply a double standard to Negroes."

She lowered her eyes, trying to disguise her swift surge of triumph. He needed her. More important, he trusted her. At least a bit. "What makes you think I can help?"

"I know you can help. The question is, will you?"

"Yes." She slapped her notebook shut. "I don't mind fighting the army." She jumped to her feet and crossed to her chest, closing her pad and stashing the sketch in the bottom. "Besides, there's an irony to it." Returning, she sat next to the mattress. Gently she examined his forehead again. "You should have seen my family's slaves." Her medicinal must have worked, as he didn't recoil from her touch. She thought, with some satisfaction, that she'd finally succeeded in making him sleepy. "They lived right behind us. Three men I never spoke to. And Dimity. A six-foot-tall woman who worked as a field hand. I still don't quite know how they managed."

"But you must have. They practically lived in your house."

"No." She stared at the sheet. She found it painful, discussing the past. She'd loved her parents, her brothers, and Philip, but after a month with Ryerson's troopers she looked at her childhood with different eyes. "I seldom went out there. Once it was flooded in two feet of water. We all worked together to empty it out. It was the only time in my life I saw how they lived."

He chucked her under the chin. "Don't look so wilted. You were a child. You didn't know better."

"Maybe." She knotted her fingers. "But it makes me ashamed, realizing how poorly we treated those people. I think of myself as a kindhearted person."

"You are." He tried to sit up, but her herbal must have taken effect. He could barely lift his head off the pillow. Softly he touched the frill on her sleeve. "In fact, that's your problem. If you had even the littlest mean streak, I'd be dead, and you'd be living out on the prairie."

She smiled in spite of herself. "Perhaps, but I find it ironic that I should learn a sense of compassion from a man I thought of—" She stopped.

"—as monstrous?" he asked cheerfully.

She wished she could kiss him, but stifled the impulse, remembering his earlier request. She squeezed his fingers instead.

He brushed a lock of hair back from her cheekbone. "And if you make my troopers more fit for fighting? If we make war on your precious Cheyenne?"

She captured his hand. She knew what he was asking. She liked him, maybe too much. Because she did she answered with the truth. "I'll defend my friends to the end. Your worries about my safety are totally baseless. When I figure out how to make you see that, I'll ask you to take me back to the prairie and I'll do what I can for the Indian children."

Elizabeth found Ryerson's troop crowded into a small building, tucked in the fort's farthest corner. He had drawn her a map, showing in a bold, soldierly hand the path to the barracks. As she approached, Elizabeth studied the white clapboard structure. It didn't look much different from all the others. Impersonal, neat, and surprisingly civil, at least until one got close. Then the illusion vanished in a sea of mud, shimmering beneath silvery puddles. As she attempted to enter, Elizabeth lifted her skirts. Her boots sank into a quagmire, a fetid muck clinging sullenly to them.

She wrinkled her nose. "Miasma."

Dixon appeared in the doorway. "Hello, mistus. We've been waitin' for you." He held out his hand. He helped her over the puddle, dropping her arm as soon as she stepped onto the threshold. She paused. A rhythmic movement caught her attention. Dixon had set the whole troop to cleaning, but the wash of fresh lime couldn't disguise the reek of swamp water.

She scrunched her face up in disgust. "And humors."

He nodded. "A dog shouldn't live in this place."

Skirting around a sweeping trooper, Elizabeth plunked herself down on one of the bunks. "Is anyone hurt?"

"Just me." Dixon held up his knuckles. "I got in a good punch."

She opened her brown leather medicine bag. "Have you sent for the doctor?"

"No." Dixon pulled up a chair, sat down, and held out his hand. "I waited for you. I like your nursin' much better." He grinned.

She frowned.

He grinned again. "That's how we ended up on the prairie. That quack nearly killed us the first time we stayed here."

Stifling a scowl, she lowered her eyes and examined his cuts. His knuckles were raw and bleeding, but not seriously hurt. "Bring me some water," she said to the private who'd nearly died of pneumonia. He nodded, scurrying off.

She opened her bag and pulled out a pair of scissors. "You know, I wouldn't wish slavery on any human, but there were some advantages to the institution."

Dixon's mouth flattened. "Like what?"

"Like medical care." She glanced at his hand, then searched for a bandage. "Our slaves lived pretty poorly, but my father guarded their health."

"No offense, mistus, but there's nothin' noble in that. The death of a slave means the loss of good money."

She cut the linen into small strips. "What does it matter why someone protects you, so long as they do a good job?"

"It matters."

"You think so?"

"Yes, mistus, I know so." The private arrived with the water. Dixon accepted the basin, laying it down in front of her feet. "That's what makes a man human—somebody loves him and values his feelings."

Elizabeth lay out her bandage strips on the cot, replaced

her scissors, then drew out a cloth for washing. "The army doesn't care what you feel."

"No, but Ryerson does."

"That seems a precarious life, depending on Ryerson's good intentions."

"Seems like an all right life to me."

"Yes, well . . ." She fished through her bag for her soap. "You know what they say about good intentions."

Dixon smiled, holding his wounded hand with his other. "I'd rather follow the major to Hades than live in paradise with the kindest white master."

She grinned, taking his fingers. "Well, he did get pretty smashed up defending your honor."

Dixon snatched back his hand and frowned at his bleeding knuckles. "You've got no reason to laugh. The fight was half over you."

"I'm sorry." She knelt and dipped her cloth in the water. "I wasn't laughing at you."

"Then what?"

She soaped up carefully. "I was thinking about him."

"Now isn't that just like a woman in love." He rolled up his uniform sleeve. "The man gets himself nearly killed, and you're kneelin' there grinnin' about it."

She took his hand softly. He had long fingers, blunt-tipped and brown, and she reflected she'd never examined the skin of a Negro so closely. "Don't twist my comment around." She scrubbed fiercely, ignoring his swift intake of breath. "I didn't say a word about love."

"Then what are you smilin' about?"

"About myself." She let go of his trembling hand, rinsed out the cloth, and twisted it dry. "About how I misjudged him."

"You like it? You and he bein' married?"

"In certain ways, yes." She searched through her bag for a salve.

"He's a good man, the major."

"Yes." She considered a tin of McCloud's Liniment. "No." She glanced at the label, discounting most of the claims, racking her brain for the times she'd used this and trying to remember whether it worked. "I actually don't know. I think he's good in certain ways."

"But at least he's not the devil incarnate?" She registered the tone in his voice, wry and amused, not the least bit accusing.

"No." She opened the lid and sniffed. "That much he isn't."

"Then I'd say you're making progress."

"Look, Sergeant Dixon." She dropped the ointment into her lap. "I know what you want, but don't get your hopes up. I like the major, I honestly do, but this—marriage—it's only a sham. This is a role he's playing in order to help me."

"Believe what you want." He leaned forward, resting his forearms on his knees. "I think he loves you."

"No." The lid clattered onto the wood floor, the sound almost drowning her protest—almost. "That can't be true." Around her, men stilled. She'd forgotten the audience of housecleaning soldiers, but the pause in their movement caught her attention. Leaning forward, she lowered her voice to a whisper. "You're wrong. He can't really —you know—that can't really be true."

"Why not?" Dixon held out his scraped knuckles.

Flushing, she reached for the top, but her former pneumonia patient had already reached it. Shyly he handed it back.

"Because it just can't be," she said fiercely to Dixon.

"Why not?"

"What would we do?" She sniffed the cream. Turpentine and camphor, lightly disguised with sassafry. "He loves the army, and I have to go back to the prairie."

"Why?" Dixon nodded to the young trooper, who lowered his eyes and returned to his broom.

She took Dixon's hand and gently dabbed on the salve. "It's my home. I can't live with civilized people."

"Why not?"

"Because—" She stopped. How could she put this? She picked at the edge of the McCloud's ointment label, trying to put her thoughts in order. "I dislike the pretense. With the Cheyenne, life was much simpler. Somehow whites sense how I feel, and they hate it. It's as if I've tasted a wildness they've left behind, and they can't bear to think about what they have lost." Swiftly she gave him one pleading look.

He grinned. "You love him."

"No!" The whole tin of unguent slipped out of her fingers. "No!" She ignored it this time, as did everyone else. Her tone had drawn the whole troop's attention. "Of course not. How could I?"

Dixon's hands twitched. Leaning forward, he retrieved the ointment. A shadow passed over his handsome features. "How could you not?"

She arched a brow in surprise. "Don't be facetious."

"I'm not jokin' with you." Dixon lowered his voice, his soft Kentucky accent turning it silky. "Plenty have loved him, includin' myself."

"Well, I don't." She grabbed back the lotion and screwed on the top. Unaccountably, she felt like weeping. "I don't," she repeated with more emphasis. Looking around, she noticed the troopers. The group made a pretense of their cleaning, but their movements had a dispirited feeling, as if someone had punched each of them in the stomach. "I don't," she said a little bit louder. No one looked her way, except the youngest. He studied her with solemn eyes. She lowered her gaze and gathered her things. "I couldn't." She meant the comment more to herself than the sergeant. "I mean, I don't." Of course not, she thought. Of course not. She could not even bring herself to consider. "I couldn't possibly." Did Dixon really believe she loved him? Hands shaking, she fumbled with the clasp of her bag. "Could I?"

Ryerson didn't think he loved her. He lazed in the bed, head tucked in the crook of his elbow, surreptitiously watching Elizabeth's breathing. He loved watching her sketch, savoring the rise and fall of her breasts, pretending to delight in the skill of her fingers as he relished the rhythmic swell of her bosom. He'd enjoyed this pleasure for almost six days. He considered his feeling a perverse obsession, sprung from a mixture of guilt and frustration, the aftereffects of his wartime sorrows and his four years of essentially celibate living.

He liked her, of course. How could he not? She devoted herself almost wholly to him. She'd established a quiet daily routine. She tended her goats, consulted with Dixon, then walked with Mary to gather wildflowers. The rest of the time, she stayed in the house, fussing and patting and coddling him.

In breaks from her nursing, she occupied herself mainly with painting, absorbed in lively interior visions that expressed themselves as delicate flowers. At first he thought the tattoos made her too shy to go out. He changed his mind later, however. Watching her bouquets bloom on the paper, he realized she was one of those rare and astonishing women who sustained themselves without company.

He liked that quite well.

Helen had been ambitious for him, always planning and plotting his rise in the world. The daughter of a powerful man, she'd never been entirely happy with Ryerson's humble teaching position. Which meant, much as he loved his wife, he'd always been a little bit angry, and never more so than after she died. At her funeral he'd sworn to himself, if he ever remarried—a prospect he thought exceedingly dim —he'd never again bend his goals for a woman. Which made Elizabeth, with her peaceable ways and her Indian-loving opinions, an impossible marital prospect, but a charming and pleasant companion.

Except at bedtime, of course.

At the thought, Ryerson flipped onto his stomach, keeping his gaze carefully lowered. She'd been driving him crazy. Not on purpose, of course. Never on purpose. Without seeming to know what she was doing, she ignored his male drives entirely. He'd noticed this trait when she cared for his troopers. She seemed to regard her patients as children. Aimed at his soldiers, he thought that a fine quality. Aimed at himself, he thought it hateful. He submitted to her. Outwardly he was civil and patient, but he mentally jumped her and tore off her clothes.

At the thought, a lewd fantasy popped into his head. In it, he mounted the chestnut and rode to the edge of a cliff overlooking the prairie. Below him, Elizabeth trembled. Stripped to the waist, she'd been tied to a tree by a dozen garishly painted Indian braves. Enraged by the sight, his fictional self charged the red devils. He howled down on the warriors, scattering them with a few vicious strokes of his saber. Elizabeth shrieked wildly and fainted, evidently undone by the mere thought of bloodshed. He had to untie her, of course. She came out of her swoon in his embrace, covering her breasts with ladylike haste.

Ryerson frowned. He bunched the sheet around his

waist. The spring air caressed his bare chest, aggravating his tension, driving his thoughts darker and downward. His imagination turned lurid. In his fantasy he took her at once, ravishing her with such violence he spent himself with no thought of her pleasure. Their coupling ended with both of them trembling. As she fought back tears, he battled to regain his composure. Suddenly she lifted her eyes and asked him to take her again. She adored his embraces and wanted more, if only he would touch her more gently. Ryerson bolted upright. He sat back on his heels, drew back his fist, and rammed the pillow into the wall.

Instantly she sprang from her drawing. "What's the matter?"

He grabbed the sheet and draped it around himself. Side aching, he pushed himself off the mattress. "I'm going out."

"You can't," she said tersely, approaching the bed. "You're under arrest."

He snarled. He didn't quite mean to, but a low growl escaped his throat. "I'm going to check on the barracks." He lurched toward his trunk. "Get out of the way or you'll have to live with the consequences."

"Like what?" She lifted her chin, moving between him and his clothes. "You'll take me back to the prairie and let the wolves eat me?"

"No," he said calmly, "I'll sneak out the window wearing only my drawers."

Standing firm, she gripped her notebook a little bit tighter. "You wouldn't."

"You think not?"

"No." Her fingers showed white at the knuckles. "What if you're caught?"

"I never get caught." He drew the sheet more closely around himself. "Though I have to admit, it wouldn't be good for my health, prowling around the barracks half-naked."

"You can't." Backing up, she sat down on the lid. The leaves of her notebook fluttered gently. "You're under arrest. You're confined to this bedroom."

"They're guarding the door." A week in bed had made him dizzy. His head throbbed, and the pain in his side stabbed like a dagger. "I won't get caught if you'll just stay quiet."

She glanced from him to the door, making little sounds of extreme agitation. "I won't help you do something this stupid."

"Fine." He strolled to the window, lifted the sash, and threw his leg over.

"Wait." She chewed on her lip. "Come back in. I'll get you some pants."

He had tried to hide his affliction by keeping the sheet over his body, but right at this moment he suspected she'd gotten a glimpse of his problem.

She threw down the notebook. Turning, she searched carefully through his storage trunk. "The barracks are fine. We can't control the miasmas, but Dixon's having the troop build a walkway. We've got the whole place aired out. I'm teaching the men about camp sanitation. I've read them the army's health regulations, as well as my Grahamite pamphlets."

"So bring me my pants."

"James." Retrieving his trousers, she pivoted back. She clutched them next to her bosom. "Please. Just relax. I'll take good care of your troopers."

He pushed away from the window and moved slowly toward her. "I appreciate what you've done for them, but I'm their commander. I want to see their condition myself."

She tried to retreat, but the trunk barred her way. Reaching behind herself, she closed the lid, then plopped down on top. "What if you're caught?"

"I never get caught."

Eyes narrowed, she gripped his trousers a little bit tighter. "You're so full of yourself. You ask for my assistance and then you don't trust me. I don't know which of us is more foolish, me for wanting to help you or you for letting me do it."

He clutched the sheet more tightly to him. He ached. He ached in almost every part of his body. His head hurt. His ribs stung. His thighs and buttocks felt tense. He'd been frustrated for days, almost absurdly priapic, a persistent state that made him incredibly crabby. He sucked in his breath. Reaching her, he sat down. He refused to fight. He refused to argue. Most of all, he refused to spend one more day cooped up with this woman. "You're teaching my troop Dr. Graham's health rules?"

"Some of them, yes."

A swift sound of dissent escaped him.

"Don't be so stubborn." She frowned prettily, letting the pants slip a little. "He had some good ideas. The crackers are sold in boys' schools, you know. The saltpeter helps with discipline problems."

He wanted to take her. She still smelled of the prairie. Two weeks at the fort couldn't erase the scent: wildflowers, earth, and her female perfume. "These are soldiers, not boys. They do not need their ardor tamped down."

She lowered her eyes, tracing the gold stripe on his pants. Outside, a mockingbird trilled. She listened through the length of its song, three rowdy bird-language verses, separated by a lovely cantata, before she raised her gaze to him. "What about their commander?"

He leaned forward slowly and slipped his trousers out of

her grasp. "It's a natural reaction." She seemed not to notice his theft. She watched, lips slightly parted, as he retreated calmly to the room's farthest corner and secreted himself behind the canvas screen. Bending down, he struggled into one leg of his pants. As he did, he heard the trunk open. There was a clatter as something scraped on the floor.

"This isn't working, is it?" Her voice sounded shaky.

"What?" To his intense displeasure, his sounded worse.

"This farce of a marriage."

He shifted his weight to the other foot. "Our—arrangement—seems to be fine to me."

His shirt appeared on the wooden frame. "I hear General Hancock's launched an offensive," she said.

"So?" It still hurt him to move, but he felt determined. He had to go out. He shouldn't have stayed this long with her. He couldn't imagine what he'd been thinking, taking her into his house. It would have been better to freeze in the shelter than to get himself cornered like this.

"Vegetarian should be safe by the end of the month." Her voice came from the far side of the room.

"What are you saying?"

"I want to go back." He heard another small burst of clatter. "I'll stick with you until you're cleared of the charges, but as soon as that's through, I want to go home."

He fastened his pants and came out. "You don't like it here?"

"I didn't say that."

"Then what are you saying?"

She stood by the door, holding his holster. Out of respect for his officer's status, the colonel had left Ryerson his weapons. Ryerson wouldn't need them tonight, but she could not be expected to know that. She held out the gun belt, her hands shaking slightly. She looked wifely to him;

pleasant, subservient, ladylike, and old-fashioned. A lovely impression, and one she ruined by lifting her chin in the most hateful way. "I want to go back to my home on the prairie. I don't like living here at the fort."

"Don't say that." He kept his voice low, seeing no point in creating a ruckus. Grabbing his gun belt from her, he slung the leather around his waist. "I made you a promise. I think I've kept it. I won't let you live in that hole on the prairie."

"But, James . . ."

"No!" He pulled back the strap and worked at the buckle. "I won't hear of you living out there. No wife of mine is subsisting like that."

She started, then glanced at the door. "But I'm not your wife."

"Perhaps." With a curse to himself, he undid the holster. Tossing the gun belt on the bed, he retrieved his shirt. "Perhaps." He lowered his voice, realizing belatedly that its tone had been rising. "You're not my wife under law, but you are in the eyes of the army. And in the hearts of my troopers. What's more, I've pledged to protect you. I'd think that would give me some rights in this matter."

"I'm sorry, truly I am, for fooling the troopers."

"Then stay and help them." He shrugged into the flannel. "Help me." He buttoned his cuff. "You said yourself you didn't mind helping."

"I don't, but the Cheyenne will need me."

He stopped. "What do you mean?"

"I told you." She averted her eyes and brought him his socks. "I help the Indian children. If General Hancock makes a raid on their village, I'm sure the children will need my nursing."

"You expect that argument to persuade me?" He accepted the wool stockings from her. "I should take you to help the Cheyenne?"

"Only the children."

He gave her a look. He thought it a ludicrous notion, helping the children of his enemies.

"What?" Two red spots bloomed in her cheeks. "Nits make lice?" She glared fiercely at him and balled up her fists. It flashed through his mind: a blow to his ribs could hurt him quite badly. Fortunately she didn't swing. She turned instead and stomped back to the chest. "Chivington's theory? Don't even think it." She snatched up his boots. "The sentiment's not worthy of you."

"Elizabeth." He let go of his breath, aware for the first time he'd been holding it back. "I didn't just bring you here for a refuge. The Indians are not your own people. You have to learn to live with the whites."

"Why?" Holding the high boots, she walked stiffly to the side of the bed. She dropped to her knees and turned her face toward him, her gaze frankly angry. "I was happy out there, I tell you. I found the peace I'd been seeking. The first serenity I'd found since the war." She held up one boot.

"Good." With a flash of dismay he strode toward her. Reaching the bed, he stopped, bending his knees to bring himself even with her. "And I'm glad you loved it." Gently he tugged on her elbows, striving to raise her to her feet. "But the peace you describe is not really living."

She jerked away sharply. "Who are you to tell me how I should live?"

He held onto her arms, his fingers digging into the flesh. "I'm your husband."

"False husband."

"False husband, yes." Reluctantly he knelt before her. "But someone who cares." He wanted to hug her. He hated this kind of fighting. For all her obstinate, wrong-headed ways, she'd cared for him always. He wished now to the depth of his heart she'd allow him to watch over her for a while. "But I'm true enough to you in some ways." He slipped his boots out of her hands and set them down on the floor. "There's more to life than flowers and sky. You're entitled to love, to a genuine husband, to a home of your own and your very own children. You won't find them out on the prairie."

She jumped to her feet and ran toward the door. Ryerson let her. If she went out, perhaps he could ease his frustration by relieving his male needs himself. She paused, hand on the knob. For a moment she seemed to be thinking, then she let go, strode to the window, and pushed back the curtain. She opened the sash and thrust her face out into the twilight.

"What are you doing?" he asked quietly.

"Trying to get control of myself." She drew a deep, visible breath. The fading light streamed through the window, filtering through her hair and turning it crimson. She seemed to be considering something, for she stood very still, cheek to the frame, her face set and her focus turned inward. The mockingbird had halted its song. Leavenworth's trees rang with the din of sparrow and whippoorwill chatter.

Ryerson stood up and leaned on the bedpost. He supposed she needed to sort out her thoughts, so he let her. His own thinking needed unscrambling. As she stared out the window, he pulled his boots on in silence. Contrary to his early assumption, their false marriage had not been a favor to her. She spoke the truth about her life on the prairie. How she'd done it, he could not imagine, but he believed her life had been peaceful. He had upset that precarious balance. Moreover, she'd turned out to be useful. She cared for him and won the love of his troopers. It was she, not he, who was doing the favor. For exactly that reason, he said not a word. When he finished dressing, he sat down on the bed and listened to the bird conversation. The song of the sparrows made a sweet counterpoint to the distant shout of the evening guard mount.

He wasn't sure whether she listened. He studied her face, aloof and impassive, made almost foreign by the tattoos. For all its strange beauty, he found her expression easy and peaceful. That single virtue worked at his heart and made all her odd quirks seem pleasant. As the marchers fell silent, she crossed her arms over her bosom and shivered. "You said once I should know how to heal."

"Yes."

"Well, I'm thinking." She moved away from the window. Crossing over to him, she held out her hand. His heartbeat sped up. Warmth shimmered through him. He gripped her hand tightly, drawing her close. She responded by placing her hand on his chest. "Since you're giving prescriptions, perhaps you'd consider curing yourself."

Ryerson found Dixon on the steps of the barracks, sitting with Mary, the mulatto seamstress who'd helped Libbie make her new clothes. As Ryerson approached, the sergeant stood and saluted. Ryerson strode into the pooled light of a pair of kerosene lanterns.

"At ease." Ryerson nodded at the tall, handsome sergeant, then turned to the girl. She had wide, pretty eyes and a wistful expression, her light coffee complexion nicely set off by a pale yellow dress. She also appeared to be breathless.

Ryerson propped a boot on the step. "Good evening," he said to the girl.

Dixon held himself rigid, his gaze away from the seam-stress. "Suh."

"You're up after taps?"

"Yes, suh."

The girl stood up, staring in fright at Ryerson's shoulders.

Ryerson dusted the gold braid on his sleeve. "And I'm violating my house arrest." He pulled a cheroot from his pocket. "Perhaps we could take a walk by the river?"

Dixon hesitated, glancing at Mary. He wore his full uniform, the top unbuttoned. He, too, seemed breathless.

"How's the hand?" Ryerson asked.

Dixon's posture relaxed. "Not bad. Mary's been comfortin' me. And, of course, I got help from the new Mistus Major."

"Of course." The sun had gone down. The day had been cloudy, the soft Kansas dusk filled with insects, but now that darkness had fallen, God's tiniest creatures had all become silent, along with the daytime din of the fort.

Ryerson shoved the stub in his mouth. "And the troop?"

"They're mostly fine, Major." Dixon took the girl's elbow, lifted the lamp, and escorted her down the short flight of steps. "Don't you think you ought to get back to the house? A walk by the river seems kind of risky. The colonel will be awful unhappy if he finds you've come for a visit. And that's nothing compared to the mistus."

"Mrs. Ryerson knows what I'm doing. As for the colonel, I doubt very much he will find out."

"He will if you faint on our doorstep. You look kind of shaky. Why don't you let me send Mary to get the mistus?"

"No." Ryerson didn't feel shaky. He felt high-strung and nervous. He wasn't going back to that room until he'd walked off some of his temper. "I'll go back in a minute. I just wanted to see how the troopers are doing."

The pretty seamstress picked up the lamp and edged away from the small landing. "I'll come back tomorrow."

"You don't have to go," Ryerson snapped out. He spoke more angrily than he intended. He didn't like disturbing two lovers. They were breaking the rules, but that didn't much matter. Some rules were meant to be broken.

"That's all right, Major," the girl said softly. "It's getting late, really. I've got plenty of work to do in the mornin'."

She glanced shyly at Dixon, then quickly retreated, taking one of the lanterns with her. As she did, Dixon buttoned the top of his uniform jacket. To Ryerson's surprise, the sergeant's previously ill-fitting coat hung evenly from his broad shoulders. All of the wrinkles had been ironed out, and the blue wool hugged his waist tightly.

Ryerson touched one of the buttons. "I like this. Did she tack down your chevrons?"

"Women." Dixon grinned. "I surely do love them."

Ryerson smiled back. "They love you, in any event."

"That's true enough, Major."

Reaching down, Ryerson doused the remaining lamp. He opened the door and peered into the barracks and spoke to the sergeant in a low voice. "So . . . what's the new Mrs. Major been doing?"

"She's kept us real busy." Dixon stepped in, walking softly. "She's got us to scrubbing. The barracks." He gestured at the dark cavern. "Ourselves." His outstretched arm seemed to take in the sleepers. "She pokes her nose in unlikely matters, like what we do with our leavins'. But the men know she means well. She keeps us dosed up with quinine, orders up special diets for those that don't feel well, and feeds the rest of us funny brown crackers."

Ryerson grimaced. "Do the troopers complain?"

"No, suh. Not much. Except for the crackers." He lowered his voice to a whisper. "We throw them away after she's gone. But mostly we take her suggestions. Soldiering's a fine occupation, but a feminine touch can do wonders."

They walked quietly between the soldiers, their boots brushing against the wood floors. Though the low ground still made the place fetid, Ryerson could smell the freshly scrubbed walls, the soapy residue of her cleaning. "Do you think her improvements are helping?"

"Some. There's two new cases of malarial fever, but she's got the dysentery tamped down."

They'd reached the far side of the barracks. Ryerson opened the door, then took one last look at his troopers. He couldn't see much, but the night sounds were peaceful, some men snoring and nobody moaning.

Dixon stepped out. He looked to the left, descended the porch, then waited. Ryerson joined him, pulling a match out of his pocket. He nodded at the path to the river. Without a word, both men started down, strolling in companionable silence over the landscape. Neither could see well. Ryerson lit his cigar stub, creating a small flare with the match and a tiny, glowing, circular ember. Dixon didn't seem much distracted, however. He stepped in front of his wartime commander and strode down the bluff that led to the river and into a clearing that looked vaguely familiar. Ryerson stopped, looking around. He leaned his shoulder against a tree trunk. "You like the seamstress?"

"She fixes my clothes."

"That all?"

"She's got pretty eyes."

"The troop could use its own laundress."

Dixon sat down on a log and appeared to be feeling along its bark surface. "Do you like the new Mrs. Major?"

"Not for the post of troop laundress."

"I wasn't suggesting that, suh."

"Then what are you asking?" Ryerson paced to the edge of the clearing. He wasn't sure why they'd walked to this place. He realized now when he'd been here before and strongly suspected why Dixon had brought him. "You know perfectly well she's not my real wife."

"But you like her?"

Ryerson sucked in a lungful of smoke. He did not inhale often, preferring the more miserly satisfaction of just holding the stub in his mouth. But he needed distraction. He'd been cooped up too long with Libbie. He wanted to feel the burn in his chest, a sensation to keep him from longing for Libbie. "I like her, yes."

"Enough to keep her?"

"Sergeant, you presume on our friendship."

Dixon took out his whittling knife. Ryerson couldn't see him well in the darkness, but his jaunty posture seemed unrepentant. "We need her. You need her. The war was bad, but peace won't be easy, especially if we stay on the plains. We'll need a good woman just to survive."

"She's an excellent nurse, I grant you that. But do you really think that's a reason for marriage?"

"Sounds good to me."

Ryerson puffed on the cigar stub, pacing the clearing. Dixon's comments made sense. Women had uses. Soldiers lost patience with certain chores. Women, with their motherly interest in life's fundamentals, could be helpful in some situations. "We couldn't just find a good laundress? During the war, they did our nursing."

Dixon took a firm grip on the knife and peeled a long strip of the stick. "Where are we going to find that kind of help? The rules say a laundress has to be married. There's hardly any black women out here. How will we find a married white woman who wants to work as a colored troop's laundress?"

"My point exactly."

Dixon looked up. He searched Ryerson's expression, then ducked his head and inspected his whittling. "That's different."

"Why?"

"I'm not the marryin' type."

"How do you know? You've never tried it."

Dixon scraped off another long strip. Then another. Then several more. Ryerson could not see the shape of the carving, but the green stick got rapidly thinner. Leaning back on a tree, Ryerson watched his broad-shouldered sergeant in silence. Dixon whittled the stick down to a nub before he saw fit to respond to Ryerson's comment. "It would be an adjustment, settlin' down with only one woman."

"Mary looked happy."

"Sure, but did I?"

Ryerson strolled across the clearing. He held out his hand for the knife. Dixon handed it over and Ryerson pulled a cheroot out of his pocket. "I agree with your logic. The troop could use a feminine presence. But why can't it be you that gets married?" He trimmed the end off the cigar and offered the unlit cheroot to his sergeant.

"No." Dixon shook his head slowly. "I don't think so."

"Give me one good reason."

"I'm not the marryin' type."

"I think you'd like it."

"Are you saying you wouldn't?"

Ryerson scowled. He jammed the foul-tasting stub into his mouth. "I'm sure I'd survive. The question is—would my wife?"

"Yes, suh, I think so, or I wouldn't suggest it."

Ryerson gestured at the path toward the river. He couldn't think clearly stuck in this spot. It reminded him of the day with the broomstick, with apricot brandy and Libbie so lovely. He walked down the path through the thick undergrowth, listening for the sound of the river. Neither man spoke, and Ryerson reflected that this was the only good legacy of the war: the friendship he had with men like Dixon. "You think I could make Libbie get married?"

"Yes, suh." Dixon closed up the space between them. The path didn't permit walking together, but they stayed as near as the small path permitted. "I mean no insult to your first wife, but you had a bad experience with her. Mrs. Wheaton is different. She's got more style. More wit. And much, much more courage."

"A man can get tired of wit in a woman."

"Be fair, Major. Your first wife was stubborn, but she wasn't strong. Mrs. Wheaton's much tougher."

"Funny. I thought she was soft."

"She is, at least sometimes. A good woman is like that. Take my Mary. She's like the wind on the prairie. On some nights she'll caress you so softly, but in the right mood no force can stop her."

Ryerson stopped. They'd reached a view of the river. The Missouri shimmered by moonlight, a placid surface whose broad, flat expanse belied its depth and powerful current. "Very poetic. Are you comparing my new wife to a tornado?"

"That's one way to put it."

He lit the cigar. "I tend to think of her as more flame-like."

"She is kind of rosy."

"She certainly is." Ryerson felt his groin tighten. This conversation wasn't helping at all. "Rosy and flamelike, but also quite soft. And also sometimes like a tornado."

Dixon gazed out at the river. He stood next to his grizzled commander, his whittling knife folded back down but still clutched in the palm of his hand. "I used to like listenin' to you. You had a poem for every occasion."

Ryerson scowled. "I don't recite anymore."

"I remember a good one you taught me."

Ryerson glanced quizzically at him.

Dixon smiled. "I think it's by Pliny: 'Absence is to love as wind is to fire. It extinguishes the weak, but kindles the strong.'"

Ryerson jammed the cigar into his mouth. He'd come away to forget about Libbie, not to stand next to Dixon and wax poetic, but this time of the evening reminded him of her. The sergeant's interest seemed so perfectly heartfelt, he couldn't help wondering what his friend meant. "So is Mrs. Wheaton the wind or the fire?"

Dixon grinned, shoving the knife back into his pocket. "Neither, I think. The poem is just to remind you. Libbie might be different from Helen."

NINE

He should have kissed her, Ryerson thought. His boots crunched in the gravel as he made his way back from the barracks. He probably should have done more than that. Perhaps, he thought in wry amusement, he should have ravished her, just like in his daydream. Maybe then he'd have gotten her out of his system, relieved the almost permanent ache in his groin, taken the blunt edge off his temper, and given him, if only briefly, a moment of peace and relaxation.

Turning, he made his way toward the back of his house. He carried no lantern, and that suited him fine. He liked sorting out his thoughts in the darkness. He had no idea how he'd last the summer. She'd agreed to remain at the fort. He'd had to make an outrageous bargain. Negotiating with her had rankled his pride, but appealed to his sense of justice. After much argument and a long discussion, he proposed the novel idea that she'd help her friends by remaining with him.

The Cheyenne were doomed. Even Elizabeth had to admit it. So what better way to render assistance than to help arrange a peaceful surrender? He'd made her a promise, one he thought he could keep. If he beat the court-martial and went on maneuvers, he would put their false marriage to use. If she would send word to her former tribe, he would try to persuade her friends to give up.

He felt unaccountably grateful to her. He wasn't much fond of this Indian war. He thought the Cheyenne completely barbaric, but fighting them wasn't like freeing the Negro. Slavery had seemed evil to him. The Indians simply seemed different. He had no desire to destroy their race, if he might manage to avoid it while still obeying orders. He thought he could. He knew how to wield a field commander's power. He couldn't stand in history's way. He could, however, soften fate's harshness.

And pay Elizabeth back for her kindness.

She had lived up to her word. She'd worked hard for his troopers, teaching them all her unorthodox cures, as well as the army's more conventional methods. Though they still lived in substandard quarters, she'd improved the health and morale of his soldiers immensely.

Not to mention his own.

He skimmed under the trees, making his way in spite of the shadows. His sense of well-being mystified him. She frustrated him on a physical level. Not on purpose, of course, never on purpose, but with her continual presence, her touching and patting, the closeness the nursing required. He could have recovered without her care. His injured ribs and bruises were simple affairs that would have healed easily on their own.

Still, he liked the attention. And those bizarre Greek techniques. She'd lightened his heart. He had no other way to express the feeling. It cheered him to think of her waiting; to know she'd be there when he returned; that she'd care for the troopers if they were wounded. The thought of her made him a little less lonely. That by itself made her worth the frustration, the seething nights, the days of dull ache, the edgy temper and bodily anguish.

Reaching his home, Ryerson stepped up to the window and peered in. She'd fallen asleep by the light of a candle, sitting upright against one of the bedposts. A wide ribbon of moonlight bathed her in silver, gilding her white satin peignoir. The frilly concoction made her look like an angel. Only the moccasins gave her away.

He smiled as he pushed up the sash. She wore the beaded footgear quite often. She never complained about her high-buttoned boots, but he noticed she wore the Indian slippers in private.

He smiled, hitching himself over the sill. Pain flared in his side as he climbed through the window. He tried to move so as not to wake her. A spring breeze fluttered the candle. She stirred very slightly. He paused, hoping he wouldn't disturb her. She looked so pretty, propped up on the pillows, her auburn hair tumbling over her bosom. He liked the idea of touching that softness. He wouldn't undress her, of course. Maybe take off her shoes, as she did for him, but leave all the more modest garments intact. And he'd sleep on the cot. She'd given him the bed while he'd been injured, but perhaps it was time to switch back.

Tiptoeing in, he approached her. Evidently Elizabeth had been reading. Some kind of letter lay in her hand. He almost thought she had been crying, but the smudge on her face might have been shadow. He couldn't imagine who could have written, or what was said to cause her such pain. Gently he eased the paper out of her hand. He glanced at the spidery writing. Old-fashioned and formal, the style seemed familiar, and he wondered again who might be writing. Reluctantly he folded the message. He couldn't read by the light of one candle. He supposed she'd tell him first thing in the morning. If not, he'd find out for himself by reading it later.

He eased down beside her, watching her closely. As

lightly as he could, he lifted her robe, revealing her ankles. Warmth kindled in the pit of his stomach. It seemed such an intimate, illicit pleasure, touching her in this forbidden way. He'd come to enjoy these soft, beaded slippers. In the week of his healing, the gentle shuffle of their deerskin soles had become one of the sounds he associated with her.

Turning her foot, he took hold of her heel. She sighed. Using a skill he'd honed with his Jamie, he tugged on the supple leather. As he freed her toes, she toppled over, curling sideways like a wayward kitten, palms flat, knees tucked up a little. He paused again.

The candlelight flickered on the line of her cheekbone. Her hair tumbled over her bosom, curling over the delicate bones of her shoulders. He wanted to kiss her, but knew he shouldn't. Instead he leaned sideways, propping himself on his elbow. She smelled faintly herbal, as always. Lifting his hand, he skimmed her hair without touching its satin. Its surface seemed to glow, a living flame topping the silver. He cursed the devil inside him. He meant for the peignoir to make her angelic, bury her beauty in frothy white ruffles, but she seemed so alive, so pure, soft, and female that he felt for an instant he'd been put on this earth just to plunder her loveliness. A low sound escaped him.

Gritting his teeth, he loosened the second soft slipper. As the buttery leather came off in his hand, he realized with a deep sense of unease how much he liked caring for her. This has to work out, he thought angrily. The irony of it seemed almost too perfect. The Fates couldn't have sent him one of his victims unless they had something special in mind. Maybe redemption. Maybe one lovely summer. Maybe even, just once in his life, the straightforward, soldierly pleasure of coming back from a war to find somebody waiting.

With a sleepy snuffle, she kicked out one foot. He

wanted to kiss it, maybe not the game of piglets he'd played with Jamie, but something a bit more exotic, possibly involving the curve of the arch. *God*, he prayed as he unbuttoned his frock coat, *just once in my life I'd like to kiss every curve of her body.*

She opened her eyes. "James," she said sleepily.

He smiled and kissed the top of her forehead.

"James!" Bolting upright, she threw her arms around his waist. "It's you." She buried her face against his chest. "You've come back." Before he had time to react, she drew him close and snuggled in tightly. "You frightened me so. I thought you'd got caught."

He circled his arms loosely around her, not quite daring to touch. "I never get caught."

"I know you believe that." She sighed, seeming to melt against his blue flannel. "It's those wartime adventures. They've made you too full of yourself."

He pushed her back slightly. "But you like me that way."

"Yes." She hugged him again, as if she couldn't believe that he'd returned. "Yes."

"What's that?" he asked, indicating the letter.

"It's—" She snatched up the paper. The stiff parchment rattled. "It's a letter of sorts, although maybe it's orders. The colonel gave it to me. You understand. I wouldn't have read it, but I didn't realize it should be private."

"It's for me?"

She nodded, offering the heavy ivory stationery to him.

Brusquely he took it from her. "I have nothing to hide, but you shouldn't read my mail without my permission."

She peered anxiously at the paper. Her expression stopped him, and he wondered again who could have written. He cocked his head in a question.

She lowered her lashes. Wetting her lips, she made a

faint gesture of halfhearted apology. "You never told me her father still wrote to you."

With a jolt, Ryerson realized what she meant, the reason the handwriting looked so familiar. "No." He brushed at his sleeve. "I didn't. He isn't important."

"Yes. Well." She pushed a thick curl back from her cheekbone. Ryerson wondered again if she had been crying. "He seems to think differently. He wants you to join him."

Her tone caught his attention. He squinted narrowly at her. "What do you mean?"

She hung her head, almost as if she were hiding.

He flapped the letter against his thigh. "Shall I light a lamp, or do you want to tell me?"

"He's commissioned a statue of you on a horse. It's meant to honor your wartime record."

"Damn." Bolting off the mattress, he pitched the letter into a corner.

"Don't take it that way." She moved to his side. "He's trying to help you. He's petitioned the army to drop the court-martial. He wants you to join him for the unveiling."

"He what?" He unbuckled the holster and tossed the gun belt to her.

She caught it deftly. "He wants you to come to Washington."

"Damn." He tore off his coat, flinging it on the floor in angry abandon. "Goddamn. Son of a bitch. Damn."

"James!" She picked up his jacket, following him as he paced the length of the bedroom. "He's trying to help you."

"He doesn't give one good goddamn about me. He's trying to protect a woman who's gone." He turned and absently watched as she hung up his pistol. "Please understand. I don't begrudge him his grief. I'm all he has left of his Helen, but it's hard to live up to her ambitions, especially now that she's dead."

"Ambitions?" She moved to the bed and laid out his coat.

"I told you before." He shrugged out of the flannel. "Helen wanted to see me in the Senate."

"But she's gone." She folded the coat into neat quarters.

"To me, yes. But not to her father." He tossed the shirt over the screen. "He adored her. He can't let her go." Ryerson strode to the bed and sat down on the mattress.

She sank to her knees and grabbed hold of his boot heel. "Still, why does he care about your court-martial?"

He paused, leaning back on his elbows, suddenly struck by what she was doing. God, how he loved this. Someone to help him. Someone to talk to. Someone to share his worries and burdens. "Because there's no load so heavy as a debt to the dead." She pulled off the leather, freeing one foot of the heat and the weight of the knee boots. "Whatever we owe the departed, we owe them. We have no way of redressing our failures, no way of amending our bargains."

"Which means?"

He wiggled his toes, thinking perhaps he'd overreacted. Now that Washington loomed, he didn't so much mind being arrested. Whatever troubles he had with his Libbie, he still liked her company. He thrust out his left boot. "Helen wanted a powerful husband. Her father did his best to help her, but I was not cut out for political life. I became very famous, but not in the way she envisioned. She died an angry, frustrated woman." Elizabeth took the heel and toe in her hand. Her peach-colored fingers seemed precious and soft as she clamped them over supple boot leather. Reaching down, he lifted her chin, struck suddenly by her softness and beauty. "Even now, he protects me." Her gaze

did not flinch. He stifled an impulse to kiss her. "He pro-
motes my career and advances my fame, because through
me"—he skimmed a silky curl off her forehead—"he
courts her forgiveness for the thing he failed to give her—a
husband as strong as the father who raised her."

Leaning forward, Ryerson grazed his thumb over her
cheekbone. Elizabeth checked her sway of delight. She
liked the sensation of his touch. He moved with deftness
and grace that softened his skin's calloused surface and
made his caress a sensual experience. She'd miss him. She
dreaded his leaving. Like a fist in her chest, a painful longing gripped hard at her heart whenever she thought of
being without him.

Tugging gently, she pulled off his boot. "Still, it's lucky
for you in this instance. It's pretty hard to court-martial a
man with a statue."

"I'll beat the charges. I'm certain of that."

Gritting her teeth, she placed his boots next to the trunk.
She hated this war, especially when Ryerson talked with
such self-assurance. His wartime experience had given him
such wild confidence. She respected his boldness, of
course. She'd experienced enough during the war to know
how he'd earned his fierce reputation. What's more, now
that she'd seen him in action, she had a real admiration for
his personal valor. Still, survival required more than just
courage. Even a hero had to adjust. Ryerson's past could
be his undoing. In his heart he remained the Great Vandal
hurtling across history's pages, the wrath of God pushing
him forward, the whole Union army backing him up.
Which was all very nice, except that his present was different.

Standing, she moved to her dresser, thinking about how
best to help him. The past few weeks had readjusted her
thinking about him. At first she'd feared Ryerson, sure

he'd destroy her beloved Cheyenne. Now she trembled instead for his troopers. For all Ryerson's personal courage, and his men's unquestioning loyalty to him, his soldiers were a pitiful lot, ill-equipped, inexperienced, and still pretty sickly.

Concerned for their safety, she'd gotten Ryerson to promise a peaceful approach. She had little faith that he'd keep their bargain, however. He fought out of habit, and long-suppressed anger, with no more control over his instincts than a thunderstorm had over its lightning. If he beat the court-martial, and stayed on the prairie, he'd surely lead that troop into battle. She'd seen firsthand how he would die—mangled, dismembered, and riddled with arrows, his private parts stuffed in his mouth.

Suppressing a shiver, she grabbed up the vial of oil. "Would you like your back rubbed?"

He stilled. "Do you think that I need it?"

Turning, she locked her gaze with his. "Yes."

He touched his top button. A liquid heat swirled within her. She almost regretted her offer. She feared her fascination with him. The heart kept at bay by her anger. The melting need and passionate hunger. The thought of how lonely she'd be when he left. None of that mattered, however. He had to accept the senator's offer. If he stayed on the prairie, he'd never survive.

Stepping forward, Elizabeth poured a few drops of oil onto her palm. She set the cruet down and briskly rubbed her hands together. Her movement heated the oil, releasing its fragrance and subtly altering its texture. She sighed, glancing his way. He remained frozen, his gaze fixed on her, his expression a little bit softer than usual. Her heartbeat sped up. She wished she could just strip off her clothes and snuggle up to him and see if the heat in those fiery glances remotely reflected the depth of his passion.

She bit her lip, determined to find a way to convince him. "Yes. You need your back rubbed. If you want to get back your health, relaxing like this will help you."

"You're the nurse." He shrugged out of his shirt. "I'll take your advice in this matter." Half-naked, he threw himself on the mattress. "You may proceed."

She lay her hands softly on his back. Stroking gently over his sinewy muscles, she considered a way to approach this subject. Helen was clearly Ryerson's soft spot, the part of his life where he didn't think clearly. Any man with the slightest sense would have leapt at the senator's offer. But Ryerson seemed to harbor some sort of resentment, have a grudge from the past he hadn't worked out. "Have you ever been in an Indian fight?"

He shook his head.

She pressed her palm on the base of his spine. "I lived among them, you know. They're not like your Negroes. They have whole societies devoted to fighting. The fiercest is called the Dog Soldiers. Its members spend most of their adult lives as warriors."

"The Negro will fight."

"I'm not trying to insult the race." Slowly she stroked, letting pressure and rhythm control the effect. "Your troopers have a wonderful courage. They'd follow you to the death. It's not their valor I question."

She could feel him fight back, refusing to let go of his tension. "Then why are we discussing this subject?"

"Look at them. They can't ride. They surely can't shoot. Have you ever thought what will happen once you get these men in battle?"

His muscles froze beneath her touch. "I've thought of nothing else since I became their commander."

"Then you know you have a serious problem." She expected a disagreement, but he said nothing, lying beneath her hands, rigid and sullen, while she worked to help him relax. Her heart sank in her bosom. She counted twenty-five strokes before she finally found the courage to speak. "You don't dispute my observations?"

Scowling, he turned on his side. "Elizabeth, give me some credit. I'm gruff, bad-tempered, and terribly vain, but I do know about fighting. My troop couldn't defeat a boys' school militia, much less hardened Cheyenne dog soldiers."

She hopped to her feet. She wanted to go for a walk by the river. Unfortunately she couldn't match his arrogance. She didn't like prowling around in the darkness, didn't want to carry a pistol, and couldn't risk taking him with her. She settled for pacing. "Then why don't you take the senator up on his offer?"

"I told you before. I don't want his help."

She stomped to the window. "How dare you turn down an offer like that?"

The mattress creaked as he shifted his weight. "I find it easy."

"I'm disappointed. I thought you had standards."

"What?"

She faced him head-on. He looked devilish in the darkness. He sprawled on the bed, half-naked and savage. The candlelight flickered on his moist skin, painting his muscles in shadow. She drew in her breath. "You're putting your own selfish interests before those of your troopers."

He bolted out of the bed, reaching her in two strides. "Are you out of your mind?"

"You're a fraud, Ryerson." She prodded his chest with her finger. "A shallow, hypocritical, cowardly fraud."

"Woman!" His jaw muscles twitched. He grabbed her wrist, holding her tightly. A bolt of pain shot up to her shoulder.

She froze, every nerve in her body intent on evasion, but her mind still intent on her purpose. "Do you deny you're frightened of Senator Parker?"

"Of course I deny it."

She tried to twist out of his grip. "Then why would you turn down his help?"

"I told you." He held her firmly, his eyes hot with anger, his whole being tense. "His help comes with strings. He offers these favors for his own reasons."

"What does that matter?" She tugged again. "He could get your troops good horses and better equipment. How could you lead those men into battle knowing you could have done better for them?"

He let her go suddenly. He strode to the door, the trunk, then back to the window. His stocking feet made no sound. The crickets had settled down for the night, and the quiet house seemed eerie. He came to rest by the peg with the sword. Without looking at her, he slid the blade out of the scabbard, balancing the edge on his palm. "You think I'm not living up to my standards?"

She did not have to speak. She could barely make out his stance in the darkness, but she could sense it. Ferocious pride, a hell-bent sense of duty, and a rigid refusal to bend or surrender. Suddenly she wanted to hold him, to find a way to take back her words. She moved slightly toward him.

He stiffened his already strictly honorable posture, gesturing her fiercely away. "You're right, of course." He held the saber before him. The flickering light winked off its jeweled handle, accenting its cruel and elegant beauty.

Elizabeth shivered, thinking again of its past. "I'm sorry," she whispered softly.

Ryerson did not acknowledge her comment. All his fierce bravado seemed to have left him. His eyes were so dark he might have been crying, but none of the starch had gone out of his posture. She wondered what held him so straight. The strength of his muscles? The years of training? Maybe only the love of his troopers. For whatever reason, he stood there unyielding, proud, and grimly determined, his gaze fixed on the glittering sword.

"Will you come with me?" he asked.

He hated taking Elizabeth back to these ruins.

Ryerson scowled, resenting this task. As Vegetarian's remnants came into focus, he battled to keep his irritation in check. He'd brought her back home. She'd refused to go with him to Washington. They'd argued about it for more than three days. He believed her life was in danger. She insisted her friends would protect her. She'd won in the end by pointing out that a former Indian captive could never be a political asset in Washington, or anywhere else. He'd paid back his debt. For that she thanked him, but his priorities lay with his downtrodden troopers. Hers were with the beleaguered Cheyenne. He couldn't argue her out of her position. So he brought her back, traveling with her alone, refusing to risk the life of a single trooper in so misguided an effort as this.

Ryerson frowned at the moldering relics. The heat had burnt the flowers to straw, but the decaying commune remained just the same. The eight-sided building, the miserable cabins, and even the overgrown gardens were declining too slowly for their demise to be noticed. Only his feelings had changed.

With an oath to himself, Ryerson charged the chestnut the length of the streambed. Cool water splashed on his thighs. Stopping midstream, Ryerson jerked his mount to a halt. He turned to watch her efforts to follow. She should have seemed funny, but she only seemed hateful, riding astride an Indian pony in a pair of ridiculous bloomers she'd made. She flapped at her goats, arms outstretched, too softhearted to truly control either the goats or the paint pony. He stifled an impulse to ride back and help her. His annoyance growing, he damned her to hell. He refused to plead, to grovel or beg. He'd offered his name and the army's protection. If she was too much the fool to accept them, so be it.

He turned the chestnut in a wide circle, then waited again for the unwieldy procession. Dressed in the bloomers, she looked silly but pretty. She wore her own version, not the wide Turkish pants favored by most, but a pair of narrow white trousers topped by a beige muslin tunic. Sunlight glinted off her deep auburn hair. He tightened his grip on the reins. He'd always remember her heart-stopping beauty. In this desolate place, she seemed something special: a splotch of bright color in a pale, washed-out landscape; a patch of red beneath the blue sky.

With a sharp clop, she drew up beside him. The goats splashed daintily through the water. As they crossed, Ryerson scanned the distant horizon. He thought it a neat, if bitter, bargain. He'd secured a freedom he didn't want in return for a month in the glittering prison of his dubious fame as a conquering hero. The colonel had dropped the court-martial in exchange for Ryerson's agreement to attend the review, dine with General Grant, and bolster the army's political fortunes by telling war stories at an endless series of speaking engagements. The prospect would have pleased Helen, but Elizabeth had her own view of these matters. She'd pointed out the advantage to his troop, then calmly insisted on going back home.

Perversely, her indifference to these arrangements had pleased him greatly. For the first time in his life, he felt as if he were precious to someone. Not a conduit for thwarted ambition, or the pale reflection of an admired father, but the object of a simple compassion. Elizabeth's attitude made him feel cared for, a situation that might have been perfect, except try as he might, he couldn't get her to care for herself.

She was in danger. He felt certain of that. General Hancock had chased over the plains, forcing a few small Indian bands to surrender. The bulk of the Cheyenne were still out raiding, a notion that made Ryerson sick to his stomach.

He dismounted the chestnut, leading the horse into the yard. The area seemed deserted, but he thought it wise to check for signs of intruders. At the edge of the clearing, Ryerson bent down to examine the grass. A chill ran down his spine. He straightened swiftly, scrutinizing the prairie. She'd had visitors in her absence. Not many, probably only one. Someone had ridden through this field and come down off his horse to wait out here.

Ryerson glanced backward, watching Elizabeth herd her bleating goats. One corral post had fallen, and she struggled to prop it up as her three white pets circled near her. A frisson of alarm prickled Ryerson's skin. Slowly he turned. He saw him quite clearly, a lone silhouette against the horizon, dressed in a gorgeous warbonnet trailing to his pony's knees.

Ryerson whirled. He broke into a run. He grabbed Elizabeth by the waist, catching her by surprise. Without skipping a beat, he pulled her into the cabin. Slamming her against a wall, he drew out his pistol and peered out the window. Dirt filtered down from the ceiling. In the vast prairie silence, the only sound was Elizabeth's breathing.

In a soft voice she asked, "What are you doing?"

"Someone's out there," he whispered. She moved

toward the window, but he gestured fiercely. "Get back. We don't know who it is."

Ignoring his signal, she poked her head into the opening. "What did he look like?"

"Stay back, you fool." Ryerson pinned her to the wall. She squirmed. He held her securely. Pressing a thigh against hers, he tucked one forearm under her rib cage. Resolutely ignoring her struggle against him, he kept an eye on the distant horizon. The Indian had disappeared from his sight.

"James." She tried to wriggle out of his grasp, but only succeeded in writhing against him. He found the tactic extremely distracting. In spite of her struggles, his gaze never wavered from the place he'd last seen the warrior.

"Stay still." He thrust forward. His traitorous body reacted with passion. He shifted his weight. She pushed with her hands, then with her hips, evidently sensing a chance to escape. He tried to step back, but he couldn't establish a comfortable distance without giving up control of her movements. With a curse to himself, he wedged one leg between her thighs. "Stay still." His order came out as a snarl. "This could be an attack. I couldn't get a good look at our friend. He's dressed like a warrior. My guess is he's scouting." Ryerson sighted down his gun barrel, struggling to keep his attention on his Indian opponent. "I'll let you go if you'll get down on the floor."

"James." She kept her voice low, as if she were trying to calm him. "It's all right. I know who he is."

"Who?" Irritation flared through him. His neck muscles tightened. He tried to dismiss his sudden suspicion, but an irrational notion burst into his brain, and he found he couldn't ignore it. "Who?"

"A friend," she said softly.

Ryerson's breathing sped up. His heartbeat doubled,

pumping so strongly he had a vivid sense of his own agitation. "What kind of friend?" he asked tightly.

"Let me go, and I'll tell you."

He tried to ease back, but his anger held him.

She lifted her chin. Her eyes glittered in wary defiance. She tried again to slip out of his grip, but he kept her pinned to the wall.

She glanced at the gun. "An Indian friend."

"I thought you just nursed for Indian children."

"I do, but—"

"So, that's why you wanted to come back!" The dark thought slammed him again, threatening all his awareness.

"James. No. You don't understand."

"You wait here for him? For that savage?"

"No."

He knew she was frightened. He could see her pulse in her throat, could feel her wildly hammering heart. He tried to control the rush of his fury. Unfortunately a devilish idea possessed him. His fingers dug into her shoulders. "Is that your husband out there?"

She looked to the left, to the right, at the top of the cabin.

"Yes," she said suddenly.

He took leave of his senses. He couldn't see her, hear her, or feel her. His whole awareness came down to one monstrous thought. He'd played by a gentleman's rules and he'd lost her.

"For God's sake, Libbie." His voice sounded strange, as if a demon had lodged in his throat. "You can do better than that."

"James." She wet her lips, her eyes as dark as hot maple syrup. "He's not important."

"Did you think I didn't want you?"

She answered. He heard it, but whatever she said did not

penetrate the cloud in his brain. Six weeks of frustration ruptured within him. He'd given this woman his soul.

He kissed her, claiming her roughly. Caging her with both hands, he clamped his lips over hers, crushing his hips against soft calico. Anger and passion flashed through him. Some remote part of his brain knew this was foolish, but the only reaction he could control was easing his finger off his gun's trigger. He ground his hips against hers. He wasn't certain she would like this, but he was past caring. Almost.

"Libbie." He eased back his mouth, though his groin, hot and insistent, stayed pressed against her. "I want you so badly." He realized he was begging, but his pride had shattered. He would have gone down on his knees if he thought that would help. "He might have marked you, but that doesn't mean he can have you forever. I want you, Libbie. Let me show you how much."

He pulled back, watching her eyes. He thought he would die if she refused him, but he still clung to civilized standards. He did not want to do this without her permission. Outside, the goats bleated. A coil of frustration tightened within him. Her pupils darkened. A damp sheen moistened her face. Wisps of dark curls clung to her cheekbones. He thought briefly of the Indian warrior, of what would happen if he approached, then realized with a fierce joy that he'd like to have a reason to kill the bastard.

He tightened his grip on the butt of the pistol.

She said yes with her eyes. He wasn't sure he read her correctly, but she brushed her lips over his mouth. He trembled. Desire swept through him, chasing out fury and logical thought. Taking her would be risky, but he thought he could do it. He refused to lose her to her Indian husband. Ryerson nodded, indicating the floor. "Take off those damned trousers."

She lay down. He didn't see how she undressed, for he kept his eye on the door. He dropped to his knees, felt for her curls, then slipped his fingers into their moisture and softness. He smelled her fear and arousal.

"You're mine. Not his." He glanced down briefly. "You understand?"

She nodded.

"Now and forever."

She nodded again.

"And nobody else's."

She nodded a third time. Leaning back on his heels, he unfastened his pants. Remaining upright, he fixed his gaze on the horizon. He entered slowly, not wanting to hurt her, puzzled briefly by her tightness, but wildly aroused by her gasp.

"Libbie, forgive me."

He shoved firmly. Heat and moistness engulfed him. He wanted to fall, tear off their clothes, rub his hard chest against her, and lose himself in her velvety texture. Fear of the Indian restrained him.

"Lift your hips, Libbie."

She complied, taking him more fully within her. He thrust hard, propelled past manners by need and frustration. Eyes wide, she shifted beneath him. He stifled a groan. He feared he might hurt her, but he wanted so badly to feel that soft refuge surround him. "I'm sorry." He pierced her again. "But . . ." He stroked slowly, punctuating each word with a thrust. "We . . . need . . . to . . . do . . . this."

The Kansas sky filled his vision, and the world came down to those two sensations: the juncture of their almost fully clothed bodies and the infinite plane of the dazzling blue heaven. He held his back straight and let himself focus on his own motion. Animal lust pushed him forward, expressed as a low guttural grunting and a rhythmic drive toward conclusion that left little room for her pleasure and none at all for seduction.

Still, she didn't resist. In fact, she helped him. Bracing her hands under her buttocks, she received him quite sweetly. Her tightness had eased. They fit neatly together, though she still didn't surround him completely. For reasons he couldn't fathom, he wanted that experience as much as completion—to fill her, leave no recess unplundered, no intimate corner free from invasion. If he could not take her naked, he'd give himself at least that satisfaction. He'd possess her completely, more thoroughly than he'd done in the daydream.

He let his gun hand drop to his side and pressed the other against her shoulder. His gaze flickered over the horizon, leaving his hips to set their own rhythm. He plunged in and out, taking her more deeply each time. Beads of sweat formed on his forehead. He longed to throw off his uniform jacket. Pressure mounted within him as four years of frustration cried out for relief. He shuddered. The time had come to spill his seed, but he held back from the act of true mating. He'd learned with the whores. There was more than one way to finish. He pulled back, intending withdrawal. He eased slightly out, but a sense of loss caught him. From deep in his chest a growl escaped him. To his infinite horror, some beast in him recoiled from retreat. That monster knew what he wanted. He wanted deeper and farther, to bury himself to his full length and gratify his most primal impulse. He hadn't reached her innermost recess. He hadn't battered the door of her womb.

He plunged in, grunting in protest. She tensed, then gasped in a spasm. He shook in reaction, caught off guard by her trembling. The vibration shattered his fragile control. A vast shudder escaped him. He wrenched himself out, his seed bursting from him. He glanced down in despair, flustered by the ending. Panic assailed him. Blood spattered her thighs.

"What the—?" His gaze swept her body, thinking perhaps she'd been wounded, that somehow the Indian had hurt her. To his relief and confusion, the red flecked him also. "Oh, Libbie. I'm sorry." Hands shaking, he straightened the cloth beneath her buttocks. He covered her knees, trying to think what to say. He knew he'd been rough, but he didn't think that he'd hurt her so badly. In all his years of sexual experience, he'd never caused a woman to bleed.

He fastened his pants, remembering the Indian. He felt ashamed already and wondered how he could repay her. "I'm sorry. I did not mean to hurt you."

"It's all right. You couldn't know. I'm twice married. No man would have guessed I was a virgin."

He froze. Had lightning come down and struck him, he couldn't have been more deeply shocked. "What are you saying?"

She rose to her feet. He scrambled up, pushing her away from the door. "Be careful. The Indian could still be out there."

"No. He's not." She looked weary and sore as she pushed her damp curls back from her forehead. "I told you. I know him. He's a peaceable man. He doesn't come to make trouble. It's just—" She picked up her bloomers and sat, hands shaking, on a bed in the corner. "Sometimes I help him."

He glanced out the window. The flat plain seemed to mock him. The wind whistled down on the prairie, bringing with it the sound of the insects and the warble of starlings. He felt suddenly certain they were alone.

He turned. She looked down at her thighs helplessly. "Here." He crossed to the bed. "Let me help you." He lifted her swiftly, grateful for his years in the saddle. She seemed light to him. Not necessarily fragile, but delicate and easy to carry. He wanted to kiss her, fold her into his chest, and weep for the wrong that he'd done her, but that reaction didn't seem manly. Averting his eyes, he strode toward the door.

"What are you doing?" she asked.

He hefted her weight and gripped her more firmly. "Taking you down to the stream."

TEN

ELIZABETH BURIED HER FACE IN RYERSON'S SHOULDER, oddly consoled by the prickle of wool and the damp, overwhelmingly masculine scent. Ryerson ignored her. He crashed through dry grasses and into a thicket of willows. Supple branches whipped Elizabeth's legs. He gripped her tightly, in something more of a vise than a cradle. Not that he hurt her. His hold was quite tender, but she felt thoroughly vulnerable in this position. She clutched her crumpled bloomers and was painfully conscious of her uncovered bottom. Ryerson paid her no attention. Whistling low for his chestnut, he strode to the stream.

As they reached the brook, his horse cantered up. Nickering softly, he waited patiently for his master. Ryerson kicked aside a few stones, then sat her in the sandy depression he'd made. He kissed the top of her head, then walked to the chestnut. Without glancing back, he worked at the dull brass buckles of his saddlebags.

Elizabeth swallowed. His quiet assurance seemed so different from the tumultuous churning in her own stomach. She'd lost something precious. She knew she ought to be sorry, but try as she might, she still couldn't regret her decision. She'd been so frightened. Not for herself. Not even for her dear Sleeps With Eagle. She'd been fright-

ened for Major James Ryerson. She'd never seen the great
raider in a killing rage, but she had no doubt about what
she'd just witnessed. Left undistracted, the war-hardened
veteran would have slaughtered her Indian husband.

And regretted that act for the rest of his life.

She shifted. The gritty sand made pretty rough sitting.
She tried to cover herself with her tunic, but the thin material stuck to her thighs and left her legs indecently outlined. She knew she ought to wash up, but shyness had
seized her. Something profound had happened between
her and the previously civilized major. She didn't know
what it meant.

A flash of color caught her attention. Approaching the
stream, Ryerson pulled a bright yellow kerchief out of a
bundle. He set the package on the ground and plunged the
bandanna into the water. Returning, he knelt beside her.
He passed the cloth over her forehead. Cool liquid moistened her skin. He pushed back her hair, then washed her
face softly, his thumbs lingering on her cheekbones. He
had a look on his face, distant, shuttered, and utterly foreign. She didn't know how to read his expression at all.

When he'd finished, he pressed the cloth into her hands,
sat down beside her, and stretched out his legs. "So, tell
me, lady, how I came to bed a twice-married virgin."

She glanced at the sky, at the stream, at the crumbling
cabin. Ten minutes ago, this place had been home. In the
space of a few heart-stopping moments, the whole landscape looked different.

Tucking her knees under her chin, she briefly pictured
her long-ago sweetheart. "Actually, it's pretty simple.
Philip was sixteen when we married. We had only one
night. We tried, but it all happened so fast. He mostly
made a mess on my nightgown. I think he could have done

it again, but he was embarrassed. We'd been kissing since we were seven. I think that's hard on a boy."

"And the Indian?"

"Sleeps With Eagle?" She pulled out her hairpins. Her curls tumbled loose. Swinging the mass over her shoulder, she wiped the kerchief over the back of her neck. "The opposite, I suppose. He's almost sixty. I was his fourth wife."

"You're joking." Ryerson laughed, a resonant chuckle deep in his chest. "What would a sixty-year-old do with four wives?"

A twinge of annoyance flashed through her. "The same thing as a man of forty. Or twenty, if you must know. I don't think he was unable . . ." She caught her hair in the yellow bandanna. Scrambling up, she yanked a tight knot. She straightened her muslin tunic. The pale material had become pretty grubby. "Actually, I think he desired me. Luckily for me, Buffalo Woman was always so jealous. Except of the nursing, of course."

"Of course." He stood. Gripping her elbow, he clutched it tightly and steadied her with one hand to her waist. He held her so closely she could feel the heat from his body. "Buffalo Woman?"

Pulling away, she moved toward the stream, making an effort to walk with some grace, but hampered by soreness and the cobbled streambed. Embarrassed, she brushed off her shirt. "Buffalo Woman was his first wife. The second and third were her sisters." Reaching the water, she crossed her arms, grabbed the sides of her tunic, and paused. "Do you mind?"

Ryerson frowned. He scanned the horizon. He studied the prairie for what seemed like five minutes, then he shook his head, denying permission. "This doesn't seem safe. Couldn't you—clean up—without undressing?"

Exasperation flared through her. She dropped her hands to her sides. "This is my home. I'm just as safe here as I was at the fort."

He strode the length of the bank, picked out a pebble, and zinged it into a thicket. A bevy of quail fluttered out. He turned, pinning her with his gaze. "You don't know who might be lurking out there."

Elizabeth dropped her bloomers next to his bundle. "You forget. I lived here for more than two years. The prairie seems dangerous to you because it's different. But you're the first person who's ever hurt me." He scowled. Tears stung her eyes, but she leashed them fiercely. She'd grown up with six brothers. She knew better than to face down a male temper by dissolving into a fit of weeps. Frowning, she turned back to the water. She kept her voice cool and sublimely indifferent. "And I'm tired of your bullying ways. No one interferes with my bath."

Lowering her eyes, she slipped out of her moccasin slippers, but left her tunic intact. It seemed too modest and too peculiar to hide from a man who'd touched her so intimately, but it also seemed wrong to ignore his feelings. Having no better notion of what would be proper, she waded into the stream with a splash.

Once in, she paused, letting the water lap at her ankles. Its burble soothed her nerves, and she waited. Ryerson glared, first at her, then at the prairie. She felt with her toes for a wide, stable stone. He paced on the shore, a ground-eating lope that blurred his light blue cavalry pants.

Elizabeth tried not to stare, but his well-defined thighs flexed with each movement. They intrigued her, those legs. Six years on horseback had strengthened his muscles. It had come as a shock, how helpless he'd made her feel when he pressed her against the wall of the cabin. The quail wandered back, darting into their shelter after a pause. Ryerson ignored them and paced. Suddenly she wanted to laugh. She'd seen hungry wolves exhibit more patience than Ryerson did at this moment.

"He's gone. I'm sure," she said calmly.

He gazed at the distant horizon, clasping his hands behind his back. "How do you know?"

"I know him." She took a few mincing steps toward the center. "He's a peaceable man, but he's not a coward. Had he seen what you did, he would have killed you."

He stopped, pinning her with his gaze. "Is that what you wanted?"

"What?"

"To get me killed?"

"No!" Indignation flashed through her. She couldn't imagine how he could misunderstand her intentions so badly. She would have stormed back to the shore, but the stony streambed made walking quite tricky. Her fingers itched for a pebble. She stifled the impulse to throw one, though she would have liked seeing him surprised. "I was frightened for him. I know Sleeps With Eagle quite well. I'm sure he left the first moment he saw you, but you seemed so—so—" Exploring the rocks with her feet, she prospected their angles, testing, rejecting, until she found a suitable surface. She balanced herself on that broad plane. "I thought you wanted to kill him."

"I did." He splashed, still booted, into the stream. Droplets of water gleamed on black leather. He negotiated the rocks without any problem, protected by the heavy footgear. Reaching her side, he steadied her with an arm to the elbow. "What made you think he was in danger if you believed he'd already run off?"

She tried to pull back.

He gripped her more tightly. "Let me help you." Moving

behind her, he braced her leg with one thigh. "It's hard to wash while standing on rocks."

She thought his nearness vaguely improper, a liberty he ought not to take, but she couldn't quite frame her objection, distracted as she was by the cords of his muscles, the riveting heat of his touch. Ignoring her tension, he undid the bandanna. Her curls tumbled over her shoulders. He dipped the kerchief in the current. Standing behind her, he squeezed the liquid onto her neck. A trickle of water flowed over her shoulder and into the space between her breasts. Her nipples puckered, though not from the cold. She could feel his breath on her earlobe.

"If you thought he'd already gone, what made you believe he was in danger?" he repeated.

She pulled at the hem of her tunic, self-conscious about her nearly exposed bottom. "He's a fine rider, and wily. But you're many years younger and one of the army's best horsemen. You could have chased him down without very much trouble."

Bending from the knees, she dipped the bandanna into the water. She wanted soap, but felt loath to send him on another errand. His jitters affected her sense of well-being. She'd bathed here for months without any trouble. For the first time, however, she felt nervous about it. Somberly she washed off the blood. The sticky red liquid made her feel shaky. The experience had not hurt that much, but the sight made her feel wounded. She glanced up in a panic.

He steadied her with a hand to the waist. "You loved this Indian husband?"

"Yes. At least after a fashion." She rinsed out the cloth, glad for his presence. Never before had her home seemed so lonely. For all she'd been frightened, she'd never forget these last weeks with him. It pained her to think of their parting. To her profound surprise, the loss of her honor made her feel precious. Her first two husbands had been kinder, more tender, but an illogical, female part of herself thrilled at the thought that Ryerson had wanted her more. Dabbling her toes in one of the currents, she watched the play of the light on the sparkling brook. "I loved Philip, also. I've loved both my husbands in my own way."

He clung to her waist, the guardian as always, unable to give up that role, even out here, so far from the fort. "You don't include me in that assessment?"

"Yes. I do." She poked her bare foot into a muddy crevice. "At least, I'll miss you. Except for your temper, you're not a bad man."

A soft sound escaped Ryerson. "So what did he do with the sisters, this ancient warrior of yours?"

"The same things he did with Buffalo Woman. She loved her sisters and didn't mind sharing her husband with them. That's a custom, you know." Cupping her hands, she splashed the water over her forearms. The cool water chilled her hot skin, a pleasant contrast to the sizzling prairie. "The Cheyenne live better than whites like to think. There's no poverty as a white man would know it, but the men have dangerous lives. If a warrior dies on a hunt or in battle, his brother-in-law will marry the widow."

"So that's what Sleeps With Eagle did? He married two widows?"

"Yes." She searched with her fingers, seeking a seat. "And he adopted their children. Their husbands both died in fights with the Yankees. All three of us had that in common, though Otter Woman and Gap Tooth Beaver hated the blue-coated soldiers worse than I did." She plopped into a sitting position—a bit of a shock, but cooling after a second. "Are you going to join me?"

"No." Letting go, he turned in a half circle, his gaze intense, his posture perfect.

"Honestly, it's perfectly safe."

Scowling, he strode to the shore, hand on his side arm. Their gazes locked, and he smiled softly. "I'm glad you weren't truly part of his harem."

She probably turned a furious scarlet. Is that what he'd thought? Was that what they all thought? Was that why the men stared so intensely? "No." She banished the notion, pressing the kerchief over her eyes. "I was never that kind of a woman. The Comanche promoted me as a healer. I'm sure that's why he bought me. At first I lived as a slave. But Sleeps With Eagle had a soft heart. I don't think he liked seeing me beaten."

"Beaten?" A splash drew her attention. He'd stepped into the water, his face dark with anger.

She stood up, knowing his temper. "Buffalo Woman." She hopped toward the bank, keeping her balance strictly by momentum. "She hated me from the first." She reached the edge, and he caught her. "Jealousy, I suppose. She calmed down a little after the marriage."

Reaching down, he shook a towel out of the bundle. "That doesn't make sense." He glanced again at the horizon, then wrapped the soft material around her.

Heat flared within her. She still wore the tunic, now dripping wet, but the cool material wasn't enough to drown out her response to his touch. She tugged the towel out of his grasp. "Well, she took the marriage to mean he intended to keep me. So she made the best of a bad situation."

Her foot touched the package. She stifled a gasp. He had her dress, the green calico, the one she'd worn when he first met her. "Where did you get that? I threw it away."

"You did." He lifted the shabby garment and shook it out. "But I retrieved it. And I wish that you'd wear it. It's much prettier than those damnable bloomers."

"Fine." She took the dress from him. Tears threatened again, but she fought them back. She didn't want him to know that he'd touched her.

"Elizabeth." Taking her by the shoulders, he turned her to face him. She clutched the dress close to her bosom. He grazed a thumb over her cheekbone. She couldn't read his shuttered expression, but his fingers seemed slightly unsteady. Apparently mesmerized by the tattoos, he studied her from beneath lowered lashes. "You let me deflower you to save the life of the savage who marked you?"

"No. Not exactly. I wanted to save both of you, really."

For a moment she thought he'd explode. A flush darkened his sun-bronzed complexion. Tension invaded his muscles. The breeze ruffled his hair, but he seemed not to notice its gentle caress. He touched her briefly. "What do you mean?"

She kept her voice steady, her gaze on his face. "I thought you would kill him. A more civilized woman might prefer honor, but I've seen too much death to be silly. Maidenhood is a frivolous bauble when balanced against the life of a man. And besides"—she pulled her tunic down a bit farther—"you already have too much on your conscience."

He shut his eyes for a moment. His sun-lightened lashes made his face oddly tender. Heat flared within her, overcoming the light summertime breeze, the cooling path of the water. Before she had time to react, he pulled her fiercely into his chest. "You're an amazing woman, Elizabeth Wheaton. You deserve better than I can offer, but I'm the best you're likely to get."

"I'm sorry?"

"We need to get married."

"What?" She could feel his heart booming. "I mean, you don't need to ask for my hand."

"It would be a very great honor," he said quietly.

Ah, his damnable standards. Of course he'd feel pressed to make this offer. "James. You don't need to do this. I should never have allowed you to bring me. You can't help certain reactions."

"Elizabeth, this is not just a kindness. I tried to protect you, but I'm not sure I succeeded." He kissed her forehead, then drew her closer. "We might have created a baby."

Her heartbeat sped up. This was all going too fast. To some degree his comment made sense. Still, something in her rebelled. Even if he'd gotten her pregnant, she'd rather live out her life as a false widow than married on paper but not in his heart. "That's no reason to rush into marriage."

"Rush!" He pushed her back roughly. "You've lived in my quarters for more than a month."

"Oh. Well." With her free hand, she gathered up the skirt of the dress. "That's certainly reasonable grounds for a marriage." She backed toward the thicket, thinking to dress.

He followed her closely, hand on his pistol. "Give me a better reason."

"Well, there are the classics."

"Like what?"

"Like love, for example."

He froze, his face dark with anger. "Don't speak to me about that emotion. I've been loved before. Look where it got me."

Frustrated, she plunged into the undergrowth. She thought him the stubbornest man. She wasn't his wife. She'd never so much as met the woman. It seemed an illogical fate, to suffer for another female's transgressions. "Then you give me a reason."

"You're going to be killed."

"Nonsense."

"Woman, give me my due. I listened to you about the nursing. You listen to me on the subject of war." His spurs chinked against the rocks. Their harsh ring contrasted sharply with the murmuring rush of the water. "Don't you know who I am? I'm the Great Vandal. The worst of the Yankees. The most skilled and terrible of all their raiders."

She hid herself behind some ferns, stripped off the tunic, and wriggled into her dress. "So?"

"So. In the past you've been lucky." He knelt down and unbuttoned the top of his shirt. Cupping his hand, he bent from the waist and splashed water into the vee of his neck. "No one has hurt you. But no one knows better than I what becomes of war's victims."

It struck her like a physical blow, the figure of speech. The way he referred to himself. He seemed matter-of-fact and perfectly natural, describing himself in those terrible phrases. She could imagine him on his campaigns, the rigors of war reducing a civilized man to the basest, most brutal aspect of his nature. "Did you do that during the war?"

"What?"

"Dishonor women?"

"No." He jumped to his feet, turning to glare into her bower. "Don't insult me. Only you push my patience that far." He circled around, water glistening off his stubble. "But my men did much worse. Not often. And not under orders. But I've seen them by the side of the road, the broken women, dazed by their fate. I've listened to their sobbing mothers, brought in the culprits, then pardoned their misdeeds."

"You didn't."

"I did. Absolutely."

Elizabeth scrambled out of the glade, catching her skirt in the process. "How could you?"

"It was easy. You don't unleash a monster, then set up a wail about his bad manners. War isn't played by a gentleman's rules. I know better. I've seen it. Do you think that I of all men could leave my wife to that fate?"

Elizabeth stopped, struck by what he was saying. Considering how easily he could force her, it unnerved her to hear he had no scruples against it. "I'm not your wife."

"But I'm proposing, goddamn it, to grant you that status."

A chill ran down her spine at that sentence. She didn't know why he was making this offer. She could see that he was angry. She recognized the signs of his anger, the rigid expression, the tic in his jaw muscles, but she didn't know what she had done to incur his fury. She squared her shoulders, keeping her voice very calm. "That argument doesn't follow."

"It makes sense to me. Look. You speak of peace. What about me? Do I have no right to aspire to that lofty ideal?"

"What are you talking about?"

"Peace of mind. Mine. I've lost one wife and two sons to a war. Do you think I would have one moment's heart's ease if I had to worry about another?"

The little glade seemed to have gone silent. His question hung in the air. For the first time since she'd known him, he'd spoken words that hinted of feeling. She turned the conversation around in her mind. Try as she might, she could only interpret his comments one way. He equated her with Helen and Jamie. With that insight, his facade fell away. He loved her, as he had his first wife. He might never say it. He might not even know it, but she did. She thought of the vow he'd extracted. "You're mine. Not his. Now and forever. For the rest of your life." Though Elizabeth hated that he compared her with Helen, the fact that he did told her something about him. He might not have done it with a piece of paper, but in the dark recesses of a tormented heart, James Ryerson had made her his bride.

They walked hand in hand back to the cabin, the chestnut following a few paces back. She'd asked for more time to give him an answer. Ryerson had said nothing. He'd taken her hand, the tenderest of gestures, and walked her back through the fading daylight.

"Does the horse have a name?" she asked as they emerged from the thicket.

"I'm sure he does." Ryerson didn't glance back or tighten his grip on the reins. "But I don't know it."

She watched the tips of her Indian slippers, feeling awkward, self-conscious, and unwilling to ask why he hadn't learned the name of such a beautiful creature.

His spurs jingled in the rustling grass as he led her up a slight rise in the ground. He picked a piece of grass off his sleeve. "I know I sound harsh, but it makes it easier to lose them in battle."

"Have you lost so many?"

He nodded briefly. "I had three shot from beneath me at Shiloh. I refused to keep track after that."

She squeezed his hand tightly. She didn't dare look at his face. He spoke without undue emotion, as if he'd distanced himself from his memories. "I suppose it sounds silly, but it's the worst part of fighting. The sounds the horses make as they're dying."

She hadn't intended any more questions, so he'd surprised her by speaking more on this subject. Still, she was glad he'd shared some small part of his wartime experience. It helped her to know they could talk on these subjects. She'd long ago forgiven his role in her family's destruction, but the war would always be there, a painful part of her past—and his.

"Do you think the war affected you greatly?"

"I have some—peculiarities, yes." He drew her closer. "There are sights and sounds that undo me quite quickly. I can't eat undercooked meat." He flashed her a look. "If we had children, I'd depend on you to make sure they're not howlers."

She smiled. "I can do that. I know a trick I learned with the Indians. They pinch off the children's noses."

"What?"

From the tone of his voice, she knew she'd surprised him. It took her a second to gather the reason. "I mean, they pinch their noses shut. That way the child can't cry out. It seems cruel, but really it's not. It's useful on a hunt or a raid."

The chestnut blew a soft breath. His heavy hooves crunched in the grass. Nanny, Pappy, and Balthazar waited, bleating sorrowfully by the side of the cabin. The Indian pony had disappeared, and she wondered bleakly if she'd get her new clothes back, and whether Ryerson would ever like bloomers, and what she would do for a wedding dress.

"Do you want children?" she asked.

"Not really, but I suppose they'll come. Witness my performance today."

"Did the loss of your son hurt so very much?"

He stiffened, though not with pride. Rather, he turned totally inward. There were no tears in his eyes, no signs of anger. Instead he turned stoic, like the warriors she'd seen during the sun dance, seeking a vision, painful thongs piercing their chests. He flicked invisible lint off his sleeve.

"Where would we live?" she asked quietly.

He ran a calloused thumb over hers. "A soldier's wife

never knows that, but you could come to Washington with me."

"James." She stopped to pick a late-blooming flower. "Can't you see what a mistake that would be? If the tattoos make me strange out here on the prairie, what do you think I'd be in our capital city?"

"Think of it this way." He crouched down beside her. His thigh brushed against her. He seemed to pay her no attention, as he helped to gather a scraggly bouquet. "You could help your Indian friends. I'll be dining with General Grant. You probably think he's your worst enemy, but he's very fair-minded once you get to know him, and he's also likely to be the next president. I'll have you meet General Parker. He's a full Seneca and one of Grant's closest advisers. You could regale them with all your opinions and do some good for the Cheyenne."

"Look." Elizabeth pointed. The sun dipped beneath the horizon, leaving a radiant fan of gold light in the sky. "I love this moment."

They watched the sunset in silence. She'd miss these wide-open spaces. She wasn't sure when he'd convinced her, but she knew now she'd be leaving. Much as she hated the fact, Ryerson had already destroyed her idyllic existence.

He meant what he said about her. Leaving her would be torture for him. She couldn't buy her peace at that price. She supposed it a sign of how much she loved him. She couldn't hurt him without feeling pain also. Maybe that didn't justify marriage, but it destroyed her peace on the prairie. Even so, when she answered she spoke quietly, as if a small voice could soften the impact of her decision.

"I suppose I could come to Washington with you."

* * *

Ryerson glanced at the preacher, a slender young man, almost as gangly as Ichabod Crane. Ryerson tugged on his elbow, hurrying him toward the train station. As he did, he went over his plan in his mind. Elizabeth hadn't exactly agreed to a marriage. Ryerson procured the preacher in spite of that detail. From the day at the cabin to this very moment, Elizabeth had avoided the subject of marrying him. He'd proposed a whole week ago, though. She probably didn't remember the conversation exactly. Ryerson thought he could turn that fact to his advantage.

His boots clumping lightly on the wood sidewalk, the minister seemed thoroughly puzzled. Ryerson didn't care. He was going to marry Elizabeth Wheaton, and he didn't give a damn how he went about it, or where. Cornering her would be tricky, but he thought he could do it. He knew a few things about his intended. She thought quickly, but moved cautiously. Surprise would work in his favor. She wasn't impressed by his position, but she didn't like facing his temper. Peace-loving and tranquil, she'd go to great lengths to avoid confrontation.

She objected to an actual marriage because she wasn't certain how deeply she loved him. She liked him. That much she'd admitted. She even loved him by some definition, but she wasn't ready to give her whole heart unless she felt her affection returned. He regarded her pride in this regard as foolish. She'd already made the only commitment that mattered.

She'd allowed him to ruin her completely.

He tightened his grip on his sword handle, glancing speculatively at the still-baffled preacher. Ryerson had told the parson the whole story. It pained him to speak of such intimate details, especially to this pious stripling, but Ryerson needed help and he needed it badly.

He'd undertaken Elizabeth's protection and failed. He'd

not only fallen from grace himself, he'd stolen a valuable treasure from her. He'd bedded her like a rutting fool, giving her God-knows-what impression of him, and sullied her irrevocably. He knew the value of what she'd given, the ancient, irrational, powerful drive that bound a man to a virgin he'd taken. He felt it himself.

Elizabeth was his. Any child she bore would be his without question. She'd not measure him against another, a heady thought, seductive and awesome. But mostly her chastity spoke of her virtue. He knew she'd been asked. Probably often by Philip. Maybe by others. She'd given Ryerson her virginity for the oddest of reasons, but he respected her logic. He'd made up his mind to bind her to him—and not in any false marriage. He'd failed her that day in the cabin, but never again. He'd keep her safe and completely protected, which meant making her a genuine wife.

He scowled at the cleric, hoping to frighten him. He had to force a more proper marriage. Fort Leavenworth was close to the borders of civilization. No one inquired too closely into personal matters and lived. But Washington was completely different. The capital city loved intrigue and scandal. His unorthodox wife was bound to incite speculation and rumor.

If Ryerson wanted to do the best for his troopers, he couldn't afford a hidden weakness. The North might have won the late war, but rebuilding the country hadn't been easy. Every fool politician had his own idea on what should be the fate of the Negro. The scalawags fought for control of the South, using the new colored voters for personal power. Ryerson's fame was a potent weapon that each faction would claim for a purpose. He only cared about the fate of his troopers, but fighting for them would make enemies. He had to protect them, as well as Elizabeth, and that meant binding her legally.

A fate she resisted.

Ryerson glanced at the cleric. "Go over the plan."

The lanky young man clutched a black leather-bound Bible. "You're going to surprise her."

"Exactly."

"She's going to protest."

"Correct."

The minister's head bobbed above his white collar. He was as jittery as a tubbed apple at a harvest party. "But the train's leaving in thirty minutes."

Ryerson nodded.

"And she's going to be married, no matter."

"Good, good." Ryerson flicked at his sleeve. He wished he had a good wartime chaplain, some true-blue man, battle-hardened and tested, but this awkward preacher would have to do. Ryerson was determined to marry Elizabeth Wheaton, whether she wanted marriage or not. Fortunately he had Dixon.

Ryerson smiled at the thought. When he'd outlined the plan, his old friend had been ecstatic. Dixon would bring her to the train station. Ryerson would procure the preacher. Senator Parker had abetted his purpose. Not that Ryerson's former father-in-law intended the perfect trap. He knew nothing of Ryerson's marriage intentions. The senator wanted Ryerson's favor, an endorsement with the new Negro voters, and a way of easing his grief over the death of his daughter. So he'd sent a palace car, lavish, secure, and completely private, to bring his ex-son-in-law home in the style of a hero.

Dixon's joy at the impending marriage had somewhat abated Ryerson's worry at leaving the troopers. None of the troop could come East, a fact that troubled James Ryerson. But Dixon had been surprisingly happy.

"We'll be all right," he said quietly. "You can get us ordered out to Fort Riley. Things'll be better farther out on the prairie. They got too many real problems out there to spend their time bedevilin' Negroes. You come back with good guns and horses, and the whole troop will have an adventure. Rescue some captives. Get up a flirt with some Indian maidens. Meanwhile"—he'd flashed his neat row of white teeth—"you take care of the missus. She saved this whole troop. We can give her a small taste of freedom before we get her tied down permanently."

As Ryerson guided the preacher around a corner, the train station came into focus. A hulking monster of a steam engine puffed quietly on the siding. Small knots of passengers milled next to the building, but Ryerson paid these people little attention. He knew Dixon would follow orders and take her right into his little mousetrap.

Sedate and ornate, the palace car gleamed in the sunlight, gilt glinting off its emerald siding. It was the kind of privilege Ryerson hated, but one that had its uses in this case.

Preacher in tow, he mounted the steps. Inside, Elizabeth waited, fidgeting nervously in the lavish surroundings. She wore a chocolate-colored traveling dress. Ryerson flinched when he saw it. She ought to wear white. No matter that she was not a virgin, she was close enough in his estimation.

Ryerson nodded at Dixon, who stood at attention. Hell, she ought to have a proper wedding, in a lovely church with bridesmaids and flowers. Not this brief ceremony with less tradition to recommend it than the jerry-rigged ritual of the broomstick. Still, he couldn't fix the wedding's shortcomings, and he made up his mind not to regret them.

"There you are, darling." Hand on her waist, he planted a confident kiss on her lips. "I've brought the preacher. Sergeant Dixon will witness." Removing his hat, Ryerson took Elizabeth by the elbow and turned her toward the pale, frightened cleric. "I know you deserve a much better wedding, but this was the best I could arrange." He straightened his saber and pulled on the hem of his uniform coat. "You haven't changed your mind, have you?"

All her feelings showed in her face. Suspicion, fear, and disorientation. She slipped her arm out of his grasp, gawked at the preacher, opened her mouth, shut it abruptly, then turned and walked the length of the car. Reaching a plush purple settee, she crossed her arms under her bosom and stared up at a high, tiny window. The light fell over her face, accenting the glow of her flawless complexion, the exotic, peculiar line of the tattoos. Glancing back, she studied the preacher speculatively.

"I should have brought you some flowers," Ryerson said as he held out a gloved hand, "but I couldn't get proper orange blossoms."

She eyed Ryerson narrowly, blinked, then sat down on the purple tufting. Outside, the steam engine hooted, sending a steady stream of white smoke past the window.

Ryerson pulled out a silver pocket watch and scowled. "We have just twenty minutes. I know you don't care about your reputation, but it doesn't seem proper to proceed any further without making our arrangement more formal."

He straightened his posture, rested his hand on his gun belt, and fixed her with his most fearsome glare. She paled and lifted her chin. He liked that about her, though he'd never admit it. In his years as a soldier, he'd made a long study of moral courage. Only fools never trembled. True valor consisted of learning to think through chattering teeth and shooting straight while your knees were knocking. Elizabeth measured up well by that standard. Ryerson's glare intimidated most men and almost all the women he'd met. Whatever terror Elizabeth felt, she held her ground calmly enough.

"Could I have a minute with Sergeant Dixon?" she asked, so softly that Ryerson barely made out the question. Suppressing a grin, he hesitated a moment. It helped to have allies. This scheme, after all, had started with Dixon. Ryerson had forgiven his friend's many transgressions in the name of arranging this marriage. Nevertheless, Ryerson thought it fitting to leave the task of persuading the recalcitrant Libbie to his loyal, Machiavellian, skirt-chasing sergeant. Quelling an urge to war whoop in triumph, Ryerson considered her words with a solemn expression. He allowed the watch hand to sweep thirty seconds, then gestured the preacher back toward the steps.

"Three minutes." He bolted out of the carriage. His spurs banged as he crossed the threshold. "You've got three minutes to make up your mind."

The car door slammed shut with a sharp clash of metal.

Elizabeth glared at Dixon. "Did you arrange this?" She charged the length of the car. Stopping abruptly, she peered out the window. She glanced anxiously at the siding. "Where did you two come up with this car?"

"Don't know, missus." The sergeant brought his head even with hers. "The major found it. He thought you'd like it for your honeymoon."

"As well I might have." She touched the ornate mahogany frame of a chair. "If I'd agreed to the marriage."

"Now settle down, missus." Dixon picked up her small bag and deposited it on the settee. "You don't want to disappoint the major. He's been real excited. You'll break his heart if you change your mind."

"Ha!" She sat down on the couch and opened her bag, pawing desperately through its contents. "This is a trap. I'm on to your ways."

"Now, missus." Dixon fished his pipe out of his pocket. "What makes you think we'd do somethin' so devious?"

"I know you. I know him." Elizabeth glared out the window. "You've cooked up this scheme together. You think I'll never go East in this palace car unless I'm legally married." Elizabeth dumped her bag's contents onto the mattress. "He knew—*knew*—I didn't want this. But he thought he'd show up with a preacher, and I'd be too polite to contradict him. Well, it won't work. It won't work, I tell you. Because for once I'm one step ahead. He's going to regret being so sneaky. I don't care how badly it hurts him, he's going to back down from this marriage proposal."

Dixon pulled a small piece of fuzz-covered wire from his pocket. "You've got a plan, do you?"

"Oh, yes." She searched through her bag. "And you're going to help me. You're going to talk him out of this marriage."

"I am?"

"Yes." She slipped out a package wrapped in white linen. "He's too bullheaded to listen to me. Undoubtedly figures I'm just a woman. But you're his friend, his old wartime buddy. You're going to make him listen to reason."

"Now, missus, why should I do that?" Dixon poked the slender reed through the pipe stem. "I think it's a fine thing, this marriage."

She moved to a small cherrywood table and unlaced three tiny bows of red ribbon. She spread the cloth out, unrolling a delicate bunch of dried flowers she'd saved from the prairie. "You're going to do this because you love him."

"I am?"

"Yes." She held a dull green sprig up to her nose. A light scent of mint wafted to her. "Then let me put it this way—if you loved a white woman, would you ask for her hand in marriage?"

Dixon drilled the pipe stem methodically. "I'm not the marryin' type."

"I understand, but pretend for a minute." She crushed a leaf between her fingers. The scent gave her courage. An irrational fact, but true enough. "You love, truly love, a woman who's white. Suppose she brings up the subject of marriage. What would you say?"

Pausing, Dixon eyed her suspiciously for a moment. She could see his brain working in his expression, wondering what trick she was up to and whether he could trust her with an honest answer.

"I'd tell her forget it," he said finally. "I wouldn't consent."

"Why not?"

"Because." He held up one hand. "I can't cut myself out of my skin. And she might think that she loves me, but she has no idea how much pain being that different would bring her."

She brushed her fingers over the tattoos on her cheekbones. "My point exactly."

"No." Dixon shook his head. "Your situation is different."

She turned her face slightly and looked at the window. Her faint reflection painted the glass. She could barely see the tattoos in this light. But she could not ignore them. "How? I can't cut these off, either."

He reached over and tilted her chin. "Because you weren't born this way. He put these there, in a manner of speakin'."

A swirl of despair spiraled through her. "And that makes me a suitable wife?"

"It does if you love him."

"You and he have been friends too long. You make arguments that don't follow."

"Look," he said as he swiveled her face toward the pane. "You survived. You've learned to like, respect, and forgive him. When he sees the tattoos and the love lighting those pretty brown eyes, it helps him remember not to be so hard on himself." A shimmer of light danced in her reflection. Dixon's arguments seemed so seductive.

"No." Frowning, she turned angrily away from her image. "I don't believe you."

"Well, you ought to." Dixon touched her shoulder briefly. "No other woman can give him that comfort."

"Can't you see what a mistake we'd be making?"

"You seem like a fine couple to me."

She picked out three faded flowers and a delicate branch of dried butterfly weed. Rerolling the linen, she slipped the sachet into a pouch in the satchel, then rifled again through her carpetbag's contents. "What kind of a life would we have together? He'd spend his career risking his life. I'd spend mine waiting and being frightened."

Dixon grinned. "You don't think risk makes love that much sweeter?"

"No." She wanted to punch him. He seemed so young, male, and foolhardy to look at a soldier's existence that way. She fished a lace-edged handkerchief out of her bag. "No. I don't believe that. But I don't want to hurt you. I know the troop needs his protection." She folded her hands to keep them from trembling. "So go out there and persuade him. Inform him I'll go to Washington with him, but I want to be free to part from him after. Remind him how much the troop needs him and use that fact to talk him out of this marriage."

Dixon shoved the fuzzy wire in his pocket. "Now who's not being clear?"

"Then let me speak more plainly. If Major Ryerson becomes my husband, your precious troop will lose its commander."

The pipe stopped halfway to his mouth. "Beg pardon, missus?"

"It will. I'll see to it. I promise." Pretending indifference, she picked up stems and fussed with her flowers. "I don't want to be cruel, but if the major becomes my true husband, I'll move heaven and earth to get him out of the army."

Dixon leaned on the cold stove as calmly as if he were discussing the weather. "Missus, you wouldn't do that."

"I would." She wanted to weep. She didn't like making these threats, but Ryerson's intransigence drove her to it. He'd never give up. She knew he wouldn't. He'd send Dixon, then come back himself. He'd fuss during the trip. At every stop he'd seek out a preacher. And somewhere, by Pennsylvania maybe, he'd work himself into a terrible temper. Not that she feared him exactly. But he seemed so stubborn, so intent and determined, it seemed easier to give him his way. Frowning, she wrapped the branches in the red ribbon. "I guarantee it."

Dixon studied her from the corner. For a moment she thought he would bolt, but he merely sucked some air through the pipe stem, then rapped the bowl on the stove. "You don't want to cause us soldiers that trouble."

She tried a fierce look, but somehow suspected it didn't work. "I mean it. I don't really want to, but he's made his proposal so tempting. I can go to Washington with him, use my position to help the Cheyenne. That's a fine idea as far as it goes. It's what comes after that has me worried."

Scowling, Dixon got up. "What's wrong with what comes after? Is there somethin' wrong with his kissin'?"

"No!" She blushed furiously. "That's not the problem." Eyes lowered, she picked at the edge of the lace handkerchief. "Don't you see? We'd make the world's worst married couple. I've already lost one soldier husband. He's lost his wife to the pressures of waiting. The troop deserves a fine commander, but don't I deserve to be happy?" She turned her gaze frankly to him, daring him to look at her face and still ignore the impact of her question. "Doesn't he, for that matter?"

He returned the look without flinching. "Yes, missus, he does."

"Then help me talk him out of this marriage."

Dixon shoved the pipe back in his pocket. Rising, he strode toward the door.

She stopped him with a gesture. "Are you going to help me?"

He tugged on his uniform sleeve, frowning angrily at the yellow vee of his chevron. "No, missus, I won't."

"Why?" She couldn't keep her voice from breaking upward. "Why would you force me to be hurtful?"

He paused, hand on the doorknob. "Because I love him."

The lace handkerchief fluttered. She crumpled it into a ball in her fist. "You said it yourself—there are many who love him. Surely there must be some other woman."

He smiled slightly. "There's others that have thrown themselves at him."

"Well, then, hop him over a broomstick with one of them."

"No, missus, can't do that."

"Why not?"

"Because"—Dixon tipped his hat slightly—"there are many that love him, and me among them, but there's no other woman who'd suit him so well."

ELEVEN

She married him with ten minutes to spare. Ryerson didn't know how Dixon did it, but his stubborn sergeant talked Elizabeth into the wedding. She made a bouquet out of a hanky and a sprinkling of dried blossoms she'd found somewhere. The lanky preacher came through like a trooper. He'd recited the vows beautifully and produced the license without questioning Dixon about the propriety of a Negro witness.

Of course, she seemed frightened. The broomstick business had suited her better. Ryerson thought about that as the train whistle shrieked and the palace car rumbled out of the station. She'd mumbled through her part of her vows, as though secretly fearful and too proud to admit it. To some degree her anxiety dented his ego. Helen had counted him as a conquest. So, he knew, had other women. As with everything else, Elizabeth measured him by her own values, however. He found it sobering to think he didn't come up to her standards.

Scowling, Ryerson peered out the window and saluted Dixon. The sergeant waved back, a dark, dapper figure shrinking rapidly into the distance. Ryerson jerked back a purple curtain, seeking one last glimpse of his friend. He hated leaving his troopers. He'd miss all of them, especially

Dixon, but Senator Parker had bluntly requested that Ryerson come by himself. Ryerson frowned. Like many a northern politician, his former father-in-law liked the idea of rights for coloreds better than he liked Negroes personally. The hypocrisy rankled, but Ryerson judged it more useful to leave his sergeant to look after the troopers. And Dixon agreed.

"Besides," he'd pointed out gaily, "if you want to make a true, soulful marriage, you've got to be alone with your woman." Ryerson smiled to himself. He turned away from the small square of glass. Elizabeth sat opposite him, eyelashes lowered, still holding the fragile bouquet, refusing to look either at him or the grasslands rapidly slipping past.

A slight movement caught Ryerson's attention. Elizabeth drew in her breath and stifled an audible sigh. Her bosom lifted the neat row of buttons curving up the front of her traveling suit. Ryerson found himself fighting a hardening groin.

"So." She raised her cinnamon eyes to his face. "You finally have me just where you want me."

"Yes." He angled away, removing his hat. "It's been a long chase." He tossed the stiff headgear on a side table. Sunlight glinted off its tiny crossed sabers. "And sporting."

"It doesn't seem so long to me."

He plunked down on the settee. His knees poked up awkwardly, and the carved frame pressed into his back. The couch had clearly been made for a woman, or, at the very least, a more civilized man.

"Are you frightened?" he asked.

"Not exactly."

"Elizabeth." Ryerson stood. He paced to the stove, acutely aware of the close quarters, of the fact that she did not want to be here, and of what had gone on in the cabin. "I know what happened before . . ." He groped for the words, uncertain of how to express his idea. He wanted to reassure her, to promise her that he would be gentle. This was all very well, except he also wished to be truthful. He knew he'd not hurt her, exactly, but he understood the nature of masculine ardor. He'd reached his limit. Long ago, to be honest. He wanted her. He didn't care how he got her. He wouldn't force her. He understood well enough the difference between a war and a battle, but he intended to have her. And soon. "What happened . . . between us . . . out there in the cabin . . ." He shucked off his gauntlets and tossed them onto the cold metal stove top. "I know I hurt you . . ."

"Don't." She hopped to her feet and crossed the car to him. "Don't apologize for it. I mean . . ." She blushed, a lovely peach tinted with scarlet. "I mean . . . I liked it, at least I think I did. Perhaps I shouldn't. I mean, civilized women—"

"Hang civilized women!"

He pulled her to him, crushing her words with a kiss. Well, not just a kiss, but a hot brand of impassioned possession. He hadn't intended to move so quickly, but her closeness enticed him. She had this softness, this dizzying sweetness, a scent like wildflowers, and a pillowy bosom. He wanted her closer, to drown in her essence, to fill his senses with her feminine presence. He pushed his tongue into her mouth. She tasted of mint and chocolate candy, and he reveled in the tang and the sweetness. Opening her mouth slightly, she grazed her teeth over his lower lip. A surge of lust powered through him. He pressed his hips into her pelvis. She flinched. He pulled back with a curse to himself, straightened his tunic, and tore at his gun belt. "If you promise me nothing else, promise me this."

"What?"

"You'll never become a civilized woman."

"But—"

"Promise." He shot her a glance, then worked at his belt buckle with unsteady fingers. "To never become a civilized woman. To love me always, just the way that you have been." The leather tongue caught, and he had to jerk it. "That doesn't seem like such a hard commitment."

"Ha!" Reaching forward, she tugged at the holster, yanking it off him. "You always say that." She walked to the tiny ornate couch and sat down. The kiss had aroused him. He felt almost naked, stripped of the weight of leather and metal. He wondered if she'd noticed his hardness, then decided it didn't much matter. Whatever was going to happen would happen. He strode to the window and pulled shut a curtain. The heavy velvet turned the world dusky, and she watched silently as he moved down the car and finished his task. He completed a circuit of all the side windows, then sat next to her and unbuttoned the top of his tunic.

"Am I asking too much?" He kept his voice soft, expressive and tender.

"Not exactly." Placing the gun on the table, she removed her own gloves and lay them next to her flowers. For the briefest of moments her gaze lingered on the metallic glint of the barrel. She sucked in a breath, turned, and took his bare hands in hers. "But it's hard to be the first one to say it."

He lifted her palm to his lips and kissed it. "Then let me go first." He brushed his thumb over her cheekbone. "Look at me, Libbie." He tried to seem a little less fearsome, but he doubted sincerely that he succeeded. The years of war had hardened his face, stamped him with a weathered complexion, and given him a mien so ferocious that even powerful men quailed under his glance. Gently as he could, Ryerson locked their fingers together. "I'm hardened to war, and it is well that I am, but I am not stone. The deaths of your loved ones meant nothing to me. The deaths of my soldiers meant little enough." She started to speak. He silenced her firmly, determined to unburden his mind on this subject. "Ah, but it's true. By the end of the war, I lost sixty boys in one assault on Kennesaw Mountain and regarded that charge as a dash before breakfast. But with you, I'm quite different. Look." He held up his hands, which he knew to be shaking. "I tremble before you. My heart stops when you enter the room." He clasped her small hands tightly in his. "I can't promise I'll always be pleasant, but I swear I'll never touch you in anger. You have nothing to fear from my hands or my weapons. It's a hard thing to marry a soldier. I can't promise to always be with you, but I'll always protect you and—"

"Be quiet." She pressed her finger over his lips. "You don't have to say these things to me."

He lifted his gaze to those wonderful eyes. To his eternal surprise, they gleamed with affection. And maybe—dare he read even this into her look?—he saw the glow of desire in them. "I want to."

"No." She shook her head softly. "I can see this speech hurts you."

"Maybe it does." He cleared his throat. In spite of his effort, his voice came out husky, thick with desire or terror or both. "But I still need to say this. I thought I'd lost the poet in me, but you dragged that poor fellow back from the grave. I don't think I can do this in meter, but I would like to express my feelings in words." He went down on one knee, an extravagant gesture, but heartfelt. "I love you, Libbie. Let me show you how much."

She nodded. He'd lowered his eyes, so he wasn't sure he had seen the gesture, but he knew she'd consented. The idea transfixed him, and for the tiniest moment he pan-

icked. Sooner or later there'd be more children, more grief
and more worry, maybe more horror, and worse. The idea
pained him. He tried not to think about it too closely. If he
proceeded a little more slowly, he could finish the way he'd
intended last time. They hadn't talked a lot about children,
but he didn't suppose she'd want to get pregnant just yet.

He rose to his feet, bent over the sofa, pulled her close
to his chest, and kissed her. She kissed him back, her warm
lips soft against his. The depth of her passion surprised
him. She came alive in his arms, sweet, eager, and breathless, her kisses wet as a child's, but fierce and far more
erotic. He wondered briefly where they would do this, then
decided he didn't care. He lifted her to him, crushing her
along the length of his body. She felt soft and vibrant,
supple and pliant, curving in all the right places. He deepened his kiss. To his absolute shock, she hiked up her dress
and curled a leg over his thigh. Panic, pride, and hunger
stormed through him. She seemed to want to be taken
right there. He knew he could do it, though he couldn't
imagine a civilized woman being so forward.

Then again, he'd just asked her to promise not to become a civilized woman.

He sank into the velvet and centered her squarely over
his lap. As he cupped his hands under her buttocks, she
twined her legs tighter and opened her mouth. He thrust in
his tongue. The heat made a welcoming foretaste of the
place she'd opened so wantonly to him. He strained his
hips upward. She dangled above him, close enough that
she could be entered, except, of course, for the clothes. He
had an impulse to tear off her garments, undo his buttons,
and take her, but he'd promised himself he would be
tender. No matter how much she tempted, he intended to
keep his vow to himself. He slipped her down slightly and
lifted his thigh, still balancing her on one of his legs.

Squeezing tight, she squirmed against him. He thought it improper, exciting, and novel for her to be so wildly responsive. Heat and softness teased at his hardness. Warm liquid moistened her thin undergarments. The rush of the train obscured her breathing and created its own sensual vibration. Though he found the resonance lovely, he'd begun to regret the palace car. He worried about how and where they should lie down.

"Stop." He disentangled himself from her embrace. "We need to slow down." His hands truly were shaking. He gripped her waist and looked around for the newfangled contraption. "As I understand it, some of these seats make into a bed."

She glanced around in confusion, her sun-shot curls wildly awry.

"How about the settee?" she asked raggedly.

He knew he should wait. He'd promised himself that he'd do this right, but she looked so lovely, so wanton and fetching, that he drew her into his chest and kissed her again. Every muscle in him tightened and hardened. Every nerve cried out for her touch. His blood rushed, as fast as in battle, and the pulsing rhythm created a heat. He unfastened her jacket, eager to feel her. He'd waited so long for this intimate contact. She sighed, delicate, dreamy. He slipped his hand under her blouse.

He breathed his thoughts into her earlobe. "Oh, Libbie. So soft. So lovely." The words rose in him like bubbles. "My bonny, my pretty, my bright, burning lady. My Libbie."

She pulled back for a minute, her cheeks as bright as the summertime roses that sometimes bloomed wild on the coast of New England. "It's not fair. A poet does not need to look at his subject. With artists, it's different."

He felt dreamy himself, and her little speech didn't make sense. "What are you talking about?"

"I've been doing these sketches. You've been posing half-naked." Passion pooled in eyes like dark honey, but the ardor in them couldn't disguise the joy and peace in her expression. She rested her hands on the planes of his chest and pressed her hips a little bit closer. "That's hard on someone whose mind likes to make pictures. There are parts of you I've just imagined."

Hand on her waist, he cocked one eyebrow. "Like what?"

"Thighs." She nuzzled her face in his chest.

"What?"

"Thighs," she repeated. "I know it's barbaric, but for weeks I've wanted to look at your thighs."

He threw back his head and laughed. "I'm afraid you'll be disappointed."

"Oh, I don't think so." She eased back and rested her hands on his biceps. "I've a fine eye for shadows and masses and a real feeling for proper proportion."

"Should I be frightened?" he asked mockingly. "I'm afraid an artist might judge me quite harshly."

She slipped off his lap, her smile a small half-moon of challenge. "There's only one way to find out."

He stood and stripped briskly, proud of his body. War might corrode a man's soul, but life in the field hardened the muscles, kept off the fat, and made a man limber. He knew perfectly well she'd like what she saw.

Stepping out of his undergarments, he wondered what she thought of the view. Certainly he had her diverted. She stared wide-eyed at his rock-hard erection and gasped. He let her look. He'd already hurt her, and he knew this part of lovemaking often frightened a novice. Proud and upright, it just didn't look like it would fit in a woman. He was about to recite a speech of disclaimer when, to his pure shock, she reached out and touched it, then planted a soft kiss on the tip.

A bolt of passion jolted straight through him. "Don't do that, Libbie."

"Why not?" She looked up, surprised.

"Because." He filled his hands with those fiery curls. "Like it or not, our situation is different than it used to be. From this day forward, I won't be put off. You've stripped me down to pure nakedness, while you sit there covered up to the neck. Stand up now, Libbie. I'm going to undress you."

She obeyed him, slowly, eyes slightly wary, but moving as always with unflinching courage. He considered briefly how this should go, then decided on languid calculation. Anything less he couldn't control. He kissed her briefly, then unbuttoned her jacket. Her breasts shifted beneath white cotton tucking, making voluptuous lines in the neat pleating. His pulse sped up.

"Do you know how long I've thought about this?" He slid the dark blazer down to her elbows, then let it pool on the floor beneath them.

She shook her head.

"From the first time I touched you." He pulled her blouse out of her waistband.

As if in a dream, she feathered her fingers over his chest. "An inauspicious beginning, I think."

"I disagree." Leaving the cool cotton blouse as a buffer, he cupped his hands under her breasts. Her lips parted slightly, and he ran a finger over one nipple. The nub puckered, and she sucked in a breath. He repeated the motion on the other side. As he did, the train swayed beneath them, and she tilted slightly. Her soft cotton grazed his hard chest. He stifled a gasp. Reaching behind her, he undid her back buttons and pulled the snowy white sleeves over her arms. A silk camisole shielded her from him, but the garment clung to the curve of her breasts and outlined the perky tilt of her nipples. He swept up the satin and captured the rosy bud with his mouth.

"Oh!" She curved her fingers into his shoulders. He supposed her grip ought to be painful, except that his nerves had gone past that feeling and on to the plane where pain became pleasure.

He suckled slowly, entranced by the feeling, the little nub on his tongue, the exquisitely tender circle around it.

"Libbie," he whispered with kisses all over her breasts, the creamy sides and the gorgeous swell of her cleavage, "I knew you'd be just like this."

He stood, pressing his nakedness into her skirt. The wool prickled slightly, but he scarcely noticed. He could feel the heat from her body as well as the fullness, texture, and weight of her breasts. He might have swelled a little bit larger, though he didn't know how he could have. Still, he reacted in some way, in heat and tightness, in the depth of his passion. The need to finish rose up within him. He squelched it.

Pulling back, he unbuttoned her skirt and slipped it down over her hips. She wore no hoop, as always, and he thanked heaven for her odd sense of fashion. Her loose petticoat came off with the motion. Sweet and disheveled, she stood before him in her moist camisole and thin pantalets. She blushed. He wanted to kiss her, but he thought he should look. He'd imagined this sight so many times.

He stepped back and smiled, allowing his gaze to rove over her body. "Turn around, please," he asked quietly.

She complied, turning slowly, her hands at her sides.

"I knew it." He leaned forward and planted a kiss on the curve of her bottom.

"James!"

"Sorry," he said, keeping his tone unrepentant. "After so many years of looking at horseflesh, I've developed a weakness for posterior dimples. Now," he said, stepping forward and pressing himself to her. "Let me finish—"

"This way?" She started, quivering slightly.

"No." He chuckled. "Let me finish taking your clothes off." He grazed his hands over her hips. "You really do think me beastly. I've reluctantly come to admire the brutes, but I've not yet adopted their method of mounting."

Leaving her in the same position, he plucked the satin top off, then blew a series of kisses onto her earlobe and neck. Sighing, she leaned slightly backward. He cupped his hands under her breasts, pushing the sides slightly inward and admiring the rift his pressure created. "So lovely," he murmured, "so soft and lovely. I promise you, Libbie, this time will be different."

She wondered what he meant by that comment. She liked what he'd done last time well enough, though he seemed to regret something about it. She knew little about married passion. Of course, there'd been Philip. A lifetime of kisses, tentative groping, and fervent wishes. Ryerson, however, had always been different, and never more so than that day in the cabin.

Even now, the memory stirred her. Once she'd gotten over the shock of her loss, there'd been something profoundly arousing about the experience. He wanted her. And very badly. Now he was blowing her delicate kisses and trying to win back her trust. She thought that amazing, for she liked what he'd done. She found them delicious, all the sensations swirling within her. In those beautiful, terrible moments there in the cabin, he'd bound himself to her on the most primal level. That fact seemed important to her. Some instinct told her there were only two qualities that counted in marriage. Passion and honor. Both of which Ryerson had in abundance.

"What are you thinking about?" he asked, so softly she almost didn't hear him.

"Nothing." She turned, smoothing her hands over his chest. "I think you're lovely also."

The train rumbled beneath them, creating a music, and the curtained light brushed him in purple, making him darker, more devilish, but also less grizzled than he generally appeared in the bright prairie sunlight. Slowly he rolled down her white pantalets, staring brazenly at her shadowy curls. Surprisingly she didn't feel self-conscious. There was something about his nudity, the pride with which he carried himself, that made her feel she wished to match him. As the filmy white cloth fell to her ankles, she stepped quickly out and stood naked before him.

"Wonderful," he murmured, "and astoundingly pagan. Look how she stands there with no false modesty, as if the artist knows her own beauty."

She blushed. His gaze might not have undone her, but his words overwhelmed her. She spread her arms out to embrace him. One at a time he kissed the tips of her fingers. "Ah, Libbie, I love you. I don't know why it's so hard to say it."

"I love you, too, James."

He sighed softly and pulled her the full length of his body. For the first time since she'd known him, she got a tactile impression of his life as a soldier. He was hard everyplace—his thighs, his chest, his muscular stomach, his arms, his neck, even his fingers. She could feel his strength as he caressed her. Not that he wasn't tender. He kept kissing her lips, her neck, and her earlobe, pressing his length gently against her. And she responded. Without even thinking, she twined her arms around his neck, rose on her tiptoes, and pushed up against him. But some timid part of her couldn't get over the shock of those solid male muscles straining against her, and the really tiny coward inside her wondered if he actually would fit, and if this could really be done without causing her pain. As if he sensed the drift of her thought, he cupped her against him and slipped his fingers into her moistness. She found this enticing and pushed her hips up to receive him.

"We can't do it standing," he whispered harshly.

"The settee?" The suggestion seemed to slip out of some other woman.

"No." He lifted her up, carrying her to one end of the car. She found his strength thrilling, but wondered briefly what he was doing. Still holding her closely, he grabbed something behind her and pushed it. He kicked with one foot. When he put her down, she found herself standing next to a bed. Narrow but cushioned, the little cot had appeared out of nowhere, and it took her a second to understand that he'd made it somehow from two of the chairs.

"Lie down," he ordered.

She did as he asked. The train rumbled beneath her, and she was glad for the rocking as the motion disguised some of her shakiness. As she arranged herself in a half-leaning position, he knelt on the bed, his posture erect, his spine even more than usually rigid.

"This won't hurt, I promise. Bend your knees a little." She complied, surprised by his frankness, but also surprised by her own comfort. She wanted him, and quite badly. She felt this as internal tension, a breathless desire to see what came next, and a soft, dizzying notion that she would follow wherever he led. Leaning forward, he dipped slowly, guiding himself to her entrance. Hot flesh probed her own, a heavy pressure, exquisite, not painful.

"Now lift," he commanded. "I want you to take me. If we do this slowly, this should not cause you pain."

She obeyed as best as she could. He certainly stretched her, though his thickness did not seem excessive. Instead, she felt pleasure, hot and erotic, a heady sense of natural perfection.

"You fit so nicely," she said quietly.

"Like a key in a lock."

Buoyed by his words, she inched her hips up. She watched as he entered, determined to see their joining. He looked as if he should split her in two, but her body adjusted, becoming more moist. She glanced up, surprised. His face had gone rigid, a stony mask of fierce concentration. A dark flush crept up his chest, making his nipples puckered brown pennies. A thrill of arousal swept through her. She thought herself bold to keep her eyes open, but he'd undergone a profound transformation, and the sight of him mesmerized her. His control intrigued her. He held to his word, watching her gravely from beneath lowered lashes, waiting for her to forgive him, trust him completely, and accept him freely into her body. His restraint gave her a sense of her power, and she realized with a sense of discomfort that he wanted much more than just coupling.

"Am I doing this right?" she asked anxiously.

He nodded.

She gazed upward, intent on sensation. "Talk to me, then. Tell me what you want."

He wet his lips. A trickle of sweat slid down his temple. "I want you to come to me freely. I want you to give that which I cannot take by possession."

Puzzled, she drew down her eyebrows.

"I want your heart, Libbie. The one thing in the world I

cannot gain by conquest." He leaned forward and kissed
her, deeply and possessively, filling her mouth and creating
pressure much lower. He lifted himself on his forearms.
Her nerves cried out. She tightened her thighs and
clutched at his buttocks, but he held himself rigid, his gaze
intent. Pride and pleasure rushed through her. She wanted
to take him deep into her body. She pushed hard, ac-
cepting him further. He gasped. A silvery sheen shone on
his forehead, and she suddenly realized what this was
about.

"Help me," she whispered. "I can't finish this way."

He leaned forward and took a nipple into his mouth.
The sensation felt lovely, but the position drew his hips
farther away. She surged upward, desire coiling within her.
She wanted both—the sharp pleasure his suckling induced,
the moisture, heat, and friction of joinder. Arching her
back, she drove her fingers into his buttocks, using the
pressure to draw him closer. He pressed with his thighs,
then, very gently, pulled with his teeth, as if he wanted to
take something from her at the same moment he gave it
back. She bucked, a frenzy building within her. She knew
what she wanted. She didn't know how she understood it,
but in that moment she discovered an instinct. She
pumped, creating a rhythm. He drove in response, the heat
creating a slickness, like a third skin between them. That
slippery layer fueled their passion, and desire took over,
making the two of them one, like-minded and mindless,
alive to each other and dead to the world, part of the great
natural drive to creation, but fiercely intent on an act of
great pleasure.

At first she did not comprehend what was happening,
but something in her let go. Waves of pleasure shattered
her focus, all her nerves came to the surface, and the wild
tension in her exploded.

He left. Before she quite realized they had finished, he pulled himself out and pressed his turgid manhood between them. A hot liquid spilled on her stomach, and the oddity of that detail left her indignant. She'd given him pleasure. She could feel the subsiding waves of his passion, but her mind worked over one simple fact. He intended to rob her of children. A sharp spurt of anger pushed through her.

She bolted upright, pushing him from her. "Why did you do that?"

"What?" He grabbed for his long johns, covering his crotch, as if he actually feared she would hit him. "What?"

She suddenly felt flustered. She wanted to pace, to dress and clean up, and she wanted to do all three at once. She tucked her knees under her chin instead. "You know what I'm talking about."

"Slow down." He leaned back on a window, the velvet curtain cradling his head, his chest still blowing harshly. "Let me get my breath."

She watched, furious, as his breathing subsided. She thought she should dress, then decided with a deep sense of vengeance that she wanted to have this conversation naked. "You don't want children?"

He shut his eyes, his chest still working. "How did you guess?"

She blushed, undoubtedly scarlet. "I grew up with six brothers. I learned a few unladylike facts."

He pulled on his wool long johns, still sitting on the little couch. "We discussed this subject out there on the prairie."

"Two words. One small, small conversation."

Wearily he rose from the seat. She thought he would dress, but he didn't. He picked up his pants and fumbled through one of the pockets. "Look. Settle down. You'll get pregnant one of these days. Believe me, I know. I want you too much for my own good, and I'm hardly perfect at this maneuver."

"Oh, great. That's just dandy, isn't it?" She didn't know where the crudity came from, but he had her so livid she'd forgotten even the simplest manners. "You'll give me a baby one of these days, even though you don't want one."

He retrieved a cigar and jammed the stub into his mouth. "What's wrong with that?"

"You know, you truly are monstrous. You've spent so much time around dying that you've forgotten what life is about."

"You're resorting to insults."

"You bet I am."

He sat down on the bed, crooked up one knee, and rolled the cheroot to the side of his mouth. "This tantrum will get you nowhere."

"Your temper gets you far enough."

"That's true, but I'm bigger." He dabbed a bit of tobacco off the tip of his tongue. "I suggest you try a lucid discussion."

For a moment, she wanted to hit him. She thought it would be a wild sight, the two of them fighting half naked, but her anger had robbed her of all common sense. She didn't care if she couldn't beat him. He'd not bully her on this particular subject. "Children deserve to be wanted."

"In a better world, I'm sure that they would be, but the world we live in can be pretty tough." To her total surprise, his voice came out as soft as his gentlest caress.

She picked up her crumpled pantalets, confused and astonished by his evident mildness. "What do you mean by that?"

"Unwanted children are born every day." His voice stayed gentle, though his demeanor belied it. His eyes seemed so dark, his expression so rigid.

She could barely keep herself from shaking. "Not to me, they're not."

"And what does that mean?"

This time she caught the anger, the lethal edge in his tone. She knew he hated what she was threatening, and she caught herself before she went further. Did she want to do that? To make good on the threat implied by her comment? To her complete surprise—and utter chagrin—she found pretty quickly she didn't.

She poked one foot into the thin pantalets. "It means, if I have a baby, I want you to love him. Or her, as the case may be."

All the tension went out of his posture. She didn't see it, but sensed it, and in that moment she learned something important. She had the power to hurt him. And had. Sighing, she abandoned her clothes. She moved next to him on the couch. Though the posture took a bit of maneuvering, she snuggled tightly into his chest. Beneath the sprinkling of hair, she could hear his heart hammering wildly. An air of fear lingered about him, mingled in with the earthy scent of their pleasure. That observation surprised her more than any other, for as well as she knew him, and as much as she'd come to think him human, she'd never, ever envisioned him frightened. A sharp pain stabbed in her bosom.

"I'm sorry, James. Sometimes I forget I married a person."

He chuckled. "As opposed to a beast?"

She laughed, brushing her hand over his stomach. "As opposed to a legend." Silently she vowed never to mistake him again. He'd lost the children of his first marriage. If she wanted her own, she'd have to teach him that she wasn't Helen, that life could be different. She stroked his thigh and noticed with pleasure that he hadn't entirely lost his arousal. "You'll have to forgive me. For most of my life you were an image, the terrible monster who'd destroyed my home. Even in person you seem so ferocious. It's hard to imagine you grieving, but I'm learning." She tucked herself under his arm. If she meant to love him and make him happy, she'd do well to consider his past. "Forgive me?"

He pulled her closer and laced his fingers under her breasts. "Oh, my bonny, my lovely, my Libbie. You're much too good to need my forgiveness."

TWELVE

As the train rumbled into Washington City, Elizabeth's heart tweaked at the sight of the shiny new Capitol building dome soaring above pigsties and slums, neat rows of brick houses, prosperous markets, a defunct slave quarters, and dozens of partially constructed government buildings.

Closing her eyes, Elizabeth grasped the settee's wooden armrest and leaned into Ryerson's chest. The southerner in her rebelled at the sight of the churchlike dome dominating the skyline. As the palace car swayed, she clutched his hand tightly and wondered how she would fit in with the Yankees, whether or not she could forgive them, how best to help her Indian friends, and most of all, how to protect James Ryerson from those who would hate him because he'd married a woman so different from what they likely expected.

Ryerson shifted behind her. His uniform buttons poked into her back. In spite of the minor discomfort, she wished they could stay this way forever, seated together on the velvet couch, his arms resting loosely around her, his heart pumping in time with hers, and his sinewy body creating a refuge. The train's whistle blew, disrupting her thoughts. The chugging motion slowed down, its even rhythm transformed into lurching. Beneath the screech of the brakes, a thumping boom assaulted her ears. She opened her eyes and peeked out the window. A metallic glint caught her attention. Three musicians stood on the station platform. Gold frogs circled their neat rows of buttons, and frilled epaulets swelled their straight shoulders.

"Oh, dear." Surprise jolted through her, and she tugged back the purple velvet curtain. "There's a brass band out there."

"For me," Ryerson said curtly.

Turning, she glanced, wide-eyed, at his grim expression. "Really?"

He nodded, then stiffened, looking for all the world as if he were ready to storm the tiny, Italianate station and attack his own welcoming committee. Elizabeth rested her forehead on the cool glass, scanning the crowd on the low wooden platform. A tuba player blasted out notes, accompanied by three hoo-pah-ing trumpets and the sturdy thump of a field drum. A knot of milling civilians flanked the musicians and jostled a man in a black beaver top hat. Elizabeth wanted to sketch the odd group, but she didn't dare pull out her pad. She committed the sight to memory, adjusted the dark veil of her hat, and smiled tentatively at her new husband.

He smiled back, and she suddenly felt glad she'd agreed to the bonnet. At Leavenworth Ryerson had purchased a half-dozen pretty draped hats. On the frontier she'd refused to wear them, reasoning she'd meet very few strangers, and the more people looked the sooner they'd get used to her oddness. In Washington, however, there would always be strangers. She'd argued with Ryerson at first, but in the end, she'd agreed with his point. These small confrontations would test her composure. She needed to conserve her patience for the more important social occasions.

At the thought, Elizabeth swallowed. She dreaded that aspect of her new life. She'd been schooled in ladylike manners, but the war and her years on the prairie had destroyed most of her social graces. Just as important, life as Ryerson's bride would require more than just manners. She wanted to help with the troopers and hoped she'd find a way to be useful, but her Indian friends needed her, too, and she couldn't keep her sympathies quiet.

"You look lovely, you know." Ryerson squeezed her hand hard. She could feel his warmth through two layers of gloves.

Stifling a sigh, she straightened the lace cuffs of her blouse. "This was so nice. I wish we could stay."

Leaning forward, he brushed a kiss over one earlobe. The sunlight winked off the epaulets on his shoulder. "It was pretty grand." He slanted a glance at the chairs. She would have labeled his expression nostalgic, except she could not imagine him feeling tranquil. His gaze locked with hers, and he grinned. "And you're pretty special."

Elizabeth blushed. He'd apologized for half of the journey for the supposed shortcomings of the honeymoon, for the narrowness of the bed, for the urgency of the sex, and for every time he imagined he'd hurt her. Elizabeth, however, had loved the whole interlude. They'd made love for three days. He'd been an unflagging though courteous lover, never less than a gentleman, always making it clear he would take no for an answer, but also conveying he wanted her badly. To be fair, she wanted him also, and probably in equal measure. For the first time in years, she felt truly alive, as if she'd been buried out there on the prairie. Except for the way he held back in the finishing moments, she'd awakened each morning thinking life perfect. Reality returned with the thump of a drum and the swaggering flourish of the martial trumpet. As Elizabeth peered once more out the window, she wished their honeymoon could have lasted forever.

He snugged his hand over her waist. "Buck up. You can do this. It can't be worse than Fort Leavenworth."

From behind her veil, she shot him a look. She couldn't glower as well as he could, but she had picked up his trick of scowling. The expression amused her, and she wondered vaguely if by her dotage she'd be able to glare as fiercely as he.

She stood and smoothed down the front of her traveling skirt. "Is the big man Senator Parker?"

Nodding, Ryerson joined her. "Now remember. He'll be surprised when I introduce you. He doesn't know about our marriage. And steel yourself for a bit of dissension. You've replaced his daughter, you know."

Elizabeth adjusted her hat. She tugged at the sleeves of her suit jacket and checked to make sure the whole front was buttoned. "And who are the others? Do you recognize them?"

"Newspapermen, I suppose."

Elizabeth's hands flew up to her cheekbones.

Ryerson pressed closer, leaning his thigh almost to hers. She wondered where he'd picked up the habit. He had this manner of asserting his presence, inclining toward her but not really touching, that made her feel safe, supported, and precious. He tucked a gloved hand under her elbow. "Don't be self-conscious. I see Henry Grolier—"

"The illustrator?"

"Yes." The palace car rumbled beneath her. Ryerson held her steady. Without letting go, he adjusted his gun belt and checked his own row of buttons. "He's a fine artist. He'll want to sketch you. In the long run, that will probably help us. The whole city will know about you without asking questions directly."

The train lurched to a halt. Elizabeth thought she felt sick to her stomach. "So now I'll be famous?"

"Yes, I expect so."

"Tattoos and all?"

Hand on his sword, he pressed the small of her back. "Are you unhappy?"

"No, not exactly." She sucked in a breath. She'd corresponded with Grolier, sending him drawings, though always under the name Lysistrata. He knew nothing of her personal life. Still, she supposed she'd find it peculiar being sketched by a man to whom she'd sent sketches. The fact of his presence amazed her, reminding her all too abruptly that she'd married a famous and powerful man. From this day forward her life would be tricky, and she would be wise to be cautious and smart. She took one last look at the room. It smelled of perfume, cigars, and lovemaking. She wished she could bottle the scent and carry the vial close to her heart.

Turning back, she glanced at her husband. Freshly washed and clean shaven, he looked almost relaxed. He squared up the brim of her bonnet, then lifted the veil and pinned it quickly. He brushed his thumb over her cheekbone. She lifted her chin and pivoted to greet his well-wishers. She kept her spine straight as he whispered, "I just wish we could have stayed here forever."

Ryerson hated his fame, and never more so than in the first three days after he and Libbie arrived in the city. Scowling, he glanced down at his wife. She slept under his arm, one leg thrown over his thigh, silky skin heating his own, her sunrise-shot hair swirled over the pillow and the scent of wildflowers teasing his nose. The morning should have been perfect. It wasn't. The coppery taste of dread coated his mouth.

Softly he picked out a strand of her hair. His new wife had become a sensation. The newspapers had carried Grolier's sketches. His lady's serene and remarkable face stared out of the cheap yellow pages. When she went out, people smiled and waved. No matter the hats, people recognized Libbie. Though the greetings seemed friendly, he still had to wonder how much pain this peculiar fame cost her.

He smoothed the thick lock back from her cheekbone. She bore up, of course. She always had. She always would. He had confidence in her endurance. That fact surprised him. He didn't like to think badly of Helen, but in the last few days he'd had some new insights. His wife's suicide had left him distrustful. After her death, he'd viewed women as different. Softer. Less able than men. And one of the reasons he'd married Libbie was that she helped him remember she was just as brave as the toughest soldier.

She didn't look it, of course. He loved that about her—the delicate chin, those high, finely formed cheekbones. But she'd faced the reporters head-on, lifting the veil and letting them look. And she posed for the artist, submitting with patience while a horde of scribblers shot questions at her. She defended the Indians. The tattoos hadn't hurt her, she'd pointed out. The Indians had an innate sense of beauty. They painted themselves, their horses, and their women. They'd made her a slave, but they'd not really harmed her. They'd offered her protection and friendship, which was more than she could say for most whites. And, yes, she did hate the Yankees, except for her husband, of course.

Libbie snuffled slightly, and Ryerson smiled to himself. The newspapers adored her. In the East, Indians sold papers. Long separated from red depredations, the average easterner made a pet of the Indian. Not real Indians, of course, but the fictional heroes who peopled their novels, sketches, and paintings. Elizabeth, with her exotic beauty, played into their romantic notion of an idyllic culture and the noble savage.

To Ryerson's surprise, Elizabeth hated those smug assumptions even more than she'd hated the western reaction.

"The Indians are people," she told reporters sincerely. "Sure, they make poetic symbols, but false sentiment won't solve their problems. They need to be treated as fully human, not as red devils or the objects of holy crusades." She preferred her friends be left in their homelands, but knew that to be a far-fetched solution. So she simply pleaded that the white man leave the red man in peace, and let the Indian make his own way.

Ryerson sighed, trailing a finger over a shimmering lock. He'd made a mistake. Oh, he liked sleeping with her. He loved it, in fact. Almost more than lovemaking, he adored the languid, civilized pleasure of lying abed with his wife at his side. She looked so pretty, snugged into the sheets, the snowy white cotton covering her breasts. She'd let him sleep nude and joined him that way. It seemed almost sinful, the crisp, cool, civilized sheets with the hot, naked woman beneath them. To a man accustomed to cots and wool blankets, the sensation was almost too lovely to bear. This was the part of marriage he wanted, idyllic and tranquil, a peaceful refuge from a harsh, scheming world.

But there was no escaping the other. Tonight they'd be attending a dinner, the first of many, in which he'd be featured as the primary speaker. Not that he minded speaking, in general. He'd taught school for six years, long enough to know how to please when he wanted. But Elizabeth insisted on coming. He wasn't ashamed. He still saw only her beauty. The stares pained him, however. She bore

this public life well, but now he felt foolish—and guilty—
for exposing her to so much scrutiny. She'd tried to tell
him, of course, but he'd wanted so much to protect her—
and, to be fair, he'd wanted this, too, this peaceful possession, the passion and joy that went before it—that he
hadn't given sufficient thought to all the ways this life
could hurt her. Specifically, he hadn't truly considered the
enmity of his father-in-law.

He slipped the sheet over her shoulder. Oh, she had
managed. Not that Senator Parker liked her. Ryerson had
seen the look in his eye, the shock and betrayal covered
too quickly by the false front of political wisdom. Elizabeth, he knew, must have seen it also. She'd presented the
senator with her frank gaze, daring him to find her repulsive. But Ryerson knew Parker would never forgive her.

Not that Parker was heartless. He liked Ryerson. He
probably admired Libbie, but he lived a disciplined life.
His supposed devotion to public welfare thinly covered a
profound love of power. He never let anyone out of his
circle. He never made a decision based on feeling. He'd
used his own wife, his beloved daughter, even his former
son-in-law to enhance his political standing. Elizabeth, for
all the newspapers loved her, would never make a political
wife. That frank gaze revealed Libbie's nature—proud, unbending, and stubborn, a compassionate woman ruled by
her heart, who'd spend her life as Ryerson's conscience.

Parker would never forgive that. He would have excused
a second wife—no man could succeed without the right
woman—but Libbie's expression, the way she faced the
newspapers, her honesty about all of her feelings, her obvious disdain for political caution, told Senator Parker, in a
way that words never could have, that his son-in-law had
moved out of his orbit.

Ryerson blew out a soft breath. He smoothed the locks

cascading over the pillow. He couldn't leave her in Washington now. Parker would shun her as soon as he left. Libbie might start out all right, but the tattoos made her strange to civilized people. She might not buckle, but Parker could certainly make her life harder.

Libbie turned over, presenting her back. Pain bloomed in Ryerson's chest. He snuggled more closely, holding her gently. A surge of affection rushed through him. He'd find her a place. He'd burned her plantation and couldn't replace it, but out in Virginia, not so very far from this city, hundreds of farms were falling to ruin, their slaves deserting, their owners killed in the war. Ryerson didn't much like the carpetbaggers who bought these ruined plantations, but Libbie wouldn't be that kind of vulture. She'd grown up in the South. She'd fit in with her neighbors. She knew how to live a southerner's life.

Softly he tucked her nearer. The curves of her body fit him so nicely. She needed a refuge. So he'd give her one. She didn't mind being alone. He still hoped they wouldn't have babies, but if they did, he thought she could manage. He had money—Helen's, of course. For himself, he'd never touched it, but it didn't seem wrong to use his first wife's fortune on somebody who needed his help.

He smiled to himself. Perhaps Elizabeth would find it a suitable vengeance, reviving a place destroyed by the Yankees. She could use her talent to make him a home, someplace lovely for him to come back to. And she'd be safe. She'd be protected. She'd be far away from the eyes of the city, far away from the war on the plains, far away from Senator Parker, and far away from her Indian husband.

They held the first dinner in the Decatur, one of the old federal-style mansions primarily noted for its elegant ballroom. As she looked down on the crowd from the head table, tenderness bloomed in Elizabeth's bosom. Ryerson began his speech with a story about her. He regaled the crowd with a tale—short, gruff, witty, and pointed—about how his formerly slave-owning wife had saved a group of colored troopers. He didn't dwell on her past or her hatred. Rather, he made the anecdote sentimental, just romantic enough to remind his war-weary listeners that the late war had been fought for a reason, and making it clear, without betraying the army, that freedom for Negroes ought to involve a substantial commitment to improving their lives.

As Ryerson outlined his troopers' needs, Elizabeth studied the audience below them. Proudly ensconced next to her husband, she had a good view of the exquisite throng. And they had a good view of her. The guests didn't quite stare. They were too schooled for that. Senator Parker guarded one elbow. Ryerson defended the other. Both men glared bluntly at gazes that lingered, giving Elizabeth a rare chance to watch others.

Few people moved. The audience listened intently, evidently transfixed by Ryerson's speech. Their attentiveness surprised her a little, for Ryerson's talk seemed straightforward to her. But these people were different, more formal than any she'd known before. The men were decked out in black tuxedos, the women more exquisite still. The princess-style dress she and Mary had sewn at Fort Leavenworth hardly rated a comment out here. Paris, it seems, had had the same thought. Elizabeth's daring, original outfit had accidentally come into fashion, a fact no westerner knew and every Washington dame took for granted.

As Elizabeth glanced down at the sea of rapt faces, Ryerson ended his speech with a mention of Lincoln. For the space of a heartbeat, the audience fell silent. One person clapped, then another. On a swell of sound, the crowd surged to its feet. Elizabeth stood, clapping along.

Senator Parker rose, leaned over to her, and whispered beneath the crescendo, "You know, your husband could have the late president's job."

Elizabeth turned to the cool, dignified man at her side. She lifted her hands a little bit higher, so he could see she had joined the applause. "Don't you think that a bit ambitious?"

"No, not at all. It will take a few years, but he's young enough for it." The candlelight gleamed off the sinuous waves of his hair. "First will be Grant. Then General Sherman, though old Billy says he doesn't want it. We'll see, though. We'll see. I think his modesty's overrated. After those two, the race is a toss-up. Ryerson could make the Senate, no question. He's a talented speaker. Look how they love him. And he handles power better than most."

Ryerson sat down at the height of his ovation, stern, then amused, then at last beseeching, glaring at his melting sorbet as if to say, "Leave off the clapping and let a simple soldier enjoy his dessert." The applause died off into laughter, then the pleasant tinkle of metal on glass, as those who'd not eaten during his speech cooled their tongues on the raspberry ice.

The senator's speech chilled Elizabeth's heart. Shyly she glanced at her husband. Parker's comments made sense. During the speech, Ryerson had commanded the room, blunt, good-humored, straightforward, totally at ease in this setting. "It seems so strange," she said wonderingly. "At Fort Leavenworth he was so hated."

"His troop isn't popular there?" Parker had an expressive voice, the kind she'd expect in a politician. She wanted to ignore his implication, but manners dictated a polite rejoinder.

"No, not at all." She sat down in her chair, intent on attending her own dessert. "And to make matters worse, his raids offended the regular soldiers. They didn't think them gentlemanly."

"That's not so peculiar." The senator took his seat with a flourish. "Kansas bled, but not like this city. Richmond's less than a hundred miles away. It's not only that men fought their brothers. When General Lee tried to invade us, half the government buildings were used for the wounded. Every person who lives here, from the lowest clerk to the mightiest general, had a vivid, personal experience with war. Ryerson fought back, and with a vengeance. Wait till he burns a few Indians out. He'll be a hero at Fort Leavenworth."

"I suppose." Elizabeth poked at her food, wishing that Parker would just go away. His comments made her sick to her stomach. She glanced at her husband. Ryerson sat, straight-backed as usual, his crimson sash slashing across his chest. He scanned the room with a casual gaze that subtly disguised his pride and his interest. Pressure flared in Elizabeth's bosom. She loved him so much. She found it hard to think of his past.

"And, of course, it helps that the Negroes love him."

"Yes, the troopers adore him," she answered, without looking at the senator.

"I don't mean that handful. I mean the whole race." Parker leaned closer, lowering his voice to a judicious whisper. "Half of them think he's Moses himself."

She turned at that comment. Ryerson had started out of his chair, as if he'd seen something surprising. She wanted to watch him, but Parker's remark drew her away. "I beg your pardon?"

The old senator picked up his spoon, a wily look in his eye. "They're an odd people. Religious, you know. They think of their freedom in terms of the Bible." He swirled the red ice in its frosted glass, then licked the dessert spoon discreetly. "Lincoln might have signed the proclamation that freed them, but it was Billy Sherman who roared through the South. And Ryerson helped." He flicked the ice cream onto his tongue. "Nobody liked burning those plantations, all those lovely white homes reduced to ashes. Nobody, that is, except the Negro. The slaves didn't regret them. They thought of those raids as divine retribution."

Ryerson waded into the crowd, evidently seeing someone he knew. Elizabeth wished she could go with him. She didn't like Senator Parker. She regretted the fact that he'd lost his daughter, but he'd terrified her with his remarks. He seemed so cold. Not bitter, exactly, but contemptuous of Ryerson's fame, as if having financed Ryerson's Riders, their wartime deeds had counted for nothing. Furthermore, Elizabeth didn't trust him. The senator's smile did not reach his eyes. Elizabeth didn't quite know what he wanted, but he clearly had some purpose in mind. She slanted a glance at the dark-suited politician beside her, then at her husband's indigo tunic as he worked his way through the admiring crowd. Suddenly the whole conversation fell into place. "Well, the Negro can't make him president."

"You think not? They've been given the vote. They're one-sixth of the U.S. population. I guarantee you, my new Mrs. Major, there's not one man in the Senate who wouldn't give his right arm for that kind of power."

"Yes. Well. They had their chance." Elizabeth spoke quietly. "But I doubt very much that you mean what you say. And you'd take it back if you saw his hands."

"I'm sorry?" Parker lay down his spoon.

She was determined to get away from the man. She

wanted to shout, but she stifled the impulse, restrained by
the vestige of civilized manners. She saw now what Ryerson hated. Beneath the neatly pressed lapels of that suit
beat a heart as cold as the most vicious slave trader's, and
with a purpose not so very different. Ryerson and his
troopers meant nothing to Parker, except a chance to sway
some voters. Elizabeth stood, keeping her voice under control. "You picked a bad image. Every man in the Senate
could have given an arm. Look at Stonewall Jackson—and
Hood—and even your General Howard. The major must
have come close enough, if you judge by the scars he car-
ries. He deserves the Senate more than most of the men in
it, but I don't think he's cut out for the job."

"He might be if he had the right wife."

Elizabeth crumpled her napkin, tossing it lightly on the
table. Ryerson reached a tall, handsome man with wavy
brown hair and an arrogant bearing. She couldn't read her
husband's expression, but his back had gone rigid. He saluted the stranger, who returned the gesture, even though
he wore civilian clothing. Elizabeth didn't know who the
tall man was, but his demeanor disturbed her, and she suddenly wanted to go to her husband. "Yes, well, he doesn't
have the right wife."

"How did I know that?" The senator's tone caught her
attention.

Elizabeth balled her hands, stifling the impulse to touch
her cheekbones. She faced the portly, smooth-faced senator, making a great effort to keep her voice civil. "I'm sure
I'm a great disappointment to you, but I don't have the
impression your plans make him happy. And that's what I
want for my husband—happiness, peace, maybe a family."

"Does he enjoy the army?"

"Maybe not the army, exactly, but he likes his troop."

"And you?" Candlelight played on the senator's face.

He looked younger than she supposed he should have, as if life itself had not marked him deeply. "I read your comments. It seems pretty awkward, a Southern belle and Indian-lover married to a great Yankee raider."

"We'll work it out." Elizabeth tried to find Ryerson again, but he and the soldier had disappeared. She moved to the end of the table, intent on finding her husband.

"How?" The senator stood, following her smoothly. "With Helen's money?"

"I don't know what you're talking about."

She held out her hand. Polite as always, Parker helped her off the dais. "She left him quite wealthy. Didn't you know that?"

"No," she said tersely.

As she descended, the strangers fell back. Ryerson's story had made her appealing, but it would take more than a mere anecdote to make this glittering throng truly friendly. Anxiously she searched for her husband. She felt something was wrong, and not just with Parker. It wasn't like James to leave her alone. People ebbed in her wake as she looked for the familiar slender blue figure.

Parker kept after her, as if he still wanted something from her. Holding her elbow, he guided her toward the far side of the room. "No. I don't suppose that you knew. He's never touched Helen's money. He's a strange man, your husband. He didn't deserve my daughter." He pointed out Ryerson, still with the stranger, and veered abruptly in his direction. "But I suppose in you he's got his comeuppance."

THIRTEEN

RYERSON SCOWLED AS THE SENATOR STEERED ELIZABETH through the crowd. Libbie was clearly unhappy, but the veteran politician worked the room with the grace of a master. He touched the shoulders of the men he met and kissed the hands of most of the ladies. Libbie, meanwhile, looked lost and distressed, as if she wished to be in some other place. Ryerson would have gone to her aid, but he disliked leaving Nathaniel Greenstreet. After four years of hatred, he yearned to make peace with his former comrade. So Ryerson stayed, barely listening to his old friend's narration, as the senator cruised from one influential confidant to another. And Libbie, lovely in emerald and visibly anxious, remained politely affixed to the crook of his elbow. It took half a waltz for the old politician to reach the two men. When he did, he smiled politely and abandoned his charge a little more quickly than good manners dictated. Elizabeth, though, seemed glad to leave him. She stepped forward, a sunny smile transforming her face. Ryerson reached for her arm. Greenstreet, alert as always, slipped in front of Libbie.

Taking her hand, the tall planter bowed gracefully. "Why, Major, you've denied me the pleasure of meeting your missus."

Ryerson caught the surprise in her eyes, the slight shock upon hearing the Mississippi-born soldier's accent. Still, she recovered quite well, extending her hand and returning the courtesy. "Sir, you have me at a disadvantage."

"Colonel Greenstreet." Ryerson almost snarled out the name. He didn't quite know what made him do it. He'd once loved his former schoolmate. Unfortunately a few of Greenstreet's wartime strategies rubbed Ryerson raw, and none more so than his ploy of granting no quarter to former slaves who fought with the Yankees. As the lanky soldier took Elizabeth's hand, Ryerson convinced himself that the knot in his stomach was only the rightful human response of a fair-minded man to a reputed monster, an ironic reaction considering his own tarnished image, but he preferred that thought to the one that niggled.

Soon he'd be leaving his Libbie.

He found himself jealous. The emotion surprised him, for he'd never been possessive with Helen. His former wife had been far too ambitious to jeopardize her position for something as trivial as love or affection. Libbie, however, was different. She followed her heart. Though she didn't seem fickle, the sight of Greenstreet taking her fingers left a roiling sensation in Ryerson's stomach. Lost in his own sense of bemusement, it took him a minute to register the confusion on Libbie's face. Catching himself, he nodded in his new wife's direction. "Colonel Greenstreet, let me introduce my new wife, the former Mrs. Elizabeth Wheaton."

Greenstreet feathered a kiss over Elizabeth's glove. "Not of the Wheatons of Saint James County?"

Elizabeth colored. For a brief instant, she seemed female and helpless, the opposite of Ryerson's picture of her. But she quickly revived, lifting her gaze up to meet Greenstreet's assessment. "That was my home, though long ago, to be honest."

"I should say so." Greenstreet smiled, Southern and gallant. To Ryerson's discomfort, he kept his gaze fixed on Libbie's bosom and ran his gloved thumb over her knuckles. The strains of a waltz floated out of the corner. Elizabeth looked nervous and lovely, a scoop neckline accenting one of her better features. For the first time Ryerson regretted her talent. Her dressmaking skills had made her quite stunning, a fact Greenstreet seemed quite aware of. "That's my home, also. I always said the major was clever, but this is his most diabolical move—stealing a belle from under my nose."

Elizabeth seemed taken aback. She rustled the drapery of her satin skirt. Ryerson thought she wanted her hand free, but Greenstreet still held it, pinning her with a grin.

She frowned. "I'm sure he meant no personal insult."

"Don't be so certain of that." He arched one eyebrow in Ryerson's direction. "The major and I go back a long way."

"I know, but—"

"You do?" Greenstreet tucked Elizabeth's hand in his elbow, leading her smoothly toward the dance floor. "He's mentioned my name?"

"Of course." She threw Ryerson a bewildered look. He nodded curtly for her to continue. He refused to be rude. If Greenstreet wanted to dance with his lady, he'd let her. He trusted Libbie. He hoped.

"Well." Greenstreet took Elizabeth in his arms and posed her at the edge of the dance floor. "I truly am flattered and I can't miss my chance. You must tell me what my old friend told you."

"I'm sorry—"

"No, no." He drew her closer. He moved in a supple glissade, not close enough to offend outright, but far more

seductive than good taste dictated. With a raffish glance in
Ryerson's direction, he danced her toward the room's center. "I won't brook objection." He spoke in a low voice that
carried. "Surely you haven't been married so long as to
favor a Yankee over a long-lost cousin?"

Elizabeth doubted they were cousins. As Greenstreet
guided her over the dance floor, she tried to recall what
she knew about him. Given the complex tangle of her Saint
James relations, she couldn't entirely dismiss his claim.
Back home, everyone married everyone else, and anyone
who grew up in Saint James County might very well be a
shirttail relation.

Elizabeth had seen Greenstreet as a child. Even as a girl
she'd thought him pretty, and he'd grown into a glorious
man. High-cheekboned and proud, with regular features
and an imperious carriage, he seemed every inch the gentleman farmer. Elizabeth had to push herself to remember
that, just like her husband, this man had spent four years
as a soldier.

"So, did the major mention me often?" He led from the
waist with his hand on her back, just the way boys were
taught in cotillion. She found him, like Ryerson, strong and
controlling, but a little more forceful than what was really
required.

"Not often." Had she been more fragile she would have
felt faint. People didn't stare here, but she still felt the
tension in the slanting glances and murmured reactions.
The tattoos made her strange, but dancing with Greenstreet sparked even more interest. Brilliant, daring, self-
taught, and creative, Greenstreet had been the sole
Southern colonel to thwart Ryerson's Riders consistently.
During the war, their rivalry had been famous, two former
schoolmates now sworn enemies. They'd fought many a

battle in Mississippi. What Elizabeth knew, and the spectators didn't, was the price of those victories to James Ryerson. She tightened her fingers over Greenstreet's shoulder.
"On the way here, he told me some stories."

"What did he say?"

Greenstreet smelled of bay rum, and she wondered if all
officers wore it. "I really can't say." She stiffened, hoping
to convey her sense of distance. She wasn't sure Ryerson
still liked him, though they'd been close enough at one
time. Almost more than any other person, Ryerson had
spoken of Greenstreet on the train. "He told me some
things that happened between you."

"Like what?" He squeezed tighter, but his gloved hands
did not warm her. "Surely these stories can't be so awful?"

She flushed. There must have been two hundred dancers, and the press of their bodies made the room stifling.
"No, they weren't awful at all."

"Then tell me."

"Well . . ." The raspberry taste in her mouth had
turned sour. She wanted to please James Ryerson, but she
did not really like this Southern-born planter. There was
something insincere in his touch, a coldness of heart beneath the grace. He exuded no warmth or genuine feeling,
excepting perhaps contempt for her husband. Worse, he
seemed at home in this place. Not at ease, but at home,
which was different. His gaze roved the room, as if he were
eager to make a connection with every strange face and
elegant lady. Like Parker, his smile did not reach his eyes.
He flashed his grin a little too often and seemed to seek a
bit of excitement before he returned his attention to her.
She did her best to grin bravely. "You were best friends at
Dartmouth."

"That's true." He executed a stylish turn. His velvet la-
pel brushed Elizabeth's cheek. "And did he say why?"

"You hated to study. He hated to ride."

"And?"

"He did your term papers, in return for which you served as his driver."

"And later? Did he tell you war stories?"

"Yes."

She felt him tense, though his smile never faded. "What did he say?"

She'd worn a corset, which she regretted now. He kept up a punishing pace, and she could have used the extra breath. "He thought he'd killed you at Shiloh."

"Is he sorry he didn't?" he asked quietly.

"No, I don't think so, though you surely surprised him that time after Corinth."

He grinned, as if she'd given him something special. "So he told you rather a lot about me?"

"Yes, I suppose."

She looked for her husband. A group of young ladies circled around him. A pretty blonde plucked at his sleeve, and a shorter brunette offered her elbow. He seemed embarrassed and sincerely flattered by the fluttering eyelashes and feminine sighs. Oddly, Elizabeth didn't feel jealous. She'd seen so much of the pain the war had caused him that she couldn't resent seeing him pleased.

"And you, how did you come to marry the great Yankee vandal?" Greenstreet had a soft Southern voice, not truly cultured, but slow and graceful, the product of breeding but not education.

"He burned my plantation."

He turned her again, swooping her smoothly away from her husband. The room swirled around her. She lost sight of the slender, beloved figure. As she twisted to find him, she caught sight of Greenstreet's dark eyes, moody, assessing, for a moment unveiled.

He leaned forward and lowered his voice. "I already know he destroyed your home."

She shot him a questioning look. They might have been far-distant cousins, but he had no reason to know about her plantation.

"I fought him for every inch of that county." He pitched his voice beneath the strains of the waltz. "Now they're building a statue to my former friend, and I've become an outcast and traitor." Slipping his hand from her shoulder, he straightened the knot of his perfectly tied four-in-hand. "And worse"—he attempted a grin—"he's snatched up the county's prettiest woman."

A chill ran down Elizabeth's spine. She'd worried about this since she married her husband—how she'd feel if she met a neighbor, how she'd explain how much she'd changed. His tone made her feel weak in the knees, and she stifled an impulse to rest her head on his shoulder. Suddenly the purpose of his questions fell into place. "Did he burn your home, too?"

"Of course."

"And now you think I can help you?"

"Not really. The major is nothing if not very thorough. I'm sure he has his own agenda. You're quite a great beauty beneath those tattoos. I'm sure he thinks you'll be an asset."

"An asset to what?"

"To his political ambitions." He danced without passion, his cadence perfect, but without the little surprises that signal a dancer's true feeling for music. "I knew him well before the war. He had no particular feelings for Negroes. Now he's their champion. It's not enough that he helped free them. He's trying to make them equal to whites."

"He's trying to be fair. He's got friends among them."

"Ah, yes. And he just happened to marry a Southern

woman. You don't think it's an accident, do you? One way or another, he has some appeal to every faction."

"I certainly do. I don't know where you get the idea, but the major is strictly a soldier. He has no ambition for political office—and certainly not what you suggest."

"And what about you? Surely you haven't abandoned your namesake?"

Elizabeth studied his impassive expression. His question puzzled. She could have sworn he referred to Lysistrata, but she couldn't imagine how he knew of her alter ego. She wanted to ask, but stifled the impulse. If Greenstreet had guessed her identity, it would be far better for her to figure his game out on her own.

"I'm sure my aunt would have approved." She referred to her father's sister, long dead, the lady for whom she'd been named as a baby.

"I did not refer only to dear Aunt Bessie."

Elizabeth started, thrown both by the fact that he knew Aunt Elizabeth's nickname and by his comment's possible double meaning.

He pulled her tight, speaking so near that his hot breath burned her earlobe. "Surely Saint James County still claims some of your heart?"

Elizabeth fell silent. In Washington it was hard to remember why she'd agreed to marry the major. She loved him, of course, but she made a poor enough helpmeet for a soldier. She'd never make a political wife. Parker was right. She had no exalted ambitions. She wanted a home someplace on the prairie, with a stalwart husband and a yard full of children. Life with Ryerson might not fit that description exactly, but it came closer at Fort Leavenworth.

Washington, however, was totally different. Ryerson claimed he did not like politics, but his actions did not match his words. Clearly he relished his fame, but not for the reasons Parker would have wished. Her raider had no use for power, except insofar as it would help his troopers. Public acceptance had a different meaning to her scrupulous husband. It worked like a balm on his conscience. He got to remember he was a hero and why he'd done such terrible deeds.

And in the faces of those simpering girls, Elizabeth had to face some terrible facts. There were, after all, two sides to this conflict. In destroying her home, he'd saved other women. Maybe he didn't need her forgiveness. Perhaps it would have been better to have married a woman who looked up to him as a hero. She, in her arrogant smugness, had become the last thing he needed, the living face of a receding past, a persistent reminder of deeds best left unexamined.

"Do you think he'd make a good politician?" she asked Greenstreet seriously.

"Why do you ask?" Greenstreet had a malevolent gaze, dark, penetrating, the kind that missed nothing. He focused it now on Elizabeth's eyes.

She faced him head-on and let him interpret her feelings. "The senator spoke on that subject to me. He thinks James could have a seat in the Senate."

"Your husband could have a good deal more than that, especially if he kills some Indians. It would take more than the marriage to win over the South, but if he has the West he doesn't really need us. Now that they've given the vote to the Negro, your husband's become a powerful man."

She looked incredulously at him. "You think he married me to get votes?"

"No, my dear, I didn't say that. I told you before. Beneath those tattoos you're a very great beauty, but the major has some unfinished business, and I strongly suspect that your background will help him."

* * *

She came to bed in absolute silence. Ryerson didn't know what had happened, but the dinner had sobered his Libbie. During Greenstreet's dance she'd seemed shadowed and sad, and she clearly disliked Senator Parker. She hadn't exactly asked to leave early, but she seemed so downcast, so bewildered and wary, that he'd brought her home as soon as he could, holding her close in the depths of the carriage, trying to think of something to say. She'd undressed quietly and put on a nightgown, the first time she'd donned one in the course of their marriage. She slipped softly into the bed and swathed the sheet over her bosom.

"Libbie." He stripped out of his clothes, leaving his uniform in a heap on the floor. "What are you thinking?"

"Oh, nothing." She spoke in a faraway voice that completely belied the content of her answer.

He leaned over her huddling figure and tried to think of a way to cheer her. Climbing into the bed, he ducked under the sheets and spooned her up to his chest. "Come on, Libbie, tell me about it. You're the one who preaches we have to talk."

He'd come to bed hard, but he tried to ignore it. He found the nightgown extremely erotic. Full nakedness would have been better. He'd gotten used to her fully nude body, but the gown came as a challenge. The soft material teased his nerve endings, inviting him to explore this new dimension—soft skin against satin nightgown.

"Come on." He jiggled her arm. "Tell me what happened? Did Parker spook you, or was it Greenstreet?"

She turned onto her back, her nipples poking from beneath the soft satin. His fingers itched to touch them, but he kept his hands still.

"Do you want to kill Indians?" she asked suddenly.

The question doused his ardor quite thoroughly. He knew there were men who reveled in blood lust, but he'd never quite been one of them. Bolting out of the bed, he moved to his trunk. "I never like killing. I do what I have to. What makes you ask a question like that?"

"The senator said you could get votes by killing."

"Undoubtedly true, but I don't want to."

"What?" She sat straight upright, cuddling the sheets close to her bosom. "You don't deny it? Killing Indians would help your political standing?"

He opened the lid of his traveling trunk, rifled through his belongings, and pulled out a silver flask. "Now, Libbie, hold onto your temper." Closing the lid, he sat down on top. It seemed barbaric, drinking stark naked, but he had a sneaking suspicion it was going to be a very long night. "I have no political standing, nor do I want it. But I know what he's talking about. From Julius Caesar down through Andrew Jackson, there's been many a soldier who's turned politician. I'd be a fool or a liar to deny that fact."

He took a long swig of his drink. The whiskey's fire burned down his throat, heating his chest and temporarily shutting off breath. She watched him with wary eyes. Wetting her lips, she held out her hand for the flask. Though he wasn't quite sure she should be drinking, he crossed to the bed and sat down next to her.

"Here." He gave her the container, the flat silver kind a gentleman carried. She tasted it briefly, then blew out a huff, evidently unused to drinking her whiskey straight. Clearing her throat, she squared her shoulders, and the sheets slipped to reveal her cleavage. "Are you sure you don't want a seat in the Senate?"

"I'm sure, absolutely."

The line of her spine relaxed a little. She took a second

small sip of the whiskey. "Even if power meant helping the Negro?"

He ran his hand over her back. The nightgown felt slippery against his palm, cool, then finally warming as he rubbed her lightly. " 'Helping the Negro' is much too abstract a notion for me. I've got my troopers. My duty's to them. I'd kill anyone who threatened my men, but I'd never wage war for personal gain."

"Spoken like a proper soldier." She shrugged off his touch. Scrambling forward, she turned, settling cross-legged among the sheets. Gaslight bathed her dark eyes in shadows, glinting blue off the silver as she returned the flask. "Shoot the enemy before he shoots me."

He took back the decanter. Her touch had warmed the cool metal slightly. He put his lips on the neck, thinking to drink, but the taste of her stopped him, that and the lingering warmth of her lips. With a curse to himself, he set down the bottle and clamped his mouth shut. Reaching forward, he captured her hand and pulled it firmly into his lap. "Libbie, I love you." He spoke through clenched teeth, barely in control of his temper. "I don't want to lose you, but war isn't played by civilized rules. It reduces all these complex, well-mannered notions to the simple logic of a schoolboy fight. I sympathize with your Indian friends, but if I met them in battle, I'd try to beat them."

She stared long and hard at their intertwined fingers. She seemed to be thinking, but no interior war marred her pretty face. A thick sweep of hair draped over her shoulder. He wanted to push it back from her cheekbones, but he wasn't sure she'd welcome his touch. Without warning, she flipped back a curl, then squeezed his fingers tightly in hers. "Speaking of conquering your friends in battle, how did it feel to see your friend, Colonel Greenstreet?"

The question surprised him. Of all the possible subjects

that could have absorbed her, that was the one he least expected. "I don't know." He plucked the flask from between his knees. Though the whiskey had already relaxed his senses, he needed to blunt more than perception. He craved escape from his emotions. "I don't know." He took another small swig. She held his hand lightly, still sitting cross-legged beside him. Her patience amazed him. He knew that about her by now. She had her own methods. A master tactician in her own right, she pressed with inflections, questions, and silence—parrying, thrusting, and feeling him out, then leaving him to find his own answers. Her rectitude created more tension than straightforward curiosity would have. He took a swift swig from his flask and turned his thoughts inward. "I don't know. It was hard, seeing a friend I'd defeated."

She took a slight shivery breath and slipped the bottle from him. "Do you still feel a kinship with him?"

"I'm not sure." As she drank, her thigh brushed his lightly. He felt himself quicken with interest. He wasn't sure he liked his reaction, but the afterglow of the drink had made him mellow, and he wanted her in spite of their quarrel. Leaning back on one elbow, he flicked the sheet over his bottom half. "I've something in common with any soldier, but Nathaniel, he's different from most of the others."

"Because you once loved him?"

"Maybe. It's hard to explain."

She stared into the silver, as if seeking courage, though he couldn't quite imagine what monster she saw there. "He's not in the army. Maybe that makes him seem distant."

"No." He toyed with the lace of her nightgown. He thought it an astonishing notion, that something so fragile could protect a woman. "That's the price of betrayal. I feel sorry for men in his position. The war ruined them for civilian life, but the Union army won't take them, and their own army has been disbanded."

"So what is he doing?"

"Planting, I think. Trying to worm his way into power."

She took a deep gulp of the whiskey. His spirits rose, then on second thought sank. He didn't know how whiskey affected this woman. She might be receptive. Then again, she might sleep.

With a heavy sigh, she let her arm drop. "But you'd like him better if he was a soldier?"

"I didn't say that." He leaned back on the mahogany headboard. "He was, in his day, my toughest opponent. Not to mention our former friendship. I have to respect both those characteristics. Still, it disturbs me to see him. I no longer love him. In fact, I think I might even be jealous."

"Really?" She reached over, hands shaky, and stoppered the whiskey. Her mood seemed to have brightened. She leaned into his chest. Snuggling closer, she gazed down, unfocused, and brushed her fingers over the cotton, lightly skimming the length of his shaft. He stifled a sharp intake of breath. No woman, not even Helen, had ever been quite so playful in bed. He would have been shocked, except her smile—easy, sweet, and completely relaxed—convinced him that her little erotic surprises were strictly the product of talent. She ignored his reaction completely and continued her teasing, delicious movement. Soft waves of delight crested through him. He sank his head back into the pillow.

She sighed and tucked her head next to his shoulder and skimmed her hand over his stomach and chest. "Have you ever thought about what you would do if you weren't in the army?"

"No." Waves of delight pounded through him. The nightgown piqued an immoderate interest. Satin on satin, the gown covered her breasts, its exquisite silk a pale reflection of the warmth, texture, and softness beneath, wonderfully shaped and made to suckle, perfect for pleasure, perfect for babies—surely one of nature's perfect creations.

"Never?" Her voice had an edge, but he ignored it.

"Never." With a sigh of delight, he pulled her roughly against his chest. "The army's my life."

Sometime in the last three weeks of lovemaking, she'd learned to interpret more than his thoughts. Without any prompting, she lifted her torso. In a motion any kitten would envy, she stroked her nipples over his chest. A bolt of pure pleasure flashed through him.

She bent her head slightly. Her curls tumbled down, creating a veil of fire-laced satin. "You've never thought you might leave your troop?"

"No, not since Shiloh . . . or maybe Vicksburg." He wished she'd shut up. He found it hard to answer these questions while distracted by her feathery touch. Like a symphony of erotic sensation, layers of silk played over his muscles. "I don't know when it happened, but at some point in time I became too hardened for my former life."

She rose up on her knees and tilted backward, straddling him in wanton abandon, naked as Eve beneath the satin. "How about going forward?"

"To what?"

"I don't know." She tugged on a slender pink ribbon. Her nightgown fell open. She smiled for the space of one heartbeat, then shrugged the gown in a pool to her waist, crossed her wrists, and lifted her hair off the nape of her neck. A cool breeze ruffled her tendrils. He thought it a glorious, sensual effect which she ruined completely with her next sentence. "You could try farming, maybe?"

He choked. He did not want to hurt her, but he couldn't help his astonished reaction. He paused for a moment, then regained his breath. "No, I don't think so," he said quietly.

Her arms dropped, as if she'd been shot. "Why not?"

"I don't come from a farm family."

"You couldn't try it?"

"No," he said firmly.

"But not the Senate," she said in the same tone of voice.

"No, not the Senate, not that. Absolutely."

Elizabeth wasn't sure she believed him. Though Ryerson never again spoke of the Senate, as the day of the unveiling approached, several senators spoke to him about it. At every single dinner or dance, some distinguished man found his way to them and tried to promote the idea that Ryerson should run for political office. The Fourteenth Amendment had passed. The Negro had been given the vote. With Elizabeth as a wife, he could probably have a Southerner's seat. The Negroes would love him because of the troopers, and if, meantime, he'd kill a few Indians, he'd be a hero to the rest of the nation. Somewhere down the road he'd have immense power, and there'd be no reason to limit his dreams to a mere stint in the United States Senate.

Elizabeth fought back every time this was mentioned, pointing out to powerful men that her husband had no taste for their life. She found it increasingly hard to hold her temper as soft old men with silvery temples discussed her husband's wartime record as if his fierce deeds were total abstractions, completely forgetting they'd cost men their lives, not to mention the families, women and children, who for better or worse had been sacrificed.

Even at dinner with Ely Parker, the Indian general brought up the idea. Good men were needed, he'd pointed out, to rebuild the country on a new basis. Men who'd treat the Negroes as equals and help to keep the peace with the Indian.

Elizabeth had agreed with those sentiments, but she still didn't think politics suited her husband. He was too straightforward for all this maneuvering, too blunt for proper caution. Even as she spoke the words to the general, she had the uneasy feeling that they were lies.

She knew her husband too well, and as they appeared at their final dinner, she tightened her grip on Ryerson's elbow and prayed devoutly for their future together. To all appearances, he loved this life. He walked into the hall, gracious and resplendent, squiring her with the ease of a courtier. The crowds ignored the tattoos on her face, and she knew in her heart how he had done that. Ryerson treated her with such perfect manners that everyone followed his lead. Even strangers no longer stared, and anyone who claimed a friendship addressed her with strict courtesy. To her shock and surprise, he'd accomplished exactly the object he'd promised. He'd created a refuge simply with his presence. He created a peace in the midst of the city, and the closer he came to that goal, the more she wanted to weep. Much as she loved him, she couldn't reconcile herself to this life.

As Ryerson swept her into the drawing room of another of Washington's old federal-style mansions, she watched the glittering crowd. Oh, she liked certain parts of this life. She'd never get over the dresses, the garments designed by artists in cloth. She'd not seen the like as a girl, the little touches, the exquisite details that marked really beautiful dressing. And she liked some of the people. Ryerson had some remarkable friends, and to her surprise she found most of them pleasant and endearingly human. She met General Grant, a shy little man who liked drinking. To Ryerson's chagrin, they did not get to see Sherman, but she gathered in their round of parties that old Tecumseh had been fond of her husband, and Ryerson, in turn, adored the old man. She liked General Howard, handsome enough, though missing one arm, but better humored than his staid reputation suggested. His disfigurement created an unspoken bond, and she'd helped him eat at one of the dinners. As she cut up his meat, she admired his courage. His losses were far more serious than hers, yet they didn't seem to have made him bitter. For all the tattoos' inconvenience, her markings had never made her dependent, nor had they kept her from living a normal life, except for her self-imposed isolation. Watching the general eat with one hand, she felt like the man in Aesop's fable who cried because he had no shoes until he met someone without any feet, and she wondered at the irony of it, that a Yankee general would give her a sense of perspective from which to better judge the pain of her past.

Still, she missed her old life. She wondered constantly about the troopers and even more about the Indian children. Hancock's war, the newspapers called it, after the elderly general who pursued the Cheyenne in fits and starts over wildly untamed reaches of prairie. Near as she could tell from the tabloid accounts, he had not done much damage, but she knew from first-hand experience how much suffering even the chase would cause. She wondered how much her friends needed help and what Sleeps With Eagle would say when he found out she'd married a Yankee soldier. And finally, most perversely perhaps, gorgeous dresses and spectacular buildings couldn't compete with the beauty of vivid blue sky or wide-open prairie, or even the delicate, fragile appeal of a butterfly weed or prairie bluebonnet. She might make new friends, but even the peace Ryerson had won in the city couldn't appease the place in her heart left by a hunger for wildness and beauty and silent communion with sweet prairie breezes.

As they entered the ballroom, she saw none of these new friends, however. Amidst the resplendent soldiers, tuxedoed civilians, and ballgown-draped ladies, she caught sight of only one familiar face—a tall honey-blond with high cheekbones, too elegant to be a soldier, moving with unmistakable grace. Greenstreet. Almost as soon as they entered, he bowed out of the circle of chattering men and drifted lazily in her direction.

She handed her shawl to a waiting attendant, glancing in her husband's direction. "Perhaps we could be seated." She caught the gleam in Ryerson's eye, the combative look that preceded his temper.

"Are you frightened of him?" He nodded briefly at Greenstreet.

"No, not at all." She kept her gaze forward, her chin slightly raised. "I just didn't know how you felt about him."

"I would still like to be friends," Ryerson said curtly, "though I'm not certain why." Without looking behind, he shrugged out of his greatcoat and let the valet take it. He guided her in a half circle, unobtrusively moving her toward the speaker's dais. Greenstreet followed their progress. Without being rude or staring overtly, he wandered from person to person as if he had no particular purpose. But Elizabeth knew—Ryerson, too—that his pattern of movement mirrored their own.

Ryerson frowned, gripping her elbow. "He likes you well enough."

"I'm afraid he does." She lifted her skirts, preparing to mount the steps to the head table, when Ryerson snared her, pulling her back. Before she could express the slightest opinion, he swept her into his arms and toward the room's middle. A string quartet had been tucked in a corner, its placement indicating quite clearly that the music was meant for background, not dancing.

The four musicians ignored their fate. Three dark, slender men and one small, blond, birdlike woman poured their hearts into a waltz. Two violas, a violin, and a cello strained to produce a shocking Strauss waltz. Though no other couples were dancing, Ryerson seemed to make it his business to show the crowd—or at least the musicians— that in that cold room at least one man heard their song.

He led her into the center of the drawing room. Hand snugged in the small of her back, Ryerson bent himself toward her, focused, intense, and outrageously graceful, his feet tracing the steps while he pressed her close to his chest. For all he grumbled about them, the boots did not interfere with his movement. Elizabeth followed strictly by instinct, amazed by the singular fact that for all his pride, stiffness, and posture, he danced with a supple, muscular balance that perfectly matched the pulse of the waltz. The crowd of spectators parted, then formed themselves in an approving circle. No one else took up a partner. They simply watched, surprised and entranced by the infamous soldier and his notorious lady.

She kept her hand on his shoulder, careful not to muss his gold epaulet. "Do you mind that he likes me?"

"Yes," Ryerson said roughly.

"Do you want me to snub him?"

"No." He dipped, then turned her quickly. The move made her dizzy, and the room swirled around her. She caught a brief glimpse of Greenstreet, circling warily at the edge of the crowd, then he disappeared in an impression of color—mauve, pink, and lilac, the hues that ruled this season's fashions. "At some point I have to trust you. I made a

fool of myself out there on the prairie. I never repeat a
stupid mistake. Besides, I want to be decent. I disagree
with Nathaniel's choices, but he and I shared a fellowship
once. I'd prefer to think I can still treat him fairly."

"Well," she whispered as she breathed in the clove-
scented bay rum, made sharper, more spicy, by the heat of
the dance, "if it's any help, he still seems to like you. At
least, he asked me a lot of questions about you."

He twirled her again. She caught sight of Greenstreet,
his silent gray eyes watching them closely. She closed her
fist around Ryerson's fingers.

Ryerson squeezed, then pulled her closer. His grizzled
stubble brushed the skin of her forehead. "Libbie, I appreciate that you're trying to help me. I know you don't much
like this place."

The patterned floor seemed to ripple beneath them. She
shut her eyes and let him guide her, swaying softly in time
to the music. It distressed her slightly that she'd revealed
her unhappiness, but she liked the fact that he'd noticed.
Pressing her cheek to his chest, she lowered her voice. "Do
my prejudices show quite so much?"

"Ah, Libbie, you wear your heart on your face."

One hand flew to her cheekbone.

"No, not those, foolish woman." Ryerson kissed the top
of her head. "Just your expression. You couldn't lie if you
tried. All these vapid people must wear on your patience."

She shrugged. "They're people—"

"You like most of them, don't you?" He brushed his
calloused thumb over her scars.

"Yes."

"You're a good woman; you know that?" He glanced at
her neckline, brazen enough, but he compounded his gaffe
by blowing a soft kiss on her earlobe. "You deserve so
much better than I can give you."

To her absolute horror, her whole body responded. A warm flush of desire rushed to her face. Her nipples stood up. She got weak in the knees and hot in unladylike places. "This life is fine." She didn't dare look at the crowd. She thought it a good thing they were truly married, for the kiss would create scandal enough. "I don't want anything more."

"I know. But you should have better. I burned your home."

Her gaze snapped toward his. They hadn't discussed this subject in ages.

"I'm going to replace it." He met her look with one of his own, calm, unperturbed, and deadly serious. "I understand now where I failed Helen. I promise you, Libbie, I'll always protect you—if I have to slay thousands to do it."

She felt an ache in her heart. Reaching up, she pretended to smooth a lock from his forehead. "That's not quite what I wanted from you."

"I know that. And I'm sure you think I'm a monster to make such a terrible promise. But monsters can love. Look at Quasimodo. Esmeralda's slightest rebuke would drench him in sorrow."

She smiled in spite of herself. "Are you comparing yourself to a poor, lovestruck hunchback?"

"Perhaps not the hunchback, exactly." His swift grin matched her own, then faded quickly. "But I know what you thought out on the prairie. You looked at me with pity and hatred. I was the beast who'd ruined your life. And you know what?"

"No." She touched the satin sash on his chest.

"I deserved your scorn." He straightened his shoulders, splendidly draped in crimson satin, decorated with medals the meanings of which were foreign to her. "I was a hard man, and I know it." He touched her chin softly. "But I promise you this, my bonny, my Libbie—no man, not one of your husbands, or one of these scoundrels"—he glanced around proudly, as if daring any man in the gathering to cross him—"longs for your smile with a heart more fond— or foolish—than mine."

FOURTEEN

"May I have this dance?" Greenstreet touched Elizabeth's shoulder.

Ryerson scowled, but released his wife. He'd meant what he said. He needed to trust her. He'd be leaving here in a couple of weeks. He'd already picked out a home for Libbie, a small farm near Manassas. He hoped she'd like the life he envisioned. She'd be just as alone as she was on the prairie, but out at Manassas she'd be protected. Most women liked comfort and glamour. And though Libbie wasn't like most women exactly, she needed a place to be free from the stares. He could not keep her beside him forever, so the time had come to force her choice. She'd have to switch her allegiance, abandon her hardscrabble existence, and adjust to the comfortable life of a senior army officer's wife.

As Greenstreet twirled her around, Ryerson nearly tripped over a corner settee. It terrified him to leave her behind. He'd miss her so much. He wasn't sure how he'd live without her. That feeling surprised him. He'd loved Helen, but she'd never become essential to him. Libbie was different. If Helen had been his milk and honey, Libbie was more like hardtack and coffee, those humble and indispensable staples that had carried him through many a battle. To his eternal surprise, he believed in Libbie. After the way he'd lost Helen, it took all his faith to believe in a woman. He knew how she revived his hopes. She did it at night, coming so alive in his arms that the pain Helen had caused him faded away, replaced by a hope, deep in his heart, that Libbie could not be defeated by hardship. He certainly hoped not, for even she would need to weather long separation. He doubted he'd gotten her pregnant. Even if fate surprised them with a baby, she had a resilience Helen had lacked. He prayed she'd survive the rigors of childbirth and the hardship of raising a child alone. The belief that she would was one of the reasons he'd consented to marriage. Still, he had his worries. He didn't trust Greenstreet. Though not in cahoots, Parker and Greenstreet had filled her head with political notions that appealed to her idealistic, softhearted nature. If Ryerson succeeded in turning his troopers into crackerjack Indian fighters, he might well return to a wife filled with hatred. Or worse.

He might return to a wife with a lover.

He frowned as Greenstreet glided her toward the room's center. Curling his fingers over his sword hilt, Ryerson sent up a small prayer to the muse who blessed poets, requesting she watch over his wife and help her never regret she'd married a soldier.

"Do you love her?" Senator Parker appeared without warning beside him. He looked as gray as a ghost, with his silvery hair and mournful pallor.

Ryerson tugged on a cuff, then brushed some dirt off the braid on his sleeve. He hadn't expected the senator at this party, though on second thought his attendance made sense. They'd unveil the statue day after tomorrow. Thorough as always, the wily old politician wanted to check on his former son-in-law and make sure neither he nor Libbie would botch his role as conquering hero.

Ryerson didn't reply. He stepped away from the crowd. A few other couples had joined Libbie and Greenstreet, but none of the women remotely compared with her startling and original beauty. She glowed like a painting in a renaissance palace, her lustrous curls set against emerald satin, her hair sweeping back from her face, then falling loose to her waist. He felt a swell of pride at the sight, for he believed in some secret part of himself that in some ways her marriage had freed her and helped her to be more relaxed around strangers.

"I love her. Yes." Ryerson straightened the crimson sash at his waist, then returned to his former father-in-law. "But that doesn't mean I didn't love Helen."

"I know that." Parker took Ryerson by the elbow and steered him toward a food-laden sideboard. Slipping easily through the crowd, he reached the table and the space next to the punch bowl. "But I still think she's a poor replacement."

"I suspected you would." Ryerson shifted away from his former father-in-law, trying to keep one eye on Libbie. She behaved herself well and should have been safe even with Greenstreet, but he still didn't like her out of his sight.

"I don't know what you were thinking." Parker spoke in the tones of a well-seasoned statesman. "Given the right wife as an asset, you could have had power, wealth, and vast admiration." He touched Ryerson's sleeve.

Ryerson glanced sideways. The senator held out a cup of punch. A pale pink liquid swirled in the glass, a bubbly seduction encased in fine crystal, but Ryerson wanted to keep his head clear. He never drank before a speaking engagement, and he needed his wits for dealing with Parker.

"No, thank you." He brushed the offered cup away with a gesture. "I've sent hundreds of boys to meet their maker. That's power enough for a simple soldier. Helen's money took care of the wealth. I've all the admiration I want when I look into the eyes of that lady out there."

The senator set down Ryerson's glass. He emptied the other in a long, thirsty gulp. His eyes had a drunken shine when he finished. "That's a fault in a man, needing a woman's approval."

Glancing back at the dancers, Ryerson picked out Elizabeth's figure. "I can't agree with that statement."

The senator set down the punch and picked up an oyster. "You could have done some good for the Negroes."

"Not what I wanted either." Ryerson stepped forward, watching for Libbie. "I can barely solve my own problems, much less those of another race."

"Except for your troopers."

"Of course."

"Oyster?" the old man asked softly. He slurped the meaty flesh off the shell. Ryerson's stomach roiled at the scent, fish cut slightly by lemon. As a student, he had loved the rich snack, but lately his tastes had gotten simpler, and the exotic concoction simply seemed slimy.

Ryerson turned toward the crowd with a grimace. Most of the spectators watched Libbie politely. Though she hadn't made many friends in the city, she'd attracted largely favorable attention. After four years of war, the mood of the country was peaceful, especially when it came to the Indians, and Libbie's Cheyenne-loving opinions evoked approving reactions from most of the people she met.

"You know she'll be a one-season wonder."

"I expect so."

"And how will she live after this visit?" The senator nib-

bled on an oyster cracker. "How do you know she won't
end up like Helen?"

"Because," Ryerson said, feeling the tic in his jaw, "she
won't."

"You can't keep her with you."

A twinge of annoyance streaked through Ryerson.
Helen's death had hurt the old politician quite badly, and it
pained Ryerson to disagree with her father. He would have
liked to console him, but the senator had pickled his grief
in fine liquor. Ryerson could see the signs of excess in the
senator's puffy expression, the spidery veins of his nose.
The old man's pudgy hands trembled slightly as he poured
out another cupful. "In spite of your eloquent speeches,
the army's not got much use for your troopers. No white
soldier wants to live with those people. You'll end up serv-
ing some forlorn outpost without any way to care for a
wife."

For Elizabeth's sake, Ryerson squelched the rush of his
temper. He took the speech as a threat. The senator had
friends in the War Department and could easily influence
Ryerson's assignment. He couldn't hurt Libbie directly, but
he did have the power to wound her through worry, not to
mention creating grief for the troopers. He brushed his
hand over his sword hilt. "She'll be all right."

The old man's silvery brows drew into a frown. "So
you'll use the money at last?"

Ryerson nodded curtly.

The senator took a long drink of the punch, then wiped
his lips with a linen handkerchief. "Well, I wish you good
luck. You weren't quite man enough for my daughter. I
hope you do better with this one."

Elizabeth hated dancing with Nathaniel Greenstreet.
She didn't know why. He was handsome enough, and

Southern and courtly, the *beau sabreur* of her girlhood days
and exceedingly famous in Saint James County, but he
held her too close and led her too strongly, as if he didn't
quite trust her instincts. She found it a curious fact that
Ryerson, all grim and grizzled, danced more gracefully
than this elegant man.

As he guided her the length of the room, she pondered
the reasons why she disliked him. She'd once loved this
type of man, charming and gracious, civilized at all times,
but life with Ryerson had changed her. At first his Yankee
ways had seemed gruff by contrast, but in the end he'd won
her over, because beneath his harsh surface lay a fair-
minded man with a genuine fondness for people. Though
she still didn't like his occupation, she'd come to respect
him and enjoy the fact that he loved and helped her.

Greenstreet pressed her closer, butting against her. As
she struggled to create some distance, she realized why she
didn't like him. It seemed a mockery to dance with another. That feeling surprised her, for she didn't count herself as prudish, but she'd fallen so deeply in love with her
husband that she felt awkward being held by another, even
in this innocuous way.

"Why so sad, my lady?" Greenstreet touched her chin as
he asked.

"No reason." She wanted to shrug, but remembered her
manners. If Greenstreet had not been Ryerson's friend,
she would have walked away at this moment. She didn't
like his hands on her face, his wool suit against her breast,
or his thigh brushing a little too closely. "I miss my husband," she said quietly.

"That bad?" He laughed and tightened his grip. "He
must have a way with the ladies."

She wanted to slap him. Ryerson valued his friendship,
and Greenstreet was taking advantage. Her husband didn't

approve of his boldness, but he wanted Greenstreet's forgiveness and let him closer because of that fact. "He's a fine man, my husband."

Greenstreet squeezed her waist. "I'm sure of that, lady. I remember how well he wrote a term paper. Of course, he could not get near a horse without puking. It's a real tribute to his ambition that he learned to ride them to free the Negro."

"Is that what rankles?" She stifled the urge to step on his foot. "Do you really want to go back to slavery days?"

"No, no, my dear lady." Candlelight played off the planes of his face, accenting his high and arrogant cheekbones. "I like losing property without compensation."

"They're people, not objects. They're the ones who should be paid for their losses."

Greenstreet twirled her beneath the chandelier in the ceiling, whirling her away from her husband. He lowered his voice as he spoke. "So, you've become a nigger-lover? Your uncle must be turning to dust in his grave."

"I didn't say I loved his troopers." Heat seeped through her dress and corset. All these ladylike stays made breathing a chore. "I've just come to know the coloreds have feelings. All human beings have feelings. They have their own customs—"

"I'd say so."

She jerked her chin up, which made her bump him. "I don't deny Negroes seem different, but I have this colored friend, Sergeant Dixon—"

Greenstreet arched one skeptical eyebrow.

"I count him a friend." She met his gaze and kept it. "He helped me fall in love with my husband. He thinks differently about certain subjects, but he loves life, and women—"

Greenstreet coughed, but she ignored his rude interruption. "—and he loves James, and I don't see how you could own him, or ask to be paid for the wrong that's been done him."

"He's really seduced you." He pivoted quickly, leaving her breathless. "That's such a shame. Saint James County had such high hopes for you."

In a series of turns, he danced her the length of the room. The twirling moves made her dizzy. Dozens of tapers flickered off mirrors, and the scent of damp bodies disordered her sense. But Elizabeth kept thinking. Something niggled at the back of her brain, some comment Greenstreet had made. "How do you know about my uncle?"

He grinned, his even white teeth a little too perfect. "I know a great deal about you, my sweet. I told you. I fought over every inch of that county. It's still my political base, so when I learned that a cousin had married a friend, I made it my business to find out about her."

Elizabeth's skin suddenly went clammy. No one knew about Lysistrata, except, of course, her dear Sleeps With Eagle. She couldn't imagine how Greenstreet would guess her secret, but the tone of his voice, the slant of the shadow on those slashing cheekbones, made her instantly frightened of his interest in her past. This man was clever and filled with hatred. If he found a way to hurt her he would.

She pressed her hand to her forehead, doing her best imitation of sickness. "I think I feel faint."

"Ah." He pressed his hand to the small of her back. "A female excuse. Well, a seasoned soldier knows when to retreat."

Ryerson drove Elizabeth to the farm in the guise of a picnic. He wanted to surprise her. Not that he'd bought the farmhouse exactly, but he'd made up his mind that if she liked it he'd purchase it for her before he left.

And he hoped that she'd love it. He didn't remember her family plantation. His troops had burned dozens during the war, but he had a strong impression of Mississippi and vivid memories of those fine Southern homes. This new home was smaller, less grand than the up-country Corinthians. Still, white Doric columns graced a two-story porch, a patch of grass fronted the brickwork, and roses rambled over the fencing. The crops had been burned, like most in the rolling Virginia valleys, several times during the war. The family had fled to Atlanta, then Texas, leaving the land to a brother who had his own house. Ryerson planned to buy only the house and garden. She could tame those roses or plant her own flowers, paint the columns, or redo the interior, or simply sit on the porch and gaze at the deep blue contour of the mountains. Maybe even raise more damnable goats.

He'd miss her, of course. She sat close to him in the buggy, her hips swaying in a country road rhythm. He felt tight in his chest and in his thigh muscles. He wished he could have her this close every day. But he knew that he couldn't. Parker was right. The troop was already out at Fort Riley, a primitive post, deep in the heart of Indian country. And Hancock's war had gone pretty poorly. The white man would destroy the red in the end; there would be many more years of hard fighting. And the buffalo soldiers—Dixon had written him of the troop's nickname —would draw the toughest, most difficult duty. His troops would acquit themselves well, but he could not ask a wife to share that kind of life.

Pressing his thigh close to her, he steered the buggy off to the side of the road. The house sat below them. Cradled in the slope of a gentle valley, perched at the end of a small country lane, it faced the road they drove on and commanded a view of a meandering river. He tugged on the reins of the matched bays he'd rented.

"How do you like the house?" he asked as they rumbled to a stop in the dust.

She seemed to gather his meaning by instinct. "That one?" There were two or three houses in sight, but she pointed to the pretty two-story Doric.

"Yes." He rearranged the leather thongs in his fingers. "I'm thinking of buying it for you."

Her lips parted slightly. For a moment she sat there, eyes wide and mouth slightly open, her bosom moving beneath a gray silk day dress. The valley smelled far more green than the prairie, its air summer-grass sweet and humid. He panicked.

"Oh, James, I love it." She hugged his waist, then hid her face in his chest. He thought she trembled, but she only mumbled, speaking quietly into the brown wool of his suit coat. "Can we see the inside?"

"Certainly." He paused for a moment, savoring her touch. Soon enough he'd be gone, all her softness a faint memory, with only the dry, wildflower scent of the plains to remind him of his times with his Libbie. Quickly he clicked to the bays. "Now remember, it's empty. And drab. No one's lived there since the second Bull Run."

"I see." Pulling away, she seemed sad for a moment. "Do you know what became of the people who lived there?"

"They fled," he said curtly.

"Ah." She frowned, then pushed a pin into her chignon. "I'm sure they'll be glad to see it fixed up." She smiled, then rolled her eyes upward. "As long as they don't find out who bought it."

He fell silent, but was glad to see she had some sense of

humor about the more awkward aspects of this arrangement. He drove past a broken gate, through the weed-
choked yard to a paint-peeling porch, pulled the buggy up
to the entrance, and stopped.

"It needs work," she said dryly and hopped out of the
wagon. "But nothing that money, or sweat, or both can't
help with." She flew up the steps, took in the view, filled up
her lungs, then pushed on the door. The hinges protested
her entrance, but she charged into the gloom, her voice
trailing cheerfully after. "We'll have to evict thousands of
spiders. Luckily I'm not afraid of the creatures."

"Well, I am." He looped the reins into the ring of a cast-
iron darky resplendently clothed in a scarlet jacket.

"Really?" She appeared in the doorway. "The fearless
leader of Ryerson's Riders is afraid of both spiders and
horses?"

"Don't look so smug." He grimaced as he entered the
parlor, brushing a web off his hat. "Oh, God." He jumped
back, surprised, goose bumps forming by instinct as his
mind noted the creeping sensation. Cursing, he slammed
his hat onto the floorboards. A fat, black, eight-legged
creature crawled off the brim and scuttled beneath it.
"Jesus H. Christ!" He scowled at the headgear, wondering
how to retrieve it. "Yes! I hate spiders."

"Calm down." She patted his hand, scooped up the insect, and carried it out to the porch. "Your Libbie will save
you."

"Vampire," he muttered, taking his hat and inspecting it
closely.

"Now, don't be nasty." She bounced down the steps and
into the yard, letting the spider loose in the roses. "At last,
I can do something useful for you." She scanned the horizon, then crossed to a fence and peered out at the dusty
field that bordered the home place. "I don't know what

they grow in Virginia, but I'm sure we can figure out how to farm this."

Ryerson's heart skipped a beat. He walked to within a few inches of her and rested his boot on a lower fence rail. "I'm not buying the land," he said quietly. "Only the house and gardens."

"Oh." She turned, her face suffused in confusion and worry. She smoothed down her skirt, then pulled off her gloves and made a small study of her blunt fingernails. "How did you plan on making a living?"

"The same way I am." He steadied himself on a worn wooden post. He'd come in a civilian outfit, a pair of wool pants with a matching coat, without a gun, much less a sword, and he felt suddenly naked without them. "I'm returning to Kansas in a couple of weeks. I thought you could stay and make a home in this place."

Her hands flew to her cheekbones.

"Libbie." Crossing the distance between them, he crushed her to his chest and cursed himself beneath his breath. He could be good with words when he wanted, but breaking this news made him nervous, and he'd put the proposition too bluntly. "It's not what you think." He could feel her heart beating, her body shaking. "I can't take you with me. The troop's at Fort Riley. That's much different from Fort Leavenworth. It's farther out than your home on the prairie, only half-built, and surrounded by hostiles. There's no place in that fort for a woman."

She wrenched herself out of his grasp, ducked under the rail, and stomped into the dirt field. "I've lived in worse places."

"Libbie." He threw down his hat. "Don't argue with me. You can't spend the rest of your life in hovels."

She whirled, locked her gaze with his, and stilled. Little else moved in the placid landscape, the farms having been abandoned for years. The sun had yet to heat up the valley. The morning breeze fluttered through the leaves of the trees and the few stray tendrils of her auburn hair. She waited, eyes blazing and posture expectant, her hair pulled back from her face, and he remembered the day long ago on the prairie when he'd wondered where her loyalties lay.

"You're right." Her shoulders slumped. She dropped her arms to her sides. "I don't need to live like a wild Indian."

He had been less surprised when Joe Johnston surrendered. Shutting his eyes, he made a passionate gesture he'd learned from Italians and kissed the tips of his fingers. "Thank you." He ran his hand over the nape of his neck, working the stiffness out of his muscles and missing her soft touch already. "I love you. I promise you won't regret this decision." He pressed his fingertips over his temples, already longing for comfort. "I'll always be faithful. I'll always come back. I'll send you money, more than enough. I just ask that you live here and be happy and welcome me home between tours of duty."

"And what if you're killed?"

He opened his eyes and looked straight into hers. "That's a risk a soldier's wife takes."

"Well, it's a risk I've taken before." Bending down, she scooped up a handful of dirt and ran the brown soil through her fingers. "I want to ask a favor of you."

He cocked one eyebrow, suspicious.

"I want you to leave the army." She dusted her hands and took a step toward him. "I've been thinking a great deal about this. I think of myself as quite independent, but I don't want to live by myself. I can't live here"—she gestured at the surrounding farmland—"surrounded by people like Greenstreet. They think I'm a traitor."

"What do you care what fools like him think?"

"Because it's hard enough to conquer remorse without living down public opinion."

"Do you want me to find a place in the North?"

"No. No. That's not what I'm saying." She shook out her skirt, took a step toward the house, paused, looked around, then held out her hand. "Walk with me, James."

Taking her elbow, he guided her toward the road in the distance. She kept up with his pace, striding with astonishing vigor over burnt-out, denuded furrows.

"I don't want to live with the Yankees. I'm a total stranger to your way of life, but I'll compromise. Meet me halfway. If you leave the army, I'll live anywhere with you."

He kicked a dirt clod, wishing to throw it. He understood the thrust of her logic, but couldn't agree with her reasons. "You're forgetting the troopers."

"No. I'm not. I warned Sergeant Dixon." Her fingers tightened over his elbow. "I gave him a chance. I told him before we got married that if we went through with a legal marriage I'd try to talk you out of the army."

"You didn't warn me."

"Of course not; you wouldn't have listened."

He sucked in a breath. "But you think I'll listen this morning?"

"I'd hoped you'd changed." They'd reached the road, the one they'd rode down on. She stepped onto the dusty track, looked up the hill, then headed farther down into the valley. "I was hoping you'd come to love me—"

"Libbie—" He stopped and turned her toward him. "I do. You have to believe me." He ran a thumb over her cheekbone. "But you don't know what you're asking."

She stopped his caress. "I know Dixon's your friend—"

"Of course." He recaptured her elbow and marched toward a line of trees in the distance. "But you don't understand."

"No. I don't. You told me yourself you did this for Helen. You're a talented man. I know you've got money. If you don't want to farm, you could go back to teaching. For heaven's sake, James, you don't even like horses."

He struggled to get control of himself. He didn't want to speak on this subject, did not want to remember the pain. She had no right to ask this at all, no right to make him remember. Except she did. As they strolled toward the shimmering trees, he tried to remember his marriage vows. She'd pledged to love, obey, and honor, but he'd pledged lifelong devotion. If he asked this separation from her, he at least owed her an explanation. The line of trees foreshadowed a river. As they entered the shade of a stately elm, he noticed the sheen of the slow-moving water.

He guided her up the arch of a stone bridge. "You've forgotten my Jamie."

"Your son? What's he got to do with your career in the army?"

"He's why I do this." He stared down at their reflection, distant and placid below them. They seemed like some other couple. Two shimmering figures. He sedate. She radiant and lovely. He wondered if they'd ever be peaceful, or if the war would always haunt them.

"Libbie." He stared wildly around, noting the trees. Two armies must have fought hard for this place. Though she might never notice, he took in the pockmarked tree trunks, the recovering brush, and the broken branches. His mind produced desolate fragments of the forest at Shiloh, completely denuded of all its spring growth by the fighting. He wanted to cradle his head in his hands, but he'd never flinched in genuine battle, so he refused to regret his difficult past or the fact that he could not look at this forest with quite the eyes that an innocent might. "Libbie," he said as he squeezed her hand, still unused to skin-to-skin contact, "my heart goes out to you for your losses, but the death of a child is not like that of a husband—or even a mother or father. Your child is your future." His voice seemed to belong to somebody else. He felt proud that he kept it so calm. "When Jamie left—" He fought down the catch in his throat and the memory of his son's gravestone. "When Jamie left—" Words failed him completely. The river reflection stayed totally still, and Ryerson had the odd thought that he ought to dissolve and flow down to the water, but some mysterious, perverse law of physics kept him standing upright and in one piece. "I cannot describe how I felt." The woman stirred in the reflection, ducking her head and hiding her face. "It's hard to make sense of something so crazy." His voice came out as a whisper. "Libbie, I need a way to give his death meaning. It is for us the living . . ."

Lincoln's words broke in his throat. He'd memorized them so long ago. He'd recited them weeping, and riding and fighting, and many nights instead of sleeping, but he could not speak of his son to this woman, even in another man's words. He thought of his son as a little soldier, as much a victim of war as any adult. Lincoln's speech expressed how he felt. Since the time he'd lost his Jamie, Ryerson had tried to give his life meaning by living for the cause his son died for. For him, that meant helping the Negro. He loved Sergeant Dixon and most of his troopers, but he knew they'd survive somehow without him. He was the one who'd never make it, if he came to believe his son's life had been wasted. The whole address rolled through his head, in its imagined stentorian tones, but his grief for Jamie was sacred and private, and he would not breach it even for Libbie.

"You know, I never thought about it, but in his own way Lincoln was both a soldier and poet."

He glanced, surprised, at her profile. He didn't think she'd catch his reference from such a broken fragment of quote.

She wrapped one arm around his waist. "I don't know what will become of us, James." She clung to him in silence, watching the water. He tried to listen to the whispering trees, but the forest seemed haunted by ghosts and a hushed, tomblike silence that echoed the painful memory of his son's final struggle. Libbie seemed equally stricken, her tear-stained face solemn and troubled. At length, she pressed a fierce kiss to his mouth. To his amazement, his body responded. A roar filled his ears—the rush of his blood. Beneath the cool silk, she burned like a cinder, hot and feverish, desperate with emotion or lust or maybe just the heat of the summer, but he couldn't resist returning her passion, his hands working over the dress, the soft material giving beneath them.

"Ah, Libbie, I love you so much." He flattened her against the arched stonework, using the bridge and his hips to entrap her, too strongly aroused to retain his decorum. She did not seem to care. She shifted beneath him, her arms clinging tight, her mouth moving hotly against him, intermittently gasping for breath, as if she were dying or drowning or sobbing, and a thought passed through his mind that she might be all three, for in the kiss he could feel her heart breaking.

"My bonny, my Libbie." He could take her right here. She had that wildness in her. Though he'd never experienced this passion with Helen, he knew the meaning of this desperate embrace, for he'd experienced these moments sometimes after battle, the absolutely perfect awareness of life that comes after a close brush with death—the bright, lucid realization that life could not be any more lovely. He deepened the kiss. He wouldn't make love to her on the bridge, but he wanted at least to extend this moment. He might never return. He hated that fact, but he couldn't regret his life or profession. It was an ancient, honorable impulse, the protection of those who were weaker, and once he'd discovered its pleasures, he'd never wanted to give them up. He'd carry this kiss with him into battle, and he hoped the one he gave her would see her through her own lonely nights.

She moaned. He sought out her nipples, surprised to find them outlined so clearly even beneath such ladylike clothes. He teased at their softness. She held onto his waistband. Swaying back slightly, she used the belt that circled his waist and braced herself against his pelvis. A low growl escaped him. His lips felt bruised, his muscles tense, and his lower part rigid and swollen. He wished he could cradle her gently, but this kind of passion was hard to deny, and he found himself wondering where he could take her.

She broke off the kiss, searching his eyes, and nodded. He took her hand without a word. Together they walked to the end of the bridge, then slipped quietly into the shade beneath it.

"Are you sure you want to do this?" he asked as he took off his coat.

She nodded, eyes shiny, and sat down on the brown wool of his jacket. She lifted the wide bell of her skirt and slipped out of her undergarment. He unbuttoned his pants, dazed by the sight of white thigh and the purely passionate thought that she'd offer herself so wantonly to him. He went down on his knees, preparing to enter, when a startling idea hit him. He bent at the waist, kissing her intimately, listening for her tiny whimpers, suckling until her low moans of pleasure subsided into deep, shuddering gasps.

He plunged in, aroused by the sound and the knowledge that he'd brought her to a peak, claiming her mouth and her body with deep satisfaction while the summer breeze caressed his bare buttocks and her nails dug into his muscles, and the pain and the softness brought him to climax at the very moment he pulled himself out.

She slapped him, hard, across his face. He knew by the stinging she'd left an imprint. He didn't bother to ask why she'd hit him, for he read her pain in his expression, and his own heart felt battered and bruised as he realized that even if they worked all else out, they'd still be left with the problem of children.

"Is that the price of your sympathy?" He touched the burning skin of his cheek. "Every time I open my heart, you'll seize on my weakness and try a seduction?"

She did not respond, only sat there, wild and disheveled, her eyes blazing with anger and hatred.

He stood up slowly and buttoned his pants. "I'm going to leave you for a while. I'll send back the buggy. I want you to join me at the unveiling, but you have to come of your own volition. I'm tired of trying to force you to love me. You've married me. You've taken a vow, but you haven't accepted my life or profession. I'll always protect you, but I don't have to live with a woman whose every glance rebukes my position."

True to his word, Ryerson left in a rage, made all the more frightening by his absolute silence. He hustled Elizabeth back to the house, planted her on the porch, and sprang into the buggy, tossing down the picnic basket and galloping off in a cloud of dust. Elizabeth sank onto the steps, exhausted and frightened and drained.

Ryerson had been wrong. She loved him to the core of her being, but she couldn't imagine their marriage working unless she got him out of the army. She didn't want to be widowed again. It hurt her that he belittled her loss. After all, her young husband had been her future also. Of course she'd survive, but she wanted more from life than mere existence. She wanted James. She wanted his children. She wanted a house, and liked this one fine, but not just a house to live in. She wanted a home. If she had to live by herself, she might as well go back to the prairie. There at least she had her own friends, her double identity as Lysistrata, and her work caring for Indian children. Life might be harder, but it was also more useful, and safer, at least after a fashion. On the prairie, she had a way to protect her heart from the battering effects of Ryerson's tantrums.

Sighing, she picked up the basket, amazed that even in his blackest anger Ryerson would think of a detail like leaving her lunch. She wasn't hungry, but she'd tucked a sketch pad in the basket. She pulled it out, sat down, and started to draw. For the first half hour she remained angry, but as the sun climbed in the sky, she began to enjoy the peace and quiet, the chance to draw the countryside. She felt slightly annoyed when a black dot appeared on the road. She watched the distant conveyance roll down the road and wondered vaguely if James had returned, or if he'd sent someone back so quickly, or if this was simply some stranger. Squinting into the sunlight, she noted the growing profile of the horses. She didn't think this was James and his bays. The buggy was older than the one James had driven, swaying in a lopsided rhythm to the powerful cadence of two spirited chestnuts. Still, she thought the driver must have been sent by her husband. He ignored the rickety tilt of the carriage, barreling down the road with an aggressive precision that spoke of a highly experienced horseman. She rose to meet her presumed envoy. As he turned down the lane, the cavalryman waved, seemingly friendly. She could not make him out, but he seemed to know her. She felt a slight frisson of anger at James for leaving her out here unprotected.

As the worn-out black buggy grew nearer, to her utter amazement she made out Colonel Greenstreet, tall and dashing in a dark suit. Arriving at the porch, he pulled back on his reins, then launched himself out of the carriage.

"Good afternoon, ma'am." He touched the brim of his slouch hat. "Fancy meeting you in this place."

"Fancy that." She pressed her pad to her bosom. "May I ask what brings you this way?"

The colonel looped his reins in the iron ring of a small metal darky, then held out his hand as if to help her. "I heard you needed a rescue."

She eyed him, suspicious, and moved away. "I don't know what makes you think I'm in need of your help."

Ignoring her rudeness, he peeked into the picnic basket snuggled at the foot of the porch. "The man from whom you rented your carriage does a little spying for me."

She started, astonished. "Spies? You had us followed?"

"No, no. Nothing quite so barbaric." He lifted a red-and-white napkin and fished out a piece of fried chicken. "Your husband gave orders to send you a buggy. I diverted the driver and came in his stead. What's that?" He pointed the drumstick at her notebook.

"Is this part of your service to Saint James County?" She flipped closed the cover, oddly loath to let him take a look at her drawings. "You keep track of all the belles who get lost?"

"Something like that." He mounted the porch, then leaned casually against one of the columns. "I gather you had a fight with your husband."

"That's no concern of yours, my good cousin." She lifted

the cover and shoved in the pad, then picked up the basket and tucked the handle over her elbow. She wanted to leave here, but wasn't sure how. In her mind she gave Ryerson a thorough trouncing for leaving her in this dilemma. The trouble with quarreling with cavalry raiders was that they always had horses, and she never did.

Meanwhile Greenstreet studied her closely, chewing gleefully on a small piece of chicken. "I'm glad to see how well you defend him. In the long run that makes you more useful."

She stifled the urge to pull out her pad. Greenstreet looked strangely barbaric, eating the greasy meat with his fingers. He'd be easy to caricature in this pose, languid and lethal, with the loutish manners she associated with a low class of people. Unfortunately art had to wait. He was up to something, following her here, and she was determined to figure out what.

"Useful?" she asked casually.

"To the cause, dear lady, the one you and I share."

"You're mistaken if you think we have causes in common."

"I think not." He tossed the bone into the dirt, then filched a napkin out of her basket.

"I know you think because I'm Southern—"

"No, no." He patted his mouth, fastidious again. "I don't make assumptions because of your accent or what I know of your past. You have strong feelings on certain subjects, strong enough that you expressed them, and very effectively I might add."

"I don't know what you're talking about." A sick feeling churned in her stomach. She didn't like the tone of his voice or the triumphant gleam in his eye.

"I think you do."

"If you'll excuse me." She stormed past him, an irrational effort and pointless, but he made her feel angry and trapped. She made up her mind to escape him, even if she had to do so on foot.

He let her past without trying to block her, though she felt his eyes on her as she stomped down the road.

His voice came to her, honeyed and golden. "So he doesn't know that he married his most viper-penned critic."

She stopped, her back still to him. "Don't you think that's rather harsh?"

"Not when you look at the drawings."

She turned. He'd unfolded a newspaper from his coat pocket and held one of its pages for her to read. She quelled her urge to panic and run and managed to walk forward quite calmly. It still surprised her to see her own sketch, though. James, her husband, the man that she loved, glared out of the pages, caricatured, by her hand, in the guise of a devil.

She took the sketch and examined the stiff newsprint serenely. "I find that picture quite hateful."

"You're too modest, my dear. I think it's perfect."

She crumpled the cartoon and tossed it. "Why are you bothering me with this nonsense?"

"Because I want to know why you did it."

She wanted to cry, to scream, to run, or to shoot him, but none of those seemed effective options. She settled on an arch of the eyebrow. "I don't know what you're talking about."

"I think you do." Bending down, he picked up the newspaper. "Your reputation precedes you, my dear. Your cartoons were famous in Saint James County."

"I drew a little when I was a girl." She watched him pull out another paper, a small white drawing torn from a sketch pad. "So did every other well-bred Southern woman."

"Yes, but sadly for you, you did it so well, and I was such a terrible student. Even as a girl of sixteen, you had a wicked flair for satirical portraits. Come here." He sat down on the porch and gestured her over. She sat down on the lower step, reluctant, wary, but intrigued by how he had figured this out. As she smoothed out her skirt, he made a small grunt of satisfaction, then held the pair of drawings out to her. In the girlish pen scratches, all her past came flooding back. Her childhood headmaster stared out of the paper, lampooned in a cruder, more imitative technique than the one she'd used for Ryerson's drawing. Even to an amateur's eyes, the drawings must have had much in common. She'd always had a distinctive style. She couldn't still her hammering heartbeat, but she knew Greenstreet couldn't see inside her body, so she controlled all outward reaction and stared up at him with her most open gaze.

"I'm not sure what you're implying, but I think you are sadly mistaken."

Cursing, he stuffed the drawings back into his pocket and strode to the side of the carriage. "Listen to me, Elizabeth Wheaton. I don't know why you married your husband, but I've read your statements in the newspapers and I see these drawings with my own eyes. You don't like what he did to your people, or what he's about to do to the Indians." He lifted a whip out of the buggy and paced to one end of the lane. "Perhaps you believe he can't be defeated, that no one can help the South anymore, but you're wrong." He stopped, tapping his boot with the quirt. "You can do a great deal to hurt him."

"James?"

He nodded.

She disliked the business with the whip. He was trying to frighten her, and that made her angry. James might lose his temper sometimes, but he never made her fear for her well-being. She picked up the basket and walked straight toward him, thinking the best defense lay in attack. "What kind of fool do you think I am?" She clutched the wicker handle. "I'm angry, but I'd never betray him."

"I take you for a fool who loves her husband and would rather he not be made aware of the drawings."

She stopped. He'd pegged her correctly. No matter what happened between her and James, she had changed since she'd drawn those cruel sketches. She'd rather he never knew what a hateful monster she'd been. "Aren't you taking a terrible risk, asking me to betray him?"

"Not really. I've beaten Ryerson at deadlier games." His elbow pressed close to his side. She remembered what James had told her about him. They'd nearly killed each other at Shiloh. In a rare instance of man-to-man combat, on the last skirmish of a two-day battle, Greenstreet had outcharged his own troopers and galloped alone into Ryerson's Riders. Greenstreet got off the first shot, missing Ryerson by a few inches. Ryerson pulled out his service revolver, aimed for the shoulder, and blasted his friend straight through the stomach. James had been certain he'd killed his old friend, but Greenstreet had the luck of the devil. In a performance that rivaled Old Scratch, he had plucked one of the Riders straight out of his saddle and rejoined his troop by using the man as a shield. Ryerson had been secretly grateful, but Elizabeth, seeing the hatred in Greenstreet's expression, couldn't help wishing her husband had killed him.

"And you haven't forgotten how badly he hurt you?"

He shifted his weight with an unconscious wince. "I'll never forget, not as long as I live."

She came down off the steps and kicked some dirt over the chicken bone. "What kind of help do you want?"

"Lampoon his troopers. Do cartoons like this." He patted his pocket. "Show them for the fools that they are."

Indignation flared in her. "You must be joking."

"Of course not. You know they'll never make soldiers. You can skewer all their little foibles, all their fancy dress and childish pretensions, their simpleminded, dependent ways."

"They're not that simple." She bit her lip. She couldn't think quickly enough, but some gut-level instinct kept working. She had to get home. She had to tell James. Greenstreet must have a reason for wanting these drawings. If she could just figure it out, she might find a way to help the troopers. "After all, one was sly enough to murder my uncle."

"That's the girl. Now you're thinking." He strode back to his horses, taking the head of one of the chestnuts.

She skittered away from the fidgeting pair. "But I need to know. How does it help Saint James County if I make fun of my husband's troopers?"

He untied the reins. "It fits in with our plans."

"Whose plans?"

"Before I go on, you have to choose." He arranged the long leather thongs over the horses' backs, then swiftly mounted the seat of the buggy. "Are you going to help us, or will you stick by your husband?"

"I'm leaving my husband." The scent of the chicken wafted up to her, leaving her heartsick, or homesick, or both. "Or, rather, he's leaving me. I'll do what you ask if you'll keep your promise never to reveal that I'm Lysistrata."

"That request doesn't make sense."

"Women seldom make sense, but that doesn't mean we can't be useful."

"Spoken like a true politician." He tugged on the reins, making the horses step backward in a mincing prance. "Have you heard of the Klan?"

"No."

"It's an organization—an army of whites—who are fighting to keep the Negro in his place. Slavery's gone, but the good white folks of the South don't intend to step aside for the Negro. We'll make them pay for using the ballot by using the nigger's ignorance against him."

She clutched the handle of the wicker basket, struggling to make sense of his tirade. "I'm not sure I know what you mean."

"This means night riding. It means ghosts in the yard and crosses burning. Sometimes it might even mean killing."

"You'd kill a man merely for voting?"

"I've killed men for less, and so has your husband."

She didn't believe that. The thought surprised her, for in her long-ago Saint James County days, she did believe Ryerson killed for no reason. But she knew him better now.

"Will you help me?"

She stared at his face, those arrogant cheekbones, the high-featured refinement she'd once thought of as cultured. She couldn't believe he'd ask her this favor. Then again, she supposed, he wouldn't believe she'd refuse. "Yes." She drew in a breath. "I'll lampoon the Yankees."

"Even if he's left you?"

She nodded. "I couldn't do what you ask for personal vengeance. I like his troopers. They've been good to me. I couldn't hurt them, no matter how angry I might be at my husband, but he's promised he would take care of me. I don't want to hurt my chances for that. I'm tired of living

out there on the prairie and I don't want Ryerson sending
me back. So go. I'll do what you ask. Send back the carriage my husband ordered. And never let me see you
again."

She wasn't sure she did the right thing. She worried
about it all the way back to Kansas. As the third-class carriage rolled through the green eastern forests, she watched
the scenery she'd missed when she'd come, and tried desperately not to miss her husband. It was hard on the train,
the honeymoon coming back in bright flashes so vivid that
often as not she wanted to weep, and she had to keep up a
long, hard, tense conversation between her brain and her
heart.

It would never work out. They were too different. She'd
never wanted to marry a soldier, and he still didn't want to
have children. Still, she was glad she couldn't jump off the
train. At every stop she stormed around the station, like
some half-crazed coyote, circling and circling until the time
came to leave, just to distract herself from buying a ticket
back to the East Coast.

Not that it mattered. He'd never forgive her. The steel
wheels clattered that message over and over as the train
passed midwestern cornfields and steamed through the
low-rolling hill country that announced they were approaching St. Louis. She hadn't gone to his unveiling.
Thousands had turned out for his statue, including many of
his wartime riders, the senator, naturally, and even his old
enemy, Colonel Greenstreet. She read about it in the
newspapers, the same ones that carried the cartoons she'd
promised. Well, not the cartoons she'd promised, exactly,
but the ones she'd decided to draw. They weren't what
Greenstreet wanted, she knew. She also knew they'd make
Greenstreet angry, and that he would probably tell James

about Lysistrata because she hadn't kept her end of the
bargain. But she didn't care. Or she did and she didn't. She
still loved James Ryerson, but he didn't love her—or at
least didn't trust her, did not understand that she needed
to be part of his life. She'd spent four years as a widow, two
of them as an outcast, piecing together her mangled spirit.
If her home on the prairie had been a refuge, it had also
been a self-imposed prison into which she'd retreated after
the war. To his enduring credit, Ryerson had brought her
out of that isolation and back to a state where she enjoyed
people, and, far more important, back to a state where she
liked herself. She could look in the mirror. She could see
her own beauty. She could look at her husband and know
he loved her, even with the tattoos on her face. Now he
proposed to exile her, but she had no intention of ac-
cepting that fate.

She'd left him a note. She'd left for the prairie. She was
tired of Washington and all of its intrigues and had no
intention of facing his temper. If he wanted her, he'd have
to come get her. In Vegetarian, Kansas. Right on the way
to Fort Riley.

FIFTEEN

ELIZABETH RODE HER PONY DOWN TOWARD VEGETARIAN'S ruins. The abandoned commune hadn't changed much, except it showed the effects of her absence. The corral had grown a thin cover of grasses, now turned to gold in the approaching autumn, the larkspur had given way to an indigo carpet of gentian, and four months of neglect had left the cabin a little more moldy. In spite of the difference, Elizabeth's heart swelled at the sight of the squat wooden cabin, the moldering buildings, and the lovely fringed flowers. Vegetarian's ruins might not be much, but she loved them.

Nanny must have felt the same way. Ignoring her usual dislike of water, the goat splashed across the sparkling stream and pressed forward, announcing herself with a joyful bleat and the clang of her bell. Pappy and Balthazar followed. They plunged into the water, clattering over the stones, pushing toward the corral like migrating birds heading toward home.

Elizabeth urged her pony over the creek. The goats' evident cheer lifted her spirits. She missed James so much. She'd reacquired her goats at Fort Leavenworth and spoken to Mary, the seamstress who'd helped her make those first party dresses. The pretty white fort, with its fresh memories of all that had happened, had made Elizabeth's heart ache for her husband, and wonder about the fate of the troopers.

Elizabeth dismounted at the door to the cabin. She refused to give in to Ryerson's temper. Mary had taken good care of her pets and kept track of the troopers to boot. The girl had gotten a letter from Dixon in which he described in sly, lurid detail the multiple dangers of life at Fort Riley, with many a not-so-subtle reference to lonely nights spent on the prairie and the soulful brown of Mary's dark eyes.

Elizabeth smiled as she pushed on the rough slab of wood. Some men didn't change, and she was glad they didn't, but she hoped for something different from James. She wanted him back, and in the worst way, but only if she could join him out at Fort Riley. She hoped her letters had made her concerns clear, that he wouldn't be angry about Lysistrata, that he would understand she wasn't in danger, and that she'd expressed well enough in her constrained, wifely, civilized note how much she loved him and why she believed that his plans for her life would doom their chances for a workable marriage.

Fine dirt sprinkled Elizabeth's shoulder. She peered into the darkened ruin. She figured she would have one week to wait. James should be leaving in a few days, though whether he'd have to go straight back to Fort Riley she wasn't certain. The Indian war had stretched through the summer. General Hancock had burned a Pawnee village, and the whole nation was howling for peace. The Cheyenne didn't care, at least not the dog soldiers, and they were raiding all over Kansas.

The goats bleated at the corral gate. Elizabeth stepped out of the doorway and blinked in the bright afternoon sunlight. For herself, Elizabeth didn't worry. She trusted her friends. She didn't believe the Cheyenne would hurt her. She'd taken care of plenty of children and had her own fame and wide reputation among the people who lived on the plains. She worried, though, for everyone else, for James and his troopers, and for her Indian friends. She ached to proceed on to Fort Riley, but she made this little detour, because James had to come to her freely.

She picked up the reins of her pony and walked quietly toward the goats, who milled outside their old enclosure. His insult had hurt her. If he would not leave the army, she would live with his choice, but he had to accept her appearance and make her part of his life. Marriage meant they were one being—composed, of course, of two different persons, but two who had committed their lives to each other.

His plantation suggestion made her a mistress, albeit one with a piece of paper. No matter how legal, she didn't consider theirs a legitimate marriage if she was kept in pampered seclusion, with no chance for children and no genuine place in Ryerson's life. She knew the tattoos would make his lot hard, but she wouldn't accept being hidden away. If she had to live that kind of life, she preferred living out here on the prairie, with friends who saw the markings as pretty, and her cartoons and her nursing to give her life meaning.

As she led the pony up to the corral, a dash of white splashed in the distance. Elizabeth shaded her eyes with her hand. A painted warhorse moved on the horizon, walking slowly down through the grasses. An Indian sat on his back, his features obscured by the afternoon rays of the autumn sunlight. Elizabeth could make out his slender outline, and the fact that he balanced a travois behind him. With those clues, she deduced who he was. Somehow she wasn't surprised. Her beloved Sleeps With Eagle had second sight and many spies among the whites. Of course he'd know of her comings and goings and probably of her marriage to James.

She lifted the log that served as a gate and drove the goats into the corral. They moved promptly into the shade of their lean-to and snuffled around for food and water. As the Indian moved toward the compound, Elizabeth's pony nickered a little. He raised his ears and pressed his nose forward, but both horses had excellent manners. The chief remained at a walk, the reins held loosely before him, giving no visible sign of how he controlled his pinto. He looked the same as she remembered, ancient and wise, but ineffably boyish. He stood slender and straight, weathered and frail, his white hair falling in clouds to his shoulders and a smile tucked in one side of his mouth. A small boy rode the litter behind him, peering quietly over the rawhide litter with a serious face and dark, shining eyes.

Elizabeth slipped the log back into place. Wiping her hands on her bloomers, she scooted to the travois. Bending down, she held out her arms to take the boy and spoke to Sleeps With Eagle in her pidgin Cheyenne.

"What have you brought for me, husband?" She called him that always. She would until the day that he died.

"A child with a burn. Not so very bad."

The boy held out a pudgy foot about one-third burned, the wound angry and weeping. Elizabeth stifled a wince and jerked her head toward the stream. "Take him to the water and hold his foot in it. I'll be right there with my powders."

The old chief nodded gravely. Elizabeth grabbed her medicine bag. She followed the horse to the bank of the stream.

"It's good to see you, wife." He spoke in his broken English. Sometimes they talked to each other this way, each in the other's language, most of their communication half spoken, but each trying to show respect by speaking in the other's language.

Bending down, she silenced the child, though she didn't much need to. He was a solemn young warrior, brave and intent on keeping a straight face. She took him in her arms, moved to the stream, and plunged his foot into the cooling water. The boy didn't cry out. He bore the shock with a stoic expression, then looked surprised as the pain faded.

"Did you step into a campfire?" she asked.

He sat down on the bank, amazed and curious that this simple treatment would do so much to make him feel better. "You are right, Grandfather," he addressed Sleeps With Eagle. "This woman is a fine healer." He spoke in precious, precocious tones, his face serious and hard, only his high, piping voice betraying his youth. He turned his round face to Elizabeth. "The blue-coated soldiers have burned our village. I am the youngest grandchild of Buffalo Woman. She sends her greetings and asks you to heal me."

Hands trembling, Elizabeth undid her bag. "Do you know which blue-coated soldiers?"

The boy slopped water over his ankle. "The buffalo soldiers out of Fort Riley."

Elizabeth looked up at the chief, unable to quite comprehend the boy's answer. The old warrior slipped off the side of his pony. The hair on his scalp-fringed shirt quivered lightly. He knelt next to the boy.

"A different kind of white soldier." He scrunched up a hank of his hair, then let it fall back to his shoulder. "With fur on their heads much like a bison."

Elizabeth pulled out a jar of aloe. "Do you know who leads them?"

"Two English lieutenants." He spoke matter-of-factly. "Your new husband has not come back yet. Do you think he would have done this"—he gestured toward the boy's wounded foot—"to us?"

"I think he would have." She tore her gaze from the child and looked steadily at Sleeps With Eagle. "He makes war like this. He's even burned the homes of the whites."

"So I have heard." He fingered the hair on the front of his shirt, a faded brown lock, probably from a white. "They say he is a very great soldier."

"One of the finest." His answer surprised her, but she let it stand.

"You wait here for him?" Standing, he scanned the horizon.

"Yes." She pulled out a clean linen bandage, one of the ones she'd made for the troopers. "Will you kill me for that?"

He grinned. "Why should I kill my prettiest wife?"

She knelt next to the boy and switched to English. "I've married another, your enemy."

"And you, are you my enemy also?" His voice was softer than she remembered from their marriage.

"No." She drew the boy's ankle out of the water, covering it quickly with aloe. "I went to Washington with my new husband. I spoke for you with General Parker, an Indian who serves in the white man's army."

"An Indian general?" He sounded surprised.

"Yes." She wrapped the bandage around the boy's wound, working quickly to get it covered before the cooling effects of the water wore off. "He's of the Seneca tribe."

As Elizabeth finished, a tear splashed on her hand. She glanced up, surprised, then pulled the boy into her lap. Hugging him tightly, she fished in her bag for a bottle. She removed the cork with her teeth, then let him take a deep swig of whiskey. He sputtered, sighed, then snuggled back into her shoulder. She cursed herself for not having thought of the painkiller sooner, but he'd seemed so stoic, so oblivious to the pain, that she'd lost track of how badly the burn would hurt him once the cooling effects of the water wore off.

As she rocked the boy in her arms, Sleeps With Eagle bent down, watching her closely. "And what did you ask of the Indian general?"

"That he leave you in peace."

"This is good."

"My request was good, but peace will not happen. The white man wants land. He wants the land's riches. He has a great deal of power and he will use it to get them."

The old chief smoothed back the boy's hair. The pudgy-faced child smiled sleepily, and Elizabeth gave him one more sip of whiskey.

"Buffalo Woman will send robes for this," the old chief said brusquely.

"No need." She hefted the boy into her arms. The old chief helped her onto her feet. She tucked the child farther up on her shoulder and carried him up to the cabin.

Home. It seemed so familiar, right down to the boy. She'd cared for many of the Indian children, but not yet for the victims of war. Her heart ached in her bosom as she entered the cabin and lay down the small sleeping bundle. She pressed her palms to her eyes, but removed them as the old man walked in. He moved almost as softly as a ghost, but his scalp-fringed shirt brushed Elizabeth's arm as he joined her. She shuddered at the feel of his trophies.

Ignoring her quivery reaction, he pressed his hand in the small of her back. "I need you to help me."

"Of course."

"I want you to go back to your husband."

She looked up, surprised. "Why?"

He nodded in the small boy's direction. "To keep him from hurting children this way."

She stepped back, astonished. "I don't know if I can help you. My husband is famous for fighting this way."

"You married a warrior." A kind of pride flared in his eyes, and she remembered that in his day her dear Sleeps With Eagle had been a leader of the dog soldiers. Turning, he signaled for her to follow him out. "I do not like his tactics." He moved into the sunlight. "There's more honor in coup than killing and no honor in burning down homes. But I will not listen to women's excuses. The white man and the red are two different people, and you are right in much that you say. The white man wants the land we live on. If he fights in this way, I know we cannot defeat him on the field of battle." He sat down on a small hillock and began to unlace his knee-high moccasins. "But there is more than one way to survive as a people. Sit down. I have something to show you."

She did as he asked, though she thought it crazy. She sat down in the grass and watched him.

"Do you remember how I used to do this?" He pulled one of the moccasins off by its sole.

"Yes." She broke off a sprig of purple gentian. "You drove me insane, washing your feet every morning, then walking around in the wet grass."

"You thought this habit unhealthy."

"Still do." She tickled her nose with the tassled flower.

He slipped the soft leather shoe off his other foot. "I never explained why I did it?"

"No."

He smiled, a boyish grin that never quite faded. "Take yours off, then. It's time that I show you."

Feeling foolish but game, she quickly stripped off her

boots and stockings. She knew enough about Sleeps With Eagle to guess he had some point to make.

He nodded approval, then turned toward the sun. Shutting his eyes, he threw his arms out to his sides in a spread-eagle gesture wide enough to encompass the whole horizon. "This is how I speak to the dead. I like to do it first thing in the morning, but afternoon will work quite well." He chanted a quiet prayer for a moment, then opened his eyes and walked in a circle, treading softly in the thick grass. "You must do what I am doing." He urged with his hands. "Watch me and follow."

Mystified, she followed as best as she could, stepping the way that he did, though she could see no particular pattern. Rather she felt the tickle of grass, the warmth of the afternoon earth.

"Do you feel them?" he asked. "They are sleeping beneath us."

A prickle ran up her spine as she realized what the old chief was saying. "No." But she tried to imagine the dead beneath her. It wasn't only an Indian concept, dust to dust and earth to earth, but she couldn't quite imagine an American leader getting up in the morning and trying to commune with his forebearers this way. "This is what you were doing those mornings? Speaking to the dead in the earth beneath you?"

"Yes."

She copied him for a few more minutes, focusing on the earth beneath her, the buzz and hum of the prairie, the heat of the autumn sunshine. She couldn't say she sensed any dead friends, but a certain peace settled over her spirit. It was good to be home. She'd never cared much for the city. Though she missed her Mississippi plantation, no place on earth meant quite as much as this cabin. She'd come of age in this place, grown into a woman, and learned to value her freedom. She unbuttoned the top of her high-collared blouse. "Why do you teach this ritual to me?"

He stopped, glancing down at his gnarled brown feet. "Because I wish you to know after I am gone that you may summon me when you want to talk."

She wanted to weep. The loss of the village must have made the old man heartsick. She'd never heard him speak of dying. "You will live a long life, my Indian husband."

"I am sure I will, but you will live longer." He sat down and pulled on his soft moccasins. "They say your husband's an honorable man."

"They say correctly."

He wiped his hands on his pants, walked to the travois, and pulled a piece of jerked meat from a stiff leather box, the kind of suitcase called a parfleche. "Then help me. Talk to your new warrior husband."

She sat down, astonished, her feet a bit cut from the sharp grasses. "You don't want me to come to the village? I could help with the rest of the children."

"No." Returning, he bit off a piece of the dried meat and chewed it. "You are a fine nurse, but you are a better wife. I've always valued your counsel. I need you to help me make peace with your husband. They are sending him to help with a treaty."

"James?"

He bit off a fragment of jerky, pulled it out of his mouth, and offered it to her. "Major Ryerson, the man that you married. He's coming to us, along with the Quakers."

She accepted the offering. At first his information surprised her, though upon reflection the selection made sense. She had been so outspoken in her opinions that the army must have believed James shared them. "What makes you think I can help you?"

"You've helped us before."

"Yes, but this is different." She sucked on a string of the buffalo jerky. The salty taste jolted her recall and brought back memories of her days as a slave. The man sitting before her had freed her from bondage. She'd owe him that favor for the rest of her life. "I mean, he's a wonderful man and I love him, but I'm not sure he's even coming. He's very angry at me."

"That's why you wait here without him?" He seemed unperturbed, just sat there chewing.

"Yes." She picked off a piece of dead weed and dug between her teeth for a stray morsel of the leathery concoction. "We're very different, you see. He does not understand my friendship with the Indians."

"But you believe he's a great soldier?" The breeze ruffled through the scalps on his shirt. He wore the ornate outfit, she knew, to remind her of his high status and fierce reputation. The tactic worked. The dentalium shells of his choker made a fine, almost feminine, contrast to the grisly reminders of his warrior's prowess, and she had to admit he looked splendid, if barbaric.

She shuddered, wondering if men were warlike in every culture. "I think he is a very fine warrior."

"Then he'll come get you."

"You think so?" Her heart gave a leap as she asked the question.

He rose in one fluid motion. He'd finished his jerky, so when he returned to his parfleche, Elizabeth thought vaguely that he was still hungry. "I believe you considered me a good husband."

"Yes. Of course. That's why I always helped you."

"And a fine leader?"

"Of course."

"Then listen to me." He spoke casually as he pulled a

smaller box from his Indian suitcase. "A great man needs a nag for a wife."

She laughed, surprised by his odd observation.

"It's true. Here, I brought this for you." He pulled out a necklace made of bone shells, daintily strung between American dimes. Returning, he knelt down behind her and tied the leather thong, then came around and stood before her. "A nagging wife keeps a man humble. That's why I kept Buffalo Woman. She stood up to me." He looked thoughtfully at the handmade decoration. "And the greater and more powerful the man, the more he needs a wife who will fight him. A fine warrior knows this and will always value a spirited wife."

Elizabeth brushed her fingers over her cheekbones. "There are other problems, you know."

"He does not like the markings?"

"No. Not exactly." She touched the beads on her necklace, thinking she wished the white man could give the Indians something better than trinkets. "He thinks they're lovely. It's the other whites who think they're peculiar."

"I am sorry they make your life hard with the others, but his is the only opinion that counts. Do you like the present?"

"I suppose so." She knew he was trying to bribe her, but his ulterior motives did not really matter. She was beginning to get used to the intrigues that accompanied being an officer's wife.

He stepped back, admiring his present. "You have the great gift, Many Fires, of seeing what lies in the heart of another. I always knew you would speak well of me, and I wanted people to listen to you. That's why I had you tattooed. So when you spoke well of the Indian, the whites would know that you spoke the truth." He brushed his hands on his pants. "If I take the boy to Buffalo Woman, will you go back to your husband?"

"I'll try." She stood up, glancing anxiously into the cabin where the Indian boy lay, still sleeping peacefully. "At least I'll try. I can't promise he will accept me, but I will wait here for a few days and if he doesn't come get me, I will go to Fort Riley."

"Good." He strode past and ducked under the door frame. "Help me remove him." Crouching down to the pallet that lay on the floor, he trundled the boy into his arms. As he did, Elizabeth opened her satchel and pulled out her container of aloe. Hurrying out, she stood by the chief as he lowered the boy onto the rawhide sling of the litter.

"Here." She tucked the medicine into the parfleche. "This is for the other hurt children. Tell Buffalo Woman she can use this to help them."

"I will do as you ask." With a graceful leap, the old chief vaulted onto the pony. "She never doubted your skill as a nurse."

Ryerson could barely make out the figure of a slender man, most likely an Indian, springing into his saddle. Ryerson spurred his chestnut into a gallop and squinted into the dying sunlight. The brightly painted pony looked somewhat familiar, and the female, though indistinct, had to be his errant Libbie. With a sigh of relief, he reined in the horse. Elizabeth did not seem to be hurt, and the Indian—for no white man mounted that deftly—was moving away from the cabin.

Hand on his gun, Ryerson proceeded slowly. The Indian moved in his direction, evidently dragging a travois behind him. Ryerson scowled at the sight of the slight, white-haired old man. This had to be Elizabeth's husband. Old man or not, Ryerson did not like seeing him here. He did not trust the Indian the way Elizabeth did. And, he had to admit to himself, he hated the idea of another man's husbandly interest. The old man passed Ryerson slowly, eyes to the front. Ryerson tried to ignore him, but he couldn't help casting one swift sidelong glance at the man who had preceded him in Elizabeth's favor. He ignored the boy, though he wondered where the child had come from and how he had come to be hurt.

The chief passed without speaking. When Ryerson could no longer hear hoofbeats, he touched his knees to his horse, splashed across the stream, and cantered up to the door of the cabin. Elizabeth stood there, dressed in a pretty white blouse and brown pantaloons in the damned bloomer pattern—and barefoot. He pulled the reins tight, but did not dismount. He'd practiced a speech all the way out to Kansas, but the Indian had unnerved him, and he forgot it. He'd expected to find her alone, not standing in front of her cabin, having just left her former husband and giving strong evidence of only just recently having put on her clothes.

"What was he doing here?" He jerked his head toward the departing figure. He didn't want to say the next sentence, but it snapped out before he could stop it. "And why aren't you wearing your shoes?"

"That's none of your business." She lifted up her carpetbag, tossed it inside the door frame, then stormed toward the corral and the goats.

He followed, still mounted. "A husband has a right to question his wife."

"Not if he intends to divorce her." She said something soft to the milling white goats, then picked up a bucket and strode toward the stream without glancing at him.

"I never said I meant to divorce you." He spoke from the back of his unmoving horse.

She stopped but did not turn around. "I distinctly remember our last conversation. You said you didn't have to live with a wife whose every glance rebuked your position."

"In our last conversation I was a cad." He dismounted slowly, approaching her calmly, intrigued by the long row of buttons that marched up her demure cotton blouse. He'd missed her so much. He'd been sick with worry. He couldn't make sense of the note, though he'd read it hundreds of times. She'd made him so angry, he couldn't grasp what she'd wanted exactly. He only knew he'd hurt her badly, and she'd repaid him with this departure. He found this punishment the worst kind of torture, but it had accomplished its evident aim. In her absence, he discovered a curious truth. He wanted her with him. He didn't care about the possible hardship. If she wanted to come out to Fort Riley, so be it. She'd lived for months in this desolate hovel. She'd certainly manage a frontier outpost. Reaching her, he tucked his thumbs in his belt. "I'm sorry for the terrible insult. I didn't mean a word I said."

She straightened her shoulders. He wouldn't have thought that she could do it, but she made her posture more rigid, more perfect. "Then why did you make that awful comment to me?"

"Because I was angry." Reaching out, he touched the nape of her neck. The soft tendrils caressed his calloused thumb.

She whipped around, her eyes dark with anger. "Don't touch me, please. I didn't deserve that kind of treatment and I won't be softened up by a hug."

He glanced down, remorseful, then jerked his head up. "What have you done with your shoes?"

"That's none of your business, either."

She turned heel, but he stormed around her, cutting off her route to the stream. She glanced at his side arm, took one step back, then tried to maneuver around him.

"Wait." He held up his palm, struggling to get control of his temper. He knew very well her bare feet meant nothing. She'd never made love to this old Indian. The child in the travois looked hurt. The bare feet didn't make sense, but he did not want to make an issue of them. "Just give me a second." He clasped his hands behind his back and took a swift walk toward the cabin. Reaching his horse, he removed his gauntlets and tucked them into his saddlebag. He scanned the horizon—a quick glance, but thorough—unbuckled his holster, and stuffed his gun in also. Returning, he planted himself before her. "There. Does that make you feel better?"

The line of her shoulders relaxed visibly. "It does, as a matter of fact."

"Good, because I'm trying hard to keep hold of my temper, and it would help me a lot if you'd meet me halfway."

"All right." She held out the bucket. "You help with the water. I'll listen."

He clutched the leather strap in his hand. "Now why are you walking around out here barefoot?"

"Don't change the subject." She wiped her hands on her odd pantaloons, then started back toward the stream. "You were explaining to me why you were so angry you resorted to insults I didn't deserve."

She looked wonderful from this angle, her hips flaring slightly, her bottom outlined by the weird outfit. He felt himself tighten and harden and he struggled to keep control of his temper. "God, Libbie. Must you make this so hard?"

"Yes." She minced down the path, and he wondered again why she was going barefoot. "If we don't learn to fight fair with each other, we might as well crawl back in our holes and live out our lives as reclusive loners unfit for even civilized discourse, not to mention an emotion like love."

He followed, still gripping the bucket, feeling naked without his weapons, but sensibly conscious that in a fight the steel on his hip would make her feel threatened. "Is that what you think of me? I'm a barbaric monster, unworthy of love?"

"No more you than myself, but the point is you have to be honest. I love you. I believe you love me, but you're bigger and stronger than I. When you lose your temper, I expect a discussion and some reassurance you will try to do better."

He drew in a deep, shaky breath. He hated this emotional female talk. He wanted to claim her and wished that he could, but nature had played a great joke on him. He'd commanded thousands of men in furious battles, terrorized armies, and pillaged plantations, but this fragile woman with the exquisite markings was going to control him in a way no man could have. He might be bigger, but Libbie had one unassailable power. She might not be aware of her beauty, but she treasured the life she'd made for herself. She wasn't his chattel and she'd only stay if he treated her fairly. Which meant if he wanted her, he had to learn patience.

"All right," he said and checked his stride. She had to walk rather more slowly, and he wondered again what she was doing. "I admit I was angry, and it wasn't your fault. I thought a great deal about my temper. I know how I came to this pass. I never wanted to serve in the army. I volunteered in order to please an ambitious wife, who had envisioned the glory but not the hardship, who was involved in being the wife of a soldier. She betrayed me, Libbie." Her head turned just a fraction, as if she were listening more closely. "And in the most terrible way. So, yes. I'm angry. I'll probably never forgive her, but I can't leave the army. It's truly important to me to give all my losses some meaning. And that's why I wanted you for a wife."

"Explain that to me, because I honestly don't understand where I fit in your life." They'd reached the stream, and she took the bucket, walking gingerly over the stones. She looked so pretty, more beautiful even than he remembered, curving in all the right places, her wayward tendrils aflame in the sunset.

He sighed to himself. "Because you're a survivor." She looked his way. He rubbed one sweaty hand on his thigh and took great satisfaction in seeing her blush. "At first I took your compassion as a sign of weakness, but I came to realize it's your greatest strength. There's a wonderful power in your resilience. No matter what happened, you would never hurt me the way Helen did."

He thought he saw tears in her eyes, but she turned away quickly and dipped the bucket. "All right," she said softly, "then let's have some ground rules. When we fight, no yelling, no insults, no swearing. If you resort to those tactics, I get to walk out."

"All the way back to this place?"

"No, just far enough to let your temper cool."

"Fair enough."

"Oh, and I like your improvisation." She straightened up and scrambled back to the bank. "No arguments while you're wearing your weapons."

"Agreed."

She reached the edge of the stream, and he caught her elbow, his stomach turning to mush as she nearly tripped. She steadied herself by placing one hand on his chest. His heart boomed so painfully, he thought his buttons ought to be shaking.

"Do you still want me?" he asked.

"Yes." She put down the bucket.

He clamped his hands over hers. They felt so soft, so small beneath his. "Even if I don't leave the army?"

"Yes."

She lowered her eyes and toyed with a dime on the necklace she wore. "They say you're appointed to a peace commission."

"That's true." He looked at her closely. The prairie became her, its startling fall sunset setting her hair aflame and lighting the peach blush of her cheekbones, but her beauty could not conceal the worry and grief in her expression. He realized suddenly what had happened, the reason she wanted him back.

He dropped her hand and picked up the bucket.

"Is that what you want?" Ryerson stifled the swift surge of his anger. "To help with the treaty?"

"Yes." As he balanced the water, she followed him back toward the path. "Do you think that's wrong?"

"No, not exactly," he lied. He wanted to strangle the Indian chief, but he'd come to make up and knew he'd better keep control of his temper. "But before I answer, I have a question."

"All right." She picked her way through the yellowing grasses.

"Wait here." He put down the bucket, strode through the underbrush, and whistled loudly for the chestnut. When the horse arrived at the clearing, he opened the bag on the side of his saddle.

"Did you do these?" He pulled out a sheaf of cartoons.

"So he told you?" She did not even look, so certain did she appear to be at his question.

"Greenstreet, yes." He smoothed out the drawing of Dixon, an excellent sketch of the sergeant whittling. "He was furious at you. He told me you were the infamous Lysistrata, the—lady—who's been drawing all those cartoons of me. I didn't believe him, of course."

"Why not?" She looked up, surprised.

"Because you've always hated the army." He flipped through the whole sequence of drawings—wonderful, compassionate sketches that portrayed the daily life of his troopers and gently needled the army for failing to provide for them better. "Why would you help the troopers this way?"

She took the papers out of his hands, staring thoughtfully at the pictures. "Because I learned a great deal from Greenstreet."

He brushed at his sleeve. "You've learned to like soldiers?"

"No, not exactly." She folded the papers, skirted the bucket, sank down next to a tree, and tucked her knees under her chin. "But I learned to tell them apart. Look, James. Soldiers are men, different one from another, distinguished not by their cause or color, but by their goodness of heart. I'll always wish for a world without soldiers, but I've learned to respect the choices you've made."

He frowned, his most eloquent scowl. He dropped his reins to the ground, and himself down beside her. "And how did Greenstreet teach you that lesson?"

"Because he's a beast."

He removed his hat and frowned dubiously.

"No, no. It's true. You know what he is doing?" She pulled out the last cartoon in the stack, the one that portrayed Nathaniel Greenstreet on a rearing horse, a cross burning behind him. "He is starting an army to prey on the Negro, a wicked idea if I ever heard one. He asked me to help him." She flashed him a guilty look. "Of course I refused him, but his request got me thinking. If we drive all the good men out of the army, then peace-loving people would be left to the mercy of monsters like him—true beasts with no sense of compassion."

He slipped the papers from her, tucked them into the crown of his hat, and set the makeshift container beside them. "Libbie, I love you." He drew her gently into his chest. "Your cartoons helped a great deal with the troopers. I got them horses and better weapons, and I know the sketches helped me obtain them. I'm so sorry for the comments I made."

"Do you forgive me?" She wrapped her arms around his waist. "For the drawings I made before I knew you in person?"

He threw back his head and laughed. "Forgive you? I loved them. I adored the one with the Indian maiden. She hung above my cot for a year."

She pulled back slightly. "You're joking!"

Reaching out, he drew her back. "I'm not. You made her so pretty. I might be civil in certain ways, but I do have my animal side."

Sighing, she sank into his chest. "And you'll take me with you out to Fort Riley?"

He scowled and lifted her chin with one finger. "On this subject, we'll compromise. You live at Fort Riley, but only until you get pregnant."

"Hah!" She surged to her feet. "And how do you expect that will happen?"

"In the usual way."

Her lips parted prettily. "Really?" A pink flush appeared on her cheeks. She dropped down beside him. "Truly?" He nodded. She wrapped her arms around his waist. "Oh, James. I love you." She sat back on her heels. "Listen. I promise. I'll be a good mother—" She scowled, as if his comment had only just struck her. "What do you mean— until I get pregnant?"

It was his turn to jump to his feet. He strode to the stream, then turned and marched back. "Libbie, don't push me. Losing that baby was the last straw for Helen. When the time comes for us to have children, I want you to be in the East with good doctors."

"James." She hopped up, scrabbling over the pebbles. "I don't mean to insult you, but I have no intention of losing your baby. Furthermore, you're completely mistaken in your assumptions. Those eastern doctors are quacks. Babies do very well on the prairie. Not to mention the fact that you've picked the right woman. I am, after all, an experienced nurse. I've cared for dozens of Indian children."

"Enough." He caught her waist, then folded her into a tight embrace. "We'll talk on that later." He kissed her, his mouth slanting sideways, his whole body pressing against her. "Just let me touch you," he murmured. He'd missed her so badly, all that feminine softness, the curve of her bosom, the slope of her bottom, the scent of wildflowers, the texture of cotton, that delicious, delightful combination of pleasures he never experienced except with Libbie.

She kissed him back, deeply and without reservation, seemingly lost in a bright burst of passion. He cupped his hands under her bosom and teased his thumbs over her nipples.

Gasping, she broke off the kiss. "Are you certain? I mean, if we made a baby, would you really want it?"

"Yes, Libbie, I'm certain." He undid her hair, then cradled her head with his hands. "Let's not talk anymore." He kissed her again, cursing his tunic and solid brass buttons, thankful for the absence of his gun belt. He wanted to toss

off all of her clothes and savor all her soft nakedness—
neck, bosom, earlobe, and stomach; thigh, calf, bottom,
and mouth—but he thought he should be a little more
civil. With a curse to himself, he thrust his tongue into her
mouth, taking shuddery delight in the hotness. God, how
he'd missed her. He would like to have spoken to her of his
feelings, but his body insisted he had other business. He
pulled back, whispering softly, "Would you like to go back
to the cabin?"

She grinned, then smiled shyly. "I rather liked it that
time by the river."

Afterward, James lay by the river listening to the murmuring stream. They'd made a bed out of his saddle blanket, and Libbie looked lovely drowsing on it. The fallen
leaves matched her hair color. Barren branches vaulted
above her, throwing lacy shadows that painted her skin.
She was as white as fine linen, creamy and smooth, except
for the peaks of her nipples. Draping his uniform over her
shoulder, he propped himself on one elbow. "Do you mind
if I ask you one more question?"

"Of course not." She brushed back a lock of his tousled
hair.

He responded in kind, running his fingers through her
tresses. He'd never get used to their silky texture, the cool
wash of curls in his hand. "What are you doing out here
without shoes?"

"Ah." She toyed with his chest, tracing the outlines of
his muscles. "It's a trick the old chief taught me. I'm learning to speak with the dead by treading the earth with bare
feet."

"I see." He ran his thumb over her cheekbones. "Does it
work?"

"I haven't got the way of it yet. But I thought I'd practice." She snuggled in close to his shoulder. "Perhaps you'd like to learn. Maybe you could speak to your Jamie."

"And you to your Philip."

"Maybe." She locked her gaze with his, her cinnamon eyes still darkened with passion. "James," she said as she lowered her lashes, "are you sure?" She kissed the side of his mouth. "You don't feel like you're betraying your Jamie?"

"No." He now loved the idea of making a baby. The feeling surprised him. She looked so fetching, disheveled and naked. He could have made love ten times today. "I've thought a great deal about that in your absence. I loved my boy dearly. But I need to go on with my life. And I could do him no greater honor than creating the brother he always wanted."

"I see." She tucked herself under the crook of his arm and sighed softly.

"Now what are you worried about?"

"The Indian boy." They'd littered the ground with their clothes.

Sitting up, he tossed her camisole to her. "What was wrong with that little boy's foot?"

She turned that frank gaze on him. "He'd been hurt when your troop burned down his village."

He was struck again by her astonishing beauty. A lesser perfection would not have survived them, but the tattoos accented a perfect oval. He remembered again why he loved her. "And you want to help him?"

"Yes." She chewed on her lip. "Well, not him exactly, but all the children in that situation."

He looked around for his pants. "Libbie, what would happen to me if I came home and told you I'd burned a village?"

She bolted upright, proud and stark naked, her white

undergarment pressed to her bosom. "You know very well what would happen!"

"Yes, I do."

"And will that meet with your standards? Having a wife who in certain ways acts as your conscience?"

She looked so lovely, eyes dark with passion, her tiny waist flaring into wide hipbones. For the first time in years, he could have recited a poem to a woman, but he'd learned one valuable lesson in his life as a soldier. Sometimes action worked better.

So he kissed her, letting her feel his renewal and interest. She responded, and he eased back slightly. "I gave the most thought of all to that subject." He touched his tongue to her earlobe, waited for her shiver, then ran his thumb over her cheekbone. "It seems like a suitable fate for a vandal—" He sighed, thinking of all the ways there were to caress her. And all the ways she could oppose him. "Spending his life with a true Lysistrata."

EPILOGUE

Sleeps With Eagle was given a Christian funeral, the same day Ryerson heard Custer had died. Ryerson thought it ironic that the old barbarian should outlive the golden-haired Indian killer and be buried out on the plains with four weeping wives at his grave. Libbie had nursed the ancient chieftain, of course. It had taken all Ryerson's control of his temper, and many lectures on civil behavior, to tolerate Libbie's self-imposed need to repay a debt to her former husband.

So it annoyed Ryerson, but didn't surprise him, when he awoke the day after the burial, reached for his wife, and found her missing. Scowling, he rolled off their bed and peered out the window. Libbie was walking off in the distance, strolling barefoot over the prairie, her green cotton skirt darkened with dew, a bouquet of wildflowers clasped by her side.

With a curse to himself, Ryerson flung up the sash. "Good thing she's not pregnant." He frowned at Charlie, a high-strung wolfhound curled up next to the bedpost. "I'd kill her myself." He drew back a lacy white curtain. The cool morning air touched his face. It had stormed during the night, but the dawn looked peaceful. High clouds, pink-tinged and golden, moved over the land, casting visible shadows over the stubbly prairie. Libbie's flame-colored hair drank in the light, tumbling loosely over her shoulders, enveloping her in a fiery halo that could have graced an angel or devil.

Checking an impulse to bark out an order, Ryerson turned and pulled on a boot. "What kind of a watchdog are you?" Charlie lifted his long, pointed snout. "You're supposed to growl when she goes out." Ryerson grabbed his shirt off a peg on the wall. Charlie yawned. "Keep up that attitude," Ryerson said as he glanced out the window, "and I'll trade you for an Indian blanket."

He scanned the clouds. There'd been tornadoes during the night, but he didn't see signs of one now. He pulled on his blue flannel and studied his Libbie. He could not see her face, but her posture was pensive. She moved slowly through the short prairie grass, her head cocked as if she were listening. Her starched white blouse dipped beneath her bosom, and her green cotton skirt flared over her hips. She looked lovely to him, more curved and softer after four children. Not so stiff as when he first knew her, and far, far more alluring.

Buttoning his shirt, Ryerson strode into the parlor. Charlie jumped off the bed and followed, toenails clicking on the bare floors. As Ryerson stalked through the cluttered room, he barely glanced at the walls filled with paintings. He banged open the door and charged through the yard, a scrubby enclosure whose struggling greenery barely softened the bleak prairie landscape.

Ryerson slowed down as he turned a corner. He felt a bit foolish chasing his wife down, but he rationalized his impulsiveness with the thought that the Comanche could steal her. The notion, of course, was extremely unlikely. Though a few straggling raiders still roamed the prairie, most of the poor devils had turned themselves in. The peace policy had long since failed. Even the Quakers had abandoned the Indian. The thankless job of keeping the peace had fallen to men like Ryerson's troopers. The work had never been easy, and sometimes they'd killed men, but they'd tried to do justice as they understood it. Ryerson had never come to like bloodshed, but he'd been proud of his record, proud of his troopers, and proud of the life he'd made for himself. And Libbie had learned to accept him. He hoped. Although, as he approached his barefoot wife, all his old wounds seemed to pain him, and he rubbed the scar he'd garnered at Shiloh.

Without saying a word, he fell in beside her. Charlie bounded into some bushes, scaring up a bevy of quail. At the sound of their whirring, a meadowlark discontinued his song, and a pink-winged scissortail veered in the other direction. Libbie paid no attention, just walked quietly, her eyes on the flowers.

"What are you doing?" Ryerson asked.

"Contacting the dead." She did not seem surprised by his presence and seemed to assume he remembered the morning he'd tracked her to Vegetarian and found her practicing this Indian trick.

"Do you miss him?"

"Of course."

He looked back at their home, a small limestone structure with none of Leavenworth's civilized beauty, but vastly more sturdy than Vegetarian's wreckage. "I suppose you miss that damnable cabin."

She turned from him, hiding her face behind the shimmering veil of her hair. "Sometimes."

He'd wanted a far grander life for her, but she'd steadfastly refused to live in the East. He was glad in the end she'd chosen to stay, for he'd never gotten over the joy of their children. He adored fatherhood and all that came with it. The grubby faces, the little disasters, the God-sent days when they required his guidance. He'd even lost his fear of their dying. For years he'd suffered through every sniffle, but all four had grown so sturdy—and Libbie nursed them with such skill and valiance—he'd finally come to believe they'd survive. Which is why his hand trembled as he touched her shoulder. "Have I not made you happy?"

She hugged him fiercely and buried her face in his chest. "Of course you have."

He lifted her chin, pushing a shimmering lock back from her face. "Then why are you weeping?"

"I'm not weeping."

He brushed his thumb over her cheekbone. "Then what are these droplets of water?"

"Mere self-expression."

He kissed the top of her forehead. He stood holding her for a while, then took her hand and walked beside her in silence. He wondered if the children were stirring. Mary would watch them, of course. She'd lived with them since Fort Riley, scorning Dixon's offer of marriage and the proffered position as the troop's laundress. She surprised them later by marrying Carter, then proceeded to try to outpace her mistress by producing a little brood of her own. Dixon had married only last year to a pretty girl with expressive eyes whose first baby would come in the summer. "Couldn't you paint him?"

"Perhaps."

He picked up a stick and threw it to Charlie. The dog bounded over the prairie. "Do you actually miss him?"

"In certain ways. Yes."

She brought her bouquet up to her nose and glanced tentatively over the lilies. "Are you jealous?"

"Of course not."

"Then why do you ask?"

Of course he was jealous. He'd never admit it, but he'd go to his grave hating the Indian. The savage had marked her. For all Ryerson loved the tattoos on her cheekbones, and wouldn't have changed her for the world, a dark part of his soul was far too barbaric to ever forgive the pain she'd endured. "How can you miss a man who's been so cruel to you?"

"Don't you miss the war?"

"That's different."

"Why?"

"Because. The war gave me courage. I lived. Perhaps for no reason, but the experience taught me I could survive."

She brushed the dots on the line of her cheekbone. "I see."

"All right. Perhaps it's not different. But how can you miss those ruins?"

She grinned, squeezing his hand. "Don't you remember one or two good times?"

He glanced back at the house. They'd come quite a distance. The clouds rumbled out on the prairie, a lightning storm brewing high in their reaches.

"We ought to go back."

She circled her arm around his waist. "After all, I lost my virginity there."

"It could rain anytime."

Sighing, she leaned into the soft flannel covering his chest. "Don't you remember the first time you kissed me?"

"I think we've outgrown kissing in rainstorms."

"Really?" She glanced around. They'd walked halfway toward Medicine Bluff, a small creek, and she fixed her gaze on the foliage that lined it. "Too bad. Because I wasn't thinking of only just kissing."

"You're insane."

"Only for you."

He planted a kiss on her mouth. Let the Indian rest. Let all the past rest. Somewhere in the sky, funnels were forming, and summer storms would buffet the prairie, but the cloud had passed over, and the day would be pretty. The cool morning air could waft over their bodies, and they could lie safely under the trees. He laughed, breaking the kiss.

"You find this funny?" she asked.

"No. I find it delicious."

They walked hand in hand toward the stream.

When they reached the bank, he glanced at her feet. "Do you still feel him?"

She shrugged her shoulders and smiled.

"You must be joking."

She scrambled down a small bluff and skipped toward the water, squishing her toes in the sand as she did. Ryerson hurried after her and glared at the ground. "Are you talking to him?"

She laughed but did not answer.

"Damn." Ryerson lobbed a rock at a tree. "At least before I could have killed him."

She sank down on the ground and buried her face in her hands. Her sides were shaking. He thought she was crying. He didn't know what words might comfort. He was casting about for a poem to offer when she raised her gaze. Her eyes were filled with tears of laughter. "Do you realize what you're saying?"

Ryerson frowned, not wanting to think how foolish he sounded.

A small giggle escaped her. She flattened her feet, her mouth pursing in concentration as she absently undid her blouse's pearl buttons.

"What are you doing?" he asked.

She lay her bouquet down by her side. "I'm just asking him to turn over."

Ryerson scowled. He zinged a small stone at the bluff. From back toward the fort, a mockingbird imitated a goat. Charlie had disappeared on the prairie, probably chasing a succulent bird. "Well?" He shucked off one boot. Maybe he could speak to her Sleeps With Eagle. He'd be damned if he'd spend the rest of his morning wildly frustrated because some damned dead Indian claimed the earth for himself. "Well?" He tossed the other boot in the sand.

"He says he'll do it. Though . . ." She giggled, her hands freezing on her third button.

"Though?" He pulled off the blue flannel. A prairie breeze puckered his nipples. She giggled again and lowered her eyes.

"Though?" he demanded.

"Though." She sighed, shrugging out of her crisply starched blouse. The sun glinted off a pale shoulder. "He thought we made quite a spectacle last time."

If you enjoyed this book, take advantage of this special offer. Subscribe now and...

Get a Historical

No Obligation

If you enjoy reading the very best in historical romantic fiction...romances that set back the hands of time to those bygone days with strong virile heros and passionate heroines ...then you'll want to subscribe to the True Value Historical Romance Home Subscription Service. Now that you have read one of the best historical romances around today, we're sure you'll want more of the same fiery passion, intimate romance and historical settings that set these books apart from all others.

Each month the editors of True Value select the four *very best* novels from America's leading publishers of romantic fiction. We have made arrangements for you to preview them in your home *Free* for 10 days. And with the first four books you

receive, we'll send you a FREE book as our introductory gift. No Obligation!

FREE HOME DELIVERY

We will send you the four best and newest historical romances as soon as they are published to preview FREE for 10 days (in many cases you may even get them before they arrive in the book stores). If for any reason you decide not to keep them, just return them and owe nothing. But if you like them as much as we think you will, you'll pay just $4.00 each and save at *least* $.50 each off the cover price. (Your savings are *guaranteed* to be at least $2.00 each month.) There is NO postage and handling—or other hidden charges. There are no minimum number of books to buy and you may cancel at any time.

FREE
Romance
(a $4.50 value)

Send in the Coupon Below

To get your FREE historical romance and start saving, fill out the coupon below and mail it today. As soon as we receive it we'll send you your FREE Book along with your first month's selections.
